BRUCE C BEE

Burn Me Whole

For my father, Bruce 'Buckeye' McMullen Sr., my stepfather, Robert 'Puppie' Evans III, and every man who ever stepped in and showed me how to stand.

"Not everything that is faced can be changed,
but nothing can be changed until it is faced."

- JAMES BALDWIN

Contents

Acknowledgments

Mom and Mike —

For standing by me through this whole journey and letting me be a free spirit long enough to find my own way. You may not have always agreed, but you never clipped my wings — and you were always there when I needed steady ground.

Family and Friends —

To the ones who read the earliest pages and gassed me up enough to keep going. Thank you for believing in me when this was just scribbles and late nights, and for riding shotgun the whole way here

La Jefa —

To the one who saw the light in me in my darkest hour. You spoke greatness over me when I couldn't see it for myself. You never flinched when I walked away from corporate, or when I packed up with Colombia with no plan but a prayer. You told me this would all work in my favor — and I'm finally starting to see what you saw back then. You were the spark that set this whole thing burning, and for that, I thank you.

A Note To You

There are some stories you write because you have to, and some because you hope they find a home. *Burn Me Whole* is both.

Knowing you spent your hard-earned dollars to invite my words into your space — especially as a new author — is a gift I can hardly put into words. In a world where distractions are endless and budgets are tight, your decision to read this book is the most humbling form of support I could ask for.

Without you, these pages would just be a big-ass paperweight. You didn't have to show up — but you did. You gave this story breath, weight, and a place to live. And for that, I'm grateful beyond words.

Thank you, truly, for giving this new voice a chance. I'm deeply thankful to have you along for the ride.

Sincerely,

Bruce C Bee

1

East Langford Parkway

Atlanta was quiet. Not the kind that wrapped around you like a peaceful blanket. This quiet pressed on the chest. It sat heavy in the room like unspoken tension, making every floorboard creak, every slipped sigh when you thought you were alone, acutely loud. This quiet turned the walls into mirrors, forcing a gaze longer than you were ready for.

I'd gotten used to it. Me, this house, and a playlist I never finished—songs I kept meaning to add, memories I wasn't ready to hear again. Sometimes I'd hit shuffle anyway, letting the ghosts sing. Most mornings felt like this: still air, no real plans, and the faint scent of something I couldn't name anymore. Grief, maybe. Or the absence of a voice that used to say my name like it meant something.

Last night's glass still sat on the table. A faint lip print barely visible, the waterline low. Its condensation had left a perfect, dark, damp ring on the wood—circular like the routine I'd fallen into. Get up, breathe, don't think too hard. Or think too much and do nothing at all. I used to wipe that table down religiously. Now, it just felt like proof I was here, even if I hadn't done much living.

My phone buzzed on the counter, a jolt. A text from my son—wedding reminders, flight logistics, a joke about drinking like we used to. A reminder that soon, the silence would break. A trip, a ceremony, people. And with it, this uncomfortable hush, usually clinging like a second skin, was briefly disturbed. That's why it felt heavier today. It wasn't just the absence of noise; it was the sharp contrast to the impending noise.

There was a time this place had rhythm. A morning hum. A back-and-forth between rooms. Laughter that spilled from the bathroom while the shower ran, or music bumping from the kitchen when someone felt like dancing instead of doing dishes. But that rhythm was gone now. Replaced by quiet footsteps and conversations I rehearsed in my head but never said aloud.

And maybe that's what got to me the most. The way stillness could make you confront things motion always helped you ignore. In the quiet, there was no job to distract me, no calendar full of meetings that made me feel important, no one calling my name down the hall. Just me and the echo of everything I hadn't figured out yet. And now, the approaching wedding was making those echoes even louder.

* * *

Six months into this sabbatical, all I'd found was more time to be disappointed in who I'd become. This trip to Jamaica for the wedding felt like a forced reset, a chance to find something other than silence. So far, though, it had only brought more space. More silence. And far too many hours to pick at old wounds I used to be too busy to feel. I thought stepping away from the grind would bring me back to myself. But the truth was uglier than I expected—maybe I'd been gone longer than I realized.

The job was gone now. Fifteen years. That's how long I gave them—my body, my time, my mind. I wore the company's name like a second skin. Traveled when they needed, even missing the last school play where my daughter was a singing tree. I ate shit when I had to. Smiled through meetings I should've flipped tables in. All for titles that looked good in emails and checks that never seemed to be enough once I hit the next rung.

I climbed every damn ladder they put in front of me. Promotions came like clockwork, and with each one, I was supposed to feel proud. Accomplished. Like I'd "made it." But somewhere along the way, I stopped recognizing the man I was becoming. I traded joy for strategy. Spontaneity for schedules. My son's birthday for a quarterly review – I remember the cake still warm on the counter as I pulled out of the driveway, headed back to the office. I became dependable to people who didn't know my middle name.

I used to be different. I used to stay up late for bedtime stories, not out of obligation—but because I wanted to see the way his eyes lit up when the dragon finally won. I used to dance in the kitchen with my wife—barefoot, off-beat, humming some dumb '90s R&B while the rice boiled over, her laughter echoing off the cabinets. I used to hold her just because. Just because her back looked beautiful in the morning light. Just because she was mine and I didn't say it enough.

But "doing what I gotta do" became the anthem. And somewhere between the flights, the deadlines, and the 3 a.m. Slack messages, I buried the parts of me that made me human. I replaced them with task lists and KPI dashboards. I called it sacrifice. Said it was for the family. For our future. But what future was I building if the present was hollow?

Now the job's gone. The title too. My marriage? That slipped out the back door years before I had the nerve to say it was over. And all I've got is this house full of memories I don't know what to do with—and a version of me I barely recognize staring back in the mirror.

* * *

Now I was just here. No title. No marriage. Barely a connection to my kids. Not estranged, not completely, but distant enough that I had to scroll through old photos just to remember the sound of their laughter. Distant enough that "how's school?" felt like small talk instead of a real check-in. The kind of connection you tell yourself is good enough because they text back with hearts and "love you too, Dad," but deep down, you know you're being given just enough to ease the guilt.

That trip to Colombia, a few months back, had given me a little breath, sure—different air, different women, different language. It was easy to feel new there. To pretend the weight I carried in the States didn't cross customs. I'd wake up to sun streaking through palm trees and the smell of mango from some vendor already yelling down the block. The music was louder, the colors richer, the stares softer. Women touched my arm when they spoke. Bartenders remembered my name. I could smile without explaining myself.

But even paradise goes silent. And when it does, reflection creeps in like humidity—slow, but it gets everywhere. You can try to drown it in rum or bury it between new sheets, but it always comes back when your feet hit the cold tile in the morning. Clarity doesn't care about your location. It doesn't give a damn about your passport stamps or your distractions. It'll find you on a rooftop in Medellín just as easily as it found you on the floor of your kitchen in Atlanta.

Because the mornings still came.

And no matter how late I stayed out, how many kisses I collected, or how far I flew, the morning always came—with its honest light and its sharp, unfiltered questions. *What are you doing? Who are you without the job, without the house, without the applause? Are you a good man, or just one who got good at performing?* That's the thing about stillness—it doesn't let you lie to yourself for long.

I sat on the edge of the bed, phone still in hand, scrolling out of habit more than curiosity. My feed was just noise—fake laughter, gym selfies, someone's vacation highlights stitched together with a trending song. I wasn't looking for anything. Just trying to fill the space between one slow breath and the next. The wedding reminders from my son still sat at the top of the screen, a low, persistent hum.

I cracked a smile earlier, didn't even think twice when he asked me to be part of it. Some things don't need a second thought. He says the word, I show up. Always been like that. But now, in the quiet of my house, the details of the upcoming trip—flight logistics, deciding what shoes to pack, digging through drawers for my passport—these small tasks filled my head, but under them, a different current pulled.

Somewhere between the practicalities, I caught myself hoping for something I couldn't name. Not a miracle. Not closure. I wasn't chasing clarity or expecting some life lesson to hit me mid-toast. It wasn't even about the wedding itself. That was solid—he was solid. I was happy for him, genuinely. But still, under all of that, there was this part of me leaning forward, waiting. Maybe for a shift I could feel. Maybe for a silence that didn't echo back everything I hadn't figured out.

I didn't want much. Just a second that landed differently. A pause where my chest didn't feel tight. A breath that wasn't followed by some weight I had to carry again. I wasn't even sure if that kind of peace existed anymore—but if it did, maybe I'd find it there. Not in the event, but in the in-between—the early morning before the ceremony, the walk back to the hotel alone, the clink of glasses when no one's looking. Maybe I just needed to feel like I wasn't drifting. That'd be enough. And maybe, in Jamaica, away from the familiar whispers of Atlanta, I could finally take that first real step.

I used to think I had it all figured out. I really did. Good money. Good house. Family I loved. A plan. Not some wild dream either—just a solid, step-by-step blueprint I could recite in my sleep. The kind of plan that's been drilled into Black boys since forever: *Go to school. Don't embarrass your mama. Get the job. Keep your head down. Take care of your people. Don't give them a reason. Stay out the way. Stack your paper. Die with your dignity intact.*

That's what I did. I played the game the way I was taught. Suit and tie. Yes sir, no sir. Made myself small in rooms just big enough for them to feel safe with me. Took the late shifts. Took the blame. Took the hits and called it responsibility. And for a while, it worked. Promotions, benefits, birthdays with bounce houses and catered wings. Nights where we laughed loud enough to forget how tired we were. I had arrived—or so I told myself.

But no one tells you what happens when the plan runs out. When you check off every box and still wake up feeling like something's missing. No one warns you how fragile it all really is.

Until one day, the cracks show. Quiet at first—an argument that doesn't get resolved, a missed anniversary, a smile that doesn't reach her eyes anymore. And then it happens all at once. What you built starts slipping

5

through your fingers, and you're standing there trying to hold on, but it's like grabbing at dust. It crumbled in my hands, and I had no clue what I was even holding anymore. Was it a legacy? A lie? A version of manhood that was never really mine?

I thought I was doing everything right. But maybe "right" was just survival dressed up in a three-piece suit. Maybe I was following a script written for somebody who never asked what I wanted. Who never even asked if I was okay.

And now... now I'm just here. Replaying the pieces. Trying to figure out if the man I became is anything close to the man I was supposed to be.

The divorce broke me more than the marriage. It broke something inside me I didn't even know was fragile. Something deep. Like a load-bearing beam you don't realize is essential until it snaps—and suddenly the whole damn house feels unstable.

I loved her. Even now, part of me still does. Not in a way that makes me want to go back, but in that permanent kind of way. Like a scar that stopped bleeding but still aches when the weather shifts. She was the first person who saw me when I was still trying to see myself. We had real love—real history. Inside jokes, secrets nobody else could ever understand, routines that made us feel like we had the world figured out.

But we didn't belong together in the way that mattered.

And I knew that. I knew it long before the paperwork. Before the therapist. Before our laughter thinned out and got replaced by that tension that sits in the room even when no one's saying anything. I knew it in the way I started staying later at work, making up reasons to avoid walking through the door. I'd sit in the parking lot sometimes with the car running, staring at the house like it might change if I waited long enough.

She didn't yell. Didn't cuss me out or throw plates like in the movies. That would've been easier, maybe. She just... stopped looking at me the same. Like whatever was behind her eyes when we met had gone dim. Like she was already somewhere else, emotionally packed and halfway out the door.

That part hurt the most.

Because when someone stops seeing you—really seeing you—it's a different kind of silence. You're still in the same bed, same kitchen, same everything, but you feel invisible. I started shrinking in that house. Going through the motions. Pouring coffee, folding towels, asking about her day like it wasn't the same script we'd already played out a hundred times.

And the crazy thing? We never stopped caring. But sometimes love isn't enough when the foundation's already cracked. We were two good people who just couldn't build the same future anymore.

So we let it go. Or maybe it let us go. Either way, something broke in the process—and I've been trying to figure out who I am without that version of "us" ever since.

And then there were the twins. My babies. My heartbeat split in two. Growing faster than I could keep up. Every time I blinked, they were taller, sharper, further from the version of them I swore I'd never miss. Time slipped like water through my hands—first steps, school plays, scraped knees, and late-night questions I wasn't there to answer. Gone. Traded for PowerPoints and boarding passes. For praise from people who wouldn't show up to my funeral.

I told myself I was doing it for them. That the grind had a purpose. That every missed dinner, every "I'll make the next one," was part of building something they'd thank me for later. That sacrificing the now was the cost of securing their future.

But truth is—I did it because I didn't know how not to. I didn't know how to sit still. How to exist without proving myself. Somewhere along the way, productivity became my identity. The job became my worth. And showing up at work felt easier than showing up in the places that actually mattered.

There was this night—I still remember it. It's etched in my chest like a burn. I came home late. Again. Silent house, lights off except for the kitchen. My son was already asleep. Probably tucked himself in. My daughter had left a note on the counter. Folded paper. Stick figures in marker. She'd drawn herself at soccer practice—bright red jersey, arms in the air, big toothy smile. And right next to her, she'd drawn a little empty

7

space with a name floating over it: "Daddy."

Like she saved me a seat I never showed up for.

That damn drawing hit me harder than any argument, any performance review, any voicemail I ignored while in a meeting. She didn't even write anything else. Just that little space. Like she was still hoping I'd fill it next time. I stood there in that kitchen, tie half-loosened, the hum of the fridge the only sound in the room, and I swear I felt something inside me split.

Because the worst part wasn't that I missed the game. The worst part was realizing I'd made "missing it" normal. That my absence had become routine. That my daughter had learned to talk to me through crayon and silence because words weren't enough anymore.

And I still have that note. Tucked in a drawer somewhere I only open when I'm ready to feel it all again. It reminds me who I was. Who I don't want to be anymore.

I sat down on the sofa and just stared at the fridge. Not because I was hungry. Not because I was even thinking straight. Just sat there like it might blink first. Like somehow, in the soft hum of the compressor or the old magnets curling at the edges, I'd find answers. Something to tell me what the hell I was doing. Or who I was without the titles. Without the rush. Without the weight of being needed by everyone except myself.

Nobody tells you success can feel like failure in slow motion. They don't tell you that it's not one moment—it's a thousand quiet ones stacked on top of each other. Skipped dinners. Apologies left on read. The ache in your chest when your kid calls you "sir" like you're a stranger trying to be polite. It's not dramatic. It's erosion. Bit by bit, it wears you down until you wake up and don't recognize the life you built.

Quitting wasn't a decision. It was a breaking point. I remember walking out that last day with a cardboard box in my hands. That cliché scene you see in movies—but real now. Mine. A box full of shit I didn't need. Old notebooks with ideas no one read. Cheap pens. That same damn mug I never washed. It still had coffee rings from three Mondays ago.

My assistant looked at me, wide-eyed and soft-voiced. "You sure?" I wasn't. But I lied like it was part of the job. Gave her a nod like I had it all figured out. Truth was, I didn't even know where I parked. I was floating.

At Frito-Lay we used to joke, "We're not saving lives. They're just chips." Except I treated it like a calling. Like every spreadsheet was sacred. Like the next promotion would finally make me feel like I wasn't failing at being a man. I sacrificed real moments—memories I should've been inside of—for metrics that didn't even matter outside of a quarterly call.

So I stopped. No plan. No big speech. Just silence. Me and that box. I didn't cry. Didn't scream. Just walked out, each step louder than the last, like the building was letting go of me before I could change my mind. The sunlight hit differently that day. Felt honest. Like it didn't care about my résumé. Like it was asking, "Now what?"

I didn't have an answer. Still don't, some days. But at least I stopped lying to myself. That was the first real win I'd had in years. And with my son's wedding approaching, maybe it was time for the next one.

2

La Rebelión

As I thought about packing for Jamaica, my mind drifted. Cartagena came after. It came after everything fell apart. After the desk was cleared, the papers signed, the life I thought I'd built packed into boxes I didn't care to open. One night, I just booked the flight. No plan. No farewell tour. I just needed air that didn't feel recycled. Somewhere my past couldn't follow.

Cartagena had always been one of those "one day" places. Somewhere I said I'd go when things slowed down—when the time was right. But time had stopped making sense, and my compass wasn't pointing anywhere familiar. So I landed in that city like a man trying to breathe for the first time in months.

It hit me the second I stepped outside the airport—heat like a hand to the chest. Humid, dense, alive. The air in Cartagena carries music, sweat, and spirit. It's a place that moves even when it's standing still. Yellow taxis zipped by, vendors called out "agua, coco, mango!" from pushcarts, the scent of fried fish and coconut rice trailing behind them like perfume.

But it was the people that struck me first. Brown like me. Darker. Black in ways that felt ancestral. People with skin kissed by sun and history, walking like rhythm lived in their bones. There was pride in their posture. Fire in their laughter. And suddenly, I wasn't just a tourist—I was kin. A stranger and still, somehow, a reflection.

I wandered. I let the old city pull me in with its cracked colonial walls and kaleidoscope balconies spilling over with flowers. Horse hooves clacked against cobblestone as if the city had its own drumline. At night, it all shimmered. Champeta bleeding from the clubs. Lovers tangled on benches. Street kids doing backflips in the Getsemani square for change and applause.

And then one night, I heard Joe Arroyo.

"La Rebelión" came pouring out of a speaker in Getsemaní—loud, defiant, Black. The drumline caught my spine first. Then the horn section hit. Then that voice—raspy, urgent, full of fire. I didn't know the lyrics, not yet, but I felt it. Like my body recognized it before my brain could translate.

Later, I found the meaning. A slave who fought back. A man who refused to let his wife be touched, who struck down his master. "No le pegue a la negra." Don't hit the Black woman.

And that was it. The song wasn't just music—it was a history lesson, a war cry, an anthem. Joe wasn't just singing—he was telling every Black Colombian, every descendant of the Afro diaspora, *you are powerful, you come from rebellion, from resistance, from love that fought back.*

That song gave the city texture. Suddenly, every drumbeat on the street had a deeper root. Every face I passed had a lineage I needed to respect. I wasn't just escaping anymore—I was remembering. Reconnecting. Realizing I had gone so long trying to be "safe," "palatable," "successful," that I'd almost forgotten what it felt like to simply belong without effort.

And yeah, I drank. I danced. I laughed too loud in the plaza while some old man tried to teach me how to move my hips without thinking. I kissed a stranger. Ate food with my hands. Let myself be soft, and curious, and alive.

But even in paradise, your soul will tap you on the shoulder.

It waited till I was walking back to my Airbnb barefoot, shoes in hand, sweat cooling on my skin, the echo of Joe still ringing in my head. That voice came soft this time—not accusing, just real.

"You found joy here. But can you carry it back with you? Or are you only free when no one knows your name?"

I didn't have the answer yet. Still don't. But Cartagena gave me the question in a language I could finally feel.

* * *

I came home with a tan, a new playlist, and a silence that settled in my bones like fog. People asked how the trip was, and I said what you're supposed to say—"Man, it was amazing." I smiled. I showed a few pictures. Sunset on the wall in Laguito. Me with aguardiente in hand, forehead glistening, shirt open just enough. Laughter in the background, music I didn't Shazam but could still hum.

I said all the right things.

But the truth? I brought more than souvenirs back with me. I brought back a version of myself I hadn't met before—one that had felt weightless for the first time in years. One that knew how to dance without checking the time. One that let his guard down long enough to feel sunlight on parts of his spirit that hadn't seen daylight in over a decade.

But that version of me didn't last in Atlanta.

Here, the rhythm didn't follow me. The colors faded. The air felt thin again. Distraction stopped working. I tried to keep the feeling alive— played the same songs from that Cartagena playlist, poured the same rum, closed my eyes and leaned back like I could trick myself into going back.

But it didn't stick. Not for long. I realized then that I wasn't meant to *fix* myself or *save* my past; I was just trying to remember what I'd *found* there.

I'd lie in bed at 3 a.m., shirt still smelling like sweat and cologne, halfway between memory and regret. My limbs felt heavy, like my body was trying to keep me grounded while my mind kept drifting. I'd stare at the ceiling fan spinning in slow, lazy circles and wonder if I'd ever stop feeling like a ghost in my own life.

I was there… but not really. Eating, breathing, answering texts, but not present. Like the version of me that danced in the plaza, who smiled without effort, never made it past customs. I'd come home, sure—but part of me never boarded the flight back.

Even now, I can still hear it sometimes—the echo of a woman's laugh

I don't fully remember, in a city I no longer missed. Not because she meant something. Not even because I knew her name. But because in that moment, in that sound, I felt seen. Wanted. Free. Her laugh wrapped around the night like a melody, rising over the bass, over the traffic, over the ache I'd buried too deep to explain.

And that's what haunts me now. I missed my kids with a kind of ache that didn't show up in photos or weekend visits. Not the loneliness. Not even the silence. But the fact that I found peace in a place that was never meant to be permanent—and still haven't figured out how to recreate it here.

* * *

The walls in my house were starting to feel too familiar again. Like they'd memorized me. Knew my footsteps, my sighs, the way I leaned against the counter when I couldn't decide whether I was hungry or just bored. The couch sagged where I always sat—left side, near the armrest, remote always just out of reach, a simple metaphor for how I'd been living.

I'd sink into that same spot every night, like muscle memory. Not because it was comfortable. Because it was predictable. Because it asked nothing of me.

The bed was worse. Big enough for two, but heavy with the kind of emptiness you don't always notice right away. Sheets pulled tight, but the cold always found its way in. No matter who had been in it before—no matter how warm her body, how soft her breath on my neck—by morning, it was like no one had ever been there. Like the room hit reset while I was asleep.

I wasn't lonely in the way people think. Not in the desperate, "please call me" kind of way. Not in the Instagram-captioned, "where's my person?" way. I had numbers I could dial. Company I could call over. I could laugh. I could smile in the mirror and make it look good. I could flirt over drinks and make it to morning with someone in my kitchen asking how I take my eggs.

But none of it touched me.

I just missed myself. Missed feeling like I had something real to wake up for. Something that pulled me out of bed with purpose instead of routine. Something that made the silence feel earned, not suffocating.

There was a time I'd wake up before the sun. Not because I had to—but because I wanted to. Because I had a reason. Because there were little feet running down the hallway. Because breakfast meant more than eggs—it meant presence. It meant us.

Now, the mornings were just mornings. Wake up. Breathe. Scroll. Shower. Maybe eat. Maybe don't. Nothing urgent. Nothing that couldn't be done later. And that scared me more than being busy ever did.

Because when the noise stops, the truth gets louder. And mine was this: I didn't know who I was outside of what I used to be.

* * *

My playlist switched tracks. The shuffle landed something low and slow— SiR's "John Redcorn." That first guitar lick crept in like memory, smooth and aching. I paused mid-pack, just stood there, hands hovering over a half-zipped bag, letting the sound fill the room like smoke.

That song always had a way of creeping under the skin.

It used to hit different when I had someone lying next to me—back pressed against mine, legs tangled up, breathing slow and synced like we were sharing air. Back then, the song felt like a confession we didn't need to say aloud. A little too honest, a little too close to our truth, but beautiful all the same.

Now? Now it just reminded me how long it had been since I let anyone that close. Close enough to hear me breathe in the dark. Close enough to feel me flinch when the nothing got too loud. Close enough to know the difference between my silence and my peace. I'd been keeping people at arm's length so long, I forgot what it felt like to be reached for.

The guitar looped, his voice soft but bleeding, and I let it play. I just stood there in the stillness of my room, bag wide open, clothes half-folded, pretending I had somewhere urgent to be. But I wasn't packing for a trip—I was packing for the illusion of movement. Trying to feel like I was still going somewhere, still in motion, still alive.

I zipped the bag.

I walked to the kitchen. The house felt colder than it had an hour ago. Or maybe that was just the song lingering. I opened the cabinet, pulled down the bottle of rum I'd been nursing since Cartagena. Just a few fingers left. I poured it into a short glass. No toast. No speech. No deep reflection. Just the burn. It hit the back of my throat and warmed my chest in a way that tricks you into thinking something real is happening. Like the fire inside means you're still here. Still present. Still something more than a man pacing the same house with ghosts in every corner. SiR kept singing in the background. "Alone… every night alone…" .

I didn't sing along. I just let it play. Some songs don't need your voice; they just need your silence.

* * *

The night before the flight, I lay in bed, staring at the ceiling like I always did. Same position. Same breath. Same questions that never had the decency to show up in the daytime. I wasn't restless—I was resigned. Just me, the ticking of the wall clock, and the dull hum of a city that didn't need me anymore.

Outside, Atlanta moved without me.

Headlights slid across my bedroom wall like ghosts. Tires hissed on wet asphalt. Somewhere down the street, someone was yelling—not in rage, but in that messy, desperate way people do when they still care. I listened to the words I couldn't make out and wondered if I'd ever feel that kind of urgency again. If I ever had.

I closed my eyes and let the weight of everything I hadn't said settle into my chest. Apologies that came too late. Truths I dressed up in half-lies just to keep the peace. The moments I swallowed grief like it was pride—mouth closed, back straight, like that would save me from breaking. I thought silence made me strong. But silence can rot you from the inside when you use it to hold too much.

Maybe I wasn't meant to be anything more than what I already was. Maybe the damage had already been done. Maybe this—this floating, this ache, this permanent sense of almost—was just who I was now. Some men get second chances. Some don't. And I'd learned not to expect redemption just because I finally wanted it.

But then again… maybe there was still something in me worth finding. Not saving. Not fixing. Just finding. A piece I'd buried before the job, before the divorce, before I taught myself how to disappear while still showing up. I didn't know what Jamaica had for me—wasn't chasing a fantasy, or some eat-pray-love kind of reinvention.

I just knew what Atlanta didn't.

Atlanta didn't have space for the version of me I was trying to become. It knew the man I used to be too well. Kept handing me the same mask and expecting me to smile behind it.

My phone buzzed on the nightstand — Tiff this time.

"You packed yet?"

No emoji, no softness. Just the question, sharp enough to cut through all my good excuses. I let it sit there. Watched the three dots pop up, vanish, pop up again. I flipped the phone face-down. Some answers better left on read.

And maybe that was the final sign: when the place that made you no longer feels like home, it's time to stop arguing with the feeling.

I reached over, turned off the lamp.

The darkness wrapped around me slow, like it had been waiting. Not scary. Not empty. Just honest. The kind of darkness that doesn't threaten— it just tells the truth.

And I let it take me. Not because I was tired. Not because I needed rest. But because it was finally time to go.

3

Boarding Without Wanting

I moved through the airport like a ghost with a boarding pass. Not rushed. Not dazed. Just floating between presence and absence, like I was watching myself from outside my own body. I didn't speak much. Didn't smile unless I had to. My carry-on rolled behind me with that soft, uneven thud of plastic wheels on polished tile—like it, too, had nowhere better to be. Same as me.

Atlanta's airport was its usual chaos. Families slumped in terminal seats with kids curled up in oversized hoodies, clutching iPads like lifelines. Business travelers speed-walked in fitted suits and Bluetooth headsets, eyes locked on departure boards like they could will time to bend. TSA agents barked orders with that familiar blend of authority and exhaustion—it wasn't even noon, and already their patience had clocked out.

I moved through it all like background noise. No destination energy. No vacation glow. Just another body in motion. I caught my reflection in one of the glass walls by the escalator—didn't recognize the man staring back. Shoulders tense. Hat pulled low. Eyes dull, like they were conserving light.

I used to feel important in places like this. Airports made me feel like I was going somewhere, like my time mattered. I used to strut through with status. Priority boarding. Laptop half-open at the gate while I juggled emails and affirmations about grind culture. Back then, motion felt like purpose. Now it just felt like escape.

I scanned my boarding pass at the gate, nodded at the agent like we knew each other. She didn't look up. Just motioned me through with the same tired flick of the wrist she gave the last twenty people. I didn't mind. I wasn't here to be seen.

As I walked down the jet bridge, the cold air shifted—cooler, more sterile. The kind of air that smells like recycled decisions and strangers trying not to brush shoulders. The wheels on my bag wobbled against the metal grate, stuttering like they were hesitating.

I didn't blame them.

This wasn't a bold departure. It wasn't brave. It was just... necessary. Sometimes leaving ain't about chasing something new. It's about stopping the slow death of staying where you don't belong anymore.

I found my seat. Window. Row 19. Didn't even bother with overhead space—just sat down, buckled in, and stared out at nothing. The plane hadn't moved, but I already felt like I was somewhere else.

Not free. Not yet.

But on the way.

* * *

The flight wasn't long, but it dragged like grief. Only a couple hours in the air, but the kind of stretch where time loosens and your thoughts start speaking louder than the engine. I hadn't touched the screen in front of me. I wasn't in the mood to be entertained. I just sat there, hood up, staring out the window like the clouds might offer some kind of answer if I watched long enough. From up here, the world looked too calm to be real. Neat. Far away. Like everything I left behind had shrunk without me in it.

I had a playlist queued up but didn't remember building it. Songs I hadn't listened to in months, maybe years. I hit play anyway, and the music filled the space that conversation used to.

SAINt JHN's "Sucks to Be You" was first. It didn't wait. It just cracked something open like it knew where the fault lines were.

You ain't even got the decency to give me a heads-up.

That line sat heavy. Not because of her. But because of me. Because of the way I walked out of the life I built without really explaining why. The way I disappeared piece by piece, day by day, telling myself I was still holding it together when I'd already let it fall apart.

I adjusted the air nozzle above me and closed my eyes.

Then came Kwes & Sampha. "Let Go of Your Hurt." That one crept in slowly, like fog.

You've been running in place with your trauma. You ain't moved past it, just dressed it in karma.

That lyric didn't feel like music. It felt like accusation.

Work was my excuse. Distance, my strategy. Fatherhood, my penance. Until I couldn't fake being okay anymore. I missed my kids with a kind of ache that didn't show up in photos or weekend visits. I missed my daughter's bedtime rambling, the way she'd talk about everything and nothing until she fell asleep mid-sentence. I missed my son's questions—half logic, half magic—like he still believed I had the answers.

And somewhere in all that missing, my mind drifted. Back to a different kind of missing, perhaps. My high school girlfriend, Imani. Years with her, with her family, meant I picked up more than just a love for dancehall; I learned the cadences, the bending of English into patois, the way a phrase could carry a whole history . The sun had been relentless, the kind that clung to your skin no matter how much shade you chased. Everything smelled like salt and sunscreen and grilled fish from the beachside vendors. We smiled for the pictures. Let strangers take them even—offering our best angles, our most convincing grins. We laughed with locals, held hands when the drinks came, leaned into each other at dinners we barely tasted. On the surface, we looked like a couple in sync. But beneath it all, the closeness felt rehearsed. Every touch, every smile, every shared glance—it was all choreography. A performance of who we used to be, or maybe who we still wished we were .

There was a picture from that trip we used to have framed. It sat on the mantle for a while, before I packed it away with the rest of the lies we told each other gently. I was behind her, arms around her waist, both of us staring out at the water like we saw something worth walking toward. We looked like love. The kind of photo people post with long captions and hashtags about forever. But I remember that moment more for what I wasn't saying than anything I felt. I remember the heaviness in my chest, the numb buzz behind my eyes, the way I kept my arms around her like muscle memory. I was already drifting. She just hadn't stopped hoping yet.

She was still trying. Planning next steps, talking about another baby, pointing out houses she thought we'd grow into. She wanted to believe we were in a rough patch. I already knew we were somewhere past repair. And I hated that I didn't have the courage to say it. Hated that I let her keep believing in a version of us that had already died between business trips and polite arguments. We framed that picture like proof, but every time I looked at it, all I could see was distance. Two people performing closeness. Holding each other like a truce, not a choice.

The music shifted again.

Juice WRLD – "Lucid Dreams."

You were my everything... thoughts of a wedding ring...

I didn't flinch. I just let the words run through me like cold water. I wasn't suicidal. But I knew what it felt like to want to disappear. To want the weight to lift, even if just for an hour. I'd had moments—dark, quiet ones—where I didn't want to die. I just didn't want to be here. Not like this. Not hollow. Not pretending.

The plane hit light turbulence. A kid cried somewhere behind me. Someone ordered tomato juice. The world kept going, indifferent. But I just kept staring out the window, letting the music bleed through the cracks.

The clouds didn't say anything. But they knew.

Up here, above everything, I finally admitted it:

I wasn't running from her.

Or from them.

I was trying to find the version of me I used to believe in.

And praying he was still out there somewhere.

* * *

I thought about my kids too. What they might've been doing that day. Whether they even remembered I'd be flying out. Whether their mom had mentioned it, or if the day just moved on without me in it. I wondered if their routines had already adjusted to the holes I left behind. If my absence was still something they felt—or just something they'd gotten used to.

The cabin lights dimmed a little as we hit cruising altitude, casting everything in this soft, artificial blue that made the plane feel more like a waiting room than a vessel. I shifted in my seat, head still tilted toward the window, but my eyes were somewhere else.

My daughter used to beg me to do her hair. Saturday mornings mostly. She'd bring the brush and the beads and the little plastic barrettes shaped like butterflies. She'd sit between my knees on the living room rug, squirming and kicking her feet, full of stories about school and dreams and questions I never had full answers for. I never got the parts straight. My fingers were clumsy, and and I'd tug too hard sometimes. But she'd smile at her reflection in the hallway mirror like it was perfect. Said I did it better than Mommy. Swore by it. And for a while, I believed her. Not because it was true, but because she did.

That stopped the same year the promotions started coming faster. I'd traded in bedtime stories for conference calls. Skipped breakfast to catch flights like this one. The more money I made, the more I convinced myself I was doing it for them. But I wasn't. I was doing it to feel valuable. To feel needed somewhere. And every bonus, every corner office, every business-class ticket pulled me further from the kind of love you can't earn back once you miss it too many times.

My son used to run to the door when I got home. Full sprint. Like his day didn't start until I walked in. Like whatever happened at school, whatever fight he had at lunch or joke he wanted to tell, it all waited for me. That kind of excitement is rare. Pure. The kind you don't realize is fleeting until it fades. Now, he barely looks up from his game when I call. Says "hey" without pausing. Gives me a nod like I'm the mailman instead of the man

21

who used to carry him to bed with both shoes still on.

And I don't blame them.

I blame me.

Not for working. Not for trying to provide. But for believing presence was about proximity. That being under the same roof could substitute for actually being there. For showing up emotionally. For sitting on the floor when I was tired. For asking how their day was and actually listening instead of checking my phone halfway through.

The hum of the engine grew louder in my ears. Or maybe the music had cut off without me noticing. Either way, the silence inside me was deafening.

I rubbed my palms together and stared out at the clouds again. They didn't care. They didn't shift. They just kept floating. Like everything else in my life I hadn't held onto tightly enough.

* * *

The plane started its descent into Montego Bay, and my chest got tight—not with nerves, but with presence. Something I hadn't felt in a while. Not anticipation. Not anxiety. Just… stillness. Like my body finally realized it didn't have to outrun anything for the next few hours. For once, I wasn't thinking about what I needed to fix or prove or explain. I wasn't rehearsing the next conversation or replaying the last one. I was just breathing. Shallow, steady. In and out.

I looked out the window as the clouds thinned and gave way to color—lush green, electric blue, that warm blur of coastline that always hit different when you knew you were stepping into it, not just admiring from above. The landing gear groaned beneath us, and the plane tilted gently forward like it, too, was surrendering.

When we touched down, the jolt didn't shake me. It settled me. Like gravity had been on pause this whole time and just decided to start working again.

The moment I stepped off the plane, it hit me. The heat. Thick and familiar. It didn't wait for me to adjust—it claimed me. Wrapped around my arms, slid beneath my collar, kissed the back of my neck like an ex who still knew all the places that made me stop talking. Heavy, intimate, unbothered by personal space. It smelled faintly of jet fuel, sugarcane, and sweat already waiting to happen. Tropical heat had a way of making you feel seen. Like it knew who you were beneath your job title and your trauma. Like it didn't care what you left behind—only that you made it here.

And I let it happen. I let it press against my skin. I let my shirt stick a little. I let my shoulders drop from where they'd been living up by my ears. It didn't feel oppressive. It felt alive. Like something old that never stopped breathing.

My steps were slower now. Not because I was tired, but because I wasn't rushing anymore. Jamaica didn't invite urgency. It didn't care about calendars or time zones or to-do lists. And in that moment, neither did I.

I was here. Whole or not. Ready or not.

And for the first time in a long time, that felt like enough.

* * *

Customs was a chaos of voices and paper and heat layered thick like smoke. The lines bent and curled in every direction—no clear order, no obvious logic. Just human rhythm. Backpacks slid across tile, passports flipped open, elbows nudged forward with the tired desperation of travelers who had been here before. Security guards stood like statues with booming voices.

"Yuh can't tek di phone yah, boss—put it inna yuh pocket!"

"Line three, people! LINE THREE—move up or move out!"

The fans overhead buzzed like they were trying to work but had given up halfway through. They didn't do a damn thing for the heat. Sweat gathered at the back of my neck, rolled down my spine like the island was testing my resolve before I even stepped outside. I didn't mind it.

The noise came in layers—deep patois with sharp edges, American accents tinged with vacation entitlement, soft threads of French and Spanish drifting in and out like radio static. It was chaotic, but it had rhythm. It didn't feel random. It felt alive.

People moved like they had somewhere urgent to be, even if that somewhere was just a drink and a view. I didn't rush. I just watched.

A little boy tugged at his mother's sleeve, begging for snacks like the wait might kill him. She handed him a bag of plantain chips without even glancing down, her other hand flipping through their passports. A man in a green mesh tank top leaned too close to me in line.

"Mi boss, weh yuh stayin'? Mi sort out ride an' ting if yuh nuh book nutten yet."

I shook my head, polite but firm. "I'm good, man. Appreciate it."

He smiled like he already knew the answer, then turned to hustle the next tired-looking couple.

The line moved. Slowly. Customs booths flickered with old screens and even older clocks. The kind of space that didn't move faster just because you wanted it to.

When it was finally my turn, I stepped forward. The customs officer looked like he'd seen every type of traveler walk through—drunk spring breakers, stressed business execs, couples pretending to still be in love. His eyes scanned me quick, then dropped to my passport.

"First time in Jamaica?" he asked, flipping it open.

I nodded. "Yeah."

He looked up, held my gaze a second longer than necessary. "Well. Better late than never."

His voice was low and calm, like someone who'd lived a lot of stories he didn't tell anymore. He kept flipping through the pages.

"Business or pleasure?"

I hesitated, just for a breath. "Little bit of both. Mostly… breathing."

He cracked a small smile at that. Just barely. But it counted.

"You bringing in any food, alcohol, or more than ten thousand US?"

"No, sir."

He nodded, grabbed the stamp, and pressed it hard.

CLACK.

It landed like a checkpoint in a video game. Or a seal on a version of myself I hadn't fully realized yet .

He handed my passport back, nodding once.

"Welcome to Jamaica, mi man. Take yuh time."

And just like that, I was in. For the first time. For real.

* * *

Outside the terminal, the sun laid hands on me again—stronger this time. No more filtered air or tempered windows. This was the real thing. Direct. Intentional. Heavy like a truth that didn't need softening. It soaked into my skin, rolled across my shoulders, slipped beneath my collar like it knew me. Like it had been waiting.

The air was thick with salt, sweat, and the sweet punch of ripe fruit somewhere in the distance. Horns honked without pattern. A whistle blew once, maybe twice, with no clear reason. People were everywhere. Lines of drivers stretched along the curb, each one holding up a sign—some typed, some scribbled on cardboard, some held like afterthoughts. My name wasn't on any of them, but they still looked at me like they were sure I belonged to someone.

"Taxi, boss? I've got A/C and cold drinks, mi nah lie!"

"Ey, King! You need SIM card? Unlocked, LTE, mi sort yuh out now now!"

"First time, mi know it—come, come, best tour inna MoBay, full vibes!"

The voices stacked on top of each other. Some friendly. Some aggressive. Most somewhere in between. I didn't feel harassed. I felt invited. Like I'd just walked into the middle of something already moving, and they were offering me a chance to catch the rhythm.

A man off to the left was blasting dancehall from a scuffed Bluetooth speaker. Sound distorted at the edges, but the beat still slapped. Bass deep enough to vibrate the pavement. The track was Vybz Kartel—something off an old riddim, still infectious.

"Gal a bubble 'pon di beat—weh yuh deh?! Forward, forward—ayy!"

He shouted names between verses like it was a roll call for a party nobody told me about.

"Devin! Tasha! Braaaddyyyyy! Come fi yuh driver, man!"

He wore a gold chain that glinted like it had its own agenda and danced in place like the sun was his DJ. No shame. No pause. Just vibes.

A younger guy brushed past me, quick to pitch.

"Good kush, mi boss? Straight from di hills—fiyah."

I shook my head, half-laughing. "Nah, I'm good."

"Seen. If yuh change yuh mind, mi dey right yah," he said, already peeling away to ask someone else. Vendors wove through the traffic with baskets of peanuts, fruit bags, bracelets. One man had laminated tour brochures fanned out like playing cards. A woman passed holding a box of cold Red Stripes like a prize. Somewhere behind me, someone was arguing over pickup times in sharp Brooklyn English.

I didn't rush. I just let it all pour over me.

The heat. The smell of jerk smoke floating in from somewhere nearby. The music. The sound of language bending, flipping, breaking into patois and reassembling itself before I could keep up. The way people moved here—with intention, even if the destination was unclear.

There was a rhythm to it all. A choreography I didn't know yet, but could feel in my chest.

And for the first time in a long time, I wasn't trying to control anything. I was just… here.

In Jamaica.

And ready to let it show me who I was when I wasn't trying so hard to be anything else.

* * *

I had made arrangements with a driver—Dez or Desmond, something like that. I found the number online, quick exchange on WhatsApp, locked it in. No photo. No license plate. Just: "Seen. I'll be dey." That was it. And that was enough.

I wasn't pressed. Not today. I found a spot on a low concrete wall near the curb and sat down, letting the sun settle onto my shoulders like it had something to say. The heat was thick and close, not hostile but heavy—like it wanted me to slow down, take it in. My shirt stuck to my back already, sweat creeping under my arms and around my neck, but I didn't mind. I wasn't trying to fight it. I was letting it do what it came to do.

I pulled out my phone, held it in my palm for a minute, but didn't unlock it. Didn't care what time it was. Didn't want to know who had messaged or what I'd missed. I let the music keep playing low in my headphones. Some riddim I didn't recognize, just bass and attitude and sunshine tucked into every bar. It was perfect.

People flowed around me like currents. Tourists clutching neck pillows and rolling luggage, trying to look confident but glancing around like they'd lost something. Locals moved with a different kind of time—like the day worked for them, not the other way around. Drivers with signs in their hands and hustle in their voices called out names like roll call.

"Jerome Thomas? Ride to Ocho Rios here, ya so!"

"Island Tours! Who book with Island Tours?"

"Mr. Henderson! Yuh ready fi di beach, mi boss?"

Nobody called my name, and that was fine. I wasn't here to be found. I was already where I needed to be.

A woman passed with a tray of patties tucked under foil. The smell caught me off guard—rich, warm, peppered with just enough grease to feel honest. "Hot patties! Fresh out di oven! Beef, chicken—anyone want?" The scent hit me right in the chest, pulled something low out of me. I didn't even try to hide the sound. My stomach tightened, but I stayed where I was.

Somewhere nearby, a car door slammed. Laughter followed. The kind that came from the belly. A man walked past selling SIM cards out of a zippered pouch, already mid-pitch before he looked anyone in the eye. A coconut vendor rattled ice in his cooler and shouted over the music blaring from a speaker strapped to his cart.

"Gimme di light an' pass di dro—whoa!"

27

The bass vibrated under my feet. Sean Paul. Loud, cracked, perfect.
And me—I just sat there.

Not waiting. Not rushing. Just… arriving.

Letting the island stretch out in front of me. Letting the moment settle into my bones. Letting the sun have its way with me.

* * *

I wasn't here for reinvention. I didn't book this flight to start over, or heal, or write some cute little comeback story with a beach backdrop. I wasn't chasing clarity or peace or whatever else people think they find when they run far enough from their own mess. I wasn't looking for a new version of myself.

I just didn't want to keep dragging the old one around anymore.

I wasn't here to fall in love. Not with a place. Not with a woman. Not with myself. That kind of shit felt indulgent right now—too shiny, too forced. I wasn't interested in tropical romance or spiritual awakenings or finding some goddamn mantra to slap on a wall in vinyl cursive.

I was just here.

To be here.

To let the sun land where it wanted. To let the wind press into me without reading into it. To feel my feet on unfamiliar ground and not try to name the lesson right away. I didn't want answers. I didn't even want questions. I just wanted pulse.

Breath. Skin. Sweat. Sound.

Whatever this place gave me, I'd take it. Not as a sign. Not as a path. Just as a moment. And that… that was the most honest thing I'd done in a long, long time.

Maybe the most alive I'd felt, too.

Even if I didn't know what the hell came next.

Even if the ground beneath me was shifting.

Even if I was still figuring out how to stand still.

4

Names Don't Need Proof

I saw the sign before I saw the man.

Crooked. Handwritten in fading marker on a bent piece of cardboard: BRUCE W. The "W" looked rewritten three times—like the pen gave up but Dez wasn't about to start over. The edges of the sign were soft and curled, like it had seen weather. It leaned a little to the left, like the person holding it didn't give a damn whether I saw it or not. But I did. Somehow, that made it feel more real.

No branding. No logo. No laminated clipboard.

Just the name. My name. Scrawled like a note passed in class.

And behind it—Dez.

Tall. Dark-skinned. Maybe mid-forties. Shoulders like he used to hit people, but didn't need to now. His shirt was damp from the heat, clinging to his back like a second skin. Short locs, neatly twisted, pulled back but not tight. A single gold hoop glinted in his left ear, catching just enough sunlight to let you know he wore it on purpose. Not flash.

Just his.

His face was unreadable. Not mean, not soft. Just… settled. Like a man who'd seen enough to know when to speak and when silence would do the job better. His walk was steady, deliberate. The kind of pace that didn't need urgency. Like he knew where he was going and figured I'd catch up.

He didn't wave. Didn't smile. He just gave me a small nod and tilted his head toward the parking lot.

That was the invitation.

That was Dez.

* * *

I grabbed my bag and followed without a word.

He didn't ask if I was Bruce.

I didn't ask if he was Dez.

We both already knew.

As I stepped closer, he glanced sideways, not stopping his stride.

"Ya good?"

Voice low, gravelly. Like he'd smoked a few lifetimes and never bothered to cough.

I nodded. "Yeah. I'm good."

That was enough.

No need for a handshake.

No welcome speech.

Just two men in a moment, already moving.

* * *

We walked in silence, the kind that didn't feel awkward—just agreed upon. Dez led the way without looking back, his stride steady, measured. Like he trusted I'd follow and knew there wasn't anything to say yet. I didn't try to fill the space. I let my footsteps fall behind his, boots scuffing against sunbaked pavement as the terminal noise faded behind us.

The car came into view as we rounded the corner of the lot—a deep blue Prado SUV, clean but not polished to death. Not brand new, but well-kept. Paint smooth. No dents. Tinted windows just enough to keep the sun out and the privacy in. It wasn't the kind of vehicle that turned heads. But it was the kind of ride you noticed if you knew what to look for. Understated luxury. Confidence, not flash.

He popped the trunk with one hand and stepped aside. I tossed my bag in. The hydraulics let out a soft hiss as the lid lifted.

Inside smelled like leather, faint air freshener, and heat that had been sitting patiently all day. Dashboard clean. No clutter. No bobbleheads. No half-empty bottles. Just a small Jamaican flag on the rearview mirror, gently swaying with the breeze from the open driver's door.

"Long flight?" Dez asked as he slid into the seat, both hands on the wheel like he was about to guide something heavier than a car.

"Not too bad," I said, pulling the seatbelt across my chest. He nodded once, subtle, and pulled off without another word.

The tires rolled smooth against the lot's gravel edge before finding the paved stretch of road. The hum of rubber on asphalt became the only sound for a moment. The sun bounced off the windshield in long streaks, flickering like it was trying to get a look inside. Warm air pushed through the vents—heat mixed with salt, thick with the smell of pavement and faint engine oil. It hit the skin like a reminder: you're not home anymore.

We said nothing.

And that silence?

It didn't feel empty.

It felt like the beginning of something unspoken.

* * *

Montego Bay moved differently. It wasn't just the scenery—it was the rhythm. A tempo that didn't ask for permission. It pulsed beneath everything: the cars, the people, the air itself. Traffic flowed without rules, at least none I could see. Horns tapped quick like drum rolls—short bursts of communication that made sense only to the people who lived in it. No lines. No lanes that anyone seemed married to. But still, somehow, it worked. Nothing collided. Everything danced.

Vendors stood at intersections like they belonged there. No booths. No uniforms. Just crates and coolers and hustles passed down through generations. Men holding plastic bags of ripe mangoes, peeled sugarcane, cold bottles of water sweating through their labels. A woman waved a pack of cigarettes through a cracked car window and closed the deal in five seconds flat. They moved like the heat didn't faze them. Like standing in the sun was just part of the transaction.

Kids in school uniforms moved in packs—skirts swinging, khakis cuffed above dusty sneakers. Their backpacks hung low, dragging against their backs like anchors, but their mouths never stopped moving. Joking. Arguing. Singing. That after-school energy that buzzed like freedom. They weaved between parked cars like they owned the concrete. Maybe they did.

The streets were alive with color. Not just the kind you wear—but the kind you live in. Storefronts with hand-painted signs in bright yellows, greens, and reds. Barbershops with names like Sharp & Serious, Bless Up Fades, Chop Dem Clean. Corner bars with chipped paint and speakers mounted up high, pouring riddims into the air like seasoning. A wall mural of Bob Marley smiled out through sun-bleached dreadlocks, his eyes half-lidded like he knew everything but wouldn't say it all at once. Haile Selassie painted beside him, hands raised in a posture somewhere between prayer and power.

Cinderblock walls held it all together—unfinished, cracked in places, but standing proud. Nothing polished. Nothing sterile. Just real. No Starbucks. No Target. No shiny glass towers trying to make you forget where you are. The billboards were small, if there were any at all. The only branding here was personality. Culture painted in bold strokes. Names that meant something.

Dez drove like he'd done it a thousand times. One hand on the wheel, the other resting loose in his lap. He didn't flinch at near misses. Didn't check the mirrors more than once. He moved with the rhythm, too—part of the choreography. I leaned my elbow on the door, felt the vibration of the road beneath my arm, watched the scene play out like a film I didn't need to pause.

This wasn't a place dressed up for tourists.

This was life. Raw. Open. Unapologetic.

And I was grateful I got to see it like this—window down, no filter, nothing curated. Just a man in the backseat, letting the city speak for itself.

* * *

"Dis yuh first time inna yard?" Dez's voice cut through the music like a bassline—low, steady, right on time. Beres was still playing, soft in the background, but the words hit clear.

"Yeah," I said, watching the road roll past.

He gave a small chuckle. Not the kind that mocked. The kind that recognized something.

"You look it."

I smirked. "That obvious?"

"Yuh got dat first-day energy," he said, eyes on the road, one hand resting easy on the wheel. "Eyes wide. Neck turning too much. Like every t'ing a surprise."

I laughed. He wasn't wrong. I'd been looking at everything—signs, people, buildings, sky. Like I was trying to memorize the place before I even stepped into it.

"What brings ya here? Vacation?"

I paused.

"Wedding," I said. "My friend's getting married. I'm just... here for support."

He glanced at me, just once, then nodded slowly.

"Support," he repeated, letting the word stretch out like he was testing the weight of it in his mouth. "Yeah, man. Support strong."

He tapped his fingers against the steering wheel, eyes still forward, voice even.

"Well... Jamaica support yuh back if yuh let her. But she doesn't chase nobody."

He looked over again, this time with a little more intention. "She not America."

33

That line hit harder than I expected. He wasn't trying to be deep. Wasn't offering a sermon. He just said it.

And let it land. I didn't answer right away. I just sat with it.

Because I knew exactly what he meant.

America was always demanding something. Hustle. Productivity. Proof. Every breath felt like a transaction. If you stopped moving, you got left behind. Jamaica—at least the way he said it—sounded like somewhere that let you be. But only if you came honest.

"She not America," he repeated, softer this time. "Yuh can't come here wit plan fi fix yuhself. Yard doesn't rush healing. She doesn't hand out closure. She just… reflects yuh back to yuhself."

I looked out the window again. The streets had changed—narrower now, tighter with shops stacked close and graffiti climbing walls like vines. A man leaned into a fruit stand, passing money like it was sacred. A woman sat braiding a little girl's hair on a plastic chair, her hands moving fast and careful.

I nodded slowly. "That why you still here?"

Dez smiled without showing teeth. "Mi try leave once. Didn't like how mi spirit feel out dere."

He didn't explain. Didn't need to.

The car rolled on, the silence folding back in around us—not awkward, not final. Just space to let that conversation breathe.

And it did.

* * *

We pulled off the main road and into the hills, the pavement narrowing as the engine worked a little harder on the incline. The city fell away in layers—traffic softening, signs fewer, the energy shifting from motion to observation. Dez knew the turns without thinking. He didn't brake unless he had to. We coasted through pockets of shade, past bursts of color where hibiscus and bougainvillea climbed fences like they were trying to see what was on the other side.

Eventually, he slowed the car and nodded toward a narrow gate tucked between two tall palms.

"Dis it."

I stepped out. Gravel cracked underfoot, the sun resting heavy on the back of my neck as I looked up.

The apartment complex sat on a slope, three levels, peach-colored and weather-worn with iron balconies and flaking paint. The kind of place where the walls held sound—arguments, laughter, old music still playing somewhere past midnight. Doors didn't match, numbers were faded or missing, but the whole place stood proud like it didn't need fixing to feel like home.

My unit was on the first floor, tucked near the middle. A one-bedroom with a small covered porch that opened straight into the courtyard. No stairs. Just a few short steps and I was at the door. The space was humble, but it felt intentional—like whoever built it cared more about breeze and shade than aesthetics. The porch had enough room for a chair and a pair of sandals. Nothing fancy. Just stillness.

Clothes flapped on lines strung between balconies overhead. Pots of mint and thyme sat on ledges near open windows. Somewhere upstairs, a radio played old gospel, and the smell of fried dumplings drifted down with the music. Kids shouted somewhere out back. A dog barked once, then gave up. No one moved fast. No one looked twice at me. Past the rooftops and trees, beyond the rusted zinc and satellite dishes angled toward foreign channels, the bay opened wide. Blue and still. Cruise ships sat docked in the distance—sleeping giants under the late afternoon sun. They didn't move. Didn't flash. Just waited.

I stood there a little longer than I needed to. Bag still slung over my shoulder, sweat already creeping through my shirt. Not because it was picturesque. Not because I was overwhelmed.

But because—for the first time in a long time—it felt like the world wasn't asking anything of me. This place didn't try to impress.

It didn't announce itself.

It just... was.

And I could feel myself starting to meet it halfway.

Dez killed the engine and glanced over at me.

"No resort?" he asked, like it had just clicked. Like he expected me to say I was only up here for a detour before heading to something with a swim-up bar and folded towel swans.

I shook my head. "Nah. Booked this place myself."

He chuckled, low and knowing. The kind of laugh that didn't mock, just registered surprise.

"Yuh sure?" he said, popping the trunk. "Most people come 'round here, they head straight fi di strip. Beachfront views, buffet breakfast, likkle wristband life."

I followed him to the back of the SUV, the heat settling thick again as I grabbed my bag.

"They don't come up inna hills. Not unless they from here or looking fi somebody."

"Didn't feel right," I said. "That other stuff."

Dez nodded, easing the trunk shut with one hand.

"Yuh right," he said. "Easy to hide inna resort. Everything neat. Predictable. Staff smile 'cause dem paid to. Same rum punch, different day."

He looked around us. The complex. The people. Life happening without performance.

"Dis place?" he said, nodding toward the building. "She doesn't hide nothing. Yuh go market, yuh smell sweat and yam. Yuh hear goat bawl in di morning. Somebody argument reach yuh window same time as di rooster. But..."

He turned back toward me.

"If yuh let her, Jamaica show yuh herself. Not di postcard. Di real real."

I let that sit for a second. Felt it more than I heard it.

"That's why I picked it," I said. "Didn't come here to be served."

Dez studied me for a beat. Then gave a slow nod.

"Mi respect dat. Plenty man come to Jamaica but never see her. They scared of what they might find when the steel drum stop playing."

He cracked his neck, glanced at the sky.

"Alright, mi bredda. Mi swing back in couple hours, show yuh round a likkle. Let Jamaica whisper to yuh before she start talking loud."

I smiled. "Looking forward to it."

He opened the door, slid into the driver's seat, then leaned back out one more time.

"Yard talk when yuh quiet. So... listen."

Then he pulled off. And just like that, it was me, the porch, the heat, and a few hours to settle in.

No filters.

No schedule.

No resort.

Just the real thing.

* * *

Inside was simple. Clean. Modern, mostly.

White tile floors that carried the sound of every step. Fresh coat of paint on the walls—off-white, plain but intentional. A standing fan hummed in the corner, tall and oscillating, the kind that clicked when it turned like it had something to say but never raised its voice. The air was cooler than outside, but still warm enough to remind me where I was.

One bed. Low to the ground. Crisp white linens. A navy-blue throw folded at the foot, tucked neat like someone gave a damn. The nightstand held a single lamp, a simple switch light with a pull cord and a little tarnish at the base. The kind of detail you'd only notice if you weren't looking for anything else.

The bathroom smelled faintly of lime and old soap. Not unpleasant—just lived-in. The scent made me think of a different kind of clean. Not hotel clean. Real clean. Like someone had scrubbed the tiles with their own hands.

The kitchen was tucked into a corner of the open space. Small fridge. Two-burner stove. Electric kettle sitting next to a jar of instant coffee, and a chipped white mug turned upside down in the drying rack. The kind of mug you didn't throw away because it still worked. There were two plates in the cabinet, a fork, a knife, and a spoon.

A folded towel sat at the foot of the bed. White. Crisp. No note, no wrapper, just placed like someone figured I'd be tired and not in the mood to search.

I stood there in the doorway for a minute, bag still in my hand, staring at nothing in particular.

It didn't look like my grandmother's house. Not the furniture, not the layout. But something in the air felt the same. A softness. A muted pride. Like whoever owned this place didn't care about impressing anyone—just wanted it to feel like enough. The kind of space where time didn't rush you. It just met you where you were.

I dropped my bag by the dresser and sat on the edge of the bed. The mattress was firm. Supportive, but not inviting. No fake plushness. Just truth.

The fan clicked overhead in its rhythm—left, right, pause. Left, right, pause. A slow metronome for a moment I couldn't quite name.

I should've felt peace.

I should've felt some kind of exhale.

This was what I said I wanted—space, distance from everything that had hollowed me out.

But instead, I just felt... full. Like everything I hadn't dealt with had followed me here.

Waited until I stopped moving.

And now it was taking a seat across from me, ready to talk.

* * *

I stepped out onto the porch.

The door creaked behind me, screen swinging once before it clicked back into place. The concrete beneath my feet was warm, still holding heat from earlier in the day. I paused for a second, just standing there. No phone. No noise in my hand. Just my body, the wind, and whatever the island was about to show me.

And then I looked out.

Montego Bay stretched wide below me—an unfolding canvas of color and sound. Hills rolled down into neighborhoods stacked like thoughts, rooftops scattered in mismatched angles, zinc and tile, satellite dishes leaning toward the sky like they were listening for something. The sea beyond it all, soft and constant. The kind of view that didn't beg for attention, but earned your stillness.

People moved through the frame like brushstrokes—small but certain. A man walked with a bucket balanced on his shoulder like it was nothing, towel slung over his neck, steps unhurried. A girl tugged her little brother by the arm, her voice high and sharp, but familiar. He followed reluctantly, resisting just enough to show he had a will of his own. On a low wall nearby, an old woman in a wide-brimmed hat talked with her hands, laughing into the breeze at someone I couldn't see—her voice cutting through the air like it had purpose.

I spotted the ships farther down the coast. Cruise liners docked and silent, white against the blue, massive and unmoving. They looked out of place and perfectly settled at the same time. Sleeping giants with nowhere to be. Watching.

I eased into the single chair on the porch. Plastic. Worn smooth. It creaked under me but held its ground. I leaned back and let my arms rest on the rails, feeling the slight drag of breeze pass across my face like fingers.

The clouds above moved slow. Confident. Like they didn't owe anyone their pace. Somewhere down the hill, music played—low, rich, and full of soul. Could've been Garnet Silk. Could've been Beres again. Didn't matter. It wasn't loud. Just present. Like it had always been playing and I was just slow enough now to notice it.

The scent of jerk drifted through the air—charcoal and spice, maybe pimento. Someone was cooking, and they weren't rushing. That smell traveled like an invitation. Laughter rolled in from across the way, bouncing off a concrete wall and riding the wind up toward me. Not forced. Not polished. Just real joy, full-bodied and loud.

And I sat there, unmoving.

The island didn't ask me to understand it. Didn't explain itself. Didn't care who I was or what I came here to escape. It just… was. And maybe that was the point. To be somewhere that didn't need me to fix anything. Didn't shrink itself for my comfort. Didn't perform. Just existed. Fully. Unapologetically. And in that space, maybe I could learn how to do the same.

5

Wray & Truth

Dez was already waiting outside when I stepped out later that evening. The sun was low, bleeding gold across the buildings, softening everything it touched. His car sat idling just past the gate, headlights dimmed, engine humming like it had nowhere urgent to be. Dez leaned out the right-side window, elbow propped casually, his body language saying time didn't move the same for him. Not here. Maybe not anywhere.

It threw me off for a second—driver's seat on the right, steering wheel where my instincts didn't expect it. Just one of those subtle reminders: I wasn't in Atlanta anymore. I was somewhere that played by a different set of rules, and didn't care if I noticed.

He spotted me and gave a short nod, like we were continuing a conversation that never needed to be spoken aloud.

"Yuh ready?" he asked, voice just above the rhythm of the street—low, calm, like he knew the answer already.

I nodded. "Yeah."

The metal gate clicked behind me as I stepped out to meet him, gravel crunching under my sandals. I slid into the left-side passenger seat, the door giving a soft thud behind me. Inside smelled like the day—residual sun, worn leather, and the last trace of whatever cologne he'd put on this morning. Something familiar. Clean. Like cedar and citrus with a little road dust baked in.

We didn't say much.

We didn't have to.

No itinerary.

No reservations.

No bullet-pointed plan.

Just Dez.

And the road.

And that was enough.

Outside the windows, the neighborhood started to shift—day slipping into night, kids heading inside, porches lighting up one by one like the city was slowly catching fire. Radios buzzed from balconies. Pots clanged in kitchens. Somebody's laugh cracked loud across the street and was answered by another one before fading into the hum of it all.

Dez pulled off without a word, smooth and steady. One hand on the wheel, the other resting in his lap like it always knew what to do.

I didn't ask where we were going.

Didn't need to.

Sometimes you don't need a destination to start moving.

Sometimes you just need someone who knows how to drive when you're too tired to steer.

* * *

Dez maneuvered through traffic like he was part of it—like the car wasn't something he drove, but something he wore. No signals. No brakes unless absolutely necessary. Just a rhythm of taps and rolls, tires gliding over pavement like the road already knew where he was going.

His left hand stayed locked to the wheel—loose but sure. His right moved like it had its own soundtrack, fingers drumming on the door panel or turning the volume up just enough to make the music feel like it belonged to the moment.

Old-school dancehall hummed through the speakers—Barrington Levy, voice spilling through static like a memory. That unmistakable falsetto, elastic and playful, winding through the beat like it wasn't in a hurry to land.

"Under mi sensi... she a hold mi, and she nah let go..."

Dez sang along in pieces—just a few lines here and there, more hum than lyric, like the music was a part of his bloodwork and didn't require conscious effort.

Outside, the city moved with its own tempo. Taxis darted into tight spaces. People stood inches from traffic selling phone credit and bagged peanuts. Headlights blinked. Horns tapped. Bikes squeezed between bumpers like water through cracks. But somehow, no one crashed. No one cursed. It was chaos, sure—but it was coordinated. I leaned my head against the window, let the warmth press into my skin. The glass vibrated with the bass from the stereo and the subtle pulse of the tires rolling over patched pavement. The scent of the city slipped through the cracked window— smoke, salt, the metallic tinge of a hard day's sun cooling off.

"Where we headed?" I asked, eyes still on the blur of headlights and storefronts we passed.

Dez didn't look over.

"Yuh gon' see."

That was his favorite answer so far.

He said it like it was a promise.

Like the destination wasn't something you found—it was something that found you once you were ready to stop asking.

I nodded and didn't push it.

Somewhere behind us, the day finished dying. The sky had gone from fire to bruise, and the streetlights buzzed alive one by one like they'd just remembered their job. And still, we moved.

No rush.

No map.

Just two men, a beat, and the road opening up in front of us like it had something to say.

* * *

43

First stop was Dead End Beach. The name sounded heavier than the vibe. I expected something bleak—abandoned shoreline, wind whipping through silence. But it wasn't that. Not at all.

It was calm.

Low tide lapped gently against the sand, curling in and pulling back like it had all the time in the world. The sky was wide open, streaked with pinks and purples from the last stretch of daylight. The kind of evening where the sun didn't set so much as exhale.

A narrow road ran between the beach and the fence that marked the edge of the airport runway. No signs. No lifeguard chairs. No curated experience. Just water, sky, and people who knew. Knew what this place was. What it meant. The ones who came here because they didn't need a resort to feel ocean. They just needed this—sand, breeze, and each other.

A group of teens stood barefoot in a loose circle near the water, kicking a deflated soccer ball back and forth, talking trash and laughing like time didn't apply here. A couple sat tangled up on a low wall, arms and legs draped casually over one another, quiet, easy—like love didn't need big gestures, just proximity. A little girl ran in looping circles through the shallows, arms stretched out like wings, her giggle rising above the waves before dropping back into them.

Then the plane came.

Loud. Low. Closer than I expected.

It cut across the sky like it didn't belong there—like it had been dropped into the scene by mistake. The roar hit a second before I could find it in the clouds. It flew so low I could see the rivets on the belly, the blinking lights, the curve of the wings banking toward landing.

Nobody flinched.

Not the girl running in the surf. Not the teenagers. Not the couple on the wall.

They didn't even look up.

It was just part of the rhythm.

The tide. The breeze. The boom of metal above your head every so often.

It startled me at first.

But then I got it.

This wasn't a disruption.

It was just another layer. Another beat in the background score of the place.

I walked closer to the edge of the water, felt the sand shift under my feet. Warm in some spots, cool in others. The scent of salt hit stronger out here, mingling with car exhaust from the nearby road and the smoke from somebody's spliff drifting lazily across the breeze.

Dez stayed back by the car, leaned against the hood like he'd been here a thousand times. Like he knew not to rush this part. Knew that the first visit to a place like this wasn't something to narrate. Just something to feel.

And I did.

Didn't speak. Didn't think. Just stood there—one man in a t-shirt and sandals, watching the day end at Dead End.

No photo. No pose.

Just presence.

* * *

And then there was the guy with the cooler. He sat on the tailgate of a dented white pickup, legs swinging slow, scrolling through his phone like time had nothing to say to him. Behind him, a makeshift liquor cart leaned against the bumper—wood slats, cracked wheels, and two reused water bottles filled with clear liquid resting in a plastic ice bin that was more ambition than insulation. he

No menu. No branding. Just a presence.

It said everything it needed to.

As we walked by, he didn't look up. He just tossed the words out like bait.

"Wha yuh seh, big man—yuh want yuh chest get clean up?"

Dez let out a low laugh beside me.

"Don't answer too quick," he said. "Whole heap regret behind dat bottle."

I smirked, stepping closer. "Hit me with one."

The vendor grinned, finally setting his phone down. "Mi like yuh spirit still."

He reached for a plastic cup from a crumpled sleeve on the cart, twisted off the reused bottle cap, and poured with a tilt of the wrist that said he'd been doing this a long time.

The liquid hit the cup like it knew the way.

He handed it over with no fanfare.

I knocked it back.

The rum didn't wait.

Didn't ask permission.

It lit a fire behind my sternum like it was burning something out on purpose. My eyes watered. I coughed—once, then again. The vendor smiled like that was the reaction he was waiting for.

"Yuh good?" Dez asked, clearly amused.

I nodded through the burn. "Yeah. Felt that in my soul."

The vendor leaned forward, elbows on his knees. "Dat's di point, my boss. If it nuh mek yuh question yuh decisions, it nuh real."

I looked at the bottle.

Then at the sea.

Then back at the bottle.

Without saying anything, I held up two fingers.

Dez blinked, then laughed. "Bwoy serious now."

The vendor chuckled, already pouring.

"Mi like dis one. Him come here fi feel tings."

The second shot hit smoother—or maybe I just knew what to expect this time. Either way, I didn't cough. Didn't flinch. Just let it settle into my chest like heat finding home. Dez gave me a look—part impressed, part curious.

"Mi cyaan lie... mi neva expect yuh go back so quick."

I shrugged, wiping the sweat from my brow. "Me either."

The vendor tapped the bottle against the cart like he was sealing a deal. "Yuh deh 'pon di edge now, mi G. One more an' yuh might start confessin' yuh sins."

I laughed, stepping back. "Not tonight."

Dez clapped me on the shoulder. "Respect. But mi cyaan carry yuh if yuh drop."

We walked off again, my chest warm, the breeze cooler now against my skin. The music in the background kept playing. The waves kept moving.

And something about taking that second shot felt symbolic.

Like I was finally leaning in.

* * *

"Dis where people go to remember what matters," Dez said, his voice low, eyes forward as we walked the narrow road alongside the beach.

The sea stretched out to our left—close enough to smell the salt, feel the mist when the breeze shifted. The air was thick with that end-of-day stillness, like even the island had taken a breath.

Down on the sand, life moved without urgency.

Two older men sat on upside-down buckets near the water, casting lines into the tide. They didn't talk much. Didn't even watch the rods. Just stared out ahead like the sea was telling them something only they could hear.

A group of teens lounged nearby, ankles buried in wet sand, speaker tucked between them low and buzzing. They passed a joint back and forth as their voices flew—sharp, fast patois that snapped between laughter and argument, teasing and truth. I couldn't catch the words, but the rhythm hit hard. Like a cipher. Like church. They were present in a way I envied.

A little boy ran wide loops across the beach, the string of a makeshift kite gripped tight in his hand. It rose and dipped with the wind—scraps of plastic bag stretched across thin sticks, tied together with string that looked like it had lived a few lives already. It wasn't pretty, but it flew, and that seemed like enough. He held a piece of cane in his other hand, gnawed down and sticky, his grin wide and free.

The water came in loud, but not in a way that demanded silence. It just made room for reflection. Like it was washing something off the day. Dez didn't stop walking. He just slowed a little.

"Dis ain't no tourist beach," he said. "People don't come here fi Instagram.

47

Dem come when dem soul feel... tight."

I nodded—not because I had the words for it, but because I knew what he meant. I felt it in the back of my throat. That pressure. The kind that builds when you've been carrying too much for too long, and you're finally somewhere that lets you set it down without asking questions.

We kept moving, the beach to our left, the road unfolding ahead like it had all night to show us something.

And for the first time in a long time, just watching felt like enough.

* * *

We didn't stay long. Dez wasn't much for lingering. He moved like someone who knew the rhythm of a place, and when that rhythm changed—even slightly—he listened. Didn't wait for a reason. Didn't need one. He just followed the signal like a man who trusted instinct over invitation.

I felt it too.

Not urgency. Not discomfort.

Just... a subtle shift. Like the moment had done what it came to do, and anything after would only dilute it.

As we made our way back toward the car, we passed the rum vendor again. Still perched on the tailgate, same slouch, same phone in hand like nothing had happened and everything had.

He looked up this time.

"Mi rate how yuh move," he said. "Quiet. Watchful. Most man come here loud—leave confused."

I gave him a nod, unsure what to say.

He held my gaze, then added, softer:

"Take yuh time, star. Jamaica nuh rush nobody. But she nuh wait neither."

He smiled once, slow and crooked, then went back to scrolling like he hadn't just handed me something that might sit in my chest for a while.

We walked the rest of the way in silence.

Dez unlocked the door with a soft chirp, slid into the driver's seat like it belonged to him more than his own bed. I got in on the left, the seat still

48

warm from earlier, the scent of salt and smoke still caught in my shirt.

He didn't turn the music up this time.

Just drove.

No bassline. No riddim to fill the silence. Just the hum of the engine, the soft scuff of tires against the road, and the occasional streetlight flickering past like a pulse in the dark.

Montego Bay blurred outside the window—neighborhoods dipping into shadow, shop gates pulled down for the night, dogs patrolling yards like they had stories to protect. The energy had changed. Not heavy. Just still.

I didn't ask where we were going. I wasn't sure I cared.

There was something about that kind of silence. Not empty, not awkward. Just honest. The kind that lets you sit in your own skin without reaching for distraction. Dez didn't fill it, and I didn't need him to.

Somewhere between the curve of the road and the rhythm of nothing, I realized how loud my life had been.

How much of it had been noise.

And how good it felt to not be performing. Not explaining.

"You ever feel like you doing everything you supposed to... and still feel lost?" I didn't plan to ask it. It just came out.

Maybe it was the water earlier.

Maybe it was the silence now.

Maybe it was just Dez—how he moved like he already knew the answers weren't waiting at the end of some perfectly built plan.

He didn't answer right away.

He just let the question hang in the cab like steam off hot pavement.

Then he chuckled. Low. Not like he thought it was funny—more like he'd tasted the same truth before.

"All the time, mi bredda," he said. His tone shifted—less driver, more man.

"Especially when I was tryna live like mi life was one big race. Tryin' to be dis... thing. A good man. A provider. A rock. Di man who never complain, never need help. Jus' keep goin', no matter how tired mi feel."

He made a sharp turn down a narrow street, one hand on the wheel, body

49

moving like it had memorized the potholes years ago.

The car rocked slightly, but his voice stayed steady.

"Yuh know what mi learn? People always talk 'bout legacy—like it start when yuh dead. But legacy nuh wait for no funeral. Legacy start when yuh stop pretending."

That sat in the air. Heavy, but clean. Like rain just before it falls.

I looked over at him. He didn't look back. Just kept his eyes on the road, headlights stretching out into the dark like they were trying to find something.

"You from America," he said, softer now. "Y'all work like yuh building a monument. Brick after brick after brick. Job title. House. Family. Hustle. Always more. Always proving."

He paused, then added:

"But sometimes, mi youth... yuh don't need no monument. Sometimes... all yuh need is a shelter."

That line landed in my chest like it had been waiting there for years.

A shelter.

Not to be admired.

Not to be remembered.

Just... to rest in.

I didn't speak right away. I just watched the road slip past.

Then, without looking at him, I asked: "So how'd you know when to stop pretending?"

Dez let out a slow breath through his nose.

"When mi body start payin' fi all di lies mi mouth was tellin'."

He didn't elaborate. He didn't need to.

We drove on in silence, headlights sweeping over empty porches and shuttered shops, the sky stretched open above us like something waiting to be named.

* * *

By the time we pulled up to Scotchies, the sky was already ink-dark. The kind of night that swallowed light whole—where the glow from streetlamps felt like flickers and the air held on to heat like it didn't know how to cool down.

You could smell the place before you saw it—pimento smoke curling through the trees, thick and sharp, with just enough scotch bonnet in the air to sting your throat before the food even touched your mouth.

Dez parked the car like he'd done it a hundred times, then nodded toward the entrance. "Come see."

We walked into a cloud of smoke that didn't apologize for itself.

"Don't say nothing. Mi ordering for yuh."

I didn't argue. I just nodded.

At the counter, Dez spoke in a rhythm I couldn't fully follow, but the tone said he wasn't new here.

"Yeh, gimme two jerk, di spicy one—half chicken each. Pork if it fresh, nuh di dry cut. Festival, two sweet potato. Plenty sauce, yuh hear mi. An' mek sure di chicken nuh bun up—jus' di edge dem fi have dat crunch. Two Red Stripe. An' mi waan two sip a di real ting—Appleton dark, nuh chaser."

The woman nodded with a smirk like she liked the way he asked. Like his order was a conversation, not a transaction.

The grill was open air—a stretch of whole chickens laid out skin-down over wide, flat logs of pimento wood, not metal grates or oil drums. No gas. No shortcut. Just tradition. Flames licked slow beneath the logs, coaxing out the kind of flavor that doesn't come quick.

"Dis di real ting," Dez said, voice a little lower. "They don't rush it here. Jerk is a process. Fire, time, and patience."

The logs were from the allspice tree—pimento wood, he told me. "When yuh smell jerk, dat smokey sweetness? Dat come from dis. No pimento, no jerk."

A woman in a headwrap turned one of the birds with a long pair of tongs. The skin cracked, juice hissed on contact. Her face didn't flinch. She was focused like the fire spoke to her.

We stepped inside. If you could call it that. No walls. Just wooden benches worn smooth by sun and sweat. A few fans rattling overhead.

Plastic trays. A sauce bottle on each table like it was gospel.

Before we sat, Dez picked up the tray with two short glasses filled with something dark—Appleton, neat. No garnish. No ice. Just rum like it was meant to be taken: straight and serious.

He passed me one.

"A before-food sip," he said. "Fi cleanse di spirit."

He lifted his glass, eyes on mine. Then came the toast:

"Fi life, love, and likkle more fire." ["To life, love, and a little more fire."]

We tapped rims and knocked it back.

The rum came in smooth, but finished with a grip. It hit deep, curled around the chest like something ancient. Dez grinned when I winced, then handed me a sweating Red Stripe from the tray that followed.

"Now yuh ready." "Dis place start early 2000s," he said, sliding onto the bench. "One man just want bring back di proper way. Tony Rerrie. Him open yah first. No drum. No gas. Jus' pimento and respect fi tradition."

I sat beside him, letting the heat settle into my skin. The night felt alive here—rustling trees, meat sizzling, the wordless nods of people who knew better than to speak when the food hit the table.

"But jerk?" he added, tilting his head. "Jerk older than all a dis. Come from di Maroons. Runaways who couldn't light no fire out in di open. So dem cook underground. Covered di smoke. Slow roast. Survival food."

He paused.

"An' even before dat—di Tainos. First people. Roasting wild boar wit allspice and pepper. We just carry on di story."

The tray landed in front of us. Dark, fire-cracked chicken. Thick, crisp skin. Meat so tender it pulled with two fingers. The smell was damn near holy.

"Dis food?" he said. "Dis memory. Dis protest. Dis pride."

We ate.

And the first bite?

The skin gave way with a crackle, releasing smoke and pepper and something deeper—wood, time, labor. The meat was tender, soaked through with seasoning. Not just coated—infused. Allspice hit first—

sweet, musky. Then thyme. Then ginger. Then heat. A slow, rising warmth that spread across the tongue and down into the chest. I didn't say much after that. It didn't try to impress you. It just was.

We sat like that for a while. Eating. Breathing. Red Stripe sweating in the warm night. Letting the place work on us.

Sometimes the loudest truths come with no volume at all.

There was something sacred about eating like that—no rush, no phones, no small talk. Just hands, fire, and focus. Sweat collecting at the back of your neck. A cold beer sweating in your grip. The occasional curse muttered low when the spice hit the wrong corner of your mouth and made your eyes water.

No one was trying to impress anybody.

No one posed for a photo.

It was food the way it was meant to be—messy, intentional, rooted.

We ate slow.

Not because we had time.

But because the food asked for it.

Demanded you stay present. Demanded you feel it.

The last bite lingered—festival sweet and dense, chicken bone cleaned down to the edge, sauce staining the tips of my fingers like memory.

When we finally finished, Dez leaned back on the bench with a sharp suck of his teeth—the kind of satisfied sound that didn't need translation.

He stretched once, arms overhead, then let them fall with a slap to his thighs.

"You full..." he asked, eyes half-lidded, voice smooth, "or you fed?"

The question didn't need explanation.

I sat with it a second, licking a trace of sauce off my thumb.

"Both," I said.

Dez grinned.

But he didn't get up.

He just stayed there, looking out toward the trees swaying at the edge of the clearing. The fire crackled behind us, the grill still working on someone else's story.

Then he said, almost to himself—

"Funny how sometimes yuh gotta eat like this… slow, hand to mouth… fi even feel yuhself again."

I didn't say anything.

He looked at me.

"Mi mean, di real self. Di one beneath all di titles and responsibilities. All di noise."

I leaned back. Let the Red Stripe rest against my thigh. My stomach was full, but something deeper had just started to stir.

"I don't even know what that version of me looks like anymore," I admitted. "I've been… the man. The husband. The father. The provider. The fixer. The one who doesn't crack. I just… I wear the costume that fits the room."

Dez nodded slow, like he already knew.

"Yuh ever ask yuhself who sew di costume?"

I looked at him.

"Was it you… or somebody else?"

That hit harder than the rum.

I exhaled through my nose, slow.

"Probably both." He scratched his beard, thoughtful.

"Mi used to think bein' true to yuhself meant sayin' what yuh want. Speaking yuh mind. But mi realize… sometimes it's just learning to sit in yuh own skin without apology. Even if it quiet. Even if it soft."

I stared at the empty tray between us.

"Sounds easier than it is."

Dez chuckled, low. "Dat's why it real. Nothin easy worth callin' true."

The fire popped again. A breeze carried the smell of spice and smoke through the air, and for a second I felt weightless. Not happy. Not sad. Just… still.

For the first time in a long time, I didn't feel like I had to prove anything.

He tossed the empty Red Stripe bottle into a nearby bin, the clink echoing low. I followed, slower, my body heavy in the best way—not tired, just… full. Not just from food. From something else I couldn't name yet.

As we walked back to the car, the scent of pimento still hung on my clothes. The fire crackled behind us, still feeding whoever came next. Another man. Another story. Another bite that might remind someone who they were.

I didn't look back.

Didn't need to.

Scotchies had already done its job.

* * *

The drive back was still. Not the kind of silence that begged to be filled— just the kind that settles after something honest. We didn't need to talk. The food had already opened something. The fire had already spoken.

I leaned against the window, the glass still warm from the day. The road rolled under us, smooth in some parts, patched in others. The headlights caught flashes of color and life—a mural of Bob Marley's face faded into concrete; a shop called Bless Up Wholesale with a hand-painted sign swinging in the breeze; a kid pedaling a bicycle too big for him, barefoot and unbothered.

The same streets we'd driven earlier felt different now. Less foreign. More felt. Like I wasn't just passing through anymore—I was in it. Not home, exactly. But not apart from it either.

"You ever think about leaving?" I asked, eyes still on the road.

Dez kept one hand on the wheel, the other resting lazy in his lap.

"I did," he said. "Long time ago."

He didn't say it with regret. Just memory.

"Thought America had answers. Thought maybe mi would find some space to grow. But all mi found was pressure. System on yuh back. Clock always ticking. People ain't living there. They surviving loud."

Surviving loud.

That hit like gospel.

I thought of Spaghetti Junction back home—six layers of concrete chaos, cars stacked in lanes like they were trying to escape something. Horns screaming. Brake lights bleeding into one another.

I remembered once sitting in traffic, watching a woman in the car next to me apply her makeup with one hand and wipe tears with the other. Mascara running. Lipstick in shaky lines. Her face cracked open in a silent scream—but she was still showing up. Still performing. For what, I don't know.

That's what America felt like sometimes. A place where people were too tired to stop pretending.

And here I was now, in a place where the world moved slower. Where a man could sit on a porch with rum in his chest and call that enough. Where food didn't lie, and fire was still a method, not just a metaphor.

Where silence was allowed to be silence.

"I get it," I said quietly.

Dez didn't nod. Didn't speak. He just let the wheels hum beneath us and the night stretch wide across the windshield.

The city dimmed behind us. Hills started to roll again. The ocean no longer visible, but still there—just beyond the dark.

And for the first time in a long time, I didn't feel like I was chasing anything. I was just being carried.

When Dez pulled up to the apartment, he didn't put the car in park right away. He just let the engine hum under us, headlights casting long shadows across the gate. The air inside the car had settled—thick with salt, smoke, and everything unsaid.

Neither of us reached for the door.

I looked out the window, then back at him. "That thing you said earlier," I started, "about pretending. Legacy. Shelter."

He didn't look over. He just let the silence hang long enough to make sure I wasn't speaking out of habit.

"I've built a lot of things," I continued. "A life. A marriage. A title. Even a version of myself I thought would make me proud. And I'm sitting here wondering if any of it was mine. Or just shit I inherited and called purpose."

Dez finally looked at me. Not surprised. Just patient.

"Is di same ting mi ask mi'self," he said. "Over and over. Yuh build so much yuh forget who yuh were before di first brick."

He leaned forward, turned the key, killed the engine. The hum faded. The silence got louder.

"But hear mi now," he added. "Truth nuh need applause. It don't need to be perfect. It just haffi feel like yuh when yuh say it."

He paused. Let that land. Then gave me the smallest smile.

"Yuh start sound like yuh ready fi stop pretending."

I didn't respond. I just sat with it. Felt the truth of it settle somewhere behind my ribs. He finally opened the door, stepped out into the night, gravel crunching under his sandals.

I followed.

He didn't say goodbye. Didn't do the American thing with handshakes or closure.

He just gave me a nod and said, "Mi pass through tomorrow. Don't forget fi listen to di island."

He turned slightly, half a grin on his face.

"She nuh talk English... but she talk real clear."

Then he was gone.

The taillights curved out of sight, swallowed by the bend in the road and the dark behind it—like the end of a chapter that didn't need a final sentence.

And I stood there for a while, letting the breeze brush past me, feeling something in my chest I couldn't quite name yet.

Not peace. Not clarity.

But the beginning of both.

I went inside, dropped my things, and poured some water. Didn't bother with the lights. The hum of the fridge, the faint rattle of the standing fan, the weight of the night pressing through the screen door—all of it was enough.

I sat at the edge of the bed, elbows on my knees, glass in hand. The cool hit my throat, but the heat of the day hadn't fully left me. Neither had Dez's words.

About pretending.

About monuments.

About survival turned flavor.

I didn't write anything down. Didn't reach for my phone. I just let it sit with me—the idea that maybe I'd built a version of myself impressive enough to fool everyone but me. Eventually, I stepped back out onto the porch.

The air was cooler now, but not by much. The breeze brushed across my skin like breath. Somewhere down the hill, a dog barked once, then silence again. The island wasn't asleep—it was just settled.

I leaned against the railing, letting my body hang loose for once. No tension in the shoulders. No calendar ticking in my head.

And I thought about what it meant to stop performing.

To let the moment pass without narrating it.

To not turn grief into content.

To not dress hurt up in language just to make it easier to carry.

What would it feel like to just... be?

Not healed. Not whole. Not ready.

Just here.

Not shaping pain into purpose.

Not dressing wounds up as wisdom.

Not calling growth what was really just exhaustion.

Just... breathing.

For once, I didn't feel the need to fix the silence.

Didn't reach for clarity.

Didn't write the caption.

I just stood there.

Letting the night hold me without asking for anything in return.

And in that stillness, I realized something:

Maybe Dez wasn't talking to who I am now...

Maybe he was talking to the man I've been afraid to become.

The man who lets softness sit beside strength.

The man who doesn't need to be useful to feel worthy.
The man who listens more than he performs.
And maybe that man didn't need answers tonight.
Just space.
And the courage to finally stop explaining his way out of himself.

6

Jimmy Cliff Blvd

Montego Bay at night was a different beast. The kind that didn't stretch first—it just stood up loud. The sun dipped and something else rose—bass, heat, perfume, sweat. The air thickened. The streets pulsed. Everything moved louder. Cars rolled slower, windows down, music bleeding. People walked with purpose—like they had something to prove or something to forget.

Earlier, Dez and I had driven past the Hip Strip in the daylight. It was damn near silent. Shutters half-closed. Vendors dozing. A breeze, but no beat. The kind of quiet that made you wonder if the city had gone somewhere else.

But now? Now it had woken up like it remembered who the hell it was.

The same stretch of pavement was unrecognizable. Sidewalks filled. Neon signs blinked alive. Smoke from a roadside grill mixed with coconut oil and cologne. Girls in heels laughed too loud. Boys in tank tops leaned against parked cars like they owned time.

This wasn't a place you strolled through.

This was a place that moved through you.

Montego Bay at night didn't whisper.

It sang with its chest out.

Didn't ask if you were ready.

It just was.

This city had layers—and only some of them showed up in the sun.

* * *

I wasn't looking for anything. I'd planned to sit near the bay with a drink and let the night pass—nothing more than stillness and salt air. Just me, a bench, and the sound of the water reminding me I didn't have to rush back to being whoever I used to be.

But the Hip Strip had other plans.

There's a pull to it—not just noise or light, but rhythm. Something in the air that tugs at your feet even when your soul says be still.

I drifted forward.

Not chasing anything.

Just… following the current.

Margaritaville's neon lights flashed hard and hungry, music spilling out with bass thick enough to move your chest. Inside, I could see a bachelorette party dancing on chairs, all glitter and sweat and bad decisions. A tourist couple argued on the curb, their voices tight and sharp, the kind of fight that's been waiting to happen for months.

Across the street, a man was breathing fire.

Not metaphorically—literally.

A crowd had formed around him, tight and loud, phones up, faces glowing from the flame as he exhaled fire into the sky like it owed him something. The heat flashed across my face as I slowed, caught in the chaos of it. For a moment, all I could hear was the roar of flame and the rush of people reacting—shouts, laughter, one woman squealing like she'd seen God.

Further down, someone was selling roasted corn from a makeshift grill. Next to him, a speaker propped on a milk crate played old Buju Banton. The beat hit hard, low and righteous. Patois danced across the air, a language I understood more than I spoke, vibrant and alive.

Taboo's red sign buzzed behind a tinted door, and I could feel the energy shift the closer I got. That deep, late-night kind of tension. Velvet ropes. Men in loafers. Women in stilettos and second chances. The kind of place where secrets go to sweat.

A taxi honked.

A Red Stripe bottle clinked and shattered somewhere behind me. Someone shouted "Bumboclaat!" and the laughter that followed was thick with rum.

And me?

I just walked.

Slow.

Quiet.

Taking it in like it might not be there tomorrow.

I passed a bar with no sign, just a wooden door half-open and a speaker buzzing in the corner. A man on a stool played dominoes with ghosts. Another sat with his head down on the counter, mouth open, dreaming out loud.

Everything here was alive.

Sweating. Singing. Spinning stories at full volume.

And I was just one man drifting through it—sober enough to feel it, enough not to interrupt it.

I hadn't come looking for anything.

But the island had a way of placing you exactly where you needed to be.

Even when you didn't know you needed to be found.

Then I heard him.

"Big man. Ganja? High grade. Bad Mind, Zion Haze… mi got even di soft ting if yuh just want breeze."

I turned.

He was leaning against a streetlight like it belonged to him. Slim frame, fitted white tee, black jeans, black-and-gold sneakers too fresh for the gravel. Short locs tucked back, eyes steady. In one hand, a clear plastic cup with something brown and slow-burning, and in the other, a small black pouch, thumb on the zipper like he'd been halfway through a sale when I caught his eye.

He wasn't pushing. Just offering.

A man who moved like the Strip was his office.

I raised a hand, half-smile. "I'm good."

He nodded, not offended. "Mi overstand. Yuh just look like a man carryin' too much thought. Sometimes herb help quiet di corners, dat's all."

I smirked. "Walking does that too."

"True." He sipped from his cup. "Mi see it. Yuh move different. Not lost, just… watchin'."

He stepped forward, casually, offered a fist.

"Troy."

We dapped. His grip was light, but grounded. Intentional.

"Bruce."

"Aight. Bruce. Cool name. Yuh from America, yeah?"

"Yeah—Atlanta."

He laughed lightly. "Mi never been. Never leave Jamaica once."

That caught me. "Never?"

He nodded. "Yeh man. All mi bredren dem dreamin' of visa and plane. Me? Mi love di soil mi born pon. Mi see beauty an' struggle same place. Mi nuh need no monument fi feel alive."

I nodded. "Lot of people back home think they need to go somewhere else to find peace."

He shrugged. "Yuh cyaan run from noise. Yuh just haffi find di one dat make sense."

Troy led me down the block toward a liquor cart tucked between a shuttered gift shop and a fence painted in faded red, green, and gold. No sign. Just a man posted up behind coolers stacked with reused water bottles filled with either brown or blood-red liquor.

"Mi general!" Troy called out. "Fix two fi di usual. Di proper mix."

The vendor didn't speak. Just nodded once and started pouring—dark rum in one cup, Campari in the other, then a quick switch and swirl that turned both glasses into something burnt orange and dangerous. No ice. No lime. Just heat and history.

Troy pulled a crumpled bill from his pocket and slapped it on the counter. "Run di ting, star. Respect."

He handed me a cup and raised his own.

63

"Di bitter go down first, but yuh feel better after."

I took a sip. It was all sting and shadows—harsh on the tongue, but it opened something deep.

We walked back to the low wall and sat.

He didn't say anything for a while. He just watched the street like it owed him money.

After a beat, he pointed with his chin. "Yuh see dem two girls fightin' over one man who not even lookin'?"

I looked. He wasn't wrong.

"Street drama," he muttered, shaking his head. "Same actors. New plot."

We both laughed.

He leaned back, drink balanced on his thigh. "Mi see everything, yuh know. Nah judge. Just watch. Always watching."

I glanced over. "That get heavy sometimes?"

He gave a short nod. "Yeh. But mi don't carry it. Mi observe it. Big difference."

I let that land.

"Mi here every night," he added. "Not cause mi have nowhere else fi be. Cause here? Mi can see people without pretendin'."

I was mute for a second. Then said, "You ever feel like you're always performing? Like even your silence got choreography?"

That made him look at me. For real this time.

"You not talkin' 'bout dis place, are you."

I shook my head. "Nah. I'm talking about... back there. Back home. Atlanta. Even when I'm alone, I feel like I'm doing something for someone else. Like there's a version of me always on display. Even when nobody's watching."

Troy sipped. "Das real. Some man get so used to performin', they forget what their own voice sound like."

I stared at the liquid in my cup. It wasn't smooth. But it was honest.

"I don't want to do that no more," I said.

Troy didn't nod. Didn't rush it.

He just sat there, letting my words breathe.

Then he said, "Maybe yuh not lookin' for somewhere to belong. Maybe yuh lookin' for somewhere to fall apart."

That hit harder than the drink.

And the thing was... he didn't say it with sympathy. Just clarity. Like someone who knew what it meant to feel like you couldn't just exist.

We sat in the silence after that.

Street noise around us. A bottle clinking behind the cart. A horn two blocks down.

Laughter floating on the breeze.

And me, sitting next to a man who wasn't trying to teach me anything.

He was just there. Present. And somehow, that helped me show up too.

* * *

Troy stood without saying a word and went back to the liquor cart.

Same nod. Same order.

The vendor didn't ask. Just poured. The way a barber doesn't ask if you want the usual—he just knows.

Troy returned, handed me a fresh cup, and sat back down.

We sipped in silence for a stretch.

Then he said, "Yuh ever notice how rum don't lie? She don't dress it up. Just show yuh what already inside."

I smirked. "Yeah. Dangerous honesty."

He nodded. "But better than holdin' it in."

Another pause. Not awkward. Just... building.

Then I said it, the thing I'd been circling since the moment I landed.

"You know what I envy?"

Troy raised an eyebrow.

"Y'all got culture. A way of moving. A rhythm. Language. Food. Flags that mean something. You say 'Jamaican' and people know what that means. Haiti too. Cuba. Trinidad. Even when the struggle loud, the identity louder."

I took a sip. Let it burn down.

65

"Black American?" I shrugged. "We got trauma and basketball. A hyphen where the heritage should be."

Troy stayed quiet. Not dismissing. Just listening.

"I mean, we were on the same damn boats. Y'all got dropped off and built culture. We got dropped off and built a brand."

I shook my head. "I don't even know what mine sounds like when nobody's listening." Troy tilted his cup. "Dat's heavy, mi bredda. But real."

I leaned forward, elbows on my knees. "Sometimes I feel like I'm borrowing from other people's roots. Wearing someone else's pride like a borrowed shirt. I look in the mirror and I see Black, but I don't see me. You ever feel that?"

He rubbed his jaw, eyes on the street but not really watching it anymore.

"Nah," he said slowly. "But not 'cause mi better off. 'Cause mi was allowed to feel rooted. Mi mada teach mi di words. Mi school teach mi di stories. Even di music mi dance to come from mi own history."

He looked over at me.

"But yuh not lost, star. Yuh just disconnected. Dem break di line before it reach yuh. That nah yuh fault."

I nodded, jaw tight.

He continued, softer now.

"But yuh here now. On a rock full a Blackness. Where yuh don't have to ask permission fi belong."

I stared at the condensation on the cup.

Then said, "I don't want to take. I don't want to appropriate. I just… want to feel close to something that doesn't feel ashamed of me."

Troy looked me in the eye for a long time.

"Then stop tryna take. Start tryna remember."

That landed in the chest.

Not advice.

Just truth.

Delivered like a sentence my bones already knew.

We didn't say anything else for a while.

Just sat.

Two men.

Two drinks.

One bloodline split by water and history.

Trying to trace the echo of a language we both used to speak.

* * *

Troy took another sip and leaned back, one leg stretched, one foot planted.

"Mi grandfather used to talk in proverbs," he said. "Wouldn't tell yuh what to do. Just say somet'ing like, 'Tree dat grow crooked still block sun.' Then leave yuh fi figure out di rest."

He chuckled softly. "Man was full of mystery. But full of presence too. When he speak, di whole room quiet. Not 'cause he loud. 'Cause he meant it."

I nodded, slow. "We didn't have that. Most of us didn't grow up with stories. Just… survival tactics. 'Don't run.' 'Keep your hands visible.' 'Work twice as hard.' That was our inheritance."

Troy looked over. "Dat sound like silence in disguise."

"Exactly," I said. "Even when we talked, it was coded. No real emotion. Just instructions. You learn how to keep your head down. Make yourself small. Be safe."

I paused.

"I didn't inherit pride. I inherited caution."

Troy let that breathe.

"Yuh ever think," he said, "di silence was planted in y'all?"

I looked at him.

"How yuh mean?"

"Mi mean, maybe di system yuh born into designed it dat way. Cut di tongue from di culture. So yuh can't pass down joy. Can't pass down self-love. Just rules."

That hit somewhere deep. Somewhere wordless.

I stared into the street, the movement starting to blur. Same music. Same bodies. But I wasn't watching anymore. I was feeling it.

"So what'd you inherit?" I asked.

Troy thought on it.

"Noise," he said finally. "But chosen noise. Di kind yuh dance to. Argument on di veranda. Auntie cussin' bad word while stirrin' stew. Laughter loud enough fi wake baby."

He smiled. "Yuh grow up hearin' yuh name over and over, until yuh believe yuh real."

He looked back at me.

"Mi guess yuh grew up knowin' yuh were Black. But never bein' told what dat meant."

I nodded. "Yeah. It was always a response. Never a declaration."

Troy tapped his cup against mine, light.

"Then maybe dis di first place yuh don't have to respond to anything. Maybe now, yuh get to define it."

* * *

I sat back. That was too much to process out loud.

But inside? Something opened.

Troy slipped off the wall without a word. Nodded once toward the sidewalk like that was the signal. Whatever we were about to step into, it didn't need explanation.

He moved like he had somewhere to be, even if it didn't have a name.

Troy ducked into a liquor shop with no sign—just a rusted grate pushed to the side and a soft bassline spilling out from somewhere in the back. He came back out with two small plastic flasks, no receipt, no talk. Just a quick pound with the guy behind the counter, and we kept walking.

He handed me one without slowing down.

"Mi nah sell tours," he said, eyes scanning the block. "Mi sell time. Experience. An' vibe. Everyt'ing else come after."

We kept moving, the Strip behind us now—not gone, but quieter. Like it had given us permission to leave.

We turned down a narrow lane. Fewer lights. Less posing. The music changed too—less volume, more intention. Someone played a riddim from a Bluetooth speaker tucked in a windowsill.

A woman sat in a plastic chair outside her doorway, legs wide, parting a little girl's hair with the kind of focus only aunties have. The child sat quiet, jaw clenched like she was trying not to flinch, but her eyes darted toward us as we passed.

From the speaker, a voice I didn't recognize floated out—low, rich, and aching. Mortimer, Troy told me later. Not mainstream. Not made for playlists or poolside vibes. Just... truth, pressed to vinyl.

I didn't know the song. But it wasn't made for tourists. It was the kind of voice that sounded like it'd been broken before and still chose to sing.

No one stared. No one asked what I was doing there.

They just let us pass.

"Yuh feel dat?" Troy asked.

I did.

It wasn't peace.

It was presence.

Like the land didn't care where I was from—only how I carried myself while I was here.

"Yuh walk different now," Troy said. "Less like yuh tryna belong. More like yuh ready fi listen."

He slowed, pointed ahead.

"Come. We go see someting real."

* * *

We moved again.

Inside the club, finally.

The air hit like a wall—heat, perfume, sweat, cologne, smoke, anticipation. Everything was thick. Felt like you had to push your way into the night, not walk through it. Lights pulsed red, then blue, then disappeared altogether, leaving only strobe flashes that carved the bodies around us into silhouettes and muscle memory. The bass wasn't sound anymore—it was structure. It held the room up. Women moved like they weren't asking permission.

Like the music came from inside them.

Men hugged walls with full glasses and empty expressions—watching, calculating, trying to be cooler than they were. Some moved to the rhythm. Most waited for someone else to unlock their confidence.

I scanned the room, trying to find mine.

Not to dance. Just… to stand. But being next to Troy gave me cover. His presence was passport. It said: he's good. He moved through the crowd like a conductor—gripping shoulders, exchanging nods, whispering jokes close to ears. A dap here. A slap on the back there. One girl blew him a kiss and disappeared into the crowd like mist.

He introduced me to no one.

But everyone knew I was with him.

"Tonight, mi boss from foreign out, seen?" he shouted over the music, throwing an arm around my shoulder.

"Wi givin' him di real."

Someone handed him a drink.

He handed it to me.

I didn't ask what was in it.

Wray. Campari. Maybe juice. Maybe just heat.

I drank.

Stopped checking the time.

The night wasn't a clock anymore.

It was motion.

It was breath.

It was permission.

Troy lit another spliff, pulled once, then passed it to me without breaking eye contact.

I took it this time without a joke. No need for bad patois or self-deprecation.

Just inhale.

Let it in.

Let it work.

The DJ cut the music for a half-second to reload a drop—and the crowd roared like they were starving for it.

When the beat came back, it hit like thunder at close range.

Waists moved. Arms raised. Necks rolled.

And for the first time in longer than I could remember, I didn't feel like a visitor in my own body.

* * *

The music shifted—a slower riddim, low and thick with bass. Troy tapped my shoulder. "Stay here."

Before I could answer, he was already gone—shouldering through the crowd with purpose.

He came back with three women.

Laughing. Glowing. Hair braided, lashes long, dresses hugging curves like secrets. One of them wore yellow and moved like she was made of rhythm.

"Dis mi bredrin from foreign," Troy said loud enough for half the dancefloor to hear. "Him reserved... but him heart good."

They all giggled. The one in yellow looked me over like she was checking for cracks.

Troy leaned toward her, grinning. "Fix him up, nuh? Ease him in soft."

She smiled. "Say less."

She didn't rush.

She just stepped into the space in front of me like the floor belonged to her. Her waist already moving—not exaggerated, not begging for attention. Just real. Like rhythm was in her bloodline.

She turned her back, slid one foot between mine, and backed up slow—patient, controlled. Gave me a beat to decide if I'd flinch.

I didn't.

Her body met mine like a memory I'd never had.

Not sexual. Not innocent either.

71

Just a kind of contact that said, "I know who I am. Do you?"

"Ayyy!" I heard from the edge of the crowd.

Troy.

"Mi youth gettin' baptized! Look pon him!"

She moved her hips, deep and steady. Like she was testing if I could hold space without shaking.

I froze for half a second.

Not out of fear—but because I could feel everything.

The weight of her. The music climbing up my spine. The tension in my own breath, like I hadn't exhaled in years.

She reached back, took my hands gently, and set them on her waist. My fingers spread without thinking.

My body followed.

"Yesssss, boss from foreign!" Troy shouted.

"Yuh see mi? Mi tell di island yuh was ready!"

The crowd around us laughed, but I didn't hear it fully.

Because her hips were speaking now, and I was just learning the language.

Slow wine. Tight circle.

Then a sudden dip that made my knees bend instinctively—not out of desire. Out of reverence.

"Mi swear," Troy called, "one likkle pum pum touch, and dis man gon' move to di hills an' bun him passport!"

I couldn't even fake a smile.

Because I wasn't performing.

I was present.

Hands steady. Eyes closed. Breath low.

Moving with a stranger like I knew her pain.

Or maybe she knew mine.

The song kept going.

She kept going.

And I just let it happen.

Let myself be moved without guilt.

Without control.

Without needing to explain who I was or where I came from.

She finally peeled away—slow, respectful. Like the dance had done what it came to do.

She looked over her shoulder once. Gave me a half-smile.

Not invitation.

Just acknowledgment.

Like she knew she'd just brought something back to life in me.

Troy reappeared beside me, grinning like he'd won a bet.

"Yuh see?" he said, throwing his arm around me again. "Jamaica don't chase yuh. But when she choose yuh... she choose yuh proper."

I shook my head, still catching my breath. "Yeah, yeah," I muttered. "You been saying that all night."

He laughed. "Mi tell yuh—one more wine like dat and yuh gon' sell yuh house, move inna di hills, raise goats, an' marry a girl name Tanesha."

I sipped the rest of my drink, turned to him with a straight face.

"Yeah, maybe. But y'all Jamaican men don't eat pum pum... and I do."

Troy froze. "Ehhhh?!"

I grinned. "I move down here, I'm taking all your hoes, nigga."

Troy damn near dropped his cup.

"Yuh wild, star!" he shouted, cracking up. "A whole menace from foreign!"

He slapped my back, still wheezing. "Mi cyaan bring yuh nowhere!"

We both bent over laughing, loud and unbothered, two Black men catching joy in the middle of bass and smoke.

For once, the night didn't feel borrowed. It felt like mine.

7

Red Stripe & Asian Porn

After a while, we stepped back out into the air. The music still echoed in my bones—not in volume, but in rhythm. My chest moved different now. My shoulders sat lower. Like the beat had carved something loose in me and didn't bother asking permission first.

The night had cooled some, but the breeze wasn't enough to chase off the sweat.

Didn't matter.

My body finally felt like mine again.

The street was calmer now. Not dead. Just... different. No more show. No more performance. Just people settling into whatever version of themselves they could afford to be at 3 a.m.

A woman walked by with her heels in her hand, barefoot and smiling. A taxi honked once and kept rolling. Somewhere down the block, a dog barked like it had something to say, but no one cared enough to listen.

Troy glanced at his phone—just once—then tucked it back in his pocket.

"Mi got one more spot fi check before mi done," he said, already halfway into the next step.

I nodded. No questions.

No itinerary.

Just movement.

We started walking again, not fast. Not slow. Just enough to feel the night stretch with us. The club faded behind us, but it didn't feel like we left something behind. It felt like the night had unzipped a new layer, and we were just peeling it back.

I didn't know where we were going.

Didn't need to.

For the first time in a long time, I wasn't following a plan.

I was following the energy.

And it felt good to not be in charge.

* * *

We walked two blocks. Neither of us said much. The silence between us wasn't heavy anymore—it was earned. Comfortable. Like we'd both said what we needed to say without needing to repeat it.

We turned down an alley lit by a single flickering streetlight. Buzzing. Pausing. Coming back. Like even the light wasn't sure it should be here. The walls were tagged with names and phone numbers and one half-finished mural of a woman with her eyes closed and her mouth open like she'd just told someone the truth.

At the end of the alley, we stopped in front of a squat concrete building— low ceiling, no windows, one rusted door. A hand-painted sign hung crooked above the entrance, barely hanging on by one nail:

Moodz – Dancehall. Drinks. Women Who'll Ruin Yuh Life.

The 'Z' in Moodz leaned hard to the right like it'd had one too many. The red paint was chipped, like someone had tried to scrub the truth off but it wouldn't budge. Above the door, a single red bulb buzzed steady. Drawing moths and men in equal numbers.

Troy slapped my shoulder, grinning.

"Mi favorite likkle madness," he said.

He didn't knock. Didn't check the time. He just walked in like the door owed him respect.

I stood there for a second, staring at the sign.

Moodz.

Something about it felt accurate.

Not a place. Not a party.

A whole state of being.

I took a breath. Rolled my shoulders back. Then followed him in.

* * *

Inside was a heat wave. Not just temperature—presence. Pressure. The kind of heat that stuck to your lungs and whispered in your ear. The door swung shut behind us, muffling the outside world in one heavy click. And just like that, I wasn't in Montego Bay anymore.

I was in Moodz.

Red light soaked the room, bleeding into sweat, skin, and shadow. Clouds of smoke floated above the crowd like they'd given up on rising. The air was thick with rum, perfume, and something darker—lust, maybe. Or memory.

The bassline hit like it had a grudge. Vybz Kartel's voice growled through wall-mounted speakers, the low-end so deep it rearranged my posture. You didn't hear the music. You felt it—in your throat, your knees, your molars.

The room wasn't big—maybe twenty-five people total—but it felt packed. Like the energy came with bodies of its own. Booths hugged the edges, sticky and dim. A small stage stood at the center with a single silver pole catching just enough light to look like salvation or sin depending on how you saw it.

Girls moved through the room like heatwaves made flesh. Some slow, sensual—dancing to their own heartbeat. Others sharper, more deliberate—shoulders squared, hips low, eyes scanning like they'd seen every type of man walk through that door and knew exactly how this would go.

None of it was innocent.

None of it tried to be.

And then I noticed the TVs.

Three flat screens lined the back wall—mounted high, tilted down—each playing softcore Asian porn on a loop. Silent. Subtitled. The kind with bad acting and bodies too smooth. Soft blue light spilled over the room in flashes, glowing off bare skin and cheap leather.

It was weird.

Surreal.

Somehow made sense.

Like the place had stopped pretending long ago and just leaned all the way into its chaos.

Troy pressed a fresh drink into my hand—Wray and Campari, thick with bite. He leaned close, voice barely above the beat.

"Relax, boss. Nobody pretend in Moodz. Dis deh raw."

I nodded, eyes adjusting, pulse catching up.

No mask. No performance. Just vice.

Laid bare and waiting.

And the wildest part?

I didn't want to leave.

We posted up near the stage. Close enough to feel the heat from the lights, far enough not to be mistaken for regulars. Troy nodded to a few folks, dapped up a man in a corner who handed him a spliff like it was currency, then leaned back against the booth like this was his living room.

I stood there, cup in hand, watching. Sipping slow. Not searching. Just... letting the night come to me.

And that's when she walked up.

Mimi.

I didn't know her name yet.

But I'd remember the entrance.

Slim.

Brown skin kissed by red light.

Long legs that walked like they had history.

She didn't sashay. Didn't try too hard. She just moved like the floor had been waiting on her to arrive.

Her top barely held on—small, ribbed, clinging for dear life. Her stomach was soft, beautiful. Stretch marks curved like lightning bolts across her hips, catching the red light like war paint.

She didn't hide them. Didn't flinch.

Moved like she was built to be seen and didn't need your approval to stay that way.

She wore confidence like perfume—undetectable until you were too close to look away.

She wore heels, black and clean.

Not flashy. Not modest. Just there—supporting the way she moved like she meant it.

She didn't look at me first.

She looked at Troy.

He grinned, raised his drink.

"Trouble," he mouthed.

She smiled. Closed-lipped. Certain.

Then her eyes slid to me.

Not flirty.

Not warm.

Just… measuring.

Like she could already tell I wasn't from here.

And she was deciding if that disqualified me, or made me interesting.

And for a second?

I wasn't sure I wanted her to decide.

"Mi nah know yuh face… Yuh new?" Her voice was syrup and smoke. Sweet, but heavy. Made to linger.

"Yeah," I said, meeting her gaze. "Just visiting."

"Mmm… from where? Atlanta? Miami?"

She squinted, sipped from her cup. "Whole heap a yuh look like unnu drop outta rap video."

I smirked. "Atlanta."

She sucked her teeth. "Mek sense."

Then leaned closer, not whispering, just making sure I heard it right.

"All di ATL man dem love two tings—money… an' big batty."

I raised an eyebrow. "Is that wrong?"

She shrugged, the corner of her mouth curling just enough.

"Only if yuh cyah tell which one fulla more fake."

We both laughed.

And just like that, the tension cracked.

Not gone—just softened. Like she'd tossed the ball in my court and was curious what I'd do with it.

Troy caught the vibe and slid off without a word—off to the bar, or the next joke, or both.

Now it was just us.

She took a slow sip, letting the straw tap against her lip before she spoke again.

"Mi soon go up pon di pole. Five minutes."

She tilted her head, eyes glinting. "Yuh like di view, yeah?"

I didn't look away.

"I do."

"Mmhmm."

She leaned in, close enough for her breath to kiss my cheek.

"Watch good, now. Mi nuh jus' wine—mi tell story."

Then she winked.

Not playful. Not coy.

Like she already knew how the story ended.

She turned and disappeared behind the curtain at the back of the stage—hips still talking, heels whispering on the wood.

And I just stood there.

Cup in hand.

Pulse steady, but rising.

Like I'd just been handed a test I didn't study for—but wasn't planning to fail.

* * *

The DJ's voice cracked through the haze, sharp and smug.

"Y'all know what time it is. Comin' to di stage—di gyal weh mek man lose dem mind an' wallet—Mimi pon di pole!"

79

The crowd responded before the beat even dropped—a mix of hollers, whistles, and low, knowing groans.

Then the track flipped.

Spice. "Go Down Deh."

And it didn't play.

It arrived.

The bassline hit like a slap and a kiss at the same time, and the room leaned in.

Mimi stepped out like she wasn't walking—like she was claiming space. Her long braids swung past her waist, catching the red lights and throwing them right back. Her heels struck the stage with authority—

clack, clack, pause—

like a countdown you couldn't stop.

She didn't smile.

Didn't wave.

She just stood there for a beat, eyes scanning the crowd like she already knew the end of the story and was deciding whether we deserved to watch it unfold.

Then she moved.

Not with softness. With precision.

She dropped low—knees wide, back arched, one palm dragging slow along the stage like she was wiping away someone else's presence. Then rose just as slow—vertebrae by vertebrae—until she stood upright again, neck tilted, hips swaying like they were in on a joke nobody else had heard yet.

She didn't dance to the beat.

She controlled it.

Every move hit like punctuation—sharp, deliberate. Gritty, fluid, sharp.

She coiled around the pole like silk, then climbed it—slow and strong, thighs gripping steel like it owed her something.

At the top, she froze.

Just long enough for every pair of eyes in the room to catch up.

Then she flipped.

Upside down, legs split, heels slicing air—body held by nothing but strength and audacity.

She slammed down into a split so hard the stage thudded beneath her, and a collective breath hissed through the room.

She didn't dance for dollars.

She danced for dominance.

For reverence.

And she got it.

The men leaned forward—drinks in hand, forgotten. Mouths open like they'd just seen a miracle wrapped in sweat.

The women?

They didn't look jealous.

They looked like they knew.

Game recognized game.

She spun out of the split, back on her feet in one fluid roll, braids whipping as she landed. One final drop to the floor—not for applause, but as punctuation. A full stop.

Then her eyes locked on me.

And it felt like being chosen and warned all at once.

She tossed me a wink—not playful. Sharp. Surgical.

Like a blade sheathed in heat.

And then she disappeared behind the curtain like she hadn't just stopped time.

Troy slid back beside me with that grin he wore when he was about to talk shit.

"Yuh likkle dancer crushin' yuh head, boss?"

I didn't even try to deny it.

"She's got… presence."

Troy laughed, slapped my chest.

"Presence? A so yuh call it? Nah man—dat gyal dangerous. She nuh flirt. She conquer."

He sipped his drink, still watching the stage like the imprint of her was

81

still moving across it.

"But mi like dat yuh got taste. Good batty an' bad decision? Classic combination."

I smirked, shook my head.

That's when I felt the shift again.

Heat behind me.

Perfume—sweet with something sharp underneath. Cinnamon. Citrus. Intent.

I turned, and there she was.

Mimi.

Fresh off the stage, but not undone. Sweat glowing on her chest like highlighter, braids hanging heavy down her back. Her skin looked kissed by the music still. Like it hadn't let go of her yet.

She stepped in close. Real close.

Like proximity was part of the conversation.

She didn't say hi.

Didn't ask permission.

She reached for my phone.

Took it out of my hand like it belonged to her, held it up to my face. Face ID unlocked with a soft buzz.

She smirked.

"Easy access," she said, thumbs already moving, adding her number like she'd done it a thousand times—but not for just anyone.

She paused, typed something in the name field, then handed it back to me without a word.

I looked down.

Mimi – Don't Waste This

She leaned in, lips brushing the edge of my ear.

"Mi nah text first. So if yuh want more than memory… move brave."

Then she pulled back, gave me a look like she was sizing me up for something more than one night.

And walked away.

No hips, no extra sway—just the certainty of a woman who knew exactly

RED STRIPE & ASIAN PORN

how much she left behind.

Troy was already howling, smacking my arm.

"Lord gad—yuh in deep now, boss! She tek yuh phone like customs an' stamp her entry!"

I didn't even respond.

Still staring at my screen.

Still wondering if this was attraction...

or warning dressed like one.

Either way?

She had my number now too.

* * *

We stepped back outside after another drink. Moodz still thumped behind us, but out here?

This was the afterpulse.

The part the brochures don't print.

Just outside the building, tucked into the side like a secret the night didn't try to hide, was what Troy called the real heartbeat. A cracked-up corner where the island stretched its legs and dropped its shoulders.

Streetlight flickering overhead—buzzing like it had something to say but couldn't spit it out. A wall nearby was peeling with history—a half-ripped poster of a Jamaican flag flapping slow in the breeze, layered over an old dancehall flyer so faded it looked like it'd been crying for years.

And just above all of it, nailed into the brick like a warning and a prayer, was a hand-painted sign in red and black:

DEAD YARD — STAY SHARP OR STAY HOME.

It wasn't a threat.

It was a truth.

No security. No velvet rope. Just vibes and consequences.

Troy was in his element. He lit up the block like it owed him something—greeting everyone with hugs, handshakes, patois too fast for me to catch but heavy with laughter. Some of the slang cracked open wide enough for me to guess the punchlines. The rest? I just let wash over me.

The crew was mixed. A few dealers leaned on a wall, eyes soft but scanning. Stick-up kids posted up like statues with sneakers too clean and belts too loose. Two women in heels and harder faces stood side by side—long nails, low voices, ready for anything or nothing at all.

A man sat on an upside-down crate, opening his backpack like a general inventory—tiny bottles of rum in one pocket, plastic-wrapped herb in another. Everything was hushed hustles. Silent exchanges. Currency moving like breath.

On the curb, a man rolled dice with shoulders hunched and eyes on fire—talking to the concrete more than the people watching.

Next to him, another man danced with himself—headphones in, but one ear off. Moving to a rhythm only he knew, body jerking and swaying beside a portable speaker balanced on a milk crate. The speaker skipped every few bars like it'd been dropped a few too many times, but the music didn't stop. If anything, the flaws made it hit harder.

Troy slipped me a look.

"Dis Jamaica too," he said, voice low.

And I knew what he meant.

This wasn't on any damn tour. It wasn't curated. It wasn't polished. It was real. And it was watching me just as much as I was watching it.

Troy flicked his lighter shut, leaned his shoulder on the wall beside me.

"Ain't no freedom here, yuh know. Just new ways fi pretend."

He cracked his knuckles, watching the lights stutter over the street.

"Mi been telling miself fifteen years mi gon' buy mi mother house. Still renting. Still here."

He tilted his head at me — half-grin, half-warning.

"Circle di drain long enough, it feel like home."

The air out here was different. Thick with smoke, testosterone, and unsaid rules. Eyes that didn't linger too long. Hands that stayed ready, just in case. Laughter that could turn into something else if the vibe shifted too fast.

This wasn't the curated chaos of Moodz.

This was raw. Unfiltered. The kind of corner you don't find—you get invited to.

And it was Troy's world.

He stood with one foot on the curb, one hand cupping his drink, the other gesturing to the madness like it was home.

"Mi love it out here," he said, eyes scanning the block.

"All di lies drop off. Nobody out here got time to pretend."

I nodded, feeling it.

You couldn't fake anything in this kind of air.

It would expose you.

Quick.

And that's when she appeared.

"So dis a yuh foreign friend?"

The voice came first—husky, loud, dipped in amusement like she already knew the answer and just wanted to watch you squirm saying it.

Then she stepped into view.

Candice.

Dark skin. Heavy hips. Braids down her back. Lips painted blood red.

Crop top clinging to curves like it'd been sewn in place.

Skirt barely legal, riding the line between invitation and dare.

Thighs thick enough to start wars, end treaties, and ruin peace talks.

And her energy?

Undeniable.

She didn't approach like she was meeting someone.

She walked up like she was checking inventory.

And before I could even speak, before I could think to square up or step aside—

Her hand was on me.

Grabbed my dick—full. Firm. No hesitation. No smile.

Like she was checking a receipt.

Like it was hers and I was just being reintroduced.

"Mmm."

She squeezed—once.

"Yuh packin'. Me like dat."

I stepped back instinctively—not scared. Just caught off guard.

My breath hitched. My eyes met hers.

She didn't flinch.

Troy exploded in laughter behind her, already halfway through his second wheeze.

"Bruce," he choked out, "meet Candice. She… got a style."

She didn't even look at him.

Her gaze stayed pinned to mine, her lips slick from the drink, her hand finally gone—but her energy still on me.

"Mi tek good care of mi man dem," she said, voice dropping into something smoky.

"An' Troy say yuh need a sweet night. So mi come."

Troy leaned in close, wiping a tear from his eye.

"Mi tell har—treat mi man proper. No foolishness."

Candice rolled her eyes, but her smile curled at the edge.

"Mi don't do foolishness. Mi do feelin'."

Then she stepped even closer, so close I could smell the sweat behind her perfume, feel the heat from her chest just shy of touching mine.

"So what, foreign?" she whispered, eyes locked.

"Yuh gon' stand up all night, or yuh gon' stand up for real?"

The night had already gone sideways.

And I'd never felt more awake.

* * *

Candice stayed close—hand on my chest, nails light against the fabric, voice in my ear like a second heartbeat.

Her words didn't ask questions.

They pressed buttons.

"Yuh look like yuh need a rubdown."

She said it slow, tongue almost dragging across the syllables.

"Mi bet yuh got dat long stamina dick."

No whisper. Just fact, like she'd already decided it was true.

"Yuh like it rough?

Or slow wit pressure?"

I didn't answer.

Didn't know how to—not with my brain still playing catch-up and my body fully caught.

She pulled a mini bottle of rum from somewhere—tight jeans, small bag, magic. Who knew.

Twisted the cap, drank straight, eyes never leaving mine.

Then she passed it to me.

I took a pull. Tried to match her pace.

Coughed. Hard.

She laughed, bold and full, like the street was hers.

"Soft, but yuh cute," she said, teeth flashing.

"Mi fix dat later."

We danced under the flickering streetlight—music bleeding from the milk crate speaker like a basement party with no curfew.

Her body moved like it had memory. Like it'd been here before.

She bent low, back arched, waist rolling in slow circles that pulled me in without warning.

She pressed into me like we were already alone.

Like the rest of the block didn't matter.

Didn't exist.

Everything about her screamed wild and ready.

But nothing about her screamed cheap.

She wasn't selling anything.

She was just... offering a ride I could choose to take or miss.

Her breath hit my neck when she leaned in again.

"So we goin' now?"

No flirt in her tone. Just intent.

I nodded.

Didn't say a word.

Couldn't lie—my body was already gone.

Back at my place, it started fast. Too fast for thinking. Too fast for second-guessing. The door closed and clothes came off like they were holding us back from oxygen.

Candice stripped like she was on a countdown. Top gone. Skirt tossed. Heels still on. Bra flung without ceremony, panties peeled like she was shedding skin. She didn't wait for a signal. Tongue in my mouth. Hands on my chest, my neck, my belt. Fingers bold and greedy—owning, not asking. Her body pressed into mine, soft and strong. Thighs thick and slick against me, skin warm with the afterglow of the night.

She kissed like she was tryna prove something. Bit my lip, then my neck, then laughed—not light, not cute. Wild. Feral. Free.

She shoved me back onto the bed and climbed on top, straddling like she belonged there.

"Mi been ready fi dis all night," she growled, grabbing my dick with both hands, stroking once, then guiding me in like she'd been dreaming about it.

She sank down slow—not gentle. Just controlled. Like she wanted to feel every inch drag.

My mouth dropped open.

She moaned like it fed her.

And then she rode.

No rhythm at first—just raw grind. Forward, back, full drop. Slapping down, hips bouncing, hands planted on my chest like she was using me to rise from the dead. Sweat already blooming between us. My fingers gripped her waist. Hers clawed at my chest.

She rolled her hips in tight circles, then picked up speed, ass clapping against me with every bounce.

"Dat feel good, foreign?" she panted, head tilted back, eyes wild.

"Yuh gon' cum already?"

I growled, flipped her, slammed her down onto her back.

She laughed again—that same reckless laugh—and wrapped her legs around me like chains.

"Mi like when yuh switch up."

I slid in deep—one stroke, all the way.

She gasped. Bit her lip.

Then grabbed my face and pulled me in.

"Don't stop," she whispered.

"Don't you fuckin' stop."

And I didn't.

I gave her what she came for.

And then some.

I didn't stop. Couldn't. Not when she looked up at me like that—lips swollen, cheeks flushed, eyes begging without blinking.

I pulled out of her slow, dragging it, watching her twitch as she felt the emptiness. Her breath caught like she wasn't ready to be without me yet.

Too bad.

I stood at the edge of the bed, grabbed her by the throat, pulled her to her knees.

"Open that mouth."

She obeyed—no hesitation.

Tongue out. Eyes wide.

I fed it to her. Slow at first. Just the head. Let her lips wrap around me, let her taste the sweat, the rhythm, the residue of how deep she'd taken me before. Then I grabbed the back of her head, tangled my fingers in her braids, and fucked her throat like it owed me something.

In. Out. No warning.

The first thrust made her gag. Second—tears already building. By the third, she was choking around it, saliva spilling down her chin, nails digging into my thighs.

"Yeah," I growled, watching her try to breathe through it.

"Take it. All of it. Show me what that mouth good for."

She moaned around me, low and hungry. Tried to nod with it still stuffed between her lips. Her throat tight, working, gagging, stretching.

I pulled back.

Let her catch a gasp.

Then shoved it back down.

She gagged again, louder this time, but didn't stop.

Didn't pull away.

"You like that?" I asked, voice rough.

"You like being my nasty little slut?"

She couldn't speak, but her eyes told me everything.

Yes.

More.

All of it.

Her hands gripped my thighs tighter, trying to keep her balance as I used her mouth like it was made for this. Her drool slicked my length, spit glistening down to her chest.

She was a mess.

A beautiful, willing fucking mess.

I pulled her off with a wet pop.

Watched the spit string from her lips to the tip of my cock.

"Get on the bed," I said.

"Face down. Ass up. Let me really fuck you now."

She crawled back up without a word. Breathing heavy, eyes glazed, thighs shaking.

And I followed.

Because she asked for fire.

And I came to burn.

She got on the bed like she knew what was coming. Face down. Ass up. Back arched perfect. Her legs spread wide, glistening, begging.

I stepped behind her, grabbed her hips, and rubbed the head of my cock right against her slit—up and down, slow, dragging it over that swollen clit just to watch her twitch.

"Please," she whispered into the mattress.

Breath shaky. Voice wrecked.

"Fuck me rough."

That was all I needed.

I slammed into her in one stroke—deep, hard, merciless.

She screamed.

Not from pain.

From relief.

Her ass bounced with every thrust. Skin clapping against skin, loud and wet and filthy. My grip tightened on her hips—pulling, snapping, drilling into her like I owned the moment.

"That what you wanted?" I growled.

"You want to be fucked like this?"

She moaned into the sheets.

Didn't answer.

So I reached forward, grabbed her hair, yanked her head back till her face turned to the side.

"I said, is this what you wanted?"

"Yes, yes—fuck, yes!"

Her voice cracked on the last word, hips pushing back to meet my strokes.

I spit down on her pussy—watched it mix with her slick. Rubbed my thumb over her asshole, pressed just enough to feel her flinch.

"You take this dick like you need it."

And she did.

Every inch. Every thrust.

Her body opened for me like it was made for this—like it had just been waiting for someone to stop being gentle.

I slapped her ass—hard.

Watched the skin ripple. Redden.

"Say it," I demanded.

"Tell me who this pussy belongs to."

She gasped, tried to speak, but it came out a moan.

Another thrust. Deeper.

"Say it."

"It's yours," she whimpered.

"Yours, daddy. All yours."

That flipped something in me.

I fucked her harder.

Rammed into her like the walls might break.

Her body jolted forward with every stroke, tits pressed into the mattress, moaning like she was losing herself one scream at a time.

I gripped her throat from behind, leaned over her back.

"You gon' cum for me again?"

My voice right in her ear.

She nodded, frantic.

"Yes—yes—just like that—don't stop—please—"

I didn't stop.

I kept going.

Drilled her until her body locked up, legs trembling, toes curling, back arched like a bow.

She let out a scream—loud, broken, primal.

And then she came.

Hard.

Soaking.

Fucking ruined.

Her body was already trembling, wet beyond reason, pussy stretched and throbbing from the last round.

But I wasn't done.

Not even close.

I grabbed her hips, pulled her back onto me, and slammed in hard—deeper than before.

She screamed. Loud. Raw. Guttural.

"OH—JESUS—YES—FUCK—"

Her voice cracked, body jolting forward, hands scrambling for the sheets like she didn't know where to hold on.

I didn't let up.

I pounded her.

Relentless. Ruthless.

Straight to the fuckin' soul.

My hips slapped against her ass with vicious rhythm—fast, full, unmerciful strokes that shook the bedframe.

"Tek—tek—tek—di whole a it—oh God—mi cyaaan—mi cyaaaaan!"

Her voice climbed into something primal, something broken.

She wasn't speaking English anymore.

"Lawd mi ah buss—ahhhh—fuck mi—RUFF—jesus please mi—"

She started speaking in tongues—a mix of patois, moans, sobs, and sounds that didn't belong to language.

Her legs shook. Her thighs clenched. Her whole body locked up like she was being exorcised.

And then she came.

Loud.

Thrashing.

Soaking.

I kept going. Fuckin' through it. Pushing her over the edge again—her body jerking, her voice cracking until it was just sounds .

When she collapsed, I pulled out—soaked, glistening, throbbing.

But I wasn't done.

I grabbed her by the hair, pulled her to her knees again—eyes dazed, face wet with tears and sweat.

"Mouth," I growled.

She opened.

Weak. Obedient. Ready.

I stuffed my cock past her lips, down her throat.

No build-up.

Just face-fucked her like I'd been waiting all night for this moment.

Thrust after thrust, deep and brutal.

Her throat took it all.

Gagging, choking, spit flying, tears streaming.

Her mascara ran. Her nose dripped.

She was a disaster—beautiful and broken and fully owned.

I grabbed her head with both hands, fucked her harder—fast, deep strokes, using her mouth like it belonged to me.

"You want it?" I growled.

She tried to nod, moaned around me.

"You gon' swallow every drop?"

Her eyes rolled back, hands gripping my thighs, mouth wide, throat open.

"Good girl.

Fuckin' take it."

I slammed in one last time, groaned deep, and came—exploding down her throat, flooding her mouth, holding her there until I felt her swallow.

She gagged, swallowed again, tears running down her cheeks.

I pulled out slow.

She gasped for air, spit dripping from her lips, eyes glazed.

Wrecked.

Beautiful.

Mine.

The room was quiet in that way only a freshly-fucked room could be. Sweat cooling on my skin. Breath slowing. The air thick with the smell of sex— raw, heavy, unashamed. The kind that doesn't leave right away.

Candice lay beside me, one leg thrown over mine, her chest still rising and falling like her body hadn't caught up yet. Her skin glistened, streaked with sweat and spit and me.

I let my head fall back into the pillow, eyes on the ceiling, listening to the fan tick overhead. No words. No need. Just that stretched-out silence that comes when two people gave each other everything their bodies had to offer.

She shifted slightly, dragging a finger across my chest in lazy circles. I didn't stop her. Didn't want to. For a minute, I let myself believe it. That maybe this wasn't just about the bodies. That maybe all the wildness, the moans, the spit, the cries in patois—meant something. Not love. But maybe connection. Maybe a little piece of something real.

She sat up slowly, reached for the water bottle on the nightstand. Took a sip, then wiped her mouth with the back of her hand. Her eyes lingered on the floor, then found mine.

And that's when the tone shifted.

Like a record scratch in the middle of a slow jam.

Her voice was flat.

No heat. No buildup.

"Yuh have mi money?".

I sat up, chest still bare, breath catching in my throat.

"What?"

She was already on her feet, slipping her bra back on like it was part of the routine.

"Mi say… mi time nah free. Troy nuh tell yuh? Mi thought yuh come proper. Mi cyaah waste up mi body for nutten.".

I blinked hard, trying to process the words. The way they felt like ice water on my skin.

"I didn't know this was… a service."

My voice was flat, stunned.

"I thought we were vibing."

She turned, one eyebrow cocked, lip curled just enough to let me know she didn't buy it.

"Vibing? Boss, mi a hustla. Mi look like some cheap gyal? Mi provide service. Good one too. Mi make yuh buss two times an still walk straight."

.

There was no shame in her voice. Just business. Just brass. Something twisted in my gut. Not jealousy. Not hurt. Something else. Something I didn't want to name.

"I'm not paying you for this."

That's when her face changed. The heat dropped out her eyes. All that post-sex glow went cold.

"Mi mash up dis bloodclaat place, yuh hear?".

Her voice rose, sharp and venom-laced.

"Play wid mi?

Mi not no idiot gyal." .

She stormed toward the nightstand, snatched a glass off the table, raised it like she meant to smash it against the wall—or worse.

Instinct kicked in.

I stood, stepped between her and the lamp—bare, tense, ready.

"Look—don't. I'll get you something. Just… calm down."

She stared at me for a long second. Breathing hard. Eyes darting, reading me like she wasn't sure if I was bluffing or broken. Then she sucked her teeth hard, loud. Crossed her arms like she was holding in everything she wanted to throw.

"Make it fast.

Mi cyaah believe dis fuckry.

Waste mi good up good up time." .

That's when I snapped.

I sat up, wiped the sweat from my face, and looked her dead in the eye.

"Waste your time?"

I laughed once—dry, sharp.

"I fucked you so good, you were speakin' in tongues and beggin' to be bred. And now you wanna talk like I owe you?".

She started to open her mouth, but I cut her off.

"You lucky I ain't charge you for this dick. You damn near passed out on it.".

She froze. Eyes narrowed. Arms uncrossed like she was getting ready to say something reckless.

"Mi see. So now yuh waan disrespect mi?".

I stood up. Walked toward her slow, still bare, chest heaving.

"You disrespected your damn self when you made it a transaction after the fact. That's some weak shit.".

I paused. Let the silence stretch.

"Next time, lead with the price. Don't sell me dreams in between moans.".

She didn't respond right away. Just stood there. Top still off. Hair a mess. Thighs still wet with everything we'd just done. But the energy had soured. The room felt colder now. And it had nothing to do with the air.

I walked to my bag, pulled out my wallet. No hesitation. No drama. I peeled off a few bills—clean, folded, silent—and tossed them onto the bed between us.

"There."

She stared at the money like she expected more. I stared at her like she was already gone.

"Don't spend it all in one place."

My voice was flat. Final.

"Wouldn't want someone else to think it's worth more than that.".

That landed. I saw it in the way her jaw flexed.

She picked up the money slow, didn't fold it, didn't count it. Just slipped it into her bra and turned to grab the rest of her shit.

I stepped back. "Get the fuck out."

Flat. Dead. Final.

She didn't say shit. She just walked to the door, heels clapping like they were stomping out whatever was left between us.

And when it closed?

That silence hit harder than the sex ever did.

* * *

Montego Bay was quiet now. No bass. No horns. Just the hum of the sea and a breeze that didn't care what had gone down a few hours ago. The heat had lifted. The air was lighter. And I was still here—not broken, just… clearer.

The bed behind me was a mess. Sheets tangled. Condensation on the glass. A bra on the floor. Her scent still hanging in the room like smoke after a fire.

And yeah—I paid for it.

Not proud of that.

But if I'm being real?

It was good.

Wild. Raw. No filters.

Pussy damn near spiritual.

That wasn't romance.

That was a storm.

And maybe I needed that.

Maybe I needed to be reminded that this trip wasn't about control. It wasn't about earning peace or chasing clarity. It was about letting shit happen.

Even the messy.

Even the mad.

Even the kind of night that leaves your ego limping but your body humming.

Would I do it again?

Probably not.

But am I mad?

…Not really.

Because maybe this was part of it.

Part of the unraveling.

Part of the plan I never made.

I came here thinking I needed answers.

But maybe I just needed to feel something honest, even if it was wrapped in lies.

And that's what tonight gave me.

Not love.

Not clarity.

But sensation.

And silence.

And one hell of a story.

* * *

I took a deep breath and let the sea air work its way through my chest. Inside, the fan ticked on. The night moved past me like it had somewhere else to be.

And I smiled.

Just a little.

8

If the Price is Right

I woke up to the kind of stillness that didn't need my permission. The apartment wasn't peaceful. Just emptied out. Still in a way that didn't offer comfort—just space. The fan ticked overhead, slow and steady. The sheets beneath me were still twisted, damp in places, warm in others. And there it was—the faint smear of lipstick on the pillow where she'd buried her face. Deep red. Bold. Like everything about her.

For a second, the room started moving again. Her body flashing back in pieces—those thick thighs planted on my hips, the way she moaned with her whole fuckin' chest. Her laugh when I flipped her over. The choke. The ride. The spit. That mouth? Unreal. She gagged like it was gospel, like the tears in her eyes meant she was being baptized in sin.

I let out a short breath. Not quite a laugh. Just... acknowledgment.

She really had eaten the dick like she was mad at it.

No lie, it was one of the wildest nights I'd ever had. Top tier. Nasty in a way that made me proud to look at the sheets and see they were still clinging to the evidence. Her scent still lingered—sweet, sweaty, a little floral, a lot filthy. One of her earrings was under the nightstand. Bra half-hanging off the lamp.

Everything pointed to a woman who'd left her mark like she'd meant to. And then she dipped. No note. No text. No fake sweet talk. Just an exit.

I wasn't mad. Not even shocked anymore. Just… surprised by how fast the vibe shifted. One second she was begging to be bred, the next she was checking for payment like they'd skipped foreplay and gone straight to invoicing. It wasn't that I felt used—it was that I hadn't seen it coming.

I sat up slowly, feet planted on the floor, hand dragging over my face. My body still sore in the best ways. The night had been chaos—sweaty, reckless, fuck-me-until-I-scream chaos. And for what it was? It did what it needed to do.

No lesson. No heartbreak. Just a damn good fuck wrapped in a little confusion. Still, I couldn't deny it: she flipped the switch first.

And maybe that's what got me. Not the money talk. Not the act. Just the way she turned cold like it was easy. Like the fire between them hadn't even warmed her. I glanced over my shoulder at the lipstick stain again, then shook my head and stood up.

"Damn…"

Because if I was being real? That night was biblical.

But the sermon was over. And the sanctuary was empty.

Time to wash off the oil and keep it moving.

I cleaned up slow, like my body wasn't in a rush to be clean. Every movement dragged a little. Not from fatigue, but from that post-storm heaviness. That thick stillness that settles after something wild. I moved through the apartment barefoot.I picked up my shorts from the floor, still warm in spots from where our bodies had tangled. I stepped over her bra like it wasn't even there.

The water in the bathroom sink ran cold. I let it splash against my face, leaned in with both hands braced on the porcelain, staring at myself like I might find an answer in the mirror. But all I saw was the same man from last night—just a little less hard. A little more honest.

I brushed my teeth. Spit.

Rinsed. Didn't reach for cologne. Didn't bother to line up my beard or lotion past the ash on my elbows. This wasn't about presentation. Just maintenance.

It was too early to drink. And too late to fall back into sleep like the night hadn't happened.

My skin still felt coated—like something was clinging to me. Not regret. Just residue. The kind that stays even after the water runs hot. A layer of breath, of sweat, of memory. My thighs still ached. Jaw a little tight from how hard I'd clenched when she took me in her mouth. Hands marked faintly from how hard I'd gripped her hips. I looked around the apartment. Too unsettling. Too boxed in. The walls felt like they were holding onto last night just as much as I was.

I needed to rinse it off. Not in the shower.

Outside.

Somewhere with space. Somewhere the air could reach me.

* * *

I asked around a bit that morning, moving slow through the breeze like a man still drying off from the night before. The first few people just pointed me toward the obvious—Doctor's Cave, the hotel strip, the places built for tourists with soft feet and curated playlists. But I wasn't looking for frozen cocktails and Bluetooth speakers. I wanted something with roots. Somewhere that didn't charge for entry or demand a wristband.

I paused in front of a corner shop where two men were playing ludi on an old wooden board, the edges worn down smooth like a memory. One of them looked up—gray beard, toothpick in the corner of his mouth.

"Yuh lookin' fi beach, boss?"

"Yeah… not the resort kind. I want the real water."

The man squinted at me, then nodded slow, approving.

"Mi like dat. Yuh wan' feel di place, nuh just pose in it. Walk 'round di bend, past di jerk man dem. When yuh see di zinc fence wid di spray paint—cut through. Follow dat track till yuh smell sea and yuh cyaah hear yuh own thoughts."

I thanked him, started to walk off—but another voice called out from a few steps up the road.

"Ey, foreign…!"

101

I turned slow, shoulders slightly tight, not sure what was coming.

A man about my age leaned on a gate, grinning wide with arms crossed like he'd been waiting to say something slick. Tank top on. Slippers dragging.

"Yuh mash up dat gyal last night, eeh? Mi cyaah sleep fi real."

I froze mid-step, blinked once. My mouth opened like I might deny it, then just shut again.

The man laughed and held up his hand like he meant no harm.

"Mi na disrespect yuh. Mi jus' say—mi proud. She deh bawl out like yuh was casting out demon. Whole yard hear di thing."

I exhaled through my nose, lips twitching into a crooked grin. I gave a slight nod, finally relaxing.

"Aight… good look, then."

"Nah man, respect due. Di gyal come outta deh lookin' like she get baptized." The man clapped once. "Mi seh, dat stroke? Elite."

I kept walking, shaking my head like I wasn't tryna entertain it, but a small smirk still pulled at my cheek.

And then—another voice. Softer. Closer.

"Wish I was the one gettin' baptized," a woman murmured, just loud enough for me to catch it.

I turned, caught her on a stoop, one leg crossed over the other, mango juice glistening on her fingertips. Her eyes were locked on me, lips curved into something wicked.

I arched a brow. "You gon' say that out loud like I'm not standin' right here?"

She sucked the mango pit once, slow. "If I say it louder, you gon' invite me next time?"

I stepped back, hands in my pockets, grin lazy. "You gotta be careful with talk like that."

"Why?"

"'Cause some of us follow through."

She laughed, full and rich. "Then maybe I should come see you later—make sure all the stories I heard true."

I gave her one last look, slow and measured. "I'll be around," I said, then turned and kept walking—cool, unbothered, but the smirk stayed put.

The beach took a bit to get to—rough road, couple turns that didn't make sense unless I'd walked it before—but it was worth every step.

No signs. No security. Just shoreline and sound.

It opened up like a secret. The sand wasn't perfect, but it was honest. Kids ran barefoot, weaving through broken shells and cigarette butts. Uncles grilled fish on portable stoves, arguing over seasoning and World Cup stats. Men slapped dominoes on concrete with the kind of force that demanded attention. And the music? Not a speaker in sight—just a car parked sideways blasting Buju loud enough to stir the tide. There were no loungers. No concierge.

Just sweat and laughter. Charcoal smoke drifting thick through the salt air. The scent of jerk and fresh fry fish hitting me all at once like a memory I hadn't made yet.

I found a shaded spot beneath a crooked almond tree and let my weight fall into the sand, legs stretched, back against a smooth trunk.

It was the first time all day

I felt still.

Not paused—still.

The waves moved without effort. The wind danced between conversations. The hum of the beach wrapped around me like a soft press on the chest—not heavy, just firm enough to remind me I had a body that needed tending.

I exhaled slow.

Let the sea air unknot whatever was still holding on inside me.

Didn't even realize how much tension I'd been carrying until the sound of dominoes slamming made me flinch—then smile.

This was the real water.

And I was finally in it.

For a few hours, I didn't think about Candice.

Or Atlanta.

Or anything that waited for me at home.

I watched.

I breathed.

I belonged, quietly.

No one looked twice at me. No questions, no curiosity. Just another man soaking in salt air and sun. My body, still carrying the echoes of last night, had started to feel like mine again. Shoulders loosened. Jaw unclenched. The breath I didn't know I'd been holding released slow, steady, like the tide had pulled it out of me and replaced it with something lighter.

There was a rhythm here—kids screaming in joy, dominoes cracking like gunshots, waves lapping against shore in sync with the bass thumping from a parked car. And somewhere in that rhythm, I found room to just be. No performance. No past. Just presence.

The sand beneath me didn't ask for anything. The sea didn't offer answers. But both gave me permission to sit still—and that felt holy in its own way.

As the sun began its slow descent, dipping gold across the water like it, too, was tired of being seen, I stood and brushed the sand from my legs.

I nodded once to the men playing dominoes, caught a smile from the mango woman without returning it fully. Just enough to leave the door cracked.

The walk back into town was quiet.

Not silent—settled. I got home, rinsed off the salt, the smoke, the weight. Let the water run hotter this time, not to cleanse, but to wake me back up.

Dressed slow. Nothing flashy. Just a clean tee, fresh breath, and pockets light enough to move.

When I stepped out again, the sky was already dimming—sunset bleeding into streetlights.

I didn't have a plan.

But for the first time in days, I didn't need one.

The day had handed me something—clarity, maybe. Or space.

Enough, at least, to make me want to see what the night might offer back.

* * *

By the time I hit the Strip, the city was already shaking off the day. Sunset had folded into streetlights, and the energy had changed—gone was the lazy hum of afternoon. Now it pulsed. Neon signs blinked alive. Bass crept through concrete.

Girls in short dresses walked like they owned the block. Vendors lit coals and shouted prices over old-school riddims that fought for space between cars and conversation.

I moved through it slow, letting the rhythm of the night wrap around me. My body felt lighter than it had all day. The sea had rinsed the weight off, but the streets were what woke me back up.

I was halfway down Gloucester Avenue, passing a spot where the music spilled from open doors and the scent of rum floated past like invitation—when I heard my name.

"Yow! Bruce!"

I turned.

Troy was leaning against a wall like he'd been waiting on me the whole time—white tee, gold chain, cup already in hand.

"Mi seh... yuh look like yuh finally touch base."

I smiled, walking over. "Had to take a day. Needed to reset."

Troy nodded, pushed off the wall, and handed me a fresh cup.

"Then tonight, mi seh... we back."

The city was waking up in neon. Music spilled from every doorway. I let myself get pulled into the motion—drinks, introductions, energy. Troy moved through it all with ease, linking me with locals who greeted me like I belonged.

They posted up near a food stall, the grill snapping under a slab of jerk pork, steam rising thick into the night air.

Troy took a sip of his drink and glanced sideways. "So... yuh make it out alive, eh?" I shook my head, chuckling. "If you talkin' about Candice? Barely."

"Mi seh—she rough?"

"Not rough. Just... wild. Like possessed. Did shit that made me forget my name."

Troy started laughing before I could finish.

"And then," I said, pointing with my cup, "after all that—she hits me with the 'you got my money?' like we'd just closed a deal."

Troy leaned back, hands on his knees. "Mi try tell yuh! Candice? She doan play. Look good, fuck better, but mi tell yuh—everybody round here lookin' fi a way to make ends meet."

I sipped. "Man, I wasn't even mad. Just caught me off guard."

Troy smirked. "She threaten fi mash up di place?"

I nodded. "Said she'd tear the whole apartment down if I didn't pay."

Troy clapped once, wheezing. "Mi seh—di gyal crazy, but mi cyaah lie... hot fuck, though?"

I tilted my head. "Top tier. Hall of fame, even. But shorty flipped the switch like it was business hours."

Troy laughed again. "Welcome to di yard, mi G. Sometimes di pussy spiritual, but yuh still haffi pay tithe."

I nearly spit my drink, eyes squinting from the laugh. "Yo, you stupid."

They kept walking, weaving through crowds and speakers and open bars until the music folded into background noise.

I nudged Troy. "Yo—real talk, what's up with 2727? I'm tryna lock in something for when my people land. Wedding guests, some folks flyin' in. I need a space to set the vibe right."

"Yuh talkin' 'bout di rooftop ting?"

"Yeah. Something clean. A lil' flex. Good drinks. I just want somewhere we can all pull up, feel good, without the whole resort energy."

Troy nodded. "Mi got yuh. One ah di promoters deh pon link tonight. Come... le' we reason. Mi introduce yuh. Yuh talk to him, reserve yuh space, pattern yuh night."

I clinked my cup to Troy's. "Say less."

"Mi seh," Troy said, already leading the way, "tonight, yuh rollin' proper."

"Had to rinse the day off me first," I said, letting the city move around me. "Now I'm good."

"Bless up," Troy replied, and they disappeared into the crowd—laughing, glowing under red lights and smoke, the night wide open in front of them.

9

Didn't Expect Her

"Why you lookin' at me like that?" I asked, grinning.

She smirked. "Yuh look like somebody worth lookin' at."

Simple. Direct. Like it wasn't a pickup line, just truth. It hit soft—but deep. Like heat soaking through fabric.

I tilted my head slightly, already pulled into her current.

"You always talk like that?"

She shrugged. "Mi nuh waste words. If mi see sumn, mi say it."

She stood there—steady, unfazed, glowing under red neon like it was painted just for her. Locs pulled up. Skin dewy from the heat, but not flustered. There was a calm in the way she held herself, like she had nothing to prove because the room already knew. I didn't realize I'd stepped closer until I caught the shift in her stance—subtle, but open.

"What's your name?"

"Jovel."

She said it slow, like it mattered. Like she wanted me to remember how it sounded before I asked again.

"I'm Bruce."

"Yuh don't move like a Bruce," she said, eyes still holding mine.

"How I move then?"

She looked me over—not greedy, just curious. Like she wasn't hunting, just taking inventory.

"Like somebody who been tryin' fi disappear... but still want to be found."

That one landed. I didn't flinch, but it caught something.

Before I could respond, her friend walked up behind her—young, fly, eyes flicking between us with a look that said *I see what's happening here.* Jovel glanced over her shoulder. "Mi soon come," she said gently, and the friend nodded, stepping back without a fuss. Just enough distance to give space, but not vanish.

Jovel turned back to me. "Yuh visiting?"

"Yeah. Wedding."

"You look like you needed the trip more than di couple getting married."

I chuckled, rubbing the back of my neck. "Damn. That obvious?"

"No," she said, smiling softly. "But mi from Maroon Town. We feel things before people say them."

That changed the air between us.

She didn't say it like a flex. Just fact.

"Maroon Town, huh? That why you walk like the ground owes you something?"

She laughed at that. Not loud. Just real. "No. That's just good posture."

She stepped a little closer. Not in a rush. Just enough to close the space between intention and action.

"You always stand outside clubs making women cross the street for you?"

"Nah," I said. "Usually I'm tryna stay out the way."

She nodded once. "Yuh didn't stay out my way tonight."

"Nope," I said. "Didn't want to."

Another beat passed. The street was still moving around us, music echoing from car windows, the scent of jerk thick in the air, but none of it was touching the space we were in.

"Can I ask you something?" I said.

She leaned in, eyes soft but sharp. "Yuh already did."

"You feel that?" I asked.

She didn't ask what I meant.

She just smiled. "Mi do."

She wasn't loud. She didn't need to be. Everything about her was statement without volume—pink lips, shaped and sure, eyes that held yours just long enough to get under the skin. Her body had that grown-woman fullness—soft in the right places, toned in the ones that mattered. And the way she stood? Like the ground knew to adjust under her weight.

Tonight, she wore it well. Strapless corset top hugging her tight, black lace against pink silk, just enough skin to leave you wondering. Her waist cinched, hips wide, legs strong. Hair framed her face in a soft bob—edges laid but not stiff, that natural flow you only get when you're not trying to force anything.

And she smelled good.

Close-up kind of good.

Not perfume, but presence.

There was something in her aura that said *come correct*, even while she smiled. The kind of woman you don't talk slick to unless you're ready to back it up.

And somehow, standing there in the chaos of cars, bass, and laughter—she was the only thing that felt still.

Like the whole night had been building toward this pause.

Like I hadn't just met her—but had been supposed to.

She caught me looking. Not in a disrespectful way—just seeing her. And instead of turning coy or playing into it, she leaned into her stance like, *yeah, I know.*

I smiled. "You always pull up on strangers like this?"

She tilted her head. "Yuh look like someone who needed the interruption."

That made me laugh—low, real. "You not wrong."

She studied me a beat longer, eyes narrowing just a touch like she could see past the grin.

"You carry weight," she said.

I didn't dodge it. I just nodded. "Some days more than others."

"Mi feel it," she said. "Mi from Maroon Town. We pick up on what don't get said."

"Yeah?" I asked, shifting a little closer. "So what am I not saying?"

She didn't flinch. "That yuh tired. Not body-tired. Soul-tired. But you still tryna look like yuh good."

I exhaled, slow.

She didn't gloat. Didn't say it to expose me.

She just saw me.

"Where I come from," she continued, "seeing through people is survival. My ancestors fought off the British and made them sign peace. Whole town built by runaways who turned warriors. Wi come from blood that never waited to be saved."

That hit different. Not dramatic. Just undeniable.

Her friend waved from the corner, phone in hand, ready to dip. Jovel turned toward her and raised a hand. "Mi soon come," she called, then looked back at me like the choice had already been made.

"Come," she said, slipping her phone into her bag.

"Where we going?"

"Fi walk. Clear your head. Or fill it—depends how yuh move."

She turned without waiting, stepping into the street with that same sway that didn't ask for attention but demanded it anyway.

That's when I saw it—the full view.

Dress fitted, movement smooth, that ass sitting soft and bold like it knew exactly what it was doing.

"Girl," I muttered, half-laughing, "I ain't know you was draggin' a wagon like that!"

She stopped and looked back, lips already forming a smile. "Yuh late."

"I'm tryin' to catch up."

She twirled slow, hands out like she was showing off a full moon. "Better keep up, foreign. Night just start."

And just like that, we crossed the street—her leading, me following—into a part of the night I hadn't planned for... but suddenly felt built for.

* * *

The casino was dead—too quiet. A few bored tourists hunched over slot machines like they were waiting on luck to give a damn. No music, no vibe, no reason to stay. So we left.

We ended up at a liquor store not far from Moodz—the same area from the other night, but this wasn't a club run. Just a quick stop to grab some rum, chasers, and a couple cold beers. But the spot had a whole vibe of its own.

It was one of those corner shops with no real sign, just a hand-painted name half-faded by the sun. The kind of place you find by memory, not directions. Inside, the shelves were cluttered and tight, stocked with everything from overproof and Magnum to off-brand chips and single cigarettes in a jar by the register. You could feel the day's heat still clinging to the walls.

But outside—outside was where the scene lived.

A couple plastic chairs leaned against the wall, a speaker balanced on a bucket, and a rhythm spilling out into the night like it had somewhere to be. Popcaan's "Family" was playing—low but clear—his voice cutting through the air like prayer and warning all at once. That beat, that bass, it had people nodding, lifting their cups, talking shit and laughing like they ain't have work again tomorrow. It was the kind of song you didn't just hear—you felt it in your ribs.

These were the after-shift people.

The real ones. Bartenders with rolled-up sleeves, hotel staff still in their name tags, casino dealers with tired eyes but loose shoulders now. Folks who'd spent all day catering to tourist fantasies, and now finally had a space to just be. To laugh loud. To cuss soft. To breathe without smiling for someone else's vacation photos.

Inside the shop, it was its own little world.

"Aye bwoi, look who deh yah!" an older man said, grinning wide as he dropped a six-pack on the counter.

A younger guy turned, dreads tied back in a loose bun, gold chain sitting proud on his chest. "Jah know, Biggs? Mi swear seh yuh did dead or move foreign!"

"Mi did move foreign, fool," the man laughed, clapping him on the back.

"Brooklyn cold as fuck, but mi come home fi di holidays. Mi cyaah deal wid snow no more."

The cashier chuckled without looking up, counting bills and sliding change across the counter. "Once yard get inna yuh blood, no place sweet like it."

In the back, two women in resort uniforms were leaned up against a fridge, sipping Boom mixed with rum out of a shared Styrofoam cup.

"Yuh hear 'bout di man inna Room 317?" one said, her eyebrows raised so high they damn near touched her edges.

The other leaned in. "Wha happen?"

"Him wife fly in from Canada fi surprise him… only fi find him inna di bed wid one next gyal. Right pon di white sheets."

"No!"

"Mi swear pon mi life. Security had fi hold her back—she fling him suitcase off di balcony. Clothes all over di garden."

The two women exploded into laughter, one stomping her foot while the other bent over, gasping between cackles. "Mi did wonder why dem call housekeeping three time fi dat room!"

Outside, more workers pulled up—still in polos, some with aprons tucked in their back pockets. They grabbed cold drinks, dapped up friends, and slid right into the current like they'd never left. The stories, the music, the energy—it all moved around me like water.

It didn't matter that the spot was rough around the edges.

That was the whole point.

It felt real. And for once, I wasn't a guest. Just a man blending into the background, watching the soul of a place unfold in front of him.

* * *

We found a spot outside—two flipped crates off to the side, just past the buzz of the speaker. The music was still going, but softer now, tucked under the hum of the night. A stray breeze kicked up dust, carrying the smell of sweat, salt, and overproof rum.

She sat down first, skirt gathered just above her knee, one foot tucked behind the other like she'd done this a hundred times before. I dropped next to her, passed her the chaser, and cracked open the bottle.

The first sip hit hard, but it warmed the chest. Made it easier to talk. Or maybe harder to hold shit in.

Jovel took a slow swig, wiped her lips with the back of her hand, and looked out toward nothing in particular. "Mi lef mi son inna di country fi come here. Negril first. Den Mobay. Always chasing work."

I turned to her, but didn't rush her. I just held the moment open.

"How old is him?" I asked, voice low.

"Eight. Going nine this summer." She gave a small smile, then blinked slow. "Mi bredda and him woman keep him. Dem good to him. But mi miss him every day. Mi feel like mi missing mi own life, yuh know?"

I nodded. "Yeah... I do."

She glanced at me like she was surprised by the honesty in that. Then looked away again.

"Him father dead," she said after a beat. "Shot last year. Wrong place. Wrong people. But dat don't matter now. Gone is gone."

"Damn," I said, quietly. "I'm sorry."

She didn't ask me to be.

"Mi nah cry over it no more," she added. "Mi did cry... too much. Now mi just try stay upright."

I passed her the bottle again.

She drank, slower this time.

"You ever get to see him?" I asked.

"Couple times a year if mi lucky. Summer if mi can afford it. Mi twenty-eight now, Bruce. Had him when mi was nineteen. Everything from dat point forward was just... survival."

The number sat heavy between us—not because it was young, but because of how old it sounded coming from her mouth. Twenty-eight, and she spoke like someone who'd lived twice that.

"Mi feel like mi been adulting since mi was a child," she said, then gave a short laugh that didn't reach her eyes. "Yuh ever feel like you skipped over

113

the part where yuh get to just… live?"

I didn't even have to think. "Yeah," I said. "All the time."

She studied me then. Not in a flirtatious way—but like she was checking to see if I was built for this level of honesty.

"What about you?" she asked. "You seem like yuh running from something too."

I exhaled, not ready to lie.

"Divorce," I said. "Two kids I don't see enough. Job that ate up the best of me. One day I just… snapped. Packed a bag and left."

"Mi see it in yuh eyes," she said. "That tiredness. Not body-tired. Soul-tired."

I chuckled under my breath. "You sound like you read people for a living."

She shrugged. "Mi been through enough to know when someone else carrying weight. Mi suspended today, yuh know."

"For what?"

She rolled her eyes. "Some stupidness at di call center. Customer get vexed, mi hang up. Now HR want investigate mi like mi criminal."

I shook my head. "Sounds familiar."

"Dem treat we like we disposable. Smile for eight hours, tek insults, then say 'have a blessed day.'" Her voice grew tight. "Mi tired, Bruce. Tired fi pretend like mi alright all di time."

"I get it," I said, leaning in a little. "More than you know."

She looked up at me then, eyes wet but not breaking. There was no pity between us—just recognition. Two people who'd been worn thin by life but still showed up anyway. Still had enough heart left to sit outside a liquor store and share truth over cheap rum.

As the bottle emptied, her smile returned—slow, genuine, glowing like the damn moon found her cheekbones and didn't want to leave.

"Mi don't even usually talk like dis," she admitted, grinning now. "Yuh mus' be trouble."

"Maybe," I said, watching her. "But you feel like peace right now."

She laughed again, softer this time. "Still trying fi figure out who mi really be. Mi a mother, mi a worker… but sometimes mi wonder if mi ever get to just be Jovel."

"You will," I said, and meant it. "Maybe not all at once. But you will."

And she looked at me like maybe—just maybe—she believed that too.

The music still played in the distance. The night hadn't gotten quieter. But in that little pocket of space we carved for ourselves, nothing else existed.

Just her. Me. And the kind of connection that didn't need a name yet.

But felt real enough to change something.

As we drank and talked, the edge started to soften. The rum had done its job—unclenched shoulders, warmed the ribs, opened up spaces in the conversation that weren't just about survival. There was still weight between us, yeah, but it didn't feel so heavy now. It was just part of the rhythm.

The night around us picked up too, like someone slowly turned the volume knob on the scene.

The speaker near the shop had switched to a riddim-heavy throwback— "Bruck Off Yuh Back"—and the mood on the sidewalk shifted right with it. A group of girls by the wall started whining like the street was a dancefloor. One of the guys with a spliff behind his ear hyped them up, yelling, "Lawd gad, gyal bruk it down den!" while slapping the side of a crate like it was a drum.

Jovel laughed, leaned in. "Jamaicans nuh need invitation fi buss a wine, yuh see it?"

"I do now," I said, grinning.

She turned back to me and raised a brow. "So tell mi... what kinda music yuh listen to?"

"All over the place," I said. "Depends on the day. R&B when I'm trying to feel something. Hip hop when I'm trying not to. Reggae when I'm trying to remember the world still got soul."

She smiled, nodded like she approved. "Good answer. Mi love Beres. Can't go wrong wid Beres."

"I don't even speak patois right," I said, "but I'll sing every damn line of 'Rockaway' like I lived it."

She laughed—real and loud—and leaned back, letting it carry through the air.

"Alright, alright," she said, pointing her cup at me. "What else? Favorite food?"

I thought for a second. "Steak, medium rare. Tacos on a lazy night. But ask me again tomorrow and I might say oxtail if it's made right."

"Might?" she gasped, hand to chest. "You mad? Oxtail is right."

I raised my hands, surrendering. "I take it back."

She smirked. "Yuh better."

We sat there swapping randoms like we were catching up from a life we never lived together—best travel spot, worst date, the dumbest thing we ever did for love. I told her about the time I got stranded in Mexico 'cause I trusted a cab driver named Ice Cream. She told me about dating a man who sold weed and swore he was "building an empire."

The air between us loosened. That early tension—grief, frustration, fatigue—it was still there, but softer now. Like it had agreed to sit this part out.

More people showed up. A few curious eyes clocked me, the foreigner posted up on crates like he belonged. One guy walked past, did a double take, and asked Jovel loud enough for me to hear, "Da yute deh from 'Merica?"

She nodded. "Yeah man. Him cool."

That was enough. Next thing I knew, someone handed me a fresh Red Stripe and raised his bottle in salute. We clinked. Another guy cracked a joke about me needing to trade my sneakers for some Clarks if I planned to stick around. Laughter spilled through the crowd like smoke.

It felt like I'd slipped into another layer of the night—one that tourists never got to see. Not the resort version. Not the curated excursion. But the real version. The part where people stop performing and just live.

And somehow, I wasn't just watching it happen.

I was in it.

Jovel looked at me again, eyes soft but sharp. "Yuh holding up?"

"I'm good," I said, and meant it. "You?"

She didn't answer right away. Just bumped her cup against mine and smiled. "Mi getting there."

And for once, I didn't feel like I had to chase the moment. It was already here. Unfolding around us like a story being told in real time—one laugh, one sip, one look at a time.

*　*　*

The bottle was down to its last breath. Jovel swirled what was left and gave me a look. No words—just the universal signal that it was time to re-up.

"Let's make the run," I said, standing and dusting my palms. She stretched with a little groan, then stood beside me, already digging in her purse.

The night had thickened around us—more people now, louder music, that sweet spot between too late to be early and too early to go home. As we made our way back toward the shop, I noticed a few new faces lingering near the entrance. And one familiar one.

Candice.

Posted up just outside the liquor store, arms folded, tight dress hugging every curve like a second skin. Her eyes locked on me before I could even pretend to look away. She stared hard—deep, searching, unmoved.

I didn't break stride.

Just offered a grin. "Nice seeing you again," I said cool, walking right past her, close enough that our shoulders nearly brushed.

No response. Not even a blink.

But I caught the tension in her jaw. That look you get when someone you thought you had... just kept walking.

Jovel turned to me as we stepped inside, one eyebrow raised. "Yuh know her?"

I chuckled, rubbing the back of my neck. "Yeah... that's a wild story. I'll tell you once we escape the fluorescent lights."

"Mi cyan wait," she said, smirking as she grabbed a basket.

She moved through the store with purpose—grabbed another bottle of overproof, two cold Red Stripes, and a pack of cigarettes from behind the counter.

"You smoke?" I asked.

"Only when mi drinking and mi feelin' dangerous," she replied without looking back.

I stepped up to pay, but before I could reach into my pocket, her hand slid across my chest, stopping me.

"Mi got it," she said, smiling up at me, playful but firm. "Tonight on me."

I looked at her for a beat—trying to memorize the curve of that smile, the confidence in it. "So you just buying me drinks now?"

"Consider it a reward. Fi keeping up."

We walked back out into the thick air, the sound of laughter and bass rising with the warmth. Just a few steps from the door, a voice called out—

"Jovel?!"

Her head snapped up. "Tanya?!"

The two women collided in a hug so tight it made a few heads turn. Tanya was in high-waisted jeans and a flowy yellow top, edges laid and glowing like she never missed a beat. Beside her, a tall Black man in fresh kicks and a gold chain smiled wide.

Tanya pulled back and looked between the two of us, eyes narrowed playfully. "Lawd... who dis now? You walkin' like y'all been stuck together all week."

Jovel laughed, trying to play it cool. "Mi just meet him tonight! Chill out."

"Mmhmm," Tanya said, grinning. "Coulda fooled me."

The man stepped up and offered a handshake. "Devin," he said, American accent thick. "Looks like Jo been showing you the real Montego Bay."

"She's been holding it down," I said, nodding.

Before anyone could say more—lights.

Engines roared like judgment—four military-green pickup trucks storming in tight formation, tires screeching as they swallowed up the street. Floodlights blasted across the storefronts, sweeping over faces like heat lamps in an interrogation room.

Doors flung open. Soldiers jumped out fast, rifles in hand, camo blending into the night like shadows with triggers. Movements sharp. Intentional. No hesitation.

"Hands in di air! NOW!"

The order cracked through the crowd like lightning, and suddenly the block wasn't a party anymore—it was a checkpoint.

Music died on cue. Voices clipped. Laughter evaporated. All that was left was the rustle of panic and the clang of nerves hitting concrete.

Beside me, Jovel didn't flinch. Just whispered, steady as breath, "Jus' cool. Dem deh jus' do di checks."

Her hand brushed mine—small, firm. A grounding touch.

I lifted my hands slow, careful. One of the soldiers was already heading our way, eyes cold and unreadable, rifle angled just low enough to remind us it could rise quick. Around us, bodies were being pulled apart from the crowd. Someone was forced to the ground. Another shoved against a truck. A bottle shattered underfoot. A woman cried out, "Mi nah do nuttin! Officer mi innocent!"

Everything felt hot. Compressed. Like the night was holding its breath.

The soldier reached us, nodding toward me.

"ID."

I nodded back, just enough to signal I heard him. "I've got my passport," I said, voice calm. Neutral. I reached slowly into my pocket, every movement exaggerated, careful not to give them a reason to flinch.

Jo was already speaking before I could unzip it. "Him American. Tourist. Just drinking out here. He nah part of nuttin."

I pulled the passport free—worn, a little bent at the corners from being stuffed in too many backpacks—and held it out flat in my palm, picture page open.

The soldier took it, glanced down. Paused.

Another soldier stepped over his shoulder, checked it too. Then the first one looked at me again, then Jo, then back at the crowd like he was doing the mental math.

A beat passed.

Then came the shout—sharp, final:

"Let dem go! Him ah visitor—he clear. Di girl too. Tell dem leave now!"

Jo didn't wait.

119

She grabbed my wrist and tugged. "Come," she said under her breath. "Don't linger. Come now."

Tanya's car was already pulled up—a white Toyota with the back door open and the engine running. Devin waved us in like he'd been ready to bolt the moment we were clear.

"Get in!" Tanya barked, voice tight as the steering wheel she was gripping.

We slipped into the back seat, doors slamming just as Tanya hit the gas. The tires screeched, gripping the road like it was trying to hold us back.

I glanced back through the window—lights still flashing, soldiers still moving through the crowd, people being questioned, held, watched. All of it shrinking behind us like a bad dream in reverse.

The car was silent except for the sound of the road under us and the sudden, awkward rhythm of everyone breathing again.

Jovel turned to me, her hand still resting on my arm, her voice low but full of fire.

"Mi tell yuh. Mi said mi got yuh."

And that's when I knew—it wasn't just the cops I was walking away from. It was something else too.

Some line in the sand between being a stranger in this place… and being seen in it.

10

Mi Got Yuh

The car peeled off fast, tires cutting into the night like they had something to prove. No one said shit at first. Just breathing—tight, uneven. Devin glanced in the rearview, jaw clenched like he was still expecting one of the trucks to follow.

My passport sat in my lap, thumb still pressed against the leather like I hadn't registered we were safe yet.

The silence broke when Tanya let out a sharp exhale. "Goddamn... I hate when they roll like that."

"Is that normal?" I asked, finally finding my voice.

Jovel nodded, her gaze out the window. "Yah man. Dem do it all di time. 'Specially round dat shop. Duppy dem always hunting."

Devin cut in. "That whole strip got a rep. Dealers, robbers—everybody post up there after hours. They not there for you," he said, glancing at me, "but you just happened to be standing in the blast zone."

Jovel turned toward me, a little softer. "Mi shoulda warn yuh... but it happen random. Tonight just happen to be yuh lucky night."

"Lucky?" I raised an eyebrow, but I was already smiling. "Damn near got tackled over a Red Stripe."

She laughed at that—short and real. "Mi told yuh... stick with me, yuh get all di real parts."

The tension started to ease after that. Tanya turned the music back on—

low, some slow riddim riding the air—and the road stretched ahead like it had forgiven us.

The car hummed along the asphalt, the rhythm of the engine matching the gentle bounce beneath us. The windows were halfway down, letting in that heavy tropical air—the kind that clung to your skin but still felt sweeter than anything back home.

Jovel shifted in her seat beside me, crossing one leg over the other. The hem of her skirt slid up just a touch, catching moonlight through the window. She looked over, the corners of her mouth curving into that sly grin—the one that lit up the darkest corners of the night without even trying.

"You alright now?" she asked.

"I think so," I said, voice lower now. "I just wasn't expecting war trucks in the middle of a rum run."

"Welcome to Jamaica," she said, smirking. "Mi didn't say it was always paradise."

"Nah," I said, watching her. "But it's real. I'll take that over paradise."

She didn't look away. She just held the moment a second longer than she had to.

And maybe it was the adrenaline still working its way out of our systems. Or the music. Or just the way the night refused to end on fear. But in that small backseat, everything slowed down again. The chaos faded behind us, swallowed by distance and asphalt. And all that was left… was the way she kept looking at me like something might actually happen between us if we didn't blink too fast.

* * *

"Yuh know seh mi fren dem nuh normal, right?" Jovel said, glancing over with a mischievous glint in her eye. Her patois rolled off her tongue like melody—thick, musical, teasing. Each word felt like it was dancing barefoot across my nerves. "Dem free-spirited… always ready fi enjoy life to di fullest. Yuh ready fi dat kinda vibes?"

She said it like a challenge. Like she already knew I wasn't.

I shifted, not uncomfortable—just alert. Curious. Her words stirred something in me I couldn't name. A mix of intrigue… and the faintest buzz of warning. "What exactly does that mean?" I asked, leaning a little closer. Maybe it was the heat, or maybe the way her lips curled when she spoke—but I needed clarity. Or maybe I didn't. Maybe I just wanted to hear more of her voice.

She laughed—a deep, honeyed sound that sat warm in my chest. "It mean seh yuh cyaan come 'round dem wid di tight-pon-pon energy. Dem nuh operate like checklist people. Dem flow. Dem feel. Dem live."

I blinked, fighting a grin. "So… chaos?"

"Sweet chaos," she corrected, eyes narrowing in amusement. "Di kinda madness dat taste like freedom. Dem nuh plan nuttin. Dem jus' show up and mek a moment outta air. If music drop, dem dance. If rain fall, dem strip. Mi love dem—but mi nah go lie, dem a lot."

She leaned her head against the seat, her gold hoops catching a streetlight for half a second.

"One time," she continued, smirking to herself, "we deh pon a boat party in Negril… everybody drunk, sunset blazing… and one girl decide fi jump off and swim back to shore like she a mermaid. Boat still moving, yuh know."

I burst out laughing. "She made it back?"

"Barely," Jo said, biting her lip. "Had to pick har up from the coast guard station."

I shook my head, still laughing, still trying to picture the scene. "And you… you just chill through all that?"

She shrugged, feigning innocence. "Mi nah di leader. Mi jus'… available."

There was something about the way she said that. Not trying to impress. Not fishing for approval. Just laying the map down and waiting to see if I'd follow the road.

"So what you're saying is…" I said slowly, watching her carefully, "I should shut up, buckle in, and try not to overthink tonight?"

Her grin deepened, wide and wicked. "Mi saying… if yuh waan hang wid me, yuh affi loosen up. A lot."

She reached into the bag by her feet, cracked open a fresh beer, and handed it to me. Her fingers brushed mine—quick, casual, but enough.

"Tonight a go mad," she said, raising her own cup like a toast. "Yuh coming?"

And in that moment—with the wind in the windows, the music thumping low, and that woman daring me with her eyes—I knew whatever came next, it wasn't gonna be unforgettable.

* * *

As we turned into the gated community, the energy shifted. The road smoothed out beneath the tires, and the houses grew bigger—clean lines, glass walls, manicured hedges standing like guards. Soft halos of streetlight lit everything gold, made the world feel slower, calmer, like it had exhaled just for us.

Jovel's hand brushed against my arm—not a grab, not a claim. Just a touch. Light. Intentional.

"Dis a di kinda place weh dreams tun reality," she said, voice low and velvety, full of something that felt like more than words. Like memory. Or maybe a future she didn't dare name yet.

I didn't speak. I just watched her face as the streetlights moved across it—shadow, light, shadow again—like the world was flipping pages.

The car rolled to a stop in front of a modern two-story house wrapped in soft stone and black steel. Big windows. Dim lights glowing from within. You could feel the money on it, but not in a loud way. This wasn't "look at me" rich. This was "we good regardless" rich. The kind that moved confident.

Before we could knock, the front door opened wide like it had been expecting us. And just like that, the silence broke.

Voices rushed out into the night—laughter, music, a wave of patois thick with jokes and inside stories. The kind of banter that hit like bullets if you weren't fluent. I caught maybe one out of every five words, but the rhythm?

That I understood. It was joy. Loud. Loose. Unapologetic.

Jovel stepped in like she'd never left. "Wah gwan, mi gyal!" one woman shouted, arms flung open, long braids swinging.

"Mi deh yah, finally!" Jovel called back, already sliding into her arms for a hug.

The woman's gaze cut to me next, eyes sharp and curious. Pretty, stylish, a kind of energy that told me she clocked people fast. She looked me up and down—not rude, just scanning. Like she was trying to place the story before she even heard it.

Jovel didn't wait for introductions.

"Yuh cyaan stay quiet tonight, star," she said, spinning back toward me with that dangerous grin. "Mi waan see how yuh keep up."

Her nudge hit my arm, soft but loaded. A dare wrapped in a flirt.

I smirked, stepped inside, letting the heat and the voices swallow me whole.

"Alright then," I said, locking eyes with her. "Let's see what your world really looks like."

Because something told me… this was only the beginning.

* * *

The deck was alive with energy—thick, charged, damn near humming. It clung to the air like sweat on skin, that sticky, electric kind of vibe that made your pulse move in time with the beat before my feet even caught up.

Popcaan's "Party Shot" blasted from a set of speakers tucked in the corner, bassline deep enough to rattle ribs. That riddim didn't ask—it took. It grabbed the night by the throat and made it move. Every drop of sound rolled across the floor like thunder made sexy. The kind that made me want to drink faster, talk louder, and forget whatever weight you walked in carrying.

People were everywhere—pressed against railings, perched on couches, barefoot on the tile. Skin glowing under string lights, rum flowing like the party owed someone a debt. Someone clapped out the beat on a plastic cup.

Another person whined their waist so smooth it looked like their body was pouring itself into the music.

Laughter burst out in pockets—quick, full-bodied, sometimes doubled over. That island kind of joy, where even the jokes didn't need to land clean to be funny. Somebody said something wild in rapid-fire patois and the whole corner lost it. A man popped open a beer with his teeth, passed it to a girl in cutoff shorts who took a sip and didn't even blink.

The air smelled like rum, cologne, sweat, and grilled meat—sensual and raw, soaked in heat. That kind of cocktail only the Caribbean could shake up.

I stood near the edge, drink in hand, body slowly catching the rhythm, eyes scanning the crowd—not to find anything, but just to feel it. To breathe it in.

This wasn't a party. It was a pulse.

And somehow, it had made space for me inside of it.

"Yuh see how di vibes set up, right?" Jovel said, stepping close, her voice a little louder now to compete with the music. She pressed a shot glass into my hand—Wray and Nephew, clear as water but dangerous like fire. Her fingers lingered against mine a second too long, her eyes full of mischief and a dare.

"Dis yah ting a nuh joke, so sip light."

I held the glass up to the light. The scent hit first—sharp, herbal, almost sweet, like it was pretending to be innocent. I raised an eyebrow.

"This the part where you try to get me drunk enough to embarrass myself?" I asked.

She smirked. "Nah. Dis di part weh mi see if yuh built fi dis life. Wray tell di truth—if yuh cyan handle him, yuh cyan handle mi."

I laughed under my breath. "That right?"

"Yup," she said, stepping back, arms folded, watching me close like I was about to walk a tightrope. "Go on den, big man. Show mi yuh got stamina."

I clinked my glass against hers. "Cheers."

The rum hit like it had a personal vendetta—burned first, then bloomed fast, spreading warmth through my chest like someone lit a match behind my ribs. I hissed through my teeth, blinked the sting away, and nodded slow.

"Shit," I said. "That's not even liquor—that's language."

Jovel laughed, full and unfiltered. "Yuh feel it, eeh? Mi did warn yuh. But yuh tek it clean. Mi impressed."

She nodded toward the long table by the back wall, where Red Stripes stacked like dominos waiting to fall. Ice bucket in the center, already sweating under the heat. "When di fire start bun yuh belly, grab a beer. Mi cyaan have yuh drop out too early. Party just start."

I followed her lead toward the table, grabbing a bottle from the ice. "You always this generous with your warnings?" I asked, popping the cap.

"Mi generous when mi like what mi see," she shot back, taking another sip of her rum. "But mi nuh waste time wid weak-heart."

"I'm starting to feel like I'm on trial," I said, leaning against the table, letting the beer cool my fingers.

She leaned in beside me, close enough that I could smell the citrus in her perfume, mixed with the sharp edge of the Wray still on her breath.

"Yuh not on trial," she said, voice lower now. "But mi watching yuh. Mi haffi know if yuh can hold space. Lotta man talk good... until dem get round real energy."

I turned to face her fully, eyes narrowing just slightly. "So this your version of screening? Rum and riddim?"

"No," she said, pausing, sipping slow before continuing. "Mi screening yuh with truth. Rum just strip off di pretense. Di vibes tell mi di rest."

I nodded, taking that in. "Alright. Then here's some truth—you got me out here half-drunk on an empty stomach, surrounded by people I don't know, dancing to music I can't understand half the time... and I don't wanna be anywhere else."

She blinked. That smile came back—slower this time. "See? Dat di kinda answer mi like."

She reached out and tugged the collar of my shirt gently, just enough to bring me closer. "But mi still watching. Just so yuh know."

127

"I wouldn't want it any other way," I said, feeling the weight of her stare settle right behind my eyes.

The music pulsed around us, a deep, sexy riddim taking over. People were whining, shifting, laughing—lost in the spell of the night.

But for a minute… it felt like we were in our own little corner of the universe. Just me, her, and the fire burning in both our throats.

* * *

Her laughter spilled over me like the music—light, full, and reckless in the best way. It wasn't polite or practiced. It was real. The kind of laugh that made you want to keep saying stupid shit just to hear it again.

It wrapped around me, warmed the skin behind my ears, settled in my chest like it belonged there. I couldn't help but smile—half because of her, half because of this whole damn night.

The air was thick with life. Rum on breath. Smoke curling up from somewhere nearby—maybe a fire pit, maybe someone's spliff. Underneath it all, that mouthwatering pull of jerk chicken, spicy and smoky, sneaking through the breeze like a siren song. My stomach growled but I wasn't leaving this spot. Not with her that close. Not with the way the world was leaning into its own pulse.

Near the speakers, a small crowd had gathered, pulled in like moths to heat. Ding Dong's "Fling Yuh Shoulda" dropped in heavy—bassline deep and playful, commanding bodies before brains could catch up. The rhythm hit low in the hips, high in the shoulders. You didn't have to know the lyrics to feel it. The song moved people.

And they moved back.

Bodies twisting, swaying, flinging shoulders with precision and ease, like the dance was muscle memory passed down through bloodlines. A woman in a red romper damn near levitated the way her waist floated between beats. A guy with gold fronts and no shirt flung his shoulder so hard his drink nearly flew, but he caught it mid-whine, took a sip, and grinned like he knew he was the vibe.

Jovel leaned in close, chin almost touching my shoulder. Her breath hit my neck when she said, "Yuh see how di riddim tek dem over? Dat's what freedom look like."

I turned slightly, close enough to catch the reflection of lights in her eyes. "That what you want?" I asked. "Freedom?"

She didn't answer right away. She just watched the dance floor like it was telling a story she already knew the ending to.

"Mi want joy," she said eventually. "Joy dat don't apologize. Joy dat don't wait for permission. Same way dem dancing now? Dat's how mi waan live."

I nodded, swallowing that truth like another shot. Heavy, warm, impossible to ignore.

And as the music carried on—shoulders flung, hips rolled, hands raised in laughter—I realized I wasn't just watching anymore.

I was inside it.

This rhythm. This night. This woman who talked like a warning but moved like an invitation.

Whatever this was turning into…

I didn't want it to stop.

Jovel grabbed my hand without warning—no countdown, no permission. Just snatched me out of my comfortable lean like the night had called my name through her mouth. Her grip was firm, fingers laced, tugging me straight toward the heart of the crowd, where the bass hit harder and the air pulsed with sweat, smoke, and something holy.

"Come," she said over her shoulder, already grinning, already knowing. "Mek mi teach yuh fi move."

She didn't wait for me to say yes. Her hips were already preaching.

The crowd opened just enough for us, bodies shifting like water parting for the chosen. Ding Dong's riddim morphed into something dirtier, grittier, deeper. The kind of beat that dripped from the ceiling and soaked the floor. And Jo—she caught it like it owed her money.

Her waist rolled slow at first—smooth and calculated. Like the music had to earn her movement. Every motion built on the last, her hips swinging in tight figure eights that looped into the rhythm like she was the track.

I stood there for a second—just breathing her in. The curve of her back, the way her arms flowed out then wrapped around herself, then stretched again like she was tasting the air. Her body didn't just move. It translated the music. Like she was letting the beat live through her spine.

And me? I looked like a man trying to learn a new language mid-sentence.

I tried to mimic the motion—hips loose, knees bent, let the bass guide me—but I could already feel the clumsy edges of it. She turned to me, laughing, and it wasn't cruel. It was light. Teasing. Playful.

"Yuh nah bad," she said, stepping in close, close enough that I could feel the breeze off her words. "But mi can show yuh fi get better."

Her hands found my hips—fingertips warm, steady—and guided them into the rhythm. Not grinding. Not sexual yet. Just connected. Aligned. Her touch was instruction. Her eyes? Permission.

"Loosen di knee dem," she whispered, her lips brushing near my ear. "Stop think 'bout it. Feel it. Let di riddim carry yuh."

And then it hit.

A quick rewind spun through the air, the crowd letting out a collective "Wooooiii!" just as the opening synth of Vybz Kartel's "Clarks" cut in. That first line—"Mi waan some Clarks boot!"—hadn't even finished before the deck went off.

"Whe di Clarks deh?!" a guy shouted from the far corner, and the entire crowd became one loud, off-key, joyful choir. Everyone shouting the lyrics like the song was tattooed on their tongues. People jumped. Shoulders flung wild. A girl near the speaker started bruking out so hard her friend had to hold her drink.

Even Jo shifted. Her hips picked up tempo, sharper now, precise but reckless. She looked over her shoulder at me, eyes gleaming like mischief and moonlight.

"Dis a anthem," she said, catching the hook mid-verse, singing it into the night with everyone else.

The air thickened with heat, laughter, and that familiar chaos that only happens when everybody knows the words and nobody's watching themselves. The crowd wasn't just dancing—they were remembering.

Feeling. Living.

And me?

I let go of the idea of being good. Let go of the need to keep up. I let her guide me. Her touch. Her breath near mine. Her body always two seconds ahead of the beat and somehow pulling me with it.

She didn't want me perfect.

She wanted me present.

This wasn't just a lesson—it was a shift.

She wasn't pulling me into a dance.

She was pulling me into her world.

And I was already halfway gone.

* * *

The crowd around us faded, like someone had turned the volume down on everything that wasn't her. The bass still thumped heavy through the floor, the lights still flickered, people still moved all around us—but none of it registered. Not really.

Because the music… belonged to us now.

Jovel moved like the beat was built from her bones. Each sway of her hips told the speakers when to drop, when to pause, when to breathe. She didn't just dance—she possessed the moment. Commanded it. And without realizing, I started moving around her, with her, inside her rhythm. Drawn in like gravity had decided I was hers tonight.

She circled me slowly, not even dancing with me at first—just around me. Letting the heat between us speak. Her fingers brushed my chest as she passed, her back grazing my side as she turned. Her eyes never strayed long—always checking to see if I was still locked in. I was. God, I was.

Then the track shifted.

The crowd let out that knowing little shout people do when the right song drops. That low rumble of anticipation before it hits. Then it came—Vybz Kartel's "Fever"—slow, heavy, sticky with tension. A riddim built for hips and secrets. It wasn't hype anymore. It was heat.

The lights seemed to dim on cue. Or maybe it was just the way my focus tunneled.

Jo leaned in close—close enough for her breath to land soft on my skin, just behind my ear. Her voice came out low, wrapped in patois and promise.

"Yuh feel it, nuh true? Dis is weh di real vibes start."

And I did. I felt it everywhere.

Heart thudding like it was trying to match the riddim. The hum of rum still in my chest. Sweat cooling down my neck. My hands itching to touch her, hold her, follow her deeper into whatever this was turning into.

I turned to face her fully, but she was already one step ahead—pressing a drink into my hand before I could catch up. She held hers up in a loose toast, head tilted, that grin curling the edges of her mouth like temptation knew it was pretty.

"Ease yuhself," she said, clinking her glass against mine. "Tonight cyan rush. We just start warm up."

I sipped slow, the liquor burning smooth this time. My shoulders dropped. My breath steadied. I let the moment take me. Her body swayed back toward me again, slower now, more intimate. Less dancehall... more dance.

The party kept going—louder, sweatier, deeper. But for me, it had narrowed to one truth:

Her.

And the rhythm that only she could teach me.

And the night, stretching ahead, like it never wanted to end.

"Tek a shot an' relax yuhself. Tonight nah mek fi hesitation." Jovel's words curled around me like smoke—low, easy, but laced with something that said this wasn't a request. Her eyes held mine a beat longer than they needed to. That kind of look that could talk you into bad decisions with no apology. She handed me another shot, and I didn't think twice. The burn was expected by now, the warmth welcome.

Outside, the crowd had begun to thin. The frenzy that had lit the deck earlier was now a slow burn. People sat more than danced now—couples curled in corners, a few barefoot souls still whining with lazy rhythm near the railing. The night was shedding its wild skin. Shifting into something deeper.

Jovel's hand found mine again—no rush, no theatrics. Just firm. Intentional. Like she already knew where this was going.

"Come," she said, softer this time. Almost a secret. "Mi show yuh di real party."

Her fingers threaded through mine, guiding me inside the house. The music softened the second we crossed the threshold—no longer thumping, just pulsing in the background like a slowed heartbeat. The lights inside were warmer, dimmer, with a kind of hush that wrapped itself around your shoulders like a blanket soaked in intention.

Laughter floated through the air—low and intimate, the kind that didn't need volume to feel big. People stood in clusters, sharing joints, swapping stories with voices dipped in rum and secrets. It wasn't a crowd anymore. It was a vibe. A shift.

The air smelled different in here—less sweat, more spirit. Incense trailed lazy swirls from the corner, mixing with leftover spice from jerk chicken and a hint of coconut oil. It was rich. Heavy. Charged with something unspoken, like the room was waiting to see what you'd bring into it.

Jovel didn't let go of my hand. Her thumb brushed against my knuckles like she was grounding me, steadying my breath without saying a word. Her hips still moved as she walked—slower now, deliberate. Less dance, more invitation.

She led me past the living room, through the hum of voices and into a hallway where the noise dimmed even more. My senses narrowed—the feel of her hand in mine, the scent of her skin, the sound of her laugh still echoing faint in the back of my head.

And I realized…

The party wasn't winding down.

It was shifting gears.

Going underground.

Becoming something only the bold stayed awake for.

And I was right where I needed to be.

"Mi waan yuh fi remember tonight," she said, barely above a whisper now. The words landed soft—but held weight, like she wasn't just talking about the party. Like she was speaking it into the part of me I kept quiet.

Her fingers drifted up my arm, slow and light, leaving a trail of heat in their wake. It wasn't just touch—it was claim. Not possession, but presence. Her presence. Fully, fearlessly felt.

Then she leaned in—closer than breath. Her lips brushed mine, light and fleeting, the kind of kiss that wasn't meant to satisfy. It was meant to spark. To leave a charge sitting under the skin. And it did. Electricity snapped through my spine like a wire had been stripped and pressed raw against bone.

By the time I blinked, she'd pulled back, her grin wide now—knowing, wild, unbothered.

"Hear dat?" she asked, cocking her head toward the ceiling.

I hadn't noticed it before. But now, yeah—I heard it. Faint sounds drifting from upstairs…a mix of muffled voices, low basslines, laughter curling around some distant beat. It wasn't loud, but it cut through everything. The kind of sound that made you curious. That made your body lean forward before your mind caught up.

I nodded. "Yeah… I hear it."

"It calling yuh, innit?" she said, her accent thick again, playful but laced with intent. "Dat sound—dat energy—dat's where di night really living."

She was already stepping back, slow, letting my hand slip through her fingers like a dare.

And the way she looked at me then—eyes low, mouth still soft from that kiss—it wasn't about seduction anymore. It was invitation.

Not just to follow her.

But to surrender to the rest of the night.

No rules. No roadmap. Just… what was waiting. Upstairs. In her world. In whatever this was turning into.

And I knew—I knew—I was going.

"Den follow mi," she said, tugging my hand like she already owned where this was headed. Her steps lightened, hips swaying with each movement—part glide, part tease. That grin never left her face. Her voice carried that same playful edge, but under it was something else—promise. Like she was leading me into something sacred disguised as chaos.

"Mi tell yuh—dis a go be di maddest ting yuh ever experience."

The words didn't just sit in my head—they echoed. Sank deep. Carved space inside me and refused to leave.

We moved up the stairs, slow at first. The kind of slow that knew it was being watched. I could feel the beat vibrating through the walls now, faint but steady—thump after thump like a second heartbeat. Somewhere above us, the music lived fuller. The night wasn't over. It was just leveling up.

Each step felt heavier, anticipation pressing into my chest. Not nerves. Not quite. It was hunger. That restless kind. The kind that sits in your gut when you know you're walking into something that's gonna mark you.

The air shifted as we climbed—warmer, thicker, charged. The faint scent of shea butter and weed clung to the hallway. The laughter upstairs came in waves now, rising and falling like a tide. Not the wild, outdoor kind. This was intimate. Slower. Inside-joke soft.

Jovel glanced back once, eyes gleaming in the dim light, her fingers still looped around mine. "You good?"

I nodded. Didn't need to say anything. She could probably feel it in the way I held her hand tighter now. The way my body leaned in like it already trusted her lead.

"Alright den," she whispered. "Don't say mi never warn yuh."

And as we reached the top step, just before the doorway opened wide and the bass wrapped its arms around us, I realized—

this wasn't just the next part of the night.

It was the threshold.

And once I crossed it, there'd be no turning back.

11

The Night She Owned

The air shifts the moment we hit the first step. It's subtle at first—just a slow thickening, like the night itself is pressing closer, breathing heavier. The bass is softer here, not booming like it was downstairs. It hums through the walls now, low and deliberate, like a pulse waiting to sync with mine. But it's not just the music anymore. There's something else threading through the sound. A rhythm beneath the rhythm.

Moans.

Faint at first. Like echoes you almost mistake for your own thoughts. But they're there. Hidden between the laughter, the clink of glass, the stretch of floorboards above us. Pleasure with no shame. Bodies giving in without apology. It pulls at something deep in my gut—curiosity wrapped in a nervous edge. Anticipation, maybe. Or warning.

Jovel doesn't say much. She just glances back at me with that look—like she already knows the questions I haven't asked yet.

"You good?" she asks, not with doubt, but intention. Like she's checking the hinges before opening a door most people wouldn't dare touch.

I nod, but she holds my eyes for a beat longer. Like she's waiting for more than a gesture. Like she needs to know that I'm not just following the vibe—I'm choosing it.

She turns then, leading me up with the kind confidence that don't beg for attention but owns every step. The air wraps tighter around us as we ascend, warmer now, thick with sweat and smoke and something more primal. My hand trails the wall out of instinct, steadying myself, but it's her rhythm I fall into—step for step, breath for breath.

Halfway up, the sounds change. What was muffled becomes clearer, sharper. No longer distant. Moans now real and human. Wet. Deep. Unfiltered. A gasp here. A cry there. Someone begging low and broken like a prayer. Another voice laughing through the release. It's not chaos—it's ceremony. Every sound a drumbeat.

Jovel doesn't flinch.

She slows just enough to let me feel it. Not to shield me—but to prepare me.

"Mi nah carry yuh up deh fi spectate," she murmurs over her shoulder, voice velvet but firm. "Mi waan yuh fi see."

Another step.

"Not just with yuh eyes—wid yuh spirit."

And somehow, I know what she means. This ain't about sex. Not just that. It's about shedding. About choosing to step into something raw, unsanitized. I feel it in the tightness of my chest, the throb building low in my body, the unspoken questions rising like steam off my skin.

By the time we reach the landing, the door ahead is cracked just enough to glow. Gold light spills out, flickering with movement. Shadows dancing. Bodies swaying.

Jovel pauses, backlit and beautiful, one hand resting lightly on the doorframe. She looks at me again—not asking for permission. Just presence.

"You ready?"

I don't know if I am.

But I nod anyway.

And she smiles like she already knew I would.

* * *

The room breathes. That's the first thing I feel. Not see—feel. The way the air moves like it has lungs of its own. Thick with heat, sweat, bass, and breath. A current of something ancient and hungry.

The lighting is low but warm, casting bodies in bronze and shadow. It takes a moment for my eyes to adjust, but when they do, I realize I'm not just looking at people—I'm looking at motion. Skin moving against skin. Mouths finding flesh like they were born knowing where to land. Hands exploring landscapes mapped only by instinct. A woman with her head thrown back, jaw slack, hips grinding like the music is coming from her spine, her moans rising not from pain, but deep, unbridled pleasure. A man buried between thighs, lost in the taste of someone else's surrender.

No one's hiding. No one's performing either. That's what makes it different. No one here is trying to be sexy. They are—without trying. Without needing an audience. Like sex ain't a spectacle here—it's a birthright.

Jovel doesn't rush me. She gives me the space to take it in. To feel the surreal unraveling of the night.

I don't move at first. I just stand there at the threshold, caught somewhere between disbelief and reverence. This is the kind of moment you don't plan for. The kind that unbuttons you from the inside out.

From the club to this hallway. From her eyes locking with mine to the words she whispered on the steps. Every second has felt like a dare. And somehow, I kept saying yes without realizing I was choosing transformation.

A symphony of moans swells around us—some low and guttural, others high and trembling. It's not chaos. It's ritual. Everybody here came to worship, not perform. To give in, not just get off, but to push every limit of their own desire.

And I get it now.

This isn't a room—it's a confession. And I'm standing in the pulpit, naked in ways I haven't even undressed for yet.

Jovel steps beside me now, her hand finding mine. Her skin is warm, soft, but there's a fire pulsing underneath. She doesn't speak. She just looks at me like she sees what I've been hiding from myself. Like she knows what I need more than I do.

She leans in, her lips brushing the shell of my ear—not with urgency, but possession.

"Come," she says, voice low, body already guiding mine deeper into the room. "Tonight... mi a show yuh how fi let go."

And just like that, we cross the threshold.

The door closes behind us.

And the night begins to undress.

* * *

The scene hits like humidity—dense, intoxicating, impossible to shake. I don't know where to focus. Every corner of the room pulses with raw, unfiltered release. Women tangled together in a blur of limbs and lips, some arching into fingers, others straddling thighs with eyes half-closed in ecstasy, their bodies desperate for more. The air smells like sex and sweat and shea butter—sweet and primal. Moans layer over the music like harmonies. No rhythm but all rhythm. Just surrender. Just heat.

There are maybe six or seven women. Two men, at most. But they don't anchor the space—they orbit it. The gravity here is feminine. It's the women who lead. Who own. Who command.

And then there's Jovel.

Still beside me, but barely. I feel the shift in her before I see it. Like a storm about to break. That calm, knowing stillness she always carries starts to hum—something electric vibrating just under the skin.

Her hand slips from mine.

She steps forward, hips moving to a rhythm only she hears. Then she turns—half-lit by gold light, bare shoulders glowing—and looks at me.

That smirk?

It's damn near predatory.

She slides her one-piece dress off her shoulders with the same ease most women offer a glance. No shame. No hesitation. Just deliberate stripping. The fabric glides down her body, revealing brown skin smooth like sunset silk. No bra. No panties. Just a body built for worship—breasts full and heavy, waist soft, hips wide and unapologetic. She lets the dress pool around her ankles like it was never meant to stay on in the first place.

Then she walks.

Straight toward a woman lounging on the couch—legs parted like a question already answered, her eyes already signaling hungry anticipation. The woman's locs fall over one shoulder, her mouth curved in that post-wine, pre-orgasm haze. Her eyes flick to Jovel and widen—but she doesn't move.

Jovel doesn't just kneel—she claims space. Braids swaying gently as she lowers herself between the woman's legs, hands sliding up the inside of her thighs like she's reading a map she's already memorized.

The woman's eyes flutter open—half-lust, half-warning. But it's too late for that. Jovel's already locked in.

She grabs the woman's hips and pulls her forward in one fluid jerk, ass lifting slightly off the couch. Then without hesitation—tongue out, mouth open—she dives in, met by the woman's eager moan.

No warm-up. No teasing. Just heat.

Wet, messy, consuming.

Jovel eats pussy like it's a profession. Like she gets paid in orgasms and knows she's about to collect.

She buries her face so deep her nose disappears in the woman's folds, tongue flattening and dragging up the full length of her slit before swirling slow, torturous circles around her clit. Over and over. Pressure building. Movements controlled, precise. Not sloppy, not rushed. Just focused. Like she knows exactly how long to drag it out before the woman breaks.

The woman is shaking now, legs trembling as she tries to hold still—tries to breathe. But Jovel doesn't let up. She grinds her face in deeper, licking like she's starving, like this is her only meal and she wants every drop.

Then she moans into it.

That low, guttural sound of satisfaction that vibrates against the woman's pussy, and it sends a shudder through her whole damn body. She gasps—loud, a sound of pure release. One hand slaps the couch arm for balance, the other yanks a fistful of Jovel's braids. Not gentle. Desperate, demanding more of the exquisite pressure.

Jovel grins into the wet.

And keeps going.

She sucks the clit now—hard, rhythmic pulls between her lips, tongue flicking between every suck. The woman starts cursing, moaning louder, body twitching like she's on the edge, begging for the release only Jovel could give. Jovel slides one hand under her ass and lifts her higher, gets an even deeper angle, then presses two fingers inside—slick, smooth, curling upward like she's searching for something holy.

She finds it.

The woman arches, damn near levitates off the couch, a scream tearing from her throat as her legs clamp around Jovel's head, pulling her in tighter for the final release. But Jovel doesn't flinch. Doesn't stop.

She devours her through the orgasm.

And doesn't stop until the woman's shaking, breathless, spine limp against the cushions.

Only then does she pull back, mouth glistening, lips swollen, braids damp at the tips. Her face is wet with it—chin shiny, lips coated in satisfaction.

She looks at me.

Not with a smile.

But with hunger.

The kind of hunger that only comes after the meal—satisfied, but greedy for something sweeter. Her mouth still slick. Her eyes locked on mine.

Like I'm next.

* * *

Around us, the room doesn't slow down—it erupts. Moans stack on top of moans. Flesh slaps against flesh. The wet sounds of fucking fill the air like percussion. On the rug in the far corner, two women ride each other with desperation—one straddled low, face buried in soft thighs, while the other arches backward, tits bouncing with every thrust of her hips. On the floor beside them, another woman lies on her stomach, panting into a pillow while someone behind her—another woman, wearing a black harness—drives a thick strap-on into her with violent rhythm, the recipient twisting and bucking into every stroke, demanding more. The woman receiving it is a mess: drooling, writhing, crying out every few strokes like she's being unraveled from the inside out, and loving every single shredding moment of it.

Across the room, the two men are tag-teaming a woman bent over the ottoman. One behind her, deep strokes shaking her frame, the other in her mouth, both grunting, focused, possessive. Her eyes are glazed, spit and cum slicking her chin, her voice rising above all the others—guttural, needy. She's begging in a language that doesn't need translation: "Don't stop. Please. More." her body actively pushing for more, her pleasure undeniable.

It's porn.

But not for show.

There's nothing performative here. No camera angles. No fake moans. Just chaos, honest and earned. Every orgasm here feels like it was torn from somewhere deep—ripped free from the body like a confession. It's raw. It's holy. It's real.

And I'm in the center of it.

Hard.

So fucking hard I can barely think. My dick strains against my jeans, pulsing with every scream, every slap, every cry. I shift, try to adjust discreetly—but my hand lingers too long. The heat of my own palm pressed against the bulge, fingers twitching like I forgot where I was.

And that's when Jo sees me.

Her eyes find mine like they never stopped watching.

Sharp. Knowing. Wicked.

She doesn't say a word. She just steps back from the couch, leaving the woman she wrecked trembling and useless behind her, legs still spread, body still twitching.

Jovel turns toward me—still glistening.

Her thighs shine. Her lips are swollen. Her chin is slick with the woman's juices, mouth parted slightly like she can still taste her.

She walks.

Slow. Measured. Like a hunter who already knows the prey ain't going anywhere.

She doesn't break eye contact.

Not once.

And fuck if it doesn't freeze me in place. I can't move. Can't speak. All I can do is breathe and watch her close the space between us—hips swaying, tits bouncing gently with each step, her nipples hard and shining under the warm light.

The room is a blur around her now. All the moaning, the fucking, the rhythm—it fades into background noise.

She is the moment.

She stops inches from me. Looks down at my hand still hovering near my fly. Then up again.

And smiles.

But not sweet.

Dangerous.

Like she's about to take what's hers.

And I'm ready to give it.

She stops in front of me—close. Close enough that I can feel the heat rolling off her skin. That wild scent of sweat, pussy, and Shea butter rising off her like perfume. Her breath, warm and shallow, fans across the fabric of my jeans, and I swear it makes me twitch.

She doesn't speak. Doesn't need to.

Her eyes say it all, burning with explicit desire for me to surrender.

She reaches for me—fingers bold, but unhurried. They brush against my bulge first, tracing the outline like she's reacquainting herself with something she already owns. She palms me through the denim, slow and firm, applying just enough pressure to make my knees go soft for a second.

Then she grips the button of my jeans.

Pops it open with a flick of her thumb.

Her other hand steadies the zipper, dragging it down with an excruciating slowness—deliberate. She doesn't rush. Doesn't yank. She wants me to feel every single tooth of that zipper give way. Wants me to tremble from it.

And I do.

She slides my boxers down just enough to let me spring free. My dick stands thick and aching, the head already glossy with pre-cum. Her eyes flick down. Just for a moment. Just enough to see me. Her lips part the slightest bit—like the sight made her breath catch, a hungry intake of air.

Then she leans in.

And kisses me.

Not my mouth. My shaft.

Right in the center.

A soft, deliberate press of lips to skin—warm, reverent. Then again, higher this time. Then the tip. Just light pecks. Teasing. Testing. Tasting. Her lips wet, her mouth still glistening from the woman she just finished devouring. Now she's sampling me like a second course, her whole body radiating fierce intent.

I'm barely breathing.

And when she finally takes me in—inch by aching inch—my whole body tenses.

The heat of her mouth hits me like a fever.

Warm. Wet. Deep.

She doesn't shove me down her throat. Doesn't rush. She slides me in slowly, her lips wrapping tight, her tongue swirling in tight circles just under the crown as she sinks lower, her body inviting me deeper, explicitly demanding the full measure. My hands twitch at my sides, fingers curling into fists—I want to hold her head, want to fuck her mouth, but I can't. Because the way she's doing it? It's like art. Like something that's supposed to be watched, felt, surrendered to.

She pulls back. Lets me fall from her lips with a slick pop. Looks up at me with that same calm, knowing gaze.

Then sinks down again.

Deeper this time.

And stays.

Her throat opens just enough to cradle me, contracting around me with deliberate pleasure. She holds me there for a beat—no movement, just pressure. Warm, wet pressure that makes my thighs clench. Then she starts moving. Slow, even strokes. No hand. Just her mouth, her tongue, and that rhythm she always seems to own.

Around us, the room is chaos.

A woman screams as the two men double-penetrate her on the ottoman—one behind, one in front, her cries echoing sharp above the music, her body arching into every thrust, explicitly begging for more. Another couple near the mirror fucks like animals, the woman on all fours, strapped to a harness while another girl rides her from behind, tits slapping, hands clawing, their moans a symphony of shared aggression and escalating pleasure. The slap of skin on skin is everywhere. The scent of sex clings to every surface.

But all I can focus on is Jo.

The way her braids fall over her cheek as she works. The heat of her mouth. The tight suction when she pulls back, the swirling chaos of her tongue when she dives back in. Her moans vibrating around my dick, low and filthy like she's getting off just from the taste.

She loves this.

Loves how I taste. Loves the weight of me on her tongue. Loves the way my breath stutters, the way I whisper her name under my breath like a warning and a prayer.

And she doesn't stop.

Not when I curse.

Not when my knees nearly buckle.

Not when I groan and mutter fuckfuckfuck through clenched teeth.

Not even when my hips twitch, begging to thrust.

She keeps her pace. Steady. Relentless. Controlled.

Because this isn't a blowjob.

This is a goddamn ritual.

And I'm being worshipped.

This is unreal, I think, mind spinning, body weightless but rooted at the same time. Like I've stepped outside of myself and I'm watching this scene unfold through a warped lens—some dream sequence I don't ever want to wake from.

Nobody back home will believe this.

Fuck, I barely believe it—and I'm living it.

Feeling it.

Still pulsing from it.

Jo's mouth slides off me slow, her lips dragging against my shaft like a goodbye she almost doesn't want to give. Her tongue flicks the tip once more—light, playful, a soft slap to my overstimulated nerves. Then she places one final kiss right at the base, wet and warm and intimate.

Like a signature.

She stays crouched for a moment, lips parted, her breath brushing my skin as her eyes lift to mine again. Still wild. Still calm. Still everything.

I'm wrecked.

Chest rising too fast. Pulse thudding at my temples. My dick glistening, twitching in open air like it's still looking for her mouth.

And Jo?

Jo's unbothered.

She rises—slow, fluid, body unfolding like silk being lifted by the wind. Her thighs glisten under the golden light. Her chin is slick, lips swollen, mouth shining with the proof of what she just did. She doesn't wipe it away. Doesn't fix her hair. Doesn't flinch from the fact that half the room probably watched.

She turns that soaked mouth into a smirk.

Then says it.

"You ready to leave?"

Just like that.

Voice cool. Casual. Like she didn't just drop to her knees in a room full of fucking bodies and turn me into a goddamn altar. Like she didn't just suck my soul out slow and hand it back with a kiss.

I don't answer right away.

Because I'm not sure if I'm ready to leave…

…or if I'm just realizing I already belong to her now.

Then—

I hesitate.

I glance around the room one more time, eyes wide, heart still racing like I've been sprinting through a dream I can't quite catch. Bodies are still everywhere. Writhing. Grinding. Colliding. A living mural of sex in motion.

But Jo doesn't wait.

"Let's go," she says, already tugging my hand, already moving toward the door like it's nothing. Like this was just an interlude.

As we pass through the room, I catch one last glimpse of a woman getting absolutely wrecked—and it roots me in place for half a second.

She's on her back, legs pinned up high by two other women, one of them straddling her face while the other is strapped up and drilling into her pussy with brutal rhythm. The strap-on is thick—maybe too thick—but the woman underneath is taking it, her body eagerly pushing back into the force. Her tits bounce with each thrust, her mouth smothered in pussy as she moans into the flesh above her. Her hands clutch the woman riding her like she's drowning in it—like the only air she's getting is soaked in sweat and slick, all of it consumed with absolute pleasure.

Her eyes roll back.

Mouth open.

Screams ragged and real, born from exhilaration, not distress.

She bucks hard, body convulsing as the orgasm crashes through her, loud and uncontrolled, like a dam finally breaking. Her thighs tremble. Her voice cracks. And when her body starts to seize again, the woman on top grabs her by the hair and holds her still—don't stop now—forcing her to stay right where she is, commanding her to take every last ripple of pleasure.

It's the kind of scene that burns itself into your memory.

One I know I'll never forget.

Not because it's wild.

But because it's free.

I'm still watching when Jo squeezes my hand.

And leads me out.

We hit the stairwell—just the two of us now—and I think we're home free. I think we're finally leaving the madness behind.

But Jo's not done.

Not even close.

Halfway down the steps, she stops me. Presses me back against the wall, heat in her eyes, fire still burning under her skin, her gaze fierce with intent. Then, without a word, she drops to her knees again.

Fast.

Like gravity pulled her there.

She yanks my pants open, pulls my dick out like she missed it, like not having it in her mouth for the last five minutes was torture.

And then she devours me.

No teasing. No slow build. Just mouth open, throat ready, hunger unhinged.

She slams me down her throat, choking a little—on purpose, her body clearly relishing the depth and challenge—then pulls back, saliva dripping from her lips as she spits on it and goes again. Her hands grip my thighs, her nails digging into flesh, anchoring me as her mouth goes to work, pulling me in for more.

It's sloppy. Loud. Relentless.

Her tongue whirls around the head, then flattens and rides the underside as she takes me deeper, her throat flexing to accommodate every inch. She moans—fucking moans—like this is for her, not me. Like sucking me off in a stairwell while people fuck upstairs is exactly how she gets off.

My head hits the wall.

Legs weak.

Breath gone.

Eyes locked on the crown of her braids bouncing with each stroke.

She doesn't stop until I'm shaking, fighting every instinct to come. Then—just as my hands reach for her shoulders—she stops.

Dead still.

She slowly lets me slide out of her mouth, licking the tip one last time, then tucks me back into my pants like she's cleaning up something she owns.

Zips me up with care.

Looks up at me with that wicked grin.

"Let's go," she says again.

Same words.

But now her voice is soaked in satisfaction.

Like dessert was served.

And she's still licking her fingers.

12

Still Burning

The night hadn't let go of us.

It was still clinging to my skin—thick, hot, electric. Still in the scent of her on my fingers, still thrumming in my chest like an echo I hadn't stopped hearing. It followed us into the car like smoke. Like sin. Like something holy we hadn't finished praying through.

Jovel slid into the backseat beside me, slow and deliberate, like she knew the silence was part of the seduction. Like words would only cheapen what was already pulsing between us.

Her thigh brushed mine—bare, warm, slick from the last woman she devoured and the sweat of her own release. That scent—coconut oil, sweat, pussy, and rum—wrapped around me like a noose. Not choking. Not yet. But close enough to remind me who was in control.

Neither of us spoke.

Didn't have to.

The windows fogged up within minutes. Her body heat meeting mine in the space between. The driver's voice floated up from the front seat once or twice—directions maybe, or filler talk—but I didn't hear a damn word. My world had narrowed to this: her breath, her skin, the slow rhythm of her chest rising and falling beside me.

I reached for her.

Didn't rush.

My hand rested on her bare knee first. Testing. Waiting. Her skin twitched under my palm—so subtle, like a reflex she didn't mean to give away. She didn't look at me, just shifted slightly, angling herself in that way women do when they've already decided what comes next.

My fingers crept higher.

Up the soft inside of her thigh.

Slow.

Measured.

A warning and a question all at once.

She exhaled. Not shaky. Not surprised. Just ready.

Her legs parted a little more—enough to tell me yes without ever saying it.

I paused there. Thumb tracing slow, lazy circles on her skin.

Felt her tense.

Then relax.

Then tense again.

She laughed.

Low.

Like she was watching me try not to fall apart in public.

I clenched my jaw.

If we weren't in this car—

If the driver wasn't right there—

If the street lights weren't sliding past the windows like slow-moving temptations—

I'd already have her moaning into my mouth.

But I stayed still.

Let the tension simmer.

Because sometimes the ache was part of the ceremony.

And right now…

We were both still worshipping the night.

* * *

She bit her lip, eyes full of challenge.

She already knew.

We weren't going home yet.

Jovel had one last stop in mind.

The car curved off the main strip and into the deeper rhythm of the city—where the streets got narrower, louder, more alive. Streetlights were patchy, but the glow from oil drums and open grills lit the scene like stage lights. The smell hit me before the door even opened—thick smoke laced with pimento, jerk seasoning, meat fat dripping into flames. My stomach clenched. My senses locked in.

People were everywhere.

Some leaning against their cars, Red Stripe in hand. Others in tight clusters, cussing and laughing over the boom of bass pouring from old speakers bungee-corded to backseats. Men in mesh marinas, women in crop tops and slippers, eyes glassy and shoulders loose with rum and ganja. It wasn't chaotic. It was alive. And it moved to a beat that didn't wait for permission.

The car hadn't even come to a full stop before Jovel opened the door. She stepped out barefoot—dress still wrinkled from the heat of our night, mouth still glistening from the parts of me she hadn't fully left behind. She looked like a goddess who never needed a temple to be worshipped.

"Mi know yuh woulda come," a woman behind the grill called out, barely glancing up as she chopped something on a wood board. Her skin glistened with sweat, arm flexing as she brought a cleaver down hard. Thwack. Thwack. Thwack.

Jovel grinned. "Mi haffi show mi fren di real ting."

The woman's eyes cut to me.

Quick glance. One second.

That's all she needed.

She smirked. "Him can handle it?"

Jovel tilted her head, then turned slowly to face me. That damn smirk deepened.

"Oh, him handle everything."

I laughed, couldn't help it. "Damn right."

The woman cackled and slapped the cleaver against the board. "We wi see. Pepper or no pepper?"

"Don't go easy," Jovel said, already licking a glob of sauce from her finger like she was still thinking about earlier. "Give him full strength."

A man standing near a second stall overheard and chimed in, waving his styrofoam box like a flag. "Mi seh mi want pepper—but mi nuh want fi dead!"

The vendor behind his grill cracked up. "Den yuh fi order soup, big man. Dis a jerk, not baby formula!"

"Gwaan wid yuh crosses!" the man barked back, laughing so hard he almost dropped his food. "Mi want pepper, but mi nuh want mi nose fi peel!"

"Tek it or lef it, star," the vendor shot back. "We nuh cater fi cowards out yah."

Laughter rippled through the crowd, easy and familiar.

A woman slid past with a cooler of drinks, shouting, "Red Stripe, Guinness, Dragon! Ice cold, babes, get dem now!" She paused when she spotted Jovel. "Yow, Jo! Yuh reach back inna town, finally?"

"Mi never lef," Jovel called back, biting into a piece of fried plantain like it owed her something.

The woman whistled. "Yuh look like trouble."

Jovel winked. "Mi am trouble."

She turned back to me then, slow and sensual, fingers slick from jerk sauce. She licked one—just one—tongue swirling around the pad of her thumb like she was cleaning up more than food.

"You watching me?" she asked, voice just loud enough for me to hear over the music, but low enough to curl straight down my spine.

I clenched my jaw. She knew what she was doing. Every flick of her tongue, every glance—it was deliberate.

"You know I am," I muttered, eyes stuck on her mouth.

She bit into a piece of jerk chicken, eyes still on mine as her lips closed around it like she was giving a slow-motion demonstration. "You gon' handle dis food?"

I took the box from the vendor without looking. The heat rising off it was immediate—thick, smoky, mean. "Baby," I said, tearing into a piece, "I handle everything."

That got a couple of the oldheads nearby nodding in approval.

"Atlanta boy feelin' brave, eeh?"

"Mi wi see when him belly start cramp."

But Jovel just smiled.

Like she knew my limits better than I did.

The sauce burned the second it hit my tongue—real fire. But I didn't flinch. Couldn't. Not with her licking her fingers like that across from me.

She leaned in, whispering near my ear, her breath still sweet with pepper and rum.

"Tek yuh time, star. Tonight just a get warm."

* * *

And it was.

Until it wasn't.

The second we pulled up to the Airbnb, the mood shifted.

Not slowly. Not subtly.

Like a switch flipped.

One minute we were full of food and flirtation, lips still tingling from heat, thighs pressed together in the backseat. The next—we were hit with that static. That energy you feel in your chest before shit goes left.

The car rolled to a stop.

We should've been inside already.

Should've been on each other—tearing clothes, crashing into walls, picking up right where that stairwell ended.

But the driver had different plans.

"Five t'ousand," he said, leaning against the hood like he'd earned the right to post up.

Jovel froze mid-step.

"Eh?" she said, sharp and clipped. Her whole energy shifted. Spine straight. Shoulders back. Her voice lost every ounce of sweetness and turned to steel.

"Tonight different," the driver muttered, eyes low.

That's all he said.

Didn't even look at me—but I felt it.

And we both knew.

He saw the Atlanta on me.

The watch. The kicks. The accent.

And he thought now's the time.

He forgot one thing though.

He wasn't dealing with me.

He was dealing with Jovel.

She inhaled—slow and deliberate. The kind of breath you take right before you choose violence.

"Yuh did haffi do dis?" she asked. Her tone? Calm like gun oil. Ready to catch fire.

The driver shrugged, not meeting her eyes. "Tings raise up, man. Mi haffi eat too."

"Mi pay yuh di same ting every time," she snapped. "Yuh know dis."

"Yeah but tonight long, Jo. Mi a wait long too—"

"Wait?!" she barked. "Yuh want charge mi fi waiting pon yuh slow backside?!"

"Jo—"

"No badda Jo mi now!" she shouted. "Yuh tek me fi eediat?"

The streetlight caught the sweat forming at the driver's temple, but he stood still. Trying to play it cool. Trying not to flinch. But the tension was cracking loud in the air—thick like gunpowder.

"Mi use yuh all di time, and yuh never pull dis! A because mi bring a foreign man now, right? That a di problem?"

"Mi nah say dat—"

"Yuh nuh haffi say it! Yuh tink mi stupid? Yuh tink mi blind?"

She stepped closer, close enough her shadow swallowed his.

155

"Yuh tink mi waan man fi pay mi fare? Yuh mad?" she hissed. "Mi pay mi own fuckin' fare every bloodclaat time. Don't eva try style mi like dat again."

The driver sighed, jaw tight. "Mi jus a seh—"

"Bloodclaat!" she spat, ripping bills from her purse like they'd insulted her.

She slapped the money against his chest—hard.

Not handed. Slapped.

Like it stung her to part with it.

"Move from yasso wid yuh dutty argument!"

The sound of the slap echoed in the night—not hand to face, but hand to ego. The bills fluttered to the ground. He bent to pick them up without a word.

Jo turned on her heel, muttering under her breath, cussing teeth, sucking air, fire in every step. She stormed past me, not even looking in my direction, her braids swinging with fury.

I followed.

Not out of fear.

But respect.

Because this woman?

She didn't just stand up for herself.

She burned shit down.

And I was about to walk into the flames with her.

⁎

She stormed inside, still muttering under her breath.

"Mi cya believe di fuckery—tink mi a some eediat gal—damn disrespect…"

The door slammed behind her, echoing off the tile like punctuation. She tossed her purse hard onto the couch—didn't even look to see where it landed—then turned and started pacing. Braids swinging. Shoulders tight. Her hands were fists, flexing and curling like they didn't know what else to do with the heat in her blood.

"Mi nuh bring no man fi spend pon mi—mi nuh need no man fi dat!"

She barked it into the air like someone had questioned her worth personally.

"Five t'ousand?! All a sudden? After all dem rides? Yuh mad?!"

She turned, punching the air like the words were trying to fight their way out.

"Mi tek taxi more dan mi tek breath, and dis fool want style mi like mi a some likkle gyal wid big dreams an' no backbone?!"

I stepped toward her—slow, cautious, not trying to fix it. Just trying to be near.

She wasn't ready.

I reached for her wrist. She yanked it back.

"Don't."

Her voice cracked.

Not soft.

Just stretched from the pressure.

Her chest rose in short, sharp bursts. Her eyes were glassy—but not with tears. With rage. That deep, soul-stinging kind that comes from being underestimated too many fucking times by people who should know better.

I tried again, gently this time.

"Breathe."

She stopped pacing—but only to spin and face me full-on. Her eyes blazed. Her whole body looked like it was holding itself back from throwing everything.

"Mi tired ah it, yuh hear mi? Tired fi haffi prove miself every blasted time. Tired fi man look pon mi an' see some soft, sweet ting dem can play wid. Mi nah sweet, mi nah soft—mi real. Mi real, and mi nah let nobaddy treat me like mi easy."

Her voice cracked again. Louder this time.

And she wasn't just talking about the driver anymore.

She turned from me, leaned on the wall with both palms, head down. Shoulders tight.

I gave her space.

Let her burn.

Let her have that anger—because it was hers. And it wasn't my job to tame it. Just to witness it. To hold it without making her feel like it was too much.

She stood like that for a minute—still. Breathing heavy. Not quite done.

Then I moved closer. Not touching her yet. Just speaking.

"Jo…"

No response.

"Look at me."

She didn't.

So I stepped in behind her, not to take control—but to offer gravity. My hand hovered at her hip before resting there. Not pulling. Just grounding.

She let out one long, shaking breath.

The kind that comes after holding your whole world inside your ribcage for too long.

Then she turned.

Her eyes met mine.

Still blazing. Still alive.

But the edge had softened. Just slightly.

Her body leaned in—barely. Not surrender. Not collapse. Just… release.

And finally, I saw it.

The fire was still there.

But now it was warmth.

Not wrath.

Something hotter.

Something darker.

Something hungry.

We didn't undress.

We tore each other apart.

Buttons popped.

Straps snapped.

Fabric ripped straight down the seams.

A chair tipped over. A lamp crashed. My belt clanged against the floor as she yanked it from my jeans like she was stripping me for war, not pleasure. Her nails scraped down my chest, leaving red trails that burned even under the sweat.

The hall blurred. The walls disappeared. It was just us—heat and instinct and too much need, too long restrained.

We slammed into the bathroom door.

Burst through.

The light flickered. The mirror fogged instantly.

She spun, wild-eyed, feral.

I didn't ask.

I grabbed her.

Our mouths collided—no softness. No care. Just teeth. Tongue. Ownership. She bit me, hard enough to draw blood, and I moaned into it. I shoved her against the tile. She shoved back. We were fighting and fucking and claiming at the same time.

The water exploded to life.

Scalding.

Perfect.

Steam rose like smoke from a blaze.

And we were the matchstick.

I slammed her back against the wall.

Hard.

The impact echoed, a deep thud that rattled something in both of us.

She didn't flinch. She grinned.

Legs wrapped around me instantly.

I grabbed her ass—fistfuls—hauling her up until I felt her pussy slide against me, soaking and hot and aching. She rocked against my cock like she was trying to light it on fire, friction slick and unforgiving. She gasped into my mouth, then bit my lip again—harder. My hands moved to her throat, fingers wrapping just enough to make her eyes widen.

She nodded.

That was all I needed.

I spun her.

She hit the wall with her palms first, ass arched, back bowed, water cascading down every curve. She looked over her shoulder, eyes daring me to fucking ruin her.

"Wash mi back," she breathed.

No.

I claimed it.

I dragged my hands down her spine, my nails tracing each ridge of her backbone before gripping her hips—tight. So tight I knew she'd feel it tomorrow. I bent her further, spreading her wider, watching water glide between her cheeks and over her swollen lips.

Her breath stuttered.

She was ready.

But I wanted to hear it.

"You want it like this?" I growled, voice rasped and animal.

She didn't answer.

She reached back, grabbed my cock, and slammed it against herself.

"Fuck me like yuh vex," she snapped. "Like yuh hate mi."

I lost it.

Buried myself in one thrust—all the way.

The sound that tore from her chest wasn't human.

Her hands slapped the tile, trying to brace. I slammed into her again— harder. The slap of our bodies filled the shower. The water turned to mist from how hot we were. The glass fogged completely, streaks of her handprints smeared across it from when she reached out mid-thrust.

I pounded her.

Ruthlessly.

No rhythm. No patience. Just release.

Every thrust was payback.

For the night.

The disrespect.

The tension.

The temptation.

The fucking taxi driver.

Everything.

I grabbed her braids. Yanked. Not cruel—commanding. She arched into it, moaning like she needed more pain to match the pleasure. I slapped her ass so hard the sound cracked like lightning.

She screamed.

"Mi love it—gimme more," she growled.

I reached down, gripped her throat from behind, and fucked her deeper. Hard enough to lift her toes from the floor. Her entire body shook. I felt her unraveling, pussy clenching around me, choking my dick with every stroke.

But I didn't let her come.

Not yet.

She reached back again. Desperate. Fingertips clawing at my hip.

"Please—please," she whispered.

I grabbed her jaw, spun her around, kissed her savagely. Water dripped from our mouths. Her breasts bounced as she clawed at my back, pulling me in until I was buried inside her again—this time with our foreheads touching, breath locked between gritted teeth.

"I'm gonna fuck the rage out of you," I muttered.

She gasped. "Try."

We slammed into the wall again.

And this time—

We didn't stop.

* * *

I threw her onto the bed—gently, but with purpose.

She landed with a gasp, her legs already spreading like instinct. She knew what was coming. Begged for it without a single word.

I climbed up behind her, grabbed her thighs, and dragged her to the edge of the bed, her body skidding across the sheets. Then I dropped to my knees.

And I devoured her.

Not with caution.

With hunger.

The kind you don't apologize for.

My mouth hit her like a wave—deep, wide, wet. I licked her from base to clit in one slow, heavy drag, then circled the top with my tongue, slow and mean. She shivered. Bucked. Moaned something unintelligible—but I wasn't listening. I was consuming.

She tasted like sex and salt and sweat, and I wanted every drop.

I locked my arms under her thighs, held her down, pinned her open like she was a feast laid out just for me. My tongue moved in tight, sharp patterns. No teasing. No games. Just focused pressure.

She squirmed.

Fingers curled in the sheets, then in my hair.

She didn't know where to hold on.

Didn't know how to survive what I was doing to her.

Every flick of my tongue made her breath catch. Every slow suck sent a tremor through her thighs. Her hips started to rock against me—desperate, needy—trying to grind her way closer to the edge.

I moaned into her.

Let the sound shake through her clit. Let my hunger become vibration. Let her feel how deep I needed this.

She gasped—sharp, broken.

"Bruce—"

Her voice cracked.

That was it.

The signal.

I wrapped my lips around her clit and sucked hard, fingers digging into her thighs to keep her in place as her whole body locked up. She didn't scream—she seized. Every muscle pulled tight, every breath caught in her throat as the orgasm tore through her like a wave crashing into a glass house.

She shattered.

And I kept eating.

Slow now. Wet now. Letting her come down with my tongue still on her, still inside her. Not stopping. Not pulling away. Not letting her go.

Because I wasn't done.

Not yet.

And as I licked, sucked, flicked, I thought about something—briefly.

There's a stigma. That Jamaican men don't do this.

Maybe that was part of it. Maybe that was why her body reacted like it had never been touched right before. Like her soul was sprinting toward something it never knew it was missing.

Had no one ever taken their time?

Had no one ever worshipped her?

Tasted her like scripture?

Held her down and made her feel like she was the only thing on Earth worth consuming?

If so, they were fools.

Because right now, I was the only man in the world who knew how she tasted—perfect and ruined and mine.

Her clit was built for this.

Larger. Rounder. Swollen and sensitive as hell.

The kind you could suck—deep—roll between your lips, flick with your tongue in lazy, teasing spirals until she couldn't decide whether to come again or run from the feeling.

And she did shake.

Every flick of my tongue made her legs spasm, hips lift, breath punch out of her lungs. She chased my mouth like she couldn't bear even a half-second without it. Her moans weren't soft now—they were choked, rough, full of ragged patois and cussing like prayer.

"Oh fuck... mi cya tek dis... mi cya tek—"

I didn't let up.

I sucked harder. Tongue faster. Let her ride the edge and tip off it again. Her thighs clamped around my head like a vice.

She screamed.

"Yessss… mi a come… mi a fuckin—mi a COMEEE!"

Her whole body convulsed—violently.

Back arched.

Fists grabbing the sheets.

Toes curled, neck snapped back, mouth open in a silent wail.

I held her through it.

Mouth locked on her clit.

Moaning into it.

Feeding her more when she had nothing left to give.

And still—she came again.

No warning this time.

Just a scream from her gut—loud, raw, terrifyingly beautiful.

"Bomboclaaaat—mi a dead, Bruce… yuh kill mi—yuh fuckin kill mi!"

Her hips jolted up, damn near lifted her off the bed. Her legs trembled. Her body locked. She cried out again—this time crying, not moaning—tears on her face, maybe from release, maybe from overstimulation.

But I didn't stop.

Not yet.

One last flick.

One more roll of my tongue, right under the hood where I knew she was at her rawest.

Her body snapped.

Arms flailing, chest heaving, mouth open in one last fuck fuck fuckkkk! as she convulsed in my hands.

Only then—only then—did I slow.

My tongue softened. My lips parted from her clit with a final kiss. Gentle. Reverent.

I looked up at her.

Wrecked.

Tears on her cheeks.

Breasts rising and falling.

Thighs twitching like aftershocks.

I let her breathe.

But I stayed right there.
Mouth still between her legs.
Because when she was ready again...
I was already home.

* * *

By the time we moved to the main event, the room was dim, the only light a faint glow from the full moon creeping through the curtains.

The fabric was thin.

Anyone walking by could've seen everything—the sheets, the skin, the shadows of bodies locked in rhythm.

We didn't care.

Not even a little.

We moved like we had something to prove. Like the night wasn't just pulling us in—it was swallowing us whole.

Sweat smeared across skin.

The scent of her still fresh on my lips.

Her thighs still trembling from what I just gave her, and somehow, she wanted more.

We tangled.

Hands in hair.

Nails down backs.

Teeth to shoulders.

We switched positions like instincts were guiding us—no choreography, just need. She scratched. I gripped. She bit. I growled. Her moans filled the room, but not soft and sweet—loud, ugly, beautiful.

When she climbed on top, it was over.

She owned it.

Her thighs straddled me like she was claiming territory. Her pussy slid down slow—too slow—until I was fully inside her again. She gasped. Rolled her hips. Her body was still recovering, still soaked, still sensitive, but she used it. Weaponized it.

She rode me with precision.

Grinding in circles first—slow, deliberate, taunting.

My head tipped back, eyes slammed shut, breath caught in my chest.

"Fuck, Jo…" I hissed.

She grinned. Ruthless.

Then leaned down till her mouth was at my ear.

"Yuh feel dat?" she whispered, voice thick with sweat and sin.

"You feel what yuh missin every time yuh let one of dem uptown gyal touch yuh?"

I grabbed her ass, hard. "Nah. They never rode me like this."

"Damn right," she spat, biting my lip. "Cause mi naw ride yuh. Mi fuckin tek yuh."

She started to bounce now—wet, slapping, messy.

My dick disappeared into her with every drop of her hips. Her ass clapped against my thighs, the sound filthy, echoing in the stillness like applause.

She was dripping.

Every movement sent more slick rolling down my cock, pooling on my stomach.

I felt everything—every pulse, every spasm, every second she got lost in her own damn rhythm.

Her eyes rolled back.

She put one hand on my chest for balance, the other sliding between her legs to circle her clit as she fucked herself on me.

It was primal.

Like she was using me.

Like I was just the tool and the storm was hers to summon.

"You like watchin me fuck myself on yuh dick?" she gasped, breath breaking between moans.

"Fuck yes," I groaned, grabbing her hips tighter. "Keep going. Don't stop."

"Mi cya stop," she panted, hips moving faster now. "Mi too close… fuck… Bruce, mi close again—"

"Come on, baby. Come on. Fuckin take it."

"Mi taking it," she cried, voice cracking, body rolling like a wave was building from deep inside her. "Mi a tek all of it—"

She slammed down—once.

Twice.

*Third time—*and she screamed.

Back arched.

Hair flying.

Pussy squeezing the life out of me as her whole body went rigid.

She collapsed onto me, chest to chest, sweat to sweat, mouth open against my neck.

But her hips didn't stop.

She was still grinding.

Still wringing every drop from the high.

Still milking my cock like her body wasn't finished yet.

"Fuck," I gasped, eyes locked on the ceiling, seeing stars through the darkness. "You tryna kill me?"

She laughed. Dark. Breathless.

"Yuh nuh dead yet."

And then she rolled her hips again.

Hard.

Slow.

And I realized—

She wasn't done either.

She pulled off me.

Slid down.

And then her mouth was on me.

Wet.

Warm.

Insatiable.

But it wasn't just the sensation.

It was the intention.

The way she leaned in like she couldn't wait to taste us mixed together— me and her, slick on my skin. The way her tongue flicked the tip, then dragged slow down my shaft like she was writing her name with it. She moaned as she licked, eyes still locked on mine.

That's what undid me.

The eye contact.

The boldness. The knowing.

The way she enjoyed it.

Not just my body—but what we had just done.

She cleaned me with her mouth like she was savoring every drop. Slow, wet, reverent. Not submissive. Not performative.

Possessive.

I groaned—loud, deep, raw—hand tangled in her hair as my hips bucked. I couldn't help it. She was too good. Too focused. Her lips wrapped around the head, tongue swirling in tight little circles, dragging me to the edge with every motion.

"Goddamn," I muttered, chest heaving.

She grinned around my dick, pulled off with a pop, wiped her mouth with the back of her hand.

Then she stood.

Walked to the bed.

Climbed up.

And assumed the position.

Face down.

Ass up.

Back arched perfectly.

Knees wide.

Hands gripping the sheets.

Head turned just enough so I could see the side of her mouth curl into a smirk.

An invitation.

A challenge.

A fucking demand.

And the moonlight—

That soft, haunting blue glow—

It caught everything.

The curve of her back.

The roundness of her ass.

The shimmer of sweat still clinging to her skin.

The mess between her thighs that I put there.

If it had been a photo, it would've been frame-worthy. Iconic.

But this wasn't a photo.

This was real.

This was ours.

And I went for it.

I climbed onto the bed, lined myself up behind her. Gripped her hips. Dragged the tip of my cock through her slick folds, watching her twitch beneath me, breath already catching.

Then I slid in.

All the way.

Slow at first.

Just to feel that stretch.

That first, perfect squeeze.

She moaned—long, low, guttural.

I pulled back.

Then slammed into her.

She yelped, legs buckling slightly, ass rippling from the impact.

I did it again.

And again.

Fast. Hard. Deliberate.

The sound of my hips crashing into her ass echoed off the walls. The bed creaked. The sheets pulled loose from the corners. Her hands clawed for grip.

And her mouth—

Her mouth let go.

"Yes! Yes, mi love dat! Fuck mi just so, Bruce—jus so—jus like dat!"

I grunted behind her, sweat flying off my brow with every stroke. I gripped her tighter. Bent over her body. Fucked her with everything I had left.

She threw it back.

Harder than I gave it.

She was loud now. Gone. Her voice cracked with every thrust.

"Mi cya manage—oh God, mi feel yuh deep, mi feel yuh—"

I reached forward, grabbed a fistful of her braids, pulled her head back just enough to whisper in her ear.

"You feel me?"

"Mi feel ALL a yuh," she cried. "Mi feel yuh inna mi fuckin chest!"

I lost it.

Pounded into her.

Once.

Twice.

A third time—

And her body collapsed.

Her legs gave out. Her arms dropped. She went flat against the sheets, ass still in the air, back quivering.

But I wasn't done.

I grabbed her waist and kept going—pulling her back into me, slamming deep, low grunts tearing from my throat. She clawed at the bed, moaning into the mattress, body convulsing from aftershocks.

She looked over her shoulder, eyes half-lidded, mouth open, drenched in sweat and cum and moonlight.

"Tek it," she gasped.

"Give mi every fuckin drop."

But I wasn't ready.

Not yet.

The edge was close—dangerously close—but I gritted my teeth and held the line. That wasn't the finish she deserved. Not yet. I had more in me. More to give. More to take.

I locked my grip around her waist and kept moving—deeper, slower, meaner. Grinding through the tension like it owed me something. She shuddered beneath me, moaning into the mattress, hips twitching with every thrust. Her body was gone—nerves fried, limbs loose—but I wasn't letting her float off just yet.

She had more to feel.

And I had more to give.

The pressure kept building, thick and tight in my core, but I held it. Controlled it. Pushed it down and kept going.

Because when I came…

It wasn't gonna be now.

It was gonna be everything.

And she wasn't ready yet.

But she would be.

Soon.

Filling her.

Stretching her.

Slamming into her in deep, deliberate strokes.

The kind you feel for days.

The kind that rewire your body.

The sound of our skin clapping together was the only thing filling the room—loud, filthy, perfect.

Just us.

And all I could hear was what Dr. Lee had said—

One sound. One rhythm. One band.

That was us.

Right fucking now.

The slap of hips crashing.

The creak of the bedframe surrendering beneath us.

Her moans—high, broken, unstoppable.

My breath, ragged and sharp.

The pulse in my temples. The thud in my chest. The beat in my hips.

We were the damn rhythm section.

I played her body like an instrument.

And she responded to every note.

No hesitation.

No missed cues.

Just movement.

Fluid. Vicious. Holy.

One rhythm—

The way I drove into her, hips rolling, pounding, dragging out every stroke before slamming back in so deep she screamed into the mattress.

One band—

The way she threw it back on me, right when I needed it, her body curling, tightening, welcoming the pressure. Her hands clawing into the sheets. Her knuckles white. Her moans turning to cries.

There was no need for a conductor.

We were the sound.

The rhythm.

The band.

And I was leading this set like a motherfucker.

I could feel it building—the fire tightening in my gut. The raw, aching need to release, but not before she broke first. Not before she fell apart one more time.

She was soaking me.

Dripping down my thighs.

Gripping my dick like she didn't want to let it go.

Like her body knew this was the moment.

My fingers dug deep into her hips, pulling her back into every brutal thrust. My teeth clenched. My jaw locked. And then I said it—low, commanding, filthy.

"You feel that? All this dick stretching you out? Come for me, wicked girl."

She whimpered—wrecked—her voice nothing but breath and patois soaked in sin.

"Mi waa feel yuh breed mi deep… choke mi… mek mi cum til mi cya move."

And that was it.

The fucking trigger.

I snapped.

Hips snapped.

Everything snapped.

I buried myself inside her.

Deep.

Deliberate.

Punishing.

The sound of her scream was pure release.

"Fuck mi! Fuck mi deep! Ooh mi a cum—lawd, mi a cum—Jesus mi cya hold it—FUCK!"

Her whole body exploded.

Convulsions rippling through her like shockwaves.

Her legs shook.

Her back arched.

She collapsed forward, face buried in the sheets, gone.

But her pussy—

Her pussy clamped around me like a fucking vice.

And I couldn't hold it anymore.

My body tensed.

Muscles locked.

Nerves lit up like fire alarms.

She felt it. Felt the shift in my breath, the tremble in my hips.

And even wrecked—face down, moaning into the sheets—she reached one hand back under her body and cupped my balls.

Gentle at first.

Then tighter.

Fingertips grazing just enough to make my knees weak.

"Cum fi mi, star," she moaned.

"Gimme all a dat hot seed. Full up mi belly wid it. Breed mi deep, mi love it just so. Come like yuh cyan stop."

Her voice was filthy. Velvet soaked in sin.

Every word ripped the last bit of control from my body.

Final thrust—

I stayed buried, deep, tight, home.

And then I let go.

My orgasm hit like a fucking freight train.

White-hot.

Full-body.

Shattering.

I spilled inside her—pulse after pulse, my cock twitching as she milked every drop from me. I grunted through clenched teeth, forehead dropping to her back, hips jerking uncontrollably as I emptied myself into her completely.

She was still twitching.

Still moaning.

Still whispering curses into the sheets like she couldn't believe her own body had given out.

I pulled out slow, every inch dragging against her still-spasming walls, my body trembling from the intensity.

Collapsed beside her.

Chest heaving.

Heart pounding.

For a long time—neither of us moved.

Just the sound of our breathing.

Heavy.

Disjointed.

Alive.

Her back rose and fell beside me, slick with sweat. Her legs still jerked every few seconds—tiny, uncontrollable aftershocks.

Then she sighed.

Deep.

Wrecked.

The kind of sigh you only let out when there's nothing left to give.

A slow, lazy smile curled onto her face. The kind that could only come from satisfaction too real to fake.

She turned her head.

I turned mine.

And we locked eyes.

For half a second, we just stared at each other—stunned, wide-eyed, wrecked.

Then we burst out laughing.

Loud.

Free.

Like two people who knew exactly what the fuck they'd just survived.

13

Hot Fish, No Fuss

She was still asleep when I opened my eyes, lips slightly parted, curls pressed flat on one side. Her leg draped over mine like she'd claimed the territory overnight. I stayed there, watching her breathe, her chest rising with no effort. It felt good... being still next to her. Not trying to figure out the next move. Not needing to.

She traced her finger down my chest, lazy circles that made me feel more real than any job title ever did.

"I keep thinking," I murmured. "When this runs out — when I gotta go back..."

She didn't stop. Just watched me.

"...I know I could slide right back in. Same grind. Same suits. Same dead hours. I'm good at it. Too good."

She didn't say nothing. Just kept tracing those circles, like she knew if she spoke I'd lose my nerve.

"I'm scared," I said, softer. "Scared I'll fold. Walk back in that office like it ain't killin' me."

She leaned down, pressed her lips to my shoulder.

"Den don't," she said.

That was all. No speech. Just truth.

I shifted slightly, brushing my fingers along the curve of her thigh.

"Mm," she murmured, half-asleep. "Yuh start trouble already?"

I smiled. "Just making sure you still real."

Her eyes stayed closed. "Mi real enough fi feel that poke behind mi leg."

"Don't act surprised. You laid up on me like that and expect peace?"

"Peace? Wid you?" She opened her eyes, playful smirk rising. "You nuh look like peace. You look like sin."

"Sin feel like the only thing keeping me sane lately."

She stretched, her body sliding along mine like silk and sun and everything else I didn't know how to name yet. Then she rolled on top of me, straddling my waist, her hips settling like she belonged there.

"Mi hungry," she said.

"For food or me?"

She rocked once—slow, teasing.

"Both."

* * *

She didn't get off me right away. She just sat there, hips still in that slow sway, her hands pressed to my chest. Watching me like she already knew what I was about to do.

"Then eat," I said, hands sliding up her thighs.

She bit her bottom lip, but the smirk stayed. "Yuh sure yuh can manage both?"

"I'll die trying."

Her laugh melted into a gasp as I sat up, arms wrapping around her back, my mouth finding the soft skin just beneath her collarbone. Her hands threaded through my hair, tugged gently, guiding me lower.

When I eased her down onto the mattress, her legs opened easy—like we'd done this a thousand times. No fumbling. Just heat. Steady and certain.

I kissed her as I entered, slow and deep. Her arms wrapped around my neck. No games. No rush. Just pressure and breath. Her hips rolled with mine, matching rhythm for rhythm.

She moaned into my mouth. "Just like that."

I held her thighs, rocked into her with a pace that said I wasn't trying to dominate—just stay in it. Stay in her.

The slick slide of her body against mine. Her lips brushing my jaw. Her nails dragging down my back.

We didn't speak for a while—just listened to each other breathe.

Then, her voice in my ear: "Cum f'me, baby. Gimme all a dat pressure."

I groaned into her neck, thrusts slowing as the wave came. She tightened her grip around me like she needed every drop of it, every tremble and breath I gave her.

When it was over, we didn't move.

Her chest rose and fell under my palm, sweat glistening on her shoulder. She reached up and wiped my lip with her thumb, then grinned.

"Still hungry," she whispered.

* * *

We eventually made it to the kitchen, still naked, until she threw my shirt at me and told me to act like a guest and not a mad man.

"You don't trust me with the stove?"

She looked over her shoulder. "Yuh look like di kinda man who burn egg and claim it's gourmet."

"Wow."

"Mi wrong?"

"…Maybe."

She laughed, deep and real. "Sit down, chef. Let me fix sum'n."

She moved like she owned the space, even though it was my rental. Eggs, plantains, leftover festival, two fingers of rum in a mug. She passed it to me with that same smirk.

"Drink. Ease off yuh back."

I sipped. It burned sweet.

"You always cook for the men you climb on top of?"

"Just the good ones." She winked. "Yuh pass—so far."

We ate on the couch. Some old-ass Jamaican soap opera played in the background, and we clowned every scene.

"Why dude teeth so damn white?" I asked.

She snorted. "That's bleach and prayer."

"Nah. That's vengeance."

She laughed so hard she snorted again. I teased her for it, and she slapped my arm, then leaned against me, head resting on my shoulder.

* * *

We talked. About dumb stuff at first. Favorite cartoon villains. What we'd eat for the rest of our lives if we could only choose one dish.

Then it shifted.

"Yuh ever think," she started, "if none of this happen—divorce, job, breakdown—yuh still woulda come here?"

I paused. "Nah."

"Why not?"

"I was surviving back there. That was the only rhythm I knew."

She nodded slowly. "Sometimes we don't know we drowning until we stop swimming."

"That's exactly how it felt."

She picked up my hand. Played with my fingers while the TV hummed in the background.

"You think you'll go back?" she asked.

"I don't even know who I am yet. How can I go back to being somebody I don't recognize?"

She looked at me then, for real. No smirk. No banter.

"Mi like yuh here," she said. "Not because yuh American or different. But because yuh... honest. Even when yuh tryna hide."

I didn't say anything. I just pulled her in closer.

* * *

She shifted a little in my arms, pulled back just enough to look at me — really look.

For a second I thought she might say something soft, but her eyes cut through me instead.

"Yuh know mi can feel when yuh holding back, right?"

I tried to smile it off. "I'm here, ain't I?"

She didn't laugh. Just brushed my jaw with her thumb, voice low.

"Being here and staying here not di same ting."

She pressed her lips to my temple — gentle but final — then pulled away to stand.

Later, she stood, stretched, and kissed my cheek.

"Mi a run out. Grabba, some more weed, maybe some Magnum. Yuh want anything?"

"I'm good."

She rolled her eyes. "That mean mi bringing food. Yuh lucky mi like yuh."

"What you getting?"

"Escoveitch. Fried and peppery. Fi put back di strength mi tek."

She walked out barefoot, keys in hand.

Door closed behind her.

And just like that, the house was quiet. Still smelled like her. Sheets twisted. Her laughter still echoing somewhere in the corners. I sat on the couch, the same one she danced in front of earlier, and exhaled.

It'd only been a few days. Maybe not even that. But something had shifted. The way I was looking at the island. The way I was looking at myself.

This wasn't healing like I expected. It wasn't closure or clarity. It was something looser. Something alive.

I didn't know if she'd stay. Or if I would.

But for once, I wasn't searching. I was just... here.

* * *

Door creaked open an hour later. The smell hit me first—spicy, vinegary, sharp. Escoveitch.

"Mi bring peace offering," she called out, kicking off her sandals.

I met her at the kitchen counter, leaned in for a kiss.

She pulled back slightly. "Not before mi wash mi hands. Don't want yuh tasting fried fish and roadside fumes."

I waited. She moved through the space like she belonged to it now. Like she never really left.

When she came back, she set down the brown paper box, sweat-stained with oil. Unwrapped it carefully like it was sacred. Fish, golden and curled, still hot. Onions, peppers, pimento scattered on top like a crown.

"You spoil me," I said.

She handed me a fork. "No. Mi just balance di scale."

We sat at the table this time.She watched me eat like she was making sure I meant every chew.

"I haven't sat still this long in years," I said finally.

"Stillness don't mean yuh stuck," she said. "Sometimes it's where di real movement happen."

She picked up her phone off the counter, tapped the screen, then tucked it back in her bag.

"Mi boy. Staying with mi sister dis week. Mi tell miself mi keeping him safe from mi fire… but one day him gon' see mi whole too."

She didn't linger on it. Just tore a piece of fried fish, placed it on my plate like punctuation.

"You always talk like that?"

"Like what?"

"Like a poet who hustle jerk chicken on the side."

She laughed—real, from the gut.

"Mi just talk how mi spirit move."

"You ever think about leaving?"

"Jamaica?"

181

I nodded.

She took a sip from her drink, eyes tracing something I couldn't see. "Mi used to. But mi story too rooted here."

"Yeah?"

She nodded slowly. "Mi son's father… he was di love of mi life. First and maybe only man mi ever loved like dat."

"What happened?"

Her smile came and went fast. "Him was… deep inna street life. Fast money. Fast living. But always made sure mi was good. Never had to worry 'bout bills or mi car breaking down or di fridge being empty."

"Just had to worry about him coming home."

Her eyes met mine. "Every damn day."

Silence stretched, but it wasn't uncomfortable.

"I tried to make peace wid it, yuh know? That maybe some men just built for war, not peace. But living like that… mi spirit couldn't stay settled."

"So you left?"

"No. Life left him. Not dead, just… caught up. Locked away. Ten-year sentence. He missed our son's first steps. First words. Everything."

"Damn."

"Mi used to visit. Bring mi son. But mi couldn't raise a child in-between searches and prison walls. So mi stopped."

I studied her face. No tears. No dramatics. Just that steady strength she wore like skin.

"Mi loved him bad. But mi couldn't let that be my forever."

"That shit real," I said. "Knowing when to choose you. Even when your heart still stuck on them."

"Exactly." She tapped her glass. "Mi nah looking for a savior. Mi save myself already. Now mi just want someone mi can breathe next to."

I nodded, chest tightening. "What if I don't know how to breathe yet?"

She smiled, softer this time. "Then mi teach yuh."

Her voice didn't crack, but I could hear the weight in it. Like grief that had been lived with, not conquered.

"I've been trying to disappear my whole damn life," I said. "Even before the divorce. Even before the job started eating me alive."

"What yuh running from?"

I didn't answer right away. I didn't know how to.

"Myself, maybe. The version of me I became when I stopped believing I could ask for more."

She didn't blink. She just nodded slowly. "Mi get that."

"I think I was performing for so long—father, husband, provider—that I forgot what it meant to just be a man. Not even a good one. Just… a real one."

She leaned in. "Yuh feel more real now?"

I swallowed. "Some days. Today? Yeah."

"Good." She squeezed my hand. "Because mi don't want yuh here pretending. Mi done play dat game."

We sat in that space—not heavy, not light. Just real.

Then she asked: "What would make you stay?"

"In Jamaica?"

"In yourself."

That hit harder than I expected.

I answered slow. "If I could wake up every day and not hate the skin I'm in… the choices I made… the dreams I gave up on. If I could just look in the mirror and not flinch."

She paused for a second. Then: "Mi think yuh already on yuh way. Yuh just don't recognize di face yet."

She stood, took our plates to the sink. Washed them like it was second nature. No rush. No show.

Then she turned back to me, drying her hands on a towel.

"Yuh not broken, Bruce. Just… raw."

I looked at her. Really looked at her.

"So are you."

She nodded. "Mi know. But raw mean we not numb. Raw mean we still feel. That's where it start."

She rinsed the last plate, wiped the counter, then turned off the light over the sink. The kitchen dimmed, leaving only the soft orange from the lamp in the corner of the living room.

She came back without a word, slipped down beside me on the couch, legs draped over mine. I shifted just enough to hold her, arms folding around her waist like they'd done it a thousand times.

We didn't talk.

We didn't need to.

The show on TV played low. Some old dancehall riddim leaked through the open window from a car driving by. A dog barked down the hill. Somewhere in the distance, a horn honked twice and faded into nothing.

She yawned, tucked her head under my chin, and exhaled like she'd finally landed.

I held her like she was mine. Not because I owned her. But because, for the first time in a long time, someone chose to stay.

And I didn't need to be fixed. Or impressive. Or anything more than still.

Just... here.

14

The Island of Fimi

The next morning, we woke up in silence. Not cold. Not awkward. Just... still. No teasing, no leftover jokes from the night before. Just the slow hum of a Montego Bay sun working its way across the bed, brushing over skin that had already said everything it needed to.

She didn't look at me right away. She just stretched—long and loose—then slid out of the sheets like nothing had shifted. Like we hadn't spent the last day wrapped up in each other's breath.

"Get dressed," she murmured, voice rough with sleep. "Mi nuh wait pon yuh, Bruce."

I grinned. "You sure? You seem like you enjoy bossin' me around."

She shot me a side-eye while slipping into a snug black crop top, her waist catching the light just right. "An' yuh love followin' mi lead, so move wid it."

I let her win. Again.

We stepped outside and the heat was already thick, rising off the hillside like the city was breathing. From the upper deck, Montego Bay stretched wide—blue water teasing the edge of everything, cruise ships floating lazy near the port. It should've felt like paradise. But all I could think about was how steep the hill was to get down.

There were no sidewalks. No safety nets. Just a narrow road carved into the slope, where route taxis flew by like pedestrians were optional.

I stayed close to the edge, dodging potholes and death. Jovel? She didn't even blink. She moved like gravity bent around her.

"You good?" she asked, glancing back.

"I'd be better if we weren't playin' chicken with every damn car on this hill."

She laughed, full and loud, like she forgot to care. "Bruce, stop move like yuh fraid. Walk like yuh know where yuh goin'."

Easy for her to say. She walked this road like it was muscle memory. I followed like I'd just learned how to use my legs.

At the bottom of the hill, the city cracked open. Vendors called out to morning shoppers. Oil popped from steel pots. The smell of fried dumplings and hot breadfruit curled through the air. Men argued outside a rum shop—loud, early, already passionate about football or politics or both.

Then it happened.

* * *

"Fimi!"

Voice deep, gravel-worn, called across the street. And suddenly, the whole block lit up.

Another voice echoed her name. Then another. A fruit vendor whistled. A group of older women waved like she was their niece coming back from foreign. Everybody knew her. Not "knew of" her. Knew her.

She didn't even flinch. She just smirked and kept walking like this was normal.

"Ayyye, mi nah see yuh in weeks, Fimi! Yuh dash mi weh or wah?" the fruit man called, leaning over his stall.

Jovel sucked her teeth. "A lie yuh a tell. Mi pass ya di odda day, yuh just blind."

"Yuh betta buy supm now, mek up fi yuh disappearance."

She rolled her eyes but reached for a mango anyway. "Gimme one sweet one, nuh di likkle bruk-up ting."

She paid before he could argue, then peeled the skin back with her teeth, juice already glistening down her thumb.

I watched her, something clicking into place.

She didn't just live here.

This city loved her.

"Fimi?" I asked as we kept walking.

She looked over, lips glistening with mango juice. "What?"

I let the name sit on my tongue. "So... Fimi."

She paused mid-step. Looked at me a little too long. Then smirked.

"Yuh haffi earn dat."

It wasn't just a nickname. It was access. And I hadn't unlocked it yet.

We turned a corner, and she slipped into conversation with an old woman sitting on a stoop, shaded by bougainvillea and time.

"Miss Patsy," Jovel greeted, crouching beside her. "Yuh good?"

The woman nodded, smiling slow. "Mi deh yah, chile. Mi see yuh runnin' up an' dung di place again."

Jovel handed her a few folded bills. "Mi just a keep busy. Mi tell yuh grandson check pon yuh?"

"Yuh did, yuh did." The old woman patted her cheek. "Yuh a good gyal, Fimi."

I hung back, watching it all like a scene from a film I'd just wandered into. Jovel wasn't showing off. This was just who she was here. Montego Bay didn't just recognize her—it made space for her.

We moved again.

Every few blocks, someone else called her name.

Men flirted. Women embraced her. Shopkeepers dapped her up like she was politics and poetry wrapped into one.

By the time we hit Miss Ling's soup shop, I'd stopped counting how many times I'd heard her name.

She waved us over.

"Fimi, mi chile! Mi hope yuh hungry."

Jovel nodded toward me. "Mi bring mi fren fi try yuh good good soup. Di real ting."

Miss Ling looked me over. "Mi hope him can handle it. Yuh know mi nuh water down mi seasoning fi nobody."

Jovel laughed. "Dat's why mi love it."

She ordered two big bowls of chicken soup with spinners, extra pepper, no negotiation.

We sat on a little bench out front. People passed. Kids ran by. The soup hit hard—thick, spicy, layered like somebody's grandmother poured memory into it.

Jovel watched me, amused. "Yuh still doubtin' mi taste?"

I shook my head, sweating. "Never said that."

"Yuh didn't haffi say it."

We turned off the main road, deeper into the city's marrow.

* * *

Jovel led the way, her steps sure even as the sidewalk crumbled beneath us.

"Yuh trust mi?" she asked over her shoulder.

"Do I have a choice?"

She didn't answer. She just smiled and kept walking.

We reached a narrow staircase tucked behind a faded paint shop. No sign, just sound—laughter, slow reggae, the faint scrape of a comb tugging through thick coils of hair.

She cupped her hands and called out. "Mi come fi fix up mi fren crown!"

A woman peeked through the upstairs window, wide smile already forming. "Fimi, bout time. Yuh bring dis yankee fi come get righteous?"

Jovel laughed. "Mi couldn't let him walk roun' like a lost prophet. Him need salvation."

We climbed the stairs and stepped into a living room that had been converted into a sanctuary for hair. No posters. No loud hustle. Just incense smoke curling near a fan, and the scent of oil and shea butter settling into the walls.

She motioned for me to sit.

The loctician—small frame, big energy—walked around me once, like she was taking inventory.

"Short dreads," she said, nodding. "Good base. Not too dry. Yuh let them breathe, that's good."

"I mean... I do my best," I offered.

She raised a brow. "We gon' make yuh look like you do better."

Jovel laughed from across the room, already digging through a box of products. "Use di coconut oil mix pon him scalp. It calm."

The woman got to work. Parting. Clipping. Tightening. Fingers flying like she was stitching something sacred back together.

Jovel leaned over and kissed the top of my head. "Mi soon come. When yuh done, mi carry yuh fi get shaped up proper."

And just like that, she was gone again.

I let the moment stretch.

The chair was old but solid. The breeze from the window cooled my back. The hands in my hair weren't rushed. There was care in every twist. Every pull. Every spritz of oil.

The music shifted—Beres Hammond, slow and smooth. A kid sat on the floor playing with a broken remote. Somebody in the back was frying something that smelled like Saturday.

And me? I just sat. Still.

Let her rebuild what I'd been neglecting.

"You overthink," she said suddenly.

"Huh?"

"Mi can feel it in yuh scalp. Yuh hold tension up top. Like yuh tryna figure out things yuh can't fix yet."

I didn't respond. Didn't need to.

She kept twisting. Slower now. Almost like she was trying to undo more than just growth.

When she finished, she spun the chair toward the mirror.

There I was.

Same face. Same eyes. But different.

Grounded.

Like I'd finally arrived somewhere—even if I didn't have the words yet.

The locs were fresh. Clean. Edges still wild, but the crown? The crown was blessed.

I stepped out onto the landing and there she was, leaning against the rail with a cold drink in one hand and that knowing look on her face.

She took one slow glance at me, head to toe, and smiled.

"Mi see yuh now," she said.

"Yeah?"

"Almost." She pointed down the block. "Come. Time fi line yuh up."

* * *

We cut through a maze of alleyways behind the plaza. She didn't say where we were going. She just glanced back once to make sure I was keeping up.

The buildings got tighter, then looser. A rusted gate creaked open under her touch, and we climbed a metal staircase that didn't look like it had been trusted in a while.

But when we got to the top—

Everything opened.

No railings. No music. No crowd. Just a flat rooftop overlooking Montego Bay's spine—market stalls, zinc rooftops, people moving like rhythm.

The sea was somewhere out there, just past the haze. But from here, the city felt close. Breathing. Bruised. Alive.

Jovel sat cross-legged on the edge, pulled something cold from her bag— two bottles of Ting. Passed me one without looking.

We drank in silence for a while. The sky was bleeding orange.

She didn't try to perform. Didn't fill the quiet.

Then finally: "This place hard, yuh know."

Her voice was soft. Not broken, but something inside it bending.

"Jamaica?"

She nodded. "Di land. Di system. Di weight. Everyting about it test yuh. Sometimes mi get tired of fighting it. Fed up. Fed up til mi teeth clench."

I waited.

"But…" she continued, eyes fixed on the horizon, "every time mi think bout leavin' for good, mi chest tighten. Like mi would betray it. Like mi would betray mi self."

She took a long sip, then wiped her mouth with the back of her hand.

"Mi born here. Hurt here. Raised mi son here. Bury love here. Laugh, cry, build, lose—all pon dis rock. So when mi seh mi cyan turn mi back? It not weakness. It's loyalty."

I studied her profile. The sharp line of her jaw. The way the light kissed her skin like it remembered it.

I nodded slowly.

"I feel that."

She looked at me now.

"What yuh feel?"

I hesitated. Then: "Like maybe you and this city… ain't separate. Like when I walk with you, I'm seeing Montego Bay through your body."

She smiled, barely. "Mi is di city."

Silence again.

I let it stretch. But there was one thing I couldn't leave unsaid.

"Can I ask you something?"

Her eyebrow arched.

"Who's Fimi?" I asked. "Like… really. Is she just what people call you? Or is she someone else?"

Jovel turned her head, her eyes locking onto mine. There was no smirk this time. No deflection.

"Fimi not separate from me," she said slowly. "But she… bigger."

I waited.

"Mi government name a Jovel. But Fimi? Dat name come from people who see mi. People mi help. People mi love. It mean mi belong to dem. And dem belong to me."

She tapped her chest.

"Fimi mean mi nah leave yuh when tings get rough. Fimi mean mi stand up when mi spirit low. Fimi mean… mi yours, if yuh earn it."

I didn't move. I just listened. Let it settle.

191

"And I earned that?"

She didn't answer. She just leaned her head against my shoulder, her voice soft now. Not performative—just hers.

"Yuh close."

The sun dipped lower.

Montego Bay didn't quiet.

But somehow, right then, it felt like it had made space for us.

15

The Wedding Party Too

We woke up in the soft breath of morning—no alarms, no pressure. Just the pale hush of sun leaking in through the blinds, painting shadows across the walls. Her thigh still rested against mine, warm and effortless, like even in sleep she didn't need to claim space. She just took it. And I let her.

The air was calm. No reggae from the street. No horns. Just the low hum of the fan and the faint cling of the past few days still hanging in the room.

I stayed on my back, one hand behind my head, eyes on the ceiling. Not thinking. Not rushing. Just... existing. Something about that felt new.

She shifted beside me, a slow stretch rolling through her body, shoulder rising, then falling again. Her voice came out low, cracked by sleep but laced with mischief.

"Yuh know... di first night mi see yuh? Mi almost walk past."

I turned my head, met her eyes. She was already watching me—one arm tucked under her cheek, curls messy, mouth slightly upturned like she already knew how I'd react.

"What stopped you?"

"Yuh face," she said. "Look like yuh didn't belong." She let the words sit for a moment, then added, "But yuh eyes? Like yuh was tryin' to."

I chuckled—short and quiet. Because damn if that didn't feel like the whole trip.

"That accurate," I said.

She rolled onto her back, staring at the ceiling now. "Mi almost left early dat night. Wasn't even feelin' 2727. Whole place feel too curated. Mi fren drag mi. Said mi needed to 'get out my shell.'" She laughed. "Dat's how mi find you... leanin' up pon di wall like yuh waiting fi someone who neva show."

"I was," I said.

She glanced over.

"I just didn't know who," I added.

She didn't say anything to that. She just let the silence return, thick with something unspoken but not uncomfortable.

I reached across the bed, ran a thumb across her stomach. Her skin still smelled like soap and sex and sleep. She didn't stop me—she just closed her eyes and breathed in deeper.

"Mi glad mi didn't walk past," she said finally, voice barely audible.

I kissed her shoulder in response. Nothing dramatic. Just... presence.

After a while, I sat up, grabbed my phone off the nightstand. It lit up like a Christmas tree. Twenty-three unread messages. Missed calls. Voice notes.

The group chat was alive again.

Names flashing across the screen—Dev, Shawn, Tyler, a few numbers I didn't even recognize. One voice note from Shawn:

"Yo... you got 2727 locked, right? Big vibes tonight. Let's fkin goooooo."

I exhaled.

The shift was here.

Behind me, she was already sitting up, wrapping her arms around her knees, robe draped over her shoulders. The intimacy between us hadn't disappeared—it just stretched out into something different. Something that knew not every moment needed to be held too long.

"They landed?" she asked.

"Yeah," I said. "Crew's officially in town."

"Time fi real chaos," she said with a lazy smirk, standing up and reaching for her bag.

She moved through the room with a different rhythm now. Not

guarded—but… reoriented. Like she already knew the world outside that door was about to change the tempo.

I opened my wallet, peeled off a few folded bills. Enough to say I see you, not enough to make it a transaction. Just enough to matter.

She turned when I held it out.

"For your hair," I said. "And a dress."

Her brow lifted, but she didn't refuse it.

"Yuh tryin' fi mek mi cry dis early?"

"Nah," I said, "just want you to walk in tonight lookin' like the room not ready for you."

She took it without fanfare, slipped it into the front pocket of her bag. Walked over, leaned down, and kissed me once—slow and full, like punctuation at the end of something that didn't need to be explained.

"No stress today," she said against my lips. "Mi link yuh later."

Then she was gone. No drama. No looking back.

Just her scent lingering in the room.

And me… sitting there, letting the weight of the last few days settle into the mattress.

* * *

I laid there a while after she left. Not because I was caught up. But because the quiet felt rare. The sheets still warm where her body had been. Her scent—sweet and earthy—still curling in the air like a shadow that hadn't figured out how to leave yet.

Then the phone buzzed again. And again.

The moment cracked open.

I grabbed it off the nightstand and thumbed it open.

The fellas were alive.

24 new messages.

Dev:

Just touched down. Customs long as fk. Why Jamaicans walk so slow?

Ty:

Yo where the Henny at?!? Who bringing the hookah?

Shawn:

Bruce, you got 2727 locked? Lmk what time we pull up. We want a section and bottles ready. Biiiiig vibes.

Aaron:

I need a Red Stripe in my hand the second I land. Don't play.

Dev:

I'm not tryna wait in no line tonight either. We good on that?

Ty:

We blowin' a bag, trust. Get the bottles up early so it look right when we walk in.

Voice notes. Memes. A TikTok link captioned:

"Tonight's energy."

A man falls off a table mid-twerk.

I sighed. Let the phone fall to my chest.

It was funny. Wild. The same chaotic humor we'd always had. But something in me didn't click the way it used to.

They were landing ready to turn up. I'd just spent the last few days learning how to slow the hell down.

Another buzz—this one from Shawn directly.

Shawn:

Yo, for real. You got the section right? Just let them know we good for it. I'll collect later tonight if anything. Just make sure we locked in.

I read it again.

"I'll collect later."

Jaw clenched. Not out of anger—just recognition. Nobody was planning to handle it up front. It was all vibes. All assumption. Like I'd just cover it.

And maybe I would've—before.

I sat up. Swung my legs over the edge of the bed. Feet on cool tile. Head buzzing louder than the chat.

I messaged Troy.

Me:

Yo, you around today?

One minute later:

Troy:

Yea man. What's good?

Me:

Crew's in town. Big night at 2727. Need to get there early. You free?

Troy:

Bet. Link mi later. Let's make sure them boys eat good.

I dropped the phone on the bed. Rubbed my face.

It was starting.

Not just the night.

But the shift.

That edge that came with expectation. With old energy walking back into a version of me I wasn't sure I wanted to wear again.

I stood, stretched, walked to the window. Outside, Montego Bay moved how it always did. No urgency. No ask.

Just rhythm.

I got dressed. White tee. Black jeans. Fresh shoes. Locs still tight from the twist. Crown blessed.

Tonight would be big. Loud. Full of familiar faces I wasn't sure I recognized anymore.

But first—I needed to link with Troy.

* * *

It was well past nine when I got there. The street was thick with motion—horns blaring, heels clacking on pavement, bass leaking from passing cars. Montego Bay was wide awake now, dressed in noise and sweat and perfume. The kind of night where everybody came out for something, even if they didn't know what.

2727 already had a small line curling out front. Not long yet, but the energy was stacking. The bass inside wasn't fully turned up, but you could feel it testing the walls—low and steady, like a warning.

Troy was outside, leaned against the wall just left of the entrance, blunt tucked between his fingers, watching the crowd like security and selector all at once. His eyes clocked me before I even got close.

He didn't smile at first. He just nodded like we'd seen each other earlier that day—even though it'd been a minute.

"Mi start wonder if Jo tie yuh up inna hills somewhere."

I laughed as we dapped up. "You wouldn't be far off."

He passed the blunt toward me. I waved it off.

"You good though?" he asked, watching me closer.

I shrugged. "Just wanted to make sure everything still tight for tonight. Wristbands, bottles, section—all that."

He nodded. "Dem ready inside. Keem say everything lock from earlier. Mi just holdin' di line til vibe kick proper."

I looked around. The street was starting to swell—more heels, more chains, more cologne, more expectation.

Troy nudged me. "Group reach?"

"This morning. Group chat been reckless ever since."

He chuckled. "Dem on full-send already?"

"Worse."

He grinned. "Yuh better pray nobody vomit pon di sofa again."

I groaned. "Don't even put that in the air."

We stood like that a moment. Watching Montego Bay flex.

A car pulled up slow. Someone yelled across the road. A woman in a red dress laughed loud as hell and kissed a man's neck like she ain't care who saw. The air smelled like jerk smoke and champagne dreams.

Troy looked me over again, then shook his head like he'd just seen the full picture.

"Mi cyaan believe yuh touch down, get mash up by Candice one night, and then come back outside pon a handholdin' vibe wid Jovel like it ain't di same man."

I laughed. "Wow. You really just throwing that out there?"

He took a slow pull from the blunt, exhaled like judgment was floating in the smoke. "Mi only speak facts. Candice tek yuh soul then disappear like a DJ pack up set. Now yuh lookin' like yuh writing poetry in yuh head."

"First of all," I said, grinning, "I was writing poetry. Just didn't say it out loud."

Troy laughed loud, smacking his chest. "Mi knew it! Bro type di word 'vulnerability' in Notes app and been soft since!"

I shook my head. "And yet, somehow... I don't miss Candice at all."

He paused. "Mi wouldn't either. Yuh paid enough."

We both cracked up.

Then he cut his eyes at me. "So Jo really got you wrapped already, eh?"

"She don't have me wrapped," I said, half-convincing.

He gave me a look.

I smirked. "She just... got her own gravity. Ain't like anything I expected."

Troy nodded slow, leaned back against the wall again. "She different still. Soft edge, sharp mind. One of dem woman yuh haffi pay attention to or she gone before yuh blink."

"I been paying attention."

"Mek sure. She not one fi repeat herself."

I let that sit for a second, then pointed at him. "You sound like you speaking from experience."

He sucked his teeth. "Mi plead di fifth."

Another beat of silence.

Then he added, "But mi respect it. Jo a real one. And yuh... yuh move different since yuh been here. Like yuh finally breathing proper."

I nodded, serious now. "Been feeling that too."

Troy tilted his head. "Good. But don't go soft tonight. Vibes ago mad. Brace fi di full show."

"I'm built for it."

He grinned. "We gon' see. Just don't start crying if yuh see Jo buss a wine pon somebody else. Mi not holdin' yuh through that."

I squinted. "Why would you even say that?"

"Mi like preparation. Mental training. Yuh American boys too emotional when yuh get outclassed."

I laughed, harder than I expected. "You talk so much shit."

"Yuh need it. Keep yuh grounded."

He tapped my chest with the back of his hand, then nodded toward the street. "Come. Let's mek sure inside crisp before yuh crew touch down and claim everything expensive."

He grinned, then turned toward the door. "Come, let's link Keem before yuh crew flood di place."

* * *

Inside, the pulse was heavier. Lights low, tables being staged. The air already thick with hookah smoke and anticipation. A few early birds lounged in the corner, sipping cocktails and watching the setup like investors.

Keem saw us coming and waved. Daps all around.

"Section ready. Bottles in queue. Hookah setup too. Mi even pull out di pineapple head ting y'all like."

I nodded. "Appreciate it."

Keem leaned in. "One ting—just make sure yuh boys nuh wild out on credit tonight. Di last time…"

"I got it," I said. "They'll come correct."

I hoped.

Troy clapped me on the back. "Well then. Time fi watch di city move."

And just like that, we posted up. Frontline. Waiting for the night to show us what kind of beast it planned to be.

* * *

Inside was already humming by the time we stepped in. Lights low, music thick, bass pressing against the walls like it wanted out. Hookah smoke rising slow over velvet couches. Staff moving with that pre-rush sharpness—tight turns, eyes scanning, no wasted motion.

I walked the section, checking the setup. Three bottles staged. Two hookahs pre-packed. Ice bucket already sweating.

Everything was locked.

Troy peeled off toward the bar. I posted up near the edge of the section, drink in hand, letting the moment settle. Letting my body remember this rhythm. The pulse of a good night before it explodes.

Then came the buzz at the door.

The fellas started pouring in—loud, grinning, charged up from the plane, the street, the rum punch they definitely grabbed before changing clothes. Loud greetings. Loud cologne. Even louder outfits.

Dev was first—college boy cool in linen and loafers.

"Bruce!" he shouted, arms wide like we ain't text all day. "My guy really running things in JA!"

We hugged, the kind that smacks shoulders twice and ends in a fist.

Ty followed behind him, already with a Red Stripe in one hand and a Bluetooth speaker in the other for no reason. He nodded toward the hookah.

"This that pineapple shit?" he asked.

"Fresh packed."

"My boy."

More showed up by the minute. I knew half, recognized a few, didn't know the rest at all. But they came in like I was the nucleus—dapping me, praising the setup, telling me "this the f**king vibe, bro" like I built the building myself.

I smiled through most of it. Played the role.

But in my chest, something hovered.

Then she walked in.

Jovel.

Hair freshly styled, edges kissed to perfection. A dark green dress that didn't cling, just followed her. Slit up the side. Skin glowing like the whole city paused to make room for her entrance.

She scanned the room, eyes finding me with no effort.

I didn't move.

Just nodded.

She nodded back—cool, composed, a soft curve at the corner of her lips. Then she floated in, greeting people with that effortless warmth, but keeping her radius tight.

She didn't sit close. Didn't hover. Just… existed. Like she was watching me now.

Before I could move toward her, I caught a flash of someone else—Lora.

Hair pinned up. Off-shoulder top. Bright smile.

She spotted me instantly and headed over.

"Bruce!" she said, voice already in flirt-mode. "I almost didn't recognize you without a laptop in front of your face."

We hugged. Light. Quick.

"Didn't know you were coming," I said.

She tilted her head. "Tiff told me about the trip weeks ago. I just assumed she mentioned it."

Right.

Tiff.

The situationship I'd cleanly forgotten in the whirlwind of Jo's orbit.

"Glad you made it," I offered, eyes flicking toward Jovel.

Lora followed my gaze. Said nothing, but clocked everything.

The music shifted. DJ talking his talk now. Bass turned up.

Drinks started flowing harder. Hookah passed like communion.

The section filled.

Laughter. Hands in the air. Somebody's girl dancing too close to somebody's boy. Cameras flashing. Troy lighting a fresh blunt in the corner, vibing with two women he didn't walk in with.

I moved through it all. Took shots. Posed for a few flicks. Nodded through conversations.

But the whole time… I felt Jo on the edge of my field of vision.

She wasn't cold.

Just reserved. Like she didn't need to compete. Like she'd already seen this version of me play out before.

At one point, she caught me mid-laugh and smirked.

Not jealous.

Not distant.

Just knowing.

The night hit its stride around midnight. Bottles refilled. Hookahs relit. Somebody spilled something expensive and nobody flinched. The DJ found his rhythm—Afrobeats into dancehall into trap, weaving the crowd like thread through a needle.

Our section overflowed. Chairs dragged in from other tables. People leaning, laughing, bubbling in time with the bass. Every few minutes, someone new walked up with a hug, a story, a drink.

I played host. Gave daps. Shared shots. Smiled like I meant it.

But every time I broke free, I found my way back to her.

Jo.

Sitting cool on the leather bench, sipping something brown, her dress catching the blue lights like it was made for this room. She wasn't trying to be seen—just couldn't help it.

I slid in next to her during a lull. Our legs touched. She didn't move.

"Enjoying yourself?" I asked.

She nodded, eyes scanning the dance floor. "Mi like watching people when dem loose. Show who dey really are."

"Yeah?"

She turned to me, one brow raised. "Yuh watchin' too?"

"Always."

She smirked. "Good. Then yuh see how dat girl been eyein' yuh fi di last ten minutes?"

I laughed low. "Which one?"

"Di one walking over right now."

I turned just as Lora approached, holding a drink and wearing that same flirty smile she always led with.

"Interrupting something?" she asked, glancing between us.

Jo stayed cool. Sipped her drink. Didn't lean in. Didn't pull away.

"Nah," I said, "just catching my breath."

Lora looked at Jo, then back at me. "You been dodging me all night."

"I've been playing host."

"Mm." She raised her glass. "You're doing a great job. Place looks good. Crowd's sexy."

"Appreciate it."

She leaned in slightly—not close enough to be disrespectful, but just enough to make her point. "So… who's the girl?"

Jo's laughter came sudden, low, from her throat. She stood slowly, placed her glass down.

"I'm gonna get some air," she said, eyes flicking to me. "When yuh done entertaining, find me."

Then she was gone—just like that.

Lora watched her walk off. "She's gorgeous," she said.

"She is."

"So, what's the story?"

I sighed. "That's not tonight's conversation."

"Fair," she said. "But Tiff doesn't know, does she?"

I met her eyes. "Well, with you here? I know for a fact she does now."

That got a smile out of her. "You think I'd run and tell?"

"No," I said, "but you don't need to. Just you showing up, looking around, clocking everything? That's enough."

"Damn," she said. "That's harsh."

"It's true."

She swirled her drink, then leaned on the table with one arm. "Tiff gets in tomorrow."

I nodded. "You staying for the wedding?"

"Wasn't planning to," she said. "But now I'm curious."

I laughed. "Dangerous word."

She smirked. "I know."

We let the beat fill the space between us. Then she added, "She's not just a fling, huh?"

I didn't answer.

Didn't have to.

Lora nodded slowly, stepping back. "Alright. That's for another day."

Then she was gone—slipping back into the crowd, hips catching the beat, drink still half full.

And me?

I turned, eyes scanning for Jo.

The night was still burning.

But the temperature had changed.

I found Jo near the back lounge, where the bass softened just enough to hear your own thoughts. She stood with one leg crossed over the other, her back against the wall, staring out at the dance floor like she was watching a movie she'd already seen.

She didn't look at me right away.

"You good?" I asked, sliding up beside her.

"Mi fine."

"Really?"

She glanced over, lips twitching into a smile. "Mi not di jealous type, Bruce. Mi read energy, not wardrobe choices."

I laughed.

"But since she clearly wanted answers..." I said, pausing for effect. "I figured I should give them to you first."

That got her attention.

"Go on."

"There's someone named Tiff. We're open. Casual. Been a little on and off. She's flying in tomorrow."

Jo didn't flinch. She just nodded once.

"Alright."

"That's it?"

"What else yuh want mi fi say?" she asked. "Yuh wasn't mine when mi meet yuh. Still not mine. Mi just like yuh."

I exhaled, a soft laugh in my chest. "You really don't play games, huh?"

She sipped her drink. "Mi too grown fi pretend mi don't know what freedom feel like."

I stepped closer. "Still like you, though."

Her eyes didn't move. "Mi know."

For a second, it felt like the night had returned to form. The beat rolling back in. The smoke curling upward. Her body warming the space between us.

Then one of the waitresses approached. Not dancing. Not smiling.

"Excuse me. Who is handling the bill?"

I blinked. "What?"

"The bill," she repeated. "Bottle service, hookah, everything in the section."

I looked over—people were starting to clear out. Half the crew gone already. Some of them mid-convo outside. Some just... vanished.

Jo tilted her head. "Dem ain't pay?"

I stepped forward. "Hold on, Shawn said—"

She cut in. "Shawn nuh deh here."

The waitress handed me the check. I looked at the total.

$5,023.75

My throat tightened.

I reached for my wallet. Card in hand. Tried to stay calm.

Swiped it once.

Declined.

"Try again."

Declined again.

"Do you have another method?"

Jo stepped in, already reading my face. "What happen?"

"Card's tripping. Probably flagged for international fraud." I looked at the waitress. "It'll go through in a second."

Another man stepped close. Tall. Shirt too tight. Security.

He didn't say anything—just hovered, eyes watching, posture straight.

Jo turned toward him. "Yuh really hovering like we plan to run off?"

"Just doing my job."

Her voice rose. "Di man not even walk toward di door yet. Yuh deh here like we criminal?"

"Ma'am—"

"Mi not yuh ma'am. Mi his woman. An' if his own damn friends had any shame, we wouldn't be here explaining nothing!"

"Jo," I said quietly, hand on her arm. "Please."

She yanked away. "Nah. Mi vex now."

A few heads turned. The DJ lowered the music just enough for the tension to breathe.

Jo stepped toward the waitress now. "Y'all watching him like thief, but di real thieves is di ones who drink, dance, tek pictures and bounce."

The security guard took a step forward. I stepped in front of Jo.

"We're not running. We're not leaving. We're gonna handle it," I said. Calm. Clear. My voice solid in the air.

Another card swipe.

Nothing.

Jo fumed beside me, pacing tight, arms folded. "Mi cyaan believe this. Five thousand dollars fi people who swear dem love yuh."

"I'll get through to someone," I muttered, already dialing Shawn.

No answer.

Texted him.

Bro. They're holding me here over the tab. Call me.

No response.

Jo looked ready to throw a chair. "Mi swear if mi see Shawn tonight mi buss him head."

"Jo—please." I put a hand on her waist, trying to pull her back into my center. "Let me fix it."

"You shouldn't have to."

"I know."

But I did.

We didn't talk the rest of the walk.

* * *

Just moved through the city like we were dragging something invisible behind us. The night still buzzed around us—cars, laughter, the distant thump of music from another party already in motion—but none of it touched us.

Jo still fuming.

Me still calculating.

Not just the money.

The cost of keeping people close who only know how to show up when the bill's not in their name.

16

Let Yuhself Be Seen

We didn't say much when we got back to the apartment. The door clicked shut behind us like it was sealing something in. No shoes kicked off. No music playing. Just that soft weight of being too tired to pretend, too wired to sleep.

Jo walked past me without a word and headed for the bathroom. I heard the sink run. A cabinet close. Then silence again.

I stood in the middle of the room, looking around like I wasn't sure what I needed. Wallet? Water? Peace?

Eventually, I sat on the edge of the bed, elbows on knees, head hanging low.

She came out a few minutes later, face washed, lashes bare. Her earrings were gone. That dress she wore like a second skin had been replaced with one of my old t-shirts—oversized and slipping off one shoulder. Still stunning. But quieter now. No spotlight.

She moved around the room slow, deliberate. No edge to it. But I could feel something rising.

"Jo," I said, voice low.

She didn't answer right away. She just kept folding her dress and laying it flat across the back of a chair like she didn't want it wrinkled, like she was trying to keep order somewhere.

When she finally turned to face me, her arms were crossed tight across her chest.

"Yuh know mi hate dat, right?"

I looked up. "What?"

"Seeing yuh out there. Stressin'. Looking fi help. An' all yuh friends? Gone."

Her voice didn't raise. But it cracked a little—just enough to let the truth bleed through.

"Mi stood next to yuh, Bruce. Watched yuh try card after card. Watched yuh call man who never answer. Watched security hover like yuh was some thief tryna dip out on a bill you ain't even run up alone."

I took a breath. "I didn't expect—"

She cut in. "Exactly. Yuh didn't expect to be abandoned. But yuh was."

I stood now. Not defensive. Just needing to meet her where she was.

"I asked Shawn to collect ahead of time. He said he'd handle it."

"Well, he didn't," she said, jaw clenching. "An' now mi cyaan unsee dat. Mi cyaan unfeel it."

She stepped forward. "You ever watch someone you care about stand in the middle of a mess they didn't create and still try fi clean it up like it's theirs?"

I didn't respond. I just looked at her. Really looked at her.

Eyes still sharp. Chest rising. Hair still smelling like cinnamon and sweat and something sweet I didn't have a name for.

"I wasn't mad at dem," she said, softer now. "Mi was mad at you. Because you just took it. Swallowed it. Like dat was normal."

"I didn't know what else to do."

She nodded, eyes glistening but no tears falling. "Yuh so used to holding everybody else up, yuh forget yuh supposed to be held too."

That landed deep.

I didn't even realize I'd sat back down until she stepped between my knees and placed both hands on my face.

"You not alone, Bruce," she said. "Not if yuh let yuhself be seen."

I swallowed.

Her thumbs brushed across my cheeks—gentle, but firm. Like she was wiping off everything I tried not to carry back inside with me.

"You still want me here?" she asked.

I didn't even blink.

"Yeah. I do."

* * *

Her hands stayed on my face, warm and grounding, like she was holding me in place while the rest of the world tried to pull me apart.

"You ever hear di story of di tree dat bend too long?" she asked, voice low, rhythm slow.

I shook my head.

She didn't rush.

"Maroon elders used to tell mi when mi was young—dere's a tree that bend in storm after storm. Not because it weak. But because it strong enough to hold di weight. Every wind come, every flood rise, and it still deh pon it's root."

I closed my eyes, letting the image form.

"But one day," she continued, "dat tree bend so long, so silent... it forget it was supposed to stand."

She let that settle. Didn't rush to fill the silence. She just let the words find their place between us.

"You been bendin', Bruce," she whispered. "So long. So proud. Carryin' everybody. Holding shit up like yuh made of steel."

Her thumbs ran slow along my jawline now, eyes locked on mine.

"But steel rust too."

Something tightened in my chest. Something small but loud.

She sat on my lap now, slow and sure, never breaking eye contact.

"Mi see how yuh move. How yuh let people love yuh just enough fi stay in dey good graces, but never deep enough fi ask yuh if yuh tired."

I didn't respond.

Couldn't.

"Mi see how yuh laugh when yuh supposed to speak. How yuh stay quiet

211

when yuh really want fi shout."

She touched the center of my chest.

"Yuh heart full of echo, Bruce. Mi feel it."

My hands found her waist without thinking. Just needing to hold something that wasn't slipping away.

She leaned in, forehead pressed against mine.

"Mi not here to fix yuh. Or save yuh. But mi not gonna stand quiet while yuh keep pretending you alright when yuh drowning behind closed doors."

A beat passed.

Another.

Then she pulled back, just far enough to meet my eyes again.

"Maroon blood nuh play wid survival," she said. "We fight. We love. We stay whole. Even when di world try splinter we."

Her voice softened.

"Let me help yuh stay whole."

* * *

Jo didn't move. Still naked on my lap, her hands resting against my chest like she was reading something beneath the skin. Not just warmth—witness.

"You ever wonder why yuh so quiet when yuh hurting?" she asked, voice like steam rising from warm ground.

I swallowed. "I'm not always hurting."

"No," she said. "But yuh always hiding."

She didn't say it to cut me. There was no venom. Just knowing.

My hands slid up her back, slow. "You say that like you been watching me longer than a few days."

She tilted her head, eyes searching mine.

"Bruce… yuh wear pain like furniture. Like it belong in yuh house. Comfortable. Familiar. Nah outta place."

I sat with that. Let it sting a little. Because she wasn't wrong.

"I've always been the one people lean on," I said. "Family. Friends. Work. I'm the stable one."

She nodded. "Stable don't mean whole."

I laughed—low and bitter. "If I cracked, who was gonna step in?"

Jo leaned back slightly, resting her weight on my thighs. "So yuh became what everybody needed."

"Yeah."

"And nobody ever asked what yuh needed?"

I met her eyes. "No."

She looked at me for a long time. Not blinking. Not rushing.

"Mi hate dat," she said. "Mi hate that yuh think that's noble. That silence is strength."

I didn't have words. Just breath.

She touched my cheek again, this time softer. "When mi son's father died, mi thought mi had to be solid. For mi boy. For mi family. For everybody."

Her voice dipped.

"Mi move like stone. Hard. Still. Strong. But inside? Mi was drowning."

That landed.

She pressed her forehead to mine.

"Grief nuh always show up like cryin'. Sometimes it just feel like numb."

I closed my eyes.

"And sometimes," she whispered, "healing don't start until somebody say—yuh nuh haffi be strong right now."

My throat tightened. My grip on her waist did too.

She kissed my jaw. My neck. Slow and reverent.

"You don't owe strength to nobody tonight," she said. "Not even yuhself."

* * *

Her words didn't echo—they rooted. Anchored themselves under my ribs like they'd been waiting for the right silence to settle into.

You don't owe strength to nobody tonight.

She said it like prayer. Like permission. Like prophecy.

And I believed her.

Her hands moved first—sliding down my chest, palms warm, fingers spread like she wanted to feel every inch of me beneath them. Not to tease. Not to perform.

Just to be there.

My hands followed—up her thighs, slow and steady. Flesh warm. Breath heavier. She was still naked on my lap, but nothing about it felt rushed.

It felt earned.

She kissed my neck again. Slower this time. Mouth open. Lips soft. Her teeth scraped gently against my jaw like she was peeling back the day.

She pulled back just enough to look at me.

"You ready fi let go?" she asked.

I nodded. But she wasn't accepting that.

"Say it."

I swallowed, then met her eyes. "Yeah. I'm ready."

She kissed me deep then—tongue sliding against mine, hands gripping the back of my head like she wanted to pull the words from my throat and melt them between our lips.

She rose off my lap for a moment, fingers moving to my waistband again—unfastening, pulling, peeling fabric down my thighs until I was bare for her.

Then she climbed back onto me. Slow. Controlled.

When I entered her, we both exhaled like we'd been holding that breath for years.

She didn't move right away.

She just sat there.

Full of me.

Eyes locked on mine.

Her hands rested on my shoulders, and I placed mine on her waist like I was holding something fragile—but wanted to grip tight anyway.

"You feel that?" she whispered.

"Yeah."

"Don't run from it."

"I'm not."

She rolled her hips once. Just once. And the weight of it—slow and soaked—made me bite back a moan that came from somewhere deeper than pleasure.

This wasn't fast. Wasn't wild. Not yet.

This was her letting me unravel.

She moved with a rhythm that wasn't for show—it was reclamation. Not just of her body, but of mine. Of space. Of peace.

She rocked on top of me, slowly building a tempo that matched the breath between us.

I kissed her neck. Her chest. Ran my tongue between her breasts and held her tighter as she picked up speed—only slightly—but enough for her breath to catch.

"Mmm," she hummed into my ear. "That's it."

She pressed her forehead to mine again.

Her hips moved in lazy figure eights now—deep, slow grinds that had me damn near shaking. Not from friction.

From feeling.

"Mi love how yuh holding me," she whispered.

"Don't let go."

"Mi not."

I kissed her again. Harder. Gripped her ass and pulled her deeper onto me. Felt her pulse around me, wet and tight and warm like home. My eyes nearly rolled back when she clenched down, slow and steady, riding that line between pain and heaven.

"Fuck," I breathed.

She licked the side of my neck, then bit it. Soft, then sharp.

"Yuh always this loud when yuh give in?" she teased.

"Only with you."

That made her grind deeper.

We moved like that for a while—no rush, no chaos. Just waves. Just motion.

Just heat pressing against heat in a room where everything else had fallen away.

When it finally broke—when my hips started bucking harder, my hands gripping her like rope—it wasn't because I wanted to cum.

It was because I didn't want to lose her inside this moment.

But she led it.

She whispered to me to let go.

And when I did?

I damn near wept into her neck.

She gripped my shoulders tighter, nails dragging down my back as she picked up the rhythm—hips rolling with a new urgency, like all that restraint was finally unraveling.

"Yuh feel too fuckin' good," she hissed, head tilting back.

My hands slid to her ass, grabbing two full handfuls, pulling her down harder with every grind.

"You takin' this dick like you missed it," I muttered against her neck.

She leaned in close, lips brushing my ear. "Mi takin' it cause it mine right now. So give it."

And I did.

Thrust up into her hard—deep enough to make her yelp, breath hitching in her throat.

She rode back down on me, grinding slow with her knees pressed tight against my ribs, the heat between us soaking the sheets beneath. Our skin slapped in rhythm now, slick and wild.

Her breasts bounced with every motion. I caught one in my mouth, sucked deep while she cursed in Patois, voice breaking apart with every bounce of her hips.

"Mi cyaan—Bruce, fuck—mi cyaan tek—"

"You takin' it," I growled. "All of it."

She started to lose the rhythm, started to tremble.

That's when I flipped her—grabbed her waist, threw her on her back without warning. Her mouth dropped open but before she could speak, I slid back inside her, deep and fast.

She screamed.

Not a high-pitched wail. A gut-sound. A claiming.

I hooked one of her legs over my shoulder and buried myself to the base, slamming into her over and over, every stroke harder, deeper, wetter.

The sound of us—slap slap slap—filled the room.Just moans and curses and the creak of the bed under the weight of everything we were letting go.

"You like this?" I grunted, sweat dripping down my back.

She clawed at the sheets, nodded, gasped.

"Say it."

"Mi fuckin' love it," she panted, voice cracking.

I spat in my hand, rubbed her clit hard while I stroked deep. She bucked, body arching like her soul was trying to escape through her spine.

She was close. I could feel it in the way her thighs started to shake—tightening around my hips, then pulling me in deeper like she needed every inch buried inside her.

Her head rolled to the side, mouth open, breath jagged.

"Bruce—Bruce—mi close, mi—"

"Don't run from it," I growled, my voice already fraying.

Her back arched off the mattress. I locked one hand behind her knee and pressed it to her chest, folding her in half. My other hand slid down to her clit, rubbing tight, fast circles as I pounded into her.

"Fuck—fuck—right there—right there!"

Her whole body bucked beneath me. Then—

She broke.

Her pussy clenched hard, wetness flooding over my dick, then a sudden rush—a hot burst of liquid that sprayed against my thighs, soaked my pelvis, coated everything between us.

I froze for half a second.

Caught off guard.

The sound it made. The way her eyes flew open, wild and locked on mine. Her mouth trembling.

"Did you just—"

She nodded, dazed and breathless.

My whole body tensed. Not from surprise anymore.

From pure hunger.

That sound—all that wetness hitting me—woke something deep.

I gripped her waist with both hands and started driving into her harder. No more measured thrusts. No more slow build.

Just wet skin and raw need.

The slickness between us amplified every stroke—louder, messier, filthier.

She whimpered.

I growled.

I leaned over her, one hand on her throat, my weight pressing her into the mattress as I slammed into her soaked cunt with everything I had.

"Yuh like squirting all over this dick, huh?"

Her eyes rolled back.

"Yuh gon do it again," I whispered. "Gon make a fuckin' mess."

She clawed at my back, nails digging in as she tried to hold on—but I didn't let her.

I wanted her to feel every stroke. Every inch.

Because this wasn't about control anymore.

It was about surrender.

And Jo just gave me everything.

I didn't stop after she squirted. Couldn't. That wet sound between us—the slap of skin against soaked flesh—sent me somewhere deeper.

I wasn't just fucking. I was feeding something I hadn't touched in years.

I caught my reflection in the dark glass—hips moving, jaw clenched—like I was watching another man wear my skin.

Jo took it all.

Her legs still shaking. Her breath stuttering. But she didn't ask me to slow down.

She opened her mouth and let out a breathy, "Yes, baby… gimme all of it."

I flipped her over, rough but not reckless. Bent her at the waist, ass in the air, back arched perfectly like her body was built for this.

And when I slid back in, the heat damn near blinded me.

She was dripping—soaking. Slick running down her thighs, coating my shaft, making the thrusts louder, nastier, more urgent.

I grabbed her waist and slammed into her, hard.

Her body jolted forward.

She moaned so loud it echoed off the walls.

I locked a hand on the back of her neck and pressed her face to the mattress.

"Keep that ass up."

"F-fuck," she gasped. "Bruce—what—what is this?"

"This?" I growled, pounding into her, hips snapping with precision and power. "This is everything I've been holding in."

She tried to speak again—some broken plea—but all that came out was a moan.

I pulled out for a second, just enough to watch her pussy clench around nothing—dripping.

Then I slid two fingers inside her—fast and deep.

She screamed.

"Look at you," I said, breath thick with heat. "Drippin' all over my damn sheets."

Her walls fluttered around my fingers, her body trying to hold onto the rhythm. But I didn't let her.

I fingered her harder, faster, then leaned down and growled into her ear.

"Who's pussy is this?"

"Yours," she whimpered.

"Say it louder."

"It's yours, Bruce. Fuck—it's all yours."

I stood again, grabbed her hips, and fucked her with every ounce of frustration, passion, and possession I had left.

The sounds—the wetness, the rhythm, the heat—drowned out everything else.

Then it shifted.

She moaned differently. Her breath caught again.

And I felt it—the way her body gripped me. Tighter. Pulsing. Shaking.

She was close. Again.

But this time, so was I.

I clenched my jaw, trying to hold it—but Jo must've felt it.

She looked back at me, eyes low and wild.

Then she slid off the bed and dropped to her knees.

I froze.

She looked up, licking her lips. "Cum for me."

"Jo—"

"Don't fight it. Gimme that nut."

She gripped my dick, still slick with her juices, and stroked me slow, then fast, then back to slow—watching me, coaxing the orgasm like it belonged to her.

And it did.

My legs locked.

My breath stopped.

Then I exploded.

She opened her mouth, lips wrapped around the tip, and took all of it. Every. Single. Drop.

Didn't flinch.

Didn't miss.

Swallowed me whole like she'd been waiting for that taste since the day we met.

* * *

Even after I was done, she kept sucking—slow and warm—tongue teasing me through the twitch.

When she finally let me go, she licked her lips and wiped the corner of her mouth with the back of her hand.

Then looked up and said, "Told yuh... mi not leavin' yuh alone."

Been catching myself narrating the room lately, like I'm watching a scene I'm in instead of living it. Not dramatic—just easier sometimes to float above and call the shots from the cheap seats. Maybe that's how I keep from feeling everything at once.

17

She Don't Bend Fi No One

By morning, that habit was still on me. The city slid by outside the window and I didn't feel inside it anymore—more like I was hovering a few feet back, watching the man in the backseat and taking notes.

The city rolled past in slow frames—fruit stands, zinc fences, barefoot boys chasing shadows. The morning heat moved like syrup, thick and stubborn, bleeding through the cracked windows of Dez's car.

Dez drove one-handed, the other resting on the door, fingers drumming slow. No music. No AC. Just motion and the kind of silence that made space for thought.

Jo sat next to Bruce in the backseat, body turned toward the window. Her shades caught light. Her mouth didn't move. She'd been silent since they left.

Bruce wasn't in a rush to change that.

He leaned forward a little, elbow resting against the back of the front seat. His eyes tracked the road, but his mind drifted—back to last night, to this morning, to whatever came next.

He didn't realize Dez was watching him in the rearview until he heard the voice.

"You been listenin'."

Bruce looked up. "What's that?"

Dez didn't smile. He just nodded toward the window like it held answers.

"The island. She been talkin' to you. Took a minute, but you finally hearin' her."

Bruce didn't respond right away.

He thought about it. Thought about the beach. The breeze in Jo's hair. The way his body had stopped needing to narrate every damn thing. The stillness. The sound between sounds.

"Yeah," he said. "I think I have."

But part of him still wasn't sure what he was hearing. Or what it meant to keep listening when the noise came from inside.

Dez chuckled—low, almost private.

"Mi see it. First time you ride with me, yuh whole body was tight. Like yuh was still tryna finish a meeting in yuh head."

Bruce smirked. "Probably was."

"Now?" Dez glanced back again. "Yuh quiet. But not in that lost kinda way. More like… yuh choosin' not to talk."

Bruce nodded. "Been doin' a lot of that."

Dez took a turn without signaling. The car dipped slightly and straightened out. The road widened.

"People come here tryin' fi change the island," Dez said. "Force it to fit them. Same way they live, same way they love. They don't last long. Island don't bend fi no one."

Bruce let that sit.

Dez continued, voice softer now. "But when yuh start to listen? She hold yuh different. Show yuh yuhself. Not always gentle. But always real."

A pause.

Then Dez glanced once at Jo through the mirror—just a flicker of recognition, not curiosity. Just respect.

"Mi see yuh too, Empress," he said gently. "Whole space shift when yuh step in."

Jo didn't turn. But her fingers, which had been still for most of the ride, moved slightly—brushed against her own thigh, like an awkward acknowledgment passed between them.

They passed the sign for the RIU. Security up ahead. The gate. The uniforms. The tray of warm champagne flutes under a fake smile of sun.

Dez slowed.

"You wan mi wait?"

Bruce looked at Jo, still silent, then back toward the gate. "Nah. We're good."

Dez gave a single nod. "Aight. But remember—listenin' don't end at the shoreline."

Bruce opened the door.

"Appreciate you," he said.

Dez looked over his shoulder one last time.

"Yuh movin' better now, bredren. Don't stop just 'cause yuh reach where everybody else expect yuh to be."

Bruce nodded. Stepped out.

The heat hit him first. Then the sound—the polite hum of luxury. Glass clinking. Flip flops on tile. Someone laughing at a joke told in a voice too loud for the moment.

He turned just slightly, watching as Jo moved ahead—shoulders tall, walk easy, like she didn't need to prove anything to this space.

And then he noticed it:

The shadow of the resort's arch stretching across the pavement like a line.

She'd already crossed it.

Bruce stood there a second longer than necessary... then followed.

* * *

The lobby was designed to impress. High ceilings. Cold marble underfoot. Columns that reached up like they were trying to hold back the heat. A chandelier the size of a Kia hung overhead, sparkling like it was still auditioning for attention.

Everything felt white. The floors, the curtains, the staff uniforms, even the light had been scrubbed sterile. It didn't smell like Jamaica. It smelled like lemon polish and refrigerated fruit.

Bruce walked beside Jo, their footsteps echoing off tile. No one greeted them. No cold towel. No welcome drink. Just the murmur of front desk staff and the distant splash of tourists already drunk enough to treat the pool like a dance floor.

Jo didn't say anything. She moved with intention, eyes scanning but not lingering. The calm she wore wasn't for show. It was armor.

There were only three people ahead of them in line, but the wait dragged. Bruce adjusted the strap on his bag. Jo shifted her weight once, then went still again.

She wasn't tense.

She was bracing.

Bruce felt it in the air, in the way her mouth had settled into that tight, unreadable line. He thought about saying something. *You good? Want me to handle it?* But he didn't. Not because he was afraid—because he knew better.

Finally, the woman behind the desk looked up and smiled.

"Good afternoon. Checking in?"

"Yeah," Bruce said. "Bruce Williamson. Just one guest."

The woman typed. "Okay, Mr. Williamson… three nights, junior suite. I've got you right here."

Click-clack-click.

Bruce glanced at Jo, then back at the clerk.

"Is it possible to get a day pass for her?"

The woman's smile stiffened just slightly. She looked at Jo for the first time with real attention.

"Can I see her ID, please?"

Jo handed it over.

The clerk read it, blinked once, then glanced down at her screen.

"I'm sorry," she said, tone too practiced, too rehearsed. "Unfortunately, we're not able to issue day passes in this case."

No explanation.

Just *this case*.

Jo didn't speak at first.

She just stared at the woman for a second longer than was comfortable. Then took a single step forward. Her voice stayed low.

"I'm sorry, what exactly is 'this case?'"

The woman glanced back at the screen. "Our system doesn't allow certain profiles to be issued passes without prior management clearance. It's a resort policy."

Jo's smile wasn't a smile. "And by 'certain profiles' you mean people who live here?"

The woman didn't answer.

Didn't need to.

The message had already landed.

Jo nodded slowly. Not backing down. Not raising her voice either.

"It's always funny how we're welcome to serve, to clean, to sing onstage, to dance behind the bar—but not to stay. Not to sit in the sun and sip from the same glass."

Bruce touched her elbow lightly.

She looked at him—not angry, just awake.

He turned to the clerk. His voice stayed calm.

"Forget the day pass. Add her to the room."

The woman hesitated. "There'll be an additional charge—"

"That's fine."

He handed over his card.

The clerk began typing again. Eyes down. Jaw tight. Like the machine might save her from the discomfort.

Bruce took the keycards.

Jo didn't reach for hers.

They walked off together, past the welcome area, past the sculpture of an African queen molded in resin like a tourist prop. Past the concierge who gave a smile too delayed to mean anything.

As they reached the elevators, Bruce could still feel it—that quiet, polished violence of exclusion.

Jo finally spoke.

"Every time I start to forget," she said softly, "the island reminds me."

Bruce didn't say anything. He didn't need to.

He just reached for her hand.

And this time, she let him hold it.

* * *

Her hand was still in his when the elevator doors opened. Neither of them let go. They walked the beige hallway in step—slow and present. Bruce carried his bag in his free hand. Jo held nothing. Didn't need to. The weight of what just happened in the lobby hadn't lifted, but something had shifted. The sharpness was gone.

What remained was heat, memory, and the pressure of being watched in a space that swore it was welcoming.

Their room was halfway down the hall. Bruce slid the key in. The green light blinked once. He pushed the door open with his shoulder and held it for her.

Jo walked in first, but didn't let go until she had to.

The suite was generous but hollow. Oversized bed. Slick tile floors. A ceiling fan spinning like it was trying too hard to be tropical. The kind of decor that wanted to feel Jamaican without actually being of Jamaica. Bruce could already smell the chlorine from the pool, leaking through the balcony doors like an uninvited guest.

Jo walked over to the bed and sat on the edge, facing the far wall. Her sunglasses were still on. Her hands rested in her lap. Calm, but full.

Bruce set his bag down by the closet. He didn't move toward her yet. He just stood for a moment, watching her silhouette against the backdrop of the balcony curtains swaying in the breeze.

She took off her glasses and placed them gently on the nightstand.

Then, without looking at him, she spoke.

"I'm gonna nap."

Bruce nodded. "You want the bed?"

She shook her head, soft. "We can share it."

It wasn't an invitation. It wasn't distance either. Just permission to be

227

close without having to perform comfort.

He slipped off his shoes, walked to the opposite side, and lay down on top of the sheets. Not touching, but not far. Their bodies parallel, both staring up at the ceiling as the fan hummed above them.

The resort noise felt far away now—blunted by concrete, by fatigue, by everything the day had already said.

Bruce turned his head slightly and looked at her.

Jo's eyes were closed, but her breathing hadn't deepened yet.

She wasn't asleep.

Just resting.

Like her body needed silence before it needed dreams.

Bruce lay still beside her.

And for the first time in hours, the silence didn't feel like something between them.

It felt like something they were holding together.

* * *

They lay there for a while. Long enough for the light to shift across the ceiling. Long enough for the fan above them to hum its way into the rhythm of breath.

Bruce didn't know if Jo ever fell asleep.

But eventually, her eyes opened. She turned toward him, barely. Said nothing.

She didn't need to.

He slipped off the bed without a word, slid his shoes back on, and reached for the keycard. She didn't ask where he was going.

She just closed her eyes again like she understood.

And maybe she did.

* * *

The elevator ride down was quiet. But the silence this time wasn't heavy.

Just temporary. The kind you carry like a jacket into a room you know is already too warm.

The elevator opened onto a different kind of noise.

Laughter. Glass clinking. Pool sandals slapping against tile. The kind of volume that didn't come from chaos—it came from comfort. From knowing who you're around and how you're expected to show up.

Bruce followed the sound toward the open-air bar near the pool. Afternoon light bounced off the water and wrapped everything in a kind of artificial glow, like a filter over real life.

They were all there.

Shawn. Dev. Jay. A couple of the other guys from school. Matching polos, neon swim trunks, freshly twisted locs and shades that cost more than most people's rent. Everybody looked good. Loud. Alive.

Bruce walked up slow.

"Ayeee, Bruce Wayne in the buildin'!" Dev shouted, arms open like a preacher mid-sermon.

Bruce smiled. Dapped him up. Took the slap on the back from Shawn.

"Bout time you showed up," Shawn said, laughing. "We thought you went ghost again."

"Nah," Bruce said. "Just been… chillin."

He could feel the shift immediately.

Same crew. Same rhythm. But his body didn't move the same. The jokes hit different. The timing felt off—not because they'd changed.

Because he had.

Jay handed him a rum punch already half melted. "We celebratin', bro. Don't be on no zen retreat shit. You at the RIU now. Real life on pause."

Bruce nodded, took the cup. Sipped.

It was sweet. Too sweet.

"Where's Jo?" Dev asked, not bothering to keep his voice down.

Bruce just tilted his head toward the building. "She restin'."

Shawn raised an eyebrow but let it pass. Dev didn't.

"She aight? Or you tryna hide her from the circus?"

Bruce smirked, low. "She's good."

Lora walked up just then, sunglasses oversized, drink in hand. She didn't say anything at first—she just looked at Bruce like she already knew everything she needed to know. Then looked past him, toward the hallway leading to the rooms.

"Island girl not poolside?"

Bruce shook his head.

Lora smiled, but not in a friendly way. "Shame. I was hopin' to meet her."

Bruce didn't answer.

Shawn clapped his hands. "Aight, y'all gon let this man breathe or what? He came all the way out here to relax, not to be interrogated."

Dev raised his glass. "Facts. But we reservin' the right to ask more questions later."

Bruce smiled again. The performance kicked in easy. He knew the beats. The nods. The "y'all stupid" timed just right. The way to float on the surface without letting anyone dive too deep.

But as the conversation turned to wedding plans, group excursions, and who brought what for the weekend, Bruce couldn't stop hearing Dez's voice in the back of his head.

"Don't stop just 'cause yuh reach where everybody else expect yuh to be."

He looked down at his cup.

Felt the sugar coat his tongue.

Felt the old self trying to settle back into his skin.

And for the first time, he didn't know if that version of him even fit anymore.

He'd just laughed at something Jay said—something about who forgot to pack swim goggles like it was a survival essential—when he felt it.

Something shifted in the air.

Not tension. Not noise. Just a pause in the rhythm. Like the room had blinked.

Bruce was mid-laugh when he felt it—

That shift. That hush under the surface. Like a cymbal still ringing in a room that had gone quiet.

He turned, and there she was.

Tiff.

Approaching in a long burnt-orange sundress that moved like it had rhythm. Fresh braids, gold hoops, flats. Drink in one hand, that lazy kind of confidence in the other.

"Look who finally showed up," Bruce said, already standing.

She smiled—warm, not performative. Hugged him close, her chin grazing his shoulder.

"You act like I wasn't always coming."

When she pulled back, her hands stayed on his arms for a second too long. Familiar, not possessive.

"You good?" she asked.

"Yeah. Just been takin' it slow."

"Mmm." She tilted her head slightly. "That's new for you."

Bruce smiled.

The fellas clocked the exchange in silence—no jokes, not yet. Just watching the moment happen.

Tiff took a sip from her drink. "Y'all been out here long?"

"Couple hours," Bruce said. "Shawn had us startin' early."

"Of course he did." Her tone carried just enough amusement to let the group laugh along.

Then came Lora.

Sunglasses on. Walk slow. That oversized floaty kimono thing that made her look like she'd floated in on drama.

She passed right behind Tiff and Bruce, not stopping, but loud enough to be heard:

"Well damn, Bruce. You sure do like the scenic route lately."

She didn't wait for a response. She just kept walking—smile invisible, shade loud.

Tiff didn't turn. She just sipped her drink again, face unreadable.

Bruce exhaled through his nose. "That was unnecessary."

Tiff shrugged, soft. "Lora gon' be Lora."

Dev leaned back with a grin. "Boy, I'm just tryna make it to the wedding."

Shawn laughed. "I ain't seen this much passive tension since we rushed Alpha."

Bruce shook his head. "Y'all wild."

But in his chest, the air felt heavier. Not bad. Just full.

Tiff looked at him once more—eyes soft, steady.

No accusation.

No curiosity.

Just knowing.

"I'ma go find my room."

Bruce nodded. "You need anything, let me know."

She gave a small smile. "I always do."

Then turned and walked off, cool as ever.

The silence she left behind wasn't loud.

It was just... undeniable.

* * *

Tiff walked off, hips easy, eyes forward. Bruce watched her go for a beat, then turned back to the group. Shawn was already mid-sip. Dev raised both eyebrows, like he was trying not to say something smart but failing.

"Aight," Jay said, breaking the silence. "So... what page we on there?"

Bruce squinted. "There?"

"Yeah, bruh. There. That whole energy was like... I dunno. Some chapter we ain't read yet."

Bruce laughed under his breath. "We cool."

Shawn leaned in slightly. "Y'all still—?"

Bruce nodded once. "Still."

Dev shook his head, smiling. "Boy, y'all relationship like a jazz album. No hook, no bridge, just vibes."

Bruce sipped his drink. "Grown folks arrangements. That's all."

Jay smirked. "You say that like you the grown one."

Bruce tilted his head. "You see me out here?"

They laughed—soft, but real.

Shawn gave him a long look, then nodded slowly. "Tiff always had her own orbit. I respect that."

"Me too," Bruce said.

There was a pause. One of those stretches where everybody looked off in a different direction, letting the moment settle without smothering it.

Dev broke it. "So if y'all still cool... and she ain't trippin'..."

Jay leaned forward. "That mean somebody else got your attention?"

Bruce didn't answer. He just looked out at the pool.

Didn't smile. Didn't frown.

Just sipped slow.

Dev whistled. "Ahhh... say less."

Shawn laughed again, shaking his head. "Y'all gon get this man caught up before the rehearsal even starts."

Bruce chuckled with them, but the moment with Shawn still pressed against the back of his mind like a sore tooth.

The first call, that night—right after the party emptied out and the promoter pulled him aside with a smile gone cold.

Shawn had answered on the third ring, loud music still in the background.

"Damn, bro. I thought they got y'all squared away?"

Bruce remembered pausing. Choosing his words carefully.

"Nah. Everybody dipped. It's just me here."

Shawn's response had been light. Casual. "You got it though, right? I mean... you the one who linked it all up. Just handle it and I'll hit you tomorrow."

Click.

No follow-up. No "my bad." No thank you.

And when they saw each other earlier today, Bruce had brought it up again— just him and Shawn in passing, trying to give him a chance to acknowledge it.

Shawn laughed like he didn't hear the tension in Bruce's voice.

"You still worried about that? It's wedding week, bro. Don't trip over receipts."

That was the moment Bruce knew it wasn't an oversight.

It was a choice.

Not malicious.

But thoughtless.

And somehow, that stung more.

He didn't need the money back.

What he needed—what he had hoped for—was recognition. A simple "You held that down. I see you."

But what he got was a man floating above responsibility, riding the high of being celebrated while Bruce had been left to mop up the aftermath like staff.

He took another sip. Let the sugar sit on his tongue.

The laughter around him grew louder again.

But inside, Bruce was quieter than ever.

The sun had started slipping. The glow on the water was thinner now, breaking apart in pieces, like the day was trying to let go without making a scene.

"Yo, we supposed to be at the terrace in twenty!" Shawn called out, slapping the back of a chair like it owed him something. "Somebody find Jay's ass before they start the whole rehearsal without us."

Dev groaned, leaning heavy into the table. "Man, fuck a rehearsal. If I remember how to walk, I remember how to stand."

They laughed again—loose, careless, the way you laugh when the world's still easy and you're still sure you're the center of it.

Bruce smiled with them.

Automatic.

Like a muscle you forget you're flexing until it aches.

But under it, something burned.

It wasn't the money.

It wasn't the mistake.

It was the math nobody else seemed to be doing.

Five thousand dollars.

That was the number.

Not fifty. Not five hundred.

Five thousand.

Enough to sting.

Enough to leave a mark.

Enough that somebody should've noticed.

Should've said something.

Should've done something.

Bruce shifted his weight slightly, feeling the pull in his lower back, the stiffness that always came when you stood too long pretending you didn't mind being still.

Jo's voice floated back to him.

Not loud. Not urgent. Just steady, like breath.

"Everybody's your friend when you useful, B."

"But when you tired? When you need somebody to see you without you fixing, without you performing?"

"That's when you find out who really holding you... and who just holding space."

He swallowed against the syrupy film of rum punch still coating his tongue.

Nobody mentioned the tab.

Nobody even looked at him like anything had gone wrong.

Shawn had laughed it off.

The others had stepped around it, careful as dancers, pretending the floor wasn't cracked under their feet.

And Bruce?

He'd let them.

He wondered if that was his real role all along.

Not brother.

Not friend.

Just the one who handled it when the bill came due.

The fixer.

The cleaner.

The weight-bearer they didn't have to thank because they never asked—

because they always knew he would.

He stared out past the bar, past the lazy sway of the palm trees under the heavy sky.

Maybe Jo was right.

Maybe he hadn't been part of something real.

Maybe he'd just been really good at pretending.

Better at it than he thought.

A slow scrape of chairs broke the thought.

Dev throwing an arm around Jay's shoulders, yanking him into a half-drunken headlock.

Shawn laughing, voice loud enough to bounce off the marble columns. "Aight, fellas, let's roll out!"

They moved as a pack—still half-sloshed, still full of that easy swagger that said the world would catch them if they tripped.

Bruce moved too.

Feet falling into rhythm with the group.

Shoulders brushing. Voices echoing off the high ceilings like a song you used to know all the words to.

But inside, he wasn't floating anymore.

Wasn't treading water just to stay close.

He was walking.

Solid. Clear.

Not for them.

Not against them.

Just... for himself.

The lobby doors swung wide ahead of them, spilling out the gold-dipped light of early evening, and Bruce stepped into it without hesitating.

He wasn't trying to fit it.

Wasn't trying to fix it.

He was just moving.

And this time, he wasn't carrying anything that didn't belong to him.

The heat, the noise, the name of me—everything hit at once, and I snapped back into my body like a door slamming. I wasn't watching anymore. I was here.

18

Fuck You Say to Me?

The glass sweated in my hand as we moved out into the sun again. My body was already loose from the drinks—just enough to feel the sway of it in my chest, not enough to trip. Laughter floated somewhere behind me, low and broken up, like whatever joke we were laughing at had already faded into something else.

We walked in a loose pack—Dev, Ty, a couple of the other boys from college, some of Shawn's cousins I couldn't keep track of.

Nobody rushed.

This wasn't the wedding yet. This was still the part where you could move slow, joke loud, pretend all the little cracks you were starting to see weren't real.

The hotel grounds stretched out wide around us—white stone paths curling between patches of green that looked too manicured to be real. A golf cart zipped past, carrying a family dressed like they were auditioning for a sandals ad—matching shirts, new sandals, too many smiles.

We didn't belong to that world.

And we didn't care.

Ty bumped my shoulder with his, nodding toward the golf cart.

"Bet they got a whole matching breakfast too," he said, grinning.

Dev snorted. "Pancakes and fake-ass memories."

I laughed, letting the sound roll out easy.

It felt good to move without thinking, to let the heat stick to my skin without fighting it. The rum buzzed in my blood, smoothing out the hard edges that had been living under my skin since last night. The last couple nights, if I was honest.

We cut across a stretch of stone walkway, the sea catching the sun just out of view. Music thumped faint from the pool area—something poppy, forgettable. The breeze smelled like salt and coconut sunscreen, thick and chemical at the same time.

Shawn was walking a few steps ahead of us. Big-ass grin plastered across his face. Laughing with one of his boys from back home about something I didn't catch. Moving like everything in the world was right where it was supposed to be.

I let him have it.

For now.

* * *

The rehearsal hall was just up ahead—a big open-air structure with white drapes tied back at the corners, like they were trying to make it look more romantic than functional. A few chairs were already set up in rows. Some woman with a clipboard and a headset hovered near the entrance, looking way too stressed for somebody who wasn't the one getting married.

Dev slowed up beside me, clinking the ice in his cup.

"Hope they got real fans in there," he said. "Not tryna pass out tryna fake-smile through this shit."

"Facts," Ty said, already peeling his dress shirt open a few buttons.

The energy was still light.

Still boys being boys.

Still the easy part.

For now.

* * *

239

We were still halfway laughing when we hit the edge of the rehearsal space. White chairs in uneven rows. Silk ribbons fluttering like they were trying too hard.

The planner lady with the headset spotted us and practically jogged over, clipboard clutched to her chest like it was a life raft. She didn't even greet us. She just started rattling off directions like we were late to a job we didn't apply for.

Shawn stepped forward, big and proud, waving her off like he had it covered.

"You don't have to stress," he said, flashing that politician smile he always had. "I got them under control."

Except he didn't.

Not even close.

The man was wound tight. Tighter than I'd ever seen him outside a deadline or a fantasy football bracket. Fussing about chairs being crooked. Checking the speaker volume himself. Snapping at the poor DJ about "cue points" like he was running Coachella. At one point, he literally pulled a measuring tape out his back pocket to check the aisle width.

A damn measuring tape.

Ty leaned close, whispered just loud enough for Dev and me to hear:

"Bro got a whole Amazon wedding registry but forgot to register chill."

Dev bit back a laugh, covering his mouth with his cup.

And in the middle of all that storm —

There she was.

Nia.

Shawn's fiancée.

The eye of it.

She sat on the edge of the stage, flip-flops dangling from one foot, sipping something bright and cold from a glass like she was just glad the breeze was good today.

Her dress wasn't designer.

Hair pulled back in a bun she probably did herself.

No makeup except whatever the sun gave her.

FUCK YOU SAY TO ME?

She laughed easy — real belly laughs — at whatever her sister whispered in her ear.

Didn't even glance at Shawn huffing around like a man about to deliver a state of the union address.

The contrast was loud.

And somehow, it made both of them make more sense.

He needed something to orbit.

She didn't need orbiting at all.

The planner clapped her hands together like a desperate kindergarten teacher.

"Alright, if we can have everyone line up, we'll start walking through the processional!"

People shifted into a loose herd. Pairs started forming—bridesmaids with groomsmen, family with family. Shawn was already pacing by the altar space, checking invisible details, barking out random reminders like it was a corporate retreat instead of a wedding.

Dev caught my eye, grinning like he already knew the joke forming in my mouth.

And yeah.

I couldn't help it.

* * *

The walk down to the rehearsal field wasn't organized — it was a slow, broken river of suits and sunglasses and half-finished drinks. Shawn was already on edge, trying to herd everybody like stray cattle.

"Y'all gotta tighten up, man! Stay in pairs! Don't just be wandering off!"

Nobody moved faster.

Nobody listened.

Dev tossed a lime wedge over his shoulder like a bouquet. Ty was talking shit loud enough for his laugh to carry across the whole field. Some of the other groomsmen kept stopping to fix their shoes, to fix their drinks, to fix nothing at all.

And there was Shawn.

Pacing ahead of the group, flapping his hands like a high school drama coach trying to orchestrate a parade. Stressing over where to stand, how to walk, whether the photographers had "good angles" of the rehearsal. Micro-managing the air itself.

I hung back, sipping my drink slow. Watching him. Feeling that same burn work its way up my chest.

Same dude who dipped on a five-thousand-dollar tab like it wasn't shit. Same dude laughing with everybody now like he hadn't left me hanging.

Dev leaned over, stage-whispering, "Tell me why I feel like we rehearsin' for free right now."

He snorted.

Ty cracked up.

I smiled, tight at the edges.

Could've left it right there.

Could've laughed it off.

Swallowed it down like every other thing I was supposed to let slide.

* * *

Instead, the words slid out before I could even stop 'em.

Sharp. Casual. Dressed up like a joke — but everybody heard the blade in it.

"As long as this rehearsal don't end with another five grand on my card, I'm good."

For half a breath, it landed soft.

The kind of joke everybody wanted to laugh at but didn't know if they should.

Dev chuckled.

Ty coughed like he was covering a laugh.

A couple heads turned.

And Shawn...

Shawn didn't laugh.

He turned.

Face pulled tight.

Voice cutting through the space with no hesitation.

"Bro, ain't nobody tell you to swipe if you broke."

Sharp.

Loud enough for the whole group to hear.

Like he wanted it to sting.

And just like that, the whole energy shifted.

The jokes stopped.

The smiles froze.

Even the sun felt hotter for no reason.

Something heavy cracked open between us, and I felt it stretch my jaw tight, blood rushing straight to my fists.

The second Shawn's words hit the air, my whole body snapped tight. Not just anger — disrespect. Deep. Raw. Personal.

I stopped mid-step. Drink still in my hand, fingers tightening around the cup without thinking.

The noise around us faded. Laughter. Ocean breeze. Music in the background. All I could hear was that one word—broke.

I turned toward him slow. Not thinking. Not breathing.

"Nigga, who the fu—"

Dev was on me before the rest of it could even break loose. He grabbed my arm hard, dragging me a half step back, his grip ironclad.

"Yo! Yo, B! Chill—chill!" Dev barked, low but urgent.

I tried to shake him off, jaw clenching, shoulders tight, but Dev braced harder, arm slamming across my chest like a damn seatbelt.

"Nah, fuck that," I snapped, voice sharp enough that a few heads turned toward us. "Nigga left me stranded, Dev. Like I ain't look out for him. Like I ain't hold it down when he disappeared."

Dev locked eyes with me, pulling me another step off the path.

"I know, bro. I know," he hissed through clenched teeth. "But not here. Not now."

I could feel my blood drumming in my ears.

Chest heaving.

Fists itching.

"He brushed me off, Dev," I growled. "Like it was nothing. Like I'm some extra body. Not the same nigga that made sure his whole crew ain't get embarrassed."

Dev squeezed my arm tighter, stepping even closer.

"He know, B. He know exactly what he did," Dev said, jaw tight. "He just tryna save face, bro. Don't hand him a bigger stage to show his ass."

I glared at him, vision tunneling.

Every cell in my body was begging for smoke.

But Dev didn't blink.

Didn't flinch.

Just held me there.

"It's about her," he said, voice dropping. "Not him. Her."

I swallowed hard.

Felt the weight of it like something sinking in my chest.

I ripped my arm free — rough.

Didn't say thank you.

Didn't apologize.

Just turned.

Still burning.

Still breathing fire through my nose.

And walked back toward the rehearsal.

Every step louder than the last.

Because no matter how much I wanted to tear him apart right there — this wasn't about him anymore.

19

Silence Like Armor

The sun was still out, but it felt different now. Hotter somehow. Heavier. Like it knew what just happened and didn't care enough to give me a breeze.

The rehearsal broke up without ceremony. No handshakes. No dap-ups. No more jokes. Just a slow, uncomfortable drift — people peeling off in twos and threes, mumbling about drinks, dinner, showers.

No one said the word fight, but everyone felt it.

Like heat rising off concrete.

Dev lingered nearby for a second, gave me a look — that silent "you good?" check-in only people who really know you can give.

I didn't nod. Didn't smile.

Just looked back, long and tired, like *not now, bro.*

And that was enough.

He let me walk. Didn't follow. Didn't press.

I didn't wait for Ty either. Didn't care where Shawn went. Didn't want to hear his voice. Didn't want to see his face laughing it off with someone else like it never happened.

I slid my sunglasses on, even though the sun was already starting to dip.

Not for the light.

For the armor.

The walk from the rehearsal space to nowhere felt longer than it was. The resort wrapped around me like it was trying too hard to keep the illusion intact — perfect angles, manicured hedges, pools shaped like question marks.

Everything designed to distract you from yourself.

But I wasn't in the mood to be distracted.

Not today.

The stone paths were just damp enough to leave ghost footprints behind me. Palm trees swayed like they had nothing to do with any of this. Somewhere in the distance, a speaker looped that same beach playlist — steel drums, vague reggae remixes, something smooth for the tourists to bob their heads to.

But it didn't reach me.

I cut through a hedge-lined walkway until it opened near a cliffside.

No signs. No infinity pool.

Just a waist-high stone wall and a view of the sea behind it — raw and open and endless.

I sat on the wall.

Elbows on knees. Drink still in hand.

The one I took from the bar on the way out, like it meant something.

Like it could fix the taste in my mouth.

It didn't.

It was warm now. Watery. The rum barely showed up.

But I sipped it anyway. Because that's what you do when you've been holding something too long.

You finish it. Even if it's gone flat.

The ocean was out there, somewhere beyond the drop. I couldn't see it clearly — just a thin shimmer past the cliff — but I could hear it. The crash, the pull, the inhale and exhale of something older than my pride. Something that didn't care who said what in front of who.

And for a second, I let myself sit in that sound.

Let my shoulders slump.

Let the sun press down without resisting it.

Let the last thirty minutes loop in my head — slow and sharp, like glass dragging across a chalkboard.

That word.

Broke.

The way he said it.

Loud. Sharp. Smiling like it was just another punchline — but not looking at me while he said it.

Like he knew.

And maybe he did.

Maybe he's always known who I was under the loyalty.

Under the hush holding shit down.

Maybe I've just been too busy performing to notice he stopped seeing me as anything real.

Or maybe I never stopped performing in the first place.

Not just here.

My whole life.

* * *

The pouch was buried deep in my pocket — just where Jo said she'd leave it. A few sheets of paper folded like money, a twisted napkin with ganja inside, and a red lighter so cheap it clicked twice before catching.

I sat back against the stone wall, the one I'd found near the cliffside where the resort forgot to decorate .

Out here, the sounds were different. No dancehall remixes or clinking cocktail glasses. Just wind. And the sea slamming into the rocks below in a rhythm too old to care if you were listening .

The sun was slanting low now, dragging long shadows across the stone. Palm trees behind me rustled like they were whispering about something that happened long before I got here. A gull cut across the sky, wings wide, coasting without trying .

I pulled my shirt off — slow, deliberate. Let the heat touch my back raw. Then laid the pouch across my thigh and opened it up.

It had been a while since I rolled my own. Back home, it was always pre-rolls or passing one somebody else lit first. Out here, it felt different.

Sacred, almost. Like if I was gonna sit in my own shit, I needed to do it barehanded .

I opened the napkin and dumped the weed into my palm. Thick buds, still sticky. Smelled like citrus and fire — the kind that clings to your fingertips even after you wash your hands.

I started breaking it up slow. Pull, pinch, crumble. Little pieces falling like ash into the creases of my jeans .

The sun lit everything in amber. Made the green in my hand glow. Somewhere down below, a wave crashed hard enough to echo. And still, my head was louder .

Been playing a role.

Not just this week.

Not just at that damn club or in front of Shawn.

My whole life .

The loyal friend. The husband who held it down. The father who stayed silent for the sake of "peace." The dependable one. The strong one. The one who never needed shit but always showed up when someone else did .

Even here, I hadn't stopped. Still organizing group chats. Booking reservations. Covering the bill so nobody looked bad. Still earning my place like I hadn't already paid for it ten times over .

The words kept spinning in my head, not loud — just constant. Like a ceiling fan you don't notice until it stops .

Yuh don't haffi perform fi mi.

Dez's voice, calm and flat.

First night in Jamaica.

At the time, I didn't think much of it. Now I heard it like a mirror. He'd seen it from jump. The strain. The script. Maybe even the pieces of me that were tired of smiling through it .

I flattened the paper against my thigh. Split the leaf open with my thumb. Laid the crushed ganja down in a clean line like I was building a small altar .

The wind blew sharp once, lifting the edge of the paper, but I cupped my hand over it. Pressed it back down like a promise . Rolled it slowly. Let

248

my fingers work without thinking — tucking, sealing, shaping something whole out of something broken down .

It held.

Barely, but it held .

I lit it with the red lighter, flame licking sideways in the breeze. The first inhale scratched the back of my throat. Bitter. Rough. Like truth .

I coughed once. Then exhaled, slow. Watched the smoke curl into the sky and vanish like it didn't owe me anything .

The ocean was still moving. Still crashing. Still reminding me that things keep going — even when you break apart .

And in that smoke, I saw it.

I don't want to be this version of me anymore.

Not the one who explains.

Not the one who smooths over.

Not the one who performs love so well he forgets what it feels like just to receive it .

I just want to be.

Not needed. Not useful. Not praised.

Just real.

And whole.

And mine .

A bird cried out somewhere above me. The wind picked up again, stronger this time — sweeping the edge of the wall with a warm, salty rush .

I closed my eyes.

Let it pass over me.

Let it take whatever it could carry.

* * *

The spliff was burning slow now. The cherry glowed orange in the fading light, curling at the edge like the paper couldn't carry the weight of what I'd packed into it. I'd stopped hitting it every few seconds. Letting it rest

249

between my fingers while the smoke rose without me.

Everything felt slower out here. The breeze. The sky. Even time.

Behind me, the world kept going — some music low and steady from the pool deck, glassware clinking, a kid laughing in the distance like nothing was broken anywhere. But in front of me, there was just sea. Endless and darkening. The horizon folding in on itself as the sun dropped behind it.

And for the first time in a long time, I didn't feel the need to chase the moment or caption it. Didn't need to write it down or send it to anybody. Didn't even pull out my phone... until it buzzed in my pocket.

Once.

Then again.

Then silence.

I didn't reach for it right away. I just stared out into the dusk, letting the smoke drift from my lips in slow ribbons. The air smelled like salt and ash and something old. Like something that had been here long before I got here, and would still be here after I left.

Another buzz.

I slid the phone out, thumbed the screen without looking at the name.

But I didn't need to.

I knew who it was.

Jo.

The message was simple.

Three words.

Not dressed up. Not digging.

Just...

"You good?"

I read it twice. Not because I didn't understand it. But because it felt like a lifeline — small and steady.

I didn't want to lie. Didn't want to front like the shit didn't hit me deep. But I also didn't want to spill everything. Didn't have the language yet. Didn't even have the shape of it.

So I sent her the only truth I had.

"Nah. But I'm breathing."

There was a pause. Not long, but just long enough for me to think she might be done — that maybe silence was her way of holding space.

Then the reply lit up the screen.

"I got you."

That was it.

No questions. No fixing.

Just presence.

The kind that don't need to be loud to be heard.

And in that moment — alone with the sea, with the last of the spliff burning between my fingers — I felt something ease in my chest.

Not gone. Not healed.

But… eased.

I tucked the roach into the wall's edge and stood up slow, bones a little heavy but breath moving steady. The sky was shifting above me — blue to indigo, shadows thickening across the stone.

And as I walked back toward the room, I didn't rush. Didn't rehearse what I'd say if I saw anybody. Didn't brace for more noise.

I just moved.

Back through the dark.

Back into myself.

20

Real, Even If They Looking

The resort looked different on the way back. Same palm trees, same winding paths, same smiling couples walking hand-in-hand toward the pool bar like nothing in the world could touch them.

But it all felt off.

Like watching a memory play out from outside your body.

Maybe it hadn't changed.

Maybe I had.

The air had cooled just enough for the heat to cling instead of burn. Soft breeze, high-pitched insects starting to stir in the hedges. The blue hour wrapped around the buildings like a filter—everything dipped in that end-of-day hush that made even the drunk laughter behind me feel distant. Like it was happening on another frequency.

I followed the path back to the suite, my body heavy in a way that wasn't just physical. Every step landed a little harder than it needed to. Like my own weight was checking me.

When I reached the door, the key card didn't read the first time.

I exhaled, slow.

Slid it again.

Click.

I pushed the door open and stepped inside.

Silence.

The kind that doesn't greet you — just waits.

The room was dim, only lit by the fading spill of sun through the balcony window.

No Jo.

No Spotify playing off her phone.

No sound of shower water or the rustle of plastic from a carry-out bag.

Just space.

Still, but not empty.

Her sandals were where she left them, kicked carelessly under the desk. A towel was slung across the chair like it never got folded. Half a bottle of water sat on the sill, sweating beads onto the wood below.

It looked like she still lived here.

But the air said otherwise.

I didn't turn on the lights.

I just dropped my phone and key on the dresser with a flat clack and kicked off my shoes.

My shirt still smelled like the cliff — salt, smoke, heat.

I pulled it over my head and let it fall where it fell.

The bathroom mirror caught me on the walk in — a quick flash of my reflection before I turned away.

Eyes red around the rims.

Jaw tight.

Neck glossy with sweat.

I looked like I'd just crawled out of something, and in a way, I had.

I ran the faucet cold.

Splashed my face until the temperature cut through the fog sitting behind my eyes.

Rubbed the back of my neck.

Tried to breathe slower.

Then I stripped the rest.

Twisted the shower knob all the way to hot.

When the water hit, I didn't move.

I just let it beat down on my shoulders, arms braced against the tile.

The pressure hit like penance — like maybe if I stood there long enough, the weight of the day would rinse off with the sweat and ash.

I stayed under until the steam fogged the mirrors, until my fingertips wrinkled and my mind quieted down enough for my breath to come in full again.

When I stepped out, the air in the room had shifted again. The sky outside had dropped another shade — now that deep indigo that only shows up when the last light is fading.

I dried off in silence.

Pulled on a fresh shirt. Clean shorts.

Slid on sandals.

Sat on the edge of the bed, towel still around my neck, and grabbed my phone.

Unlocked it.

Group chat was alive.

Pictures already going up from downstairs.

Shawn, front and center — grinning like a campaign poster, arms draped over shoulders that weren't mine.

Ty throwing up peace signs in the background.

Some champagne bottle popped open mid-frame.

Some caption that said: "Run it back tomorrow!"

Flame emojis under the photo.

Laughing reactions.

Inside jokes flying like everything was still good.

I stared at it for a beat too long.

Scrolled once.

Twice.

Then set the phone down on the nightstand, screen down.

Leaned back against the bed frame and looked up at the ceiling.

No fan spinning.

No hum of AC.

Just silence.

And in that silence, it hit me:

I didn't belong in that picture.

Not anymore.

And maybe I never really had.

Maybe I was just holding the camera before.

I lay back fully, arms resting flat on the blanket, body still warm from the shower.

Eyes open.

Mind not racing — just floating.

Between the person I used to be and the one I hadn't figured out how to become.

* * *

The elevator hummed as it lowered, the light reggae track piping through the speakers doing little to move the weight off my chest. I watched myself in the chrome wall — not to admire anything, just to check what was still showing. Fresh shirt, clean shorts, beard touched up, shoulders square.

I looked like someone ready to rejoin the fun.

But I didn't feel like him.

Not even close.

The doors opened into the resort's main lobby — wide marble floors glowing soft under the gold light of early evening. Guests drifted through like extras in a movie: couples in linen fits, kids in swimsuits still dripping from the pool, a photographer snapping a posed kiss near the grand piano.

Everything looked good here.

Curated. Controlled.

I stepped out and moved toward the back patio. The closer I got, the louder the music came — some upbeat mix of Afrobeats and resort-friendly dancehall thumping through hidden speakers. The air was thicker now, wrapped in the scent of rum punch, sunscreen, grilled fish, and citrus peel.

The sky had gone from gold to deep navy.

I passed a small wedding party posing on the steps — a woman in a pale yellow dress fixing her curls before the next picture snapped. Further out, a pair of honeymooners fed each other forkfuls of jerk chicken and kissed between bites.

The bar sat glowing at the edge of the courtyard — smooth stone counters, bottles lit from behind like stained glass, and a few stools left open like they were saving space for whoever still needed a minute.

That was me.

I didn't go to the group.

Not yet.

I needed a buffer. Something that reminded me I still had a body, still had breath.

She saw me first — the bartender.

Tall, elegant.

Brown skin rich like cinnamon bark.

Hair wrapped up in a deep green scarf. Gold hoops swaying when she moved.

There was something deliberate in how she wiped the counter — like she wasn't in a rush for anyone, including me.

"What you drinking, stranger?" she asked, voice low and a little textured — like it had its own rhythm.

I eased onto the stool. "You asking what I want or what I need?"

She smiled without showing all her teeth. "Let's start with what you want. Needs cost extra."

"Something brown," I said. "No lime, no mixer, no sweetness. Just… truth."

She raised a brow. "So… trauma in a glass?"

I laughed — the first real one all day. "Exactly that."

She turned, pulled a bottle with no label from the shelf, and poured slow.

"You've been thinking too hard," she said as she worked. "I can see it. The walk, the eyes, the way you sat like the chair owed you something."

I blinked at her. "That obvious?"

"Only to someone who knows the weight."

She slid the glass to me. "Drink slow. Let it work."

I picked it up, nodded my thanks, and sipped.

It hit like memory — smoky, sharp, lingering at the edges.

"You good?" she asked, quieter now. More real.

"Trying," I said.

She wiped the counter again, not looking at me this time. "That's better than pretending."

I held her eyes for another beat. There was a whole story behind hers I wasn't gonna ask for.

Then I stood, glass in hand.

Turned toward the group.

* * *

They were loud — same as always. A collection of loungers and bar stools pulled together in a lazy circle. Shawn sat near the middle, arms wide, commanding laughter from a story I couldn't hear. His voice carried. His laugh filled the space like it paid rent.

Ty saw me first.

"Ayyyy! Look who showed up!"

He jumped up like I'd come back from the dead. "Bout damn time, island boy!"

I nodded. No smile. Just enough acknowledgment to keep it polite.

Dev gave me a small chin raise, lowkey, nothing performative.

We locked eyes for a second. He didn't blink.

Shawn?

Didn't say shit.

Didn't look surprised.

Just raised his drink like a fake-ass diplomat and turned back to the group.

I didn't walk into the center. I pulled a chair from the edge, sat where I could see them, but not be swallowed by the noise.

Ty scooted over.

"Bruh," he said, loud enough to pull eyes but not quite sincere. "That shit earlier was wild, huh?"

I sipped. Let the glass speak for me.

"You know how it is," he went on. "Big day coming. He stressed. Pressure builds."

I turned toward him slow. Met his grin with a deadpan stare.

"That what we calling it now?" I asked.

He blinked. "I mean… y'all been boys forever. It's love, man. Just tension."

"Don't matter," I said. "He said what he said."

Dev moved closer now, sliding into the seat beside me like he was checking in without making it obvious.

"You straight, B?" he asked low.

"I'm here," I said.

He nodded, took a sip, didn't push it.

Ty kept going — couldn't help himself.

"Man, that whole tab thing?" He shrugged. "Nobody knew he left. It all happened fast."

I looked at him.

"Did you know?"

His mouth opened. Closed. "I mean… we thought he had it covered. And you always solid, B. You got us."

I nodded once.

"Exactly."

The silence landed heavy.

Even the background music — some slick remix of Burna Boy — felt softer in the space that followed.

Dev leaned forward, elbows on his knees. "He was wrong for that."

Ty sipped his drink. "We didn't mean—"

I cut him off with a look.

Didn't need another half-assed excuse from someone who hadn't even checked in.

The waitress dropped another drink beside mine. Ty probably ordered it.

I left it untouched.

The rest of the crew went back to their noise, but not with the same rhythm.

There was a crack in the soundtrack now — something off-key.

And I sat in it.

Not angry anymore.

Not trying to belong.

Just... present.

Like a tourist in my own life.

* * *

I don't know how long I'd been sitting there when the air shifted. It wasn't loud. Wasn't dramatic. Just a quiet pull — like something in the atmosphere stopped pretending.

I turned my head.

Jo.

She walked in like the night belonged to her. Hair tied up. Loose linen pants brushing her ankles. Cropped top, skin catching the last shimmer of light. No jewelry, no heels — just bare confidence. Like the breeze followed her in.

Shawn noticed first.

Straightened up in his seat like he was bracing.

Ty's eyes went wide — not in lust, not exactly — more like awe mixed with caution.

One of the cousins whispered something and and got elbowed for it.

She didn't flinch.

Didn't glance at any of them.

She walked straight to me, leaned down, and kissed my cheek.

"Hey."

"Hey."

She didn't ask if I was okay.

Didn't overstep.

Just sat down next to me like she'd been there the whole time.

Her energy changed the shape of the whole circle.

Not loud. Just certain.

Ty recovered first.

"So... this Jo?" he asked, smiling too hard.

Jo turned toward him, gave a half-smile. "That's what he's been calling me, yeah."

A beat of laughter moved through the group, awkward at first, then warming.

"I'm Ty," he said, sitting up straighter. "We been looking out for your boy over here."

She raised an eyebrow. "That right?"

Ty chuckled. "Yeah, you know... holding it down."

Jo glanced at me, then back at Ty.

"Oh, that's what that was?" she said. "Sounded more like y'all were watching him get clowned and drinking through it."

The laughter this time was real — Dev snorted into his glass.

Ty coughed. "Damn. Okay."

Jo waved her hand like she was brushing crumbs off a table. "It's cool. You're cute, but you ain't subtle."

Even Shawn cracked a smile at that, though he didn't look her in the eye.

Dev leaned over, raising his glass toward her. "Respect."

She clinked his without missing a beat.

Ty tried again, shifting gears. "So Jo, where you from?"

"Earth," she said, sipping her drink.

The whole circle laughed — even a couple cousins.

Jo shrugged. "Y'all real invested. I just came to sit next to my man and steal fries."

One of the guys pushed a plate toward her. "Go crazy."

"Thanks, cousin," she said, then looked at Bruce. "I like him already."

Bruce just smiled into his drink, eyes low, but relaxed now.

Shawn finally spoke, voice even. "Glad you could join us."

Jo looked over slow. "Yeah... I almost didn't. Wasn't sure if this was a safe space for grown-ass energy."

Shawn lifted his drink again, but the smirk didn't reach his eyes. "Every space I'm in is safe."

Jo raised her glass back, mock-serious. "Mmm. That sounds like something a man says when he's the one making people uncomfortable."

Dev made a sound like he was choking.

Ty held his mouth, trying not to laugh.

Jo leaned into me again and whispered, "You said this was your crew, not your student council."

I bit back a smile.

"Nah, for real," she said louder now, sipping again. "Y'all cool. Just... real polished. Like this whole night got approved by HR."

Ty shook his head, grinning. "You dangerous."

"Nah," she said. "I just don't come with the PowerPoint."

Another round of laughter. Lighter now.

Even Shawn chuckled, though his jaw stayed tight.

The air had shifted again.

Not perfect.

But looser. Realer.

Jo had cut through the tension not by smoothing it over — but by calling it out and daring anyone to get too sensitive about it.

She wasn't trying to be liked.

She was just being herself.

And for the first time in a long time, I realized how rare that actually was.

The group was still laughing when she stood. Jo finished the last fry on the plate, wiped her fingers on a napkin, then turned to me.

"You coming?" she asked, soft but certain.

I didn't hesitate.

I just grabbed my drink and followed.

No goodbyes.

No dap-ups.

Just me and her.

Stepping into the dark, together.

21

Say Less

We didn't talk.

Didn't hold hands.

Just walked.

Out of the circle.

Out of the performance.

Into something real.

She pulled me through a break in the hedges — a narrow, half-hidden gap that opened to a dim back path behind the resort. Concrete wall. Shipping crates. A vent blowing out spice and sea air. No lights except what the moon gave us.

She turned, looked at me.

And that was it.

I moved.

Grabbed her by the hips. Kissed her like I was reclaiming something that had been stolen.

Her fingers were already in my waistband. My hand shoved her pants down to her knees. She climbed me — no hesitation — one leg wrapped high around my back. No words. Just heat.

And then I was inside her.

No condom.

No delay.

No filter.

She was already wet — soaking, hot, tight — like her body had been waiting for this all damn day.

She choked on a moan. "Fuck—Bruce."

I slammed her against the wall.

The crates rattled.

She didn't care.

She dug her nails into my shoulders and pulled me deeper.

I wasn't gentle.

Didn't want to be.

She didn't ask for that.

She wanted it like this — messy, rough, hers.

I gave it to her.

Thrust after thrust.

Slapping skin.

My name in her throat, low and strangled.

My fingers tangled in the knot of her shirt as I held her hips steady and made her take every inch.

I could feel her clenching already.

I could feel her getting close.

And that's when I heard it.

A sound — soft but sharp.

Above us.

I froze, panting, lips on her neck.

Jo stilled.

We both looked up.

Second-floor balcony.

Curtains half drawn.

Light spilling out like it knew a secret.

Two girls.

Watching.

One in nothing but a towel, pulled halfway open.

Her breasts bare. Nipples hard.

Hand deep between her legs, moving slow.

The other wore a loose robe, hair tied up, thighs spread wide on the deck chair.

She had a drink in one hand, fingers working beneath the robe with the other.

Mouth slightly open.

Eyes locked on us.

They weren't hiding.

They weren't ashamed.

They were watching.

Watching us fuck like the world couldn't hold us.

Jo looked at them, then at me.

"You stopping?"

I grinned. "Not a chance."

I tightened my grip under her thighs and started pounding her again — harder now.

Her moan cracked.

"Let them watch," she said. "Let them see what it looks like when it's real."

I fucked her like I was showing them something they'd never forget.

Every stroke was deep. Intentional.

Her body bouncing against the wall, sweat slicking between us.

My shirt tugged half off. Her top rolled up to expose her breasts, the moonlight casting them in soft shadow and shine.

I looked up at them — those girls on the balcony.

They were locked in.

One biting her lip so hard it might bleed.

The other whispering something I couldn't hear, fingers circling fast.

And I gave them a show.

Pulled Jo's leg higher.

Spat on my hand, slid it between her legs, rubbed her clit while I drove into her.

She cursed, loud, grabbed my jaw with both hands and pulled me into a kiss that tasted like possession.

I held my orgasm.

Stayed on the edge.

Didn't want to come yet — wanted them to see me hold it.

Wanted Jo to ride the build.

Wanted her to come again — and again — because this wasn't just about release.

This was about claiming space.

Her body arched. Her moans came faster, rawer.

She came with a cry that filled the alley.

And those girls?

Still watching.

Still touching.

Still wide-eyed like they knew they were seeing something they'd never get to feel.

Jo's legs trembled.

She licked sweat off her lips, then whispered, "Finish it."

I gritted my teeth.

Grabbed her hips.

Thrust hard.

Twice.

Three times—

And then I let go.

Buried deep.

Groaned into her neck.

Came so hard my knees almost buckled.

Her arms wrapped tight around my back.

Breath tangled in my ear.

We stayed like that — our bodies stuck together, twitching and wet, breath crashing in rhythm — while the air pulsed around us.

Up above, I caught one last glance.

The girl in the robe was sucking her fingers.

The other one clapped — slow, like she knew exactly what she'd just seen.

Jo turned her head, met their eyes.

Blew a kiss.

Then looked at me and said, "Let's go before they ask for an encore."

* * *

We didn't rush. Jo fixed her pants with both hands, calm like she'd just stepped out of a massage. Her hair was frizzed at the edges, lips still swollen, the top of her shirt clinging to her skin where I'd held her down. She looked like trouble, and walked like she knew it.

I was still trying to catch my breath. Shirt damp across my chest, drawstring barely holding. My thighs ached. My ribs too. And not in a bad way.

"You good, yeah?" she asked, brushing her thumb across her bottom lip. "Or mi mash yuh up too bad?"

I rolled my neck, winced. "I think you cracked something."

She smirked. "Yuh still walkin', so yuh'll live."

She stepped past me, brushing her fingers across my stomach like punctuation. I followed, slower than her, my legs not fully mine yet.

The hedges parted behind us like nothing happened. And just like that, we were back in the curated world. Polished stone. Hanging lights. Resort jazz playing low from somewhere. A light breeze stirred the palm fronds like it was trying to cover for what we'd done.

A linen cart rattled by. The staff guy pushing it glanced up, took one look at Jo's disheveled state, then dropped his eyes fast like he'd seen a ghost and didn't want to be haunted.

Jo didn't miss a beat.

"Ease up, star," she called after him. "Wi just do wi likkle part fi di environment."

I bit my lip to stop the laugh, but it came out anyway. My abs tensed and I felt the soreness deep in the muscles I didn't even know I used.

We passed a couple sharing gelato. A group of drunk bridesmaids taking turns on a swing bench. One of them stared a little too long — then looked away when she saw the sweat on my neck and Jo's smile.

266

Jo slipped her hand into mine without looking.

Palm to palm. Easy. Familiar.

"You think those girls are still up there?" I asked.

Jo shrugged, eyes forward. "Mi sure. Dem never blink. Mi seh... dem deserve a encore."

I laughed, but I was still holding that image — the towel slipping, the hand moving under silk. The way they didn't hide. Didn't flinch.

"You ever done that before?" I asked.

Jo raised her eyebrow without turning her head. "Which part? Di sex outside, or di audience?"

"Both."

She grinned. "Mi do mi part fi di arts."

I squeezed her hand. "You're a menace."

"Mi know," she said sweetly.

We rounded the back of the bar.

The crew was still posted. Shawn, Ty, the cousins — all deep in drinks and stories, loud enough to pretend the day hadn't split something open.

Their laughter didn't touch me.

Not out of bitterness.

Out of clarity.

Jo leaned into my shoulder as we passed.

"Yuh ever a go tell dem?" she asked.

"Tell them what?"

"That you not theirs anymore."

I looked at her.

The path under us was glowing faintly.

A couple frogs chirped off in the bushes.

Someone shouted something in Spanish by the beach trail, followed by a burst of laughter.

"I don't need to tell them," I said. "They'll figure it out when I stop showing up."

She nodded once. No praise. No commentary. Just confirmation.

"Yuh know yuh a go frighten di whole a dem, right?"

"Probably."

She smiled. "Good."

We reached the front doors.

Bellhop stepped forward to open them.

He didn't speak — but the look on his face said he knew. He'd heard something. Seen something. Probably both.

Jo flashed him a wave. "Bless up, king."

Inside, the air conditioning kissed our skin like a new mood.

Cold. Sharp. Clean.

Elevator opened fast. No one else inside.

We stepped in.

Jo leaned back against the mirrored wall, chest still rising slow, skin still dewy.

She looked me up and down, eyes pausing on my waistband, then crawling back up to my mouth.

"Mi feel yuh still hard," she murmured, like she was just stating facts.

I looked down. Then at her.

Her robe had slipped slightly at the collar. One breast barely tucked back in.

My shirt stuck to me. I hadn't even noticed the bruises forming on my side.

"You trying to hold a rep?" she said. "Or build one fi real?"

I stepped in close. Pressed her back against the elevator wall.

Our bodies lined up like we never left the alley.

"Right now," I said, voice low against her neck, "I'm just trying to find a bed."

She laughed once — soft, throaty.

Then whispered back: "Betta find it quick. Cause mi not finish yet."

* * *

The door shut behind us with a soft click, and the silence that followed felt loaded. The air between us was heavy and wanting.

Jo didn't speak. She dropped her purse by the door, stepped out of her sandals, and peeled her top off without breaking eye contact. Her breasts were still flushed, rising slow with her breath. Skin dewy with the leftover heat from outside. Hair wild at the edges, sweat-kissed curls falling out of their knot. She looked wrecked. Beautiful. Unapologetic.

She stood in the center of the room like she owned the night.

I pulled my shirt off, still damp with salt and her scent, and let it fall. Then walked to her — slow.

Jo didn't wait.

She sat on the edge of the bed, legs wide, spine straight, looking up at me with that half-smile that always said *I dare you*.

"Come tek me proper now," she said. Voice low. Rough. Almost tired. But there was hunger in it.

I didn't touch her face. Didn't kiss her yet.

I dropped to my knees.

She blinked, surprised — then leaned back on her elbows, legs already parting wider.

I pulled her forward by the thighs and kissed the inside of her knee first — just to watch her twitch. Then lower. My lips grazed her skin, slow. My tongue followed the trail down.

She was already wet. Still swollen from the first round. Still warm and open.

I licked her slow at first — deep, wide strokes that made her hips rise.

Jo cursed under her breath.

One hand grabbed the sheet. The other slid into my locs, holding me steady.

"Yesss... just like dat. Don't stop now."

I didn't.

I buried my tongue inside her like I'd never get another chance. Let her grind on my mouth, chase the pace. She tasted like the sweat we earned. Like salt and sin and satisfaction.

I pressed a finger inside her while I sucked her clit — slow but firm. She arched, cried out, legs trembling already.

"Fuck... Bruce..."

I flicked my tongue, circled, then flattened it and sucked again. She bucked once, twice — and I knew she was close. Right when she hit the edge, I pulled away.

She groaned loud, slapped the bed with one hand.

"Bwoy... yuh wicked."

I stood up, eyes locked on hers, wiping my mouth with the back of my hand.

"I know."

Her chest rose and fell hard. She looked dazed. Frustrated. Turned the fuck on.

I dropped my shorts, slow, letting her see all of me. Her eyes dropped, stayed there. She bit her lip. Reached down to touch herself.

I caught her wrist.

"Not yet," I said. "That's mine."

I grabbed her ankles, flipped her onto her back. She squealed, laughing once, then gasped when I dragged her to the edge of the bed. I lined myself up and slid in slow — inch by inch.

We both hissed.

Her walls clamped around me, wet and pulsing. Her back arched. She grabbed at my waist, pulling me deeper. I buried myself in her — fully. Held it. Let her feel every inch.

She looked up at me like she couldn't breathe.

"Don't stop. Mi need it just like dat."

I started to move.

Not fast. Not soft.

Deep.

Every thrust landed with weight.

She wrapped her legs around my waist, heels pressing into my back. Her hands dug into my shoulders, fingernails dragging as her moans got higher, tighter.

I watched her — all of her.

The way her lips parted.

The way her nipples stiffened against the room's soft light.

The way she met every stroke like she needed it to live.

I leaned in, kissed her slow — tongue against tongue, our breath tangled.

She held my face.

Looked right into me.

"Mi love how yuh fuck mi."

I grunted against her lips.

"Say it again."

"Mi seh mi love—how yuh—fuck—mi."

Her voice broke with every thrust.

I slid one hand under her ass and angled deeper. Hit that spot that made her cry out and jerk beneath me.

She started shaking.

Legs trembling.

Breath gone.

Her whole body locked, then let go.

She came like a wave — slow and wide, rippling through her.

No scream. Just this deep, broken moan from somewhere in her soul.

She clung to me like she was about to fall through the bed.

I held her.

Fucked her through it.

Never broke rhythm.

Her moans softened into whimpers.

Her body loose now, melted into the mattress.

And I still wasn't done.

I pulled out, flipped her over onto her stomach, and slid back in from behind.

She gasped, arching her back, hands gripping the sheets.

"You still ready?"

She looked over her shoulder. Eyes red.

"Mi never done."

I grabbed her hips, leaned over her back, and fucked her hard.

Slower now.

Controlled.

Each thrust a statement.

She reached between her legs, touched herself while I stayed deep inside her.

That sight?

It almost ended me.

But I held the edge.

Watched her.

Wanted to burn this image into my memory.

"Cum wid mi," she said, voice raw.

I grabbed her braid. Pulled her head back gently.

"Look at me," I growled.

She turned.

We locked eyes.

I slammed into her once, twice—

And came.

Long. Deep. Hard.

Her name caught in my throat.

My hand still tangled in her hair.

Our bodies stuck together, sweat slicking our skin.

We collapsed into the sheets.

No words.

Just air.

And pulse.

Her hand slid across my stomach.

Her breath steadied against my chest.

I kissed the top of her head.

Jo whispered:

"Still want dat bed?"

I laughed once, breathless.

"I'm already in it."

* * *

We didn't speak.

Didn't move for a long time.

Just lay there, our bodies tangled in heat and silence, the night still humming beneath our skin. Somewhere outside, the waves kept moving. And sleep found us before the guilt ever could.

The sun found us first. It crept in through the linen curtains, quiet but certain — like it had permission to touch us now.

Jo was still sleeping on my chest, leg thrown across mine, hair wrapped in a scarf sometime during the night. Her lips were slightly parted, breath soft and steady against my skin. Our bodies stuck together — thighs, arms, backs of knees — warm and messy and still.

I didn't want to move.

I barely blinked.

Just stared at the ceiling and breathed her in.

Salt.

Coconut oil.

The faintest trace of sex still lingering in the sheets.

I could still feel her last moan in my jaw.

Still feel her pulse in my hips.

Still felt like I was inside her somehow — not physically, just held.

Jo shifted.

"Mmm…" she hummed, voice hoarse. "Yuh chest mek a good pillow still."

"And your mouth makes a hell of an alarm clock."

She snorted and pulled her scarf tighter.

"Yuh lucky mi didn't break yuh."

"My legs still not back."

She kissed my shoulder, lazy and proud. "Mi love mi work."

* * *

We took our time getting dressed.

I showered slow.

Water beat down on the scratches she left on my back.

Jo sat in the mirror, legs crossed, wiping coconut oil across her thighs while humming something low and off-key.

Every now and then I caught her watching me.

Not in a lusty way.

Like she wanted to make sure I was still here.

The resort restaurant was calm that time of morning. No DJ yet. Just birds somewhere high up in the trees and the occasional clatter of silverware on ceramic.

We sat outside on the patio. White tablecloths. Soft breeze. Pineapple juice sweating in tall glasses. Ackee and saltfish, boiled bananas, dumplings, callaloo. A full spread neither of us needed but neither of us questioned.

Jo wore a black sundress that clung at the hips, gold hoops, and a pair of slides that said she wasn't trying too hard but still looked better than everyone else here. Her skin glowed in the sun. Her eyes behind dark lenses still told the truth. Calm. Unbothered. Like she hadn't just been fucked into a wall, a bed, and probably a new era of her life in the last 12 hours.

She was picking apart her dumpling when I saw them.

Across the patio.

Table for two.

The girls from the balcony.

No doubt.

Towel girl had her hair slicked back now, edges laid, lips glossed. She wore a two-piece and a sheer cover-up. The robe girl sat across from her, sunglasses off, sundress hitched up mid-thigh, one shoulder bare.

Both of them paused mid-bite when they saw us.

They didn't smile.

Didn't flinch.

Just watched.

The same way they had the night before.

Intent.

Open.

Still hungry.

Jo didn't react at first. She was too busy pouring hot sauce over her callaloo.

But I knew she felt it.

The heat in the air changed — not dramatic, just enough to notice.

She finally looked up.

Saw them.

Held eye contact.

And smiled.

Small. Slow.

Not flirty.

Not territorial.

Just... yeah, you saw it. And you liked it.

Robe girl shifted in her chair, uncrossed her legs, then slowly crossed them the other way — like she was still thinking about how Jo had moaned.

Towel girl stirred her tea. Bit her bottom lip.

Not shy.

Jo raised her glass slightly. Just a nod. No toast.

Then looked back down at her plate.

I didn't say anything.

Neither did they.

But everything had already been said.

A few minutes later, Jo sipped her juice and leaned toward me.

"Yuh think dem come down here fi breakfast?"

I smirked. "Think they came down to confirm it wasn't a dream."

She stabbed her dumpling with her fork. "Well... now dem know."

I leaned back, feeling the sun on my face, the food in my belly, the weight finally off my chest.

Jo took another bite, slow. "Everybody need a likkle breakfast after church."

22

Easy Like Sunday Morning

The room smelled like lotion, linen, and rum still clinging to the corners. Outside, birds chirped like they'd already had their coffee. And sunlight spilled through the balcony curtain in gold slats — cutting across the bed, the floor, the curve of Jo's leg as she stood by the mirror.

She had one foot propped up on the chair, towel still wrapped tight under her arms, edges laid, fingers moving with muscle memory. Hair in her lap. Pins between her lips. Comb in one hand, coconut oil in the other.

Barefoot. Balanced. Unbothered.

I sat on the edge of the bed in boxer briefs and black socks, pulling one shoe on slow, letting my heel press against the floor before tightening the laces.

The room was still.

No TV.

No music.

Just the hum of the AC and the occasional shift of Jo's gold bangles tapping against the dresser as she moved.

She didn't look at me when she said it.

"Mi thinkin' fi check in wid mi cousin dem later," she said around the pin in her mouth. "Dem deh a town today. Might roll out."

I didn't take it personal.

Didn't ask for details.

Didn't need any.

"Cool," I said, tying the other shoe.

She pulled the pin from her lips and spoke more clearly this time.

"No wedding show fi mi today," she said, glancing up in the mirror.

I met her eyes in the reflection.

"Didn't think you'd be the plus-one type anyway."

She smirked. "Mi don't mind showin' up. Mi just don't like pretendin' fi care."

"Then yeah," I said, "you'd hate it."

She reached for a chain — something simple and gold — and clasped it behind her neck, then rubbed the oil into her arms with slow, circular strokes.

I stood and walked toward the chair by the window, picked up my pants and belt, and started dressing in sections — pants first, then the shirt, tucking each side with deliberate ease.

Jo finished her twist, tied it back, and finally dropped the towel.

Naked for all of three seconds.

Not for show.

Not shy.

She moved with the comfort of someone who never had to be taught her worth.

Like her skin was home, not a statement.

She stepped into her wrap dress and tugged it closed with one sharp motion.

No mirror check.

No hesitation.

I was fixing the last cuff of my white shirt when she walked over and stood in front of me.

Close enough to feel the warmth of her lotion on my chest.

Close enough that her breath touched the collar of my neck.

She reached up and adjusted the top button — the one I'd left crooked.

"You look clean," she said, eyes lingering just a second longer than usual.

"You always do," I said.

She smirked, but didn't soften.

Her hands brushed invisible lint from my chest.

Then smoothed the line of my shirt down.

Then paused.

"Yuh nervous?" she asked.

I shook my head. "Not really."

"Good," she said. "Yuh not di one gettin' married."

I chuckled once. "Feels like I was just the one gettin' divorced."

"Still count," she said, under her breath.

She leaned up, kissed me on the corner of the mouth.

Not center.

Not a performance.

Just a kiss.

Her hand grazed my chest once more before she stepped back.

"I'll find yuh later," she said, already turning toward the dresser.

I didn't stop her.

She picked up her bag, slid into her sandals, grabbed her phone off the charger — and that was it.

She was gone.

I stood there for another beat.

Alone now. Shirt crisp. Shoes tight.

Still buttoning the last cuff as the lock clicked behind her.

No footsteps.

Just the low whine of the AC and the sound of the island breathing outside.

I didn't feel abandoned.

But the room held the echo of her in it — like the air remembered what we'd done, how we'd laughed, where her body had pressed against mine just hours before.

Not empty.

Just... still.

And in that stillness, I reached for my watch, fastened it around my wrist, checked the time —

Then stepped out into the day.

* * *

The music hit me before the door opened. Bass vibrating faint through the hallway walls. Laughter louder than the speaker. That familiar rhythm of men getting ready — half-dressed, overconfident, behind schedule, but still acting like time was waiting on them.

I knocked once, then let myself in.

The smell hit me next — a mix of weed, cologne, deodorant spray, and something expensive someone probably sprayed too many times.

Ty was barefoot on the couch, one sock on, dress shirt wide open, chain resting against his chest like it paid rent there. Dev stood behind the minibar pouring drinks like he was auditioning for a party scene. Shawn was already dressed — tie perfect, pocket square folded like a tutorial, pacing in front of the mirror with a glass in hand and that bright, polished grin like he'd already rehearsed it twice.

The moment I stepped in, I got clocked.

"Yo! Look who finally decided to bless the suite!" Dev called out, raising his glass.

"Bruce!" Ty shouted. "Mr. Mindfulness. Mr. Ayahuasca. Mr. I-Don't-Got-Time-for-You-Niggas-No-More."

I smirked, stepped inside, and hit the daps in a circle — Dev first, then Ty, then Shawn.

Shawn's grip lingered. He looked me up and down like he was trying to read more than my suit.

"You straight?" he asked, voice a little lower.

"I'm good," I said.

He held the eye contact for a second too long, then slapped my back and moved toward the speaker.

I walked in slow, taking the room in.

The suite was nice — high floor, wide glass windows with a view of the ocean. A tray of empty glasses on the coffee table. Jackets hanging from random spots. Ties draped over chairs. A cologne bottle rolling back and forth near the edge of the sink from someone's earlier rush.

Dev handed me a shot without asking what I wanted.

"To love," he said, grinning. "And to not fucking it up."

"Speak for yourself," Ty muttered.

"Speak for all of us," I said, raising the glass.

We clinked.

Downed it.

Tequila. Warm. Clean. Burned just enough to remind you that you still had things to forget.

Shawn picked up a second bottle from the dresser. "One more round before we get holy?"

Ty groaned. "Bruh, ain't nobody gettin' holy. This whole thing runnin' on vibes and two haircuts."

Dev laughed so hard he dropped a lime wedge on the floor.

I eased back onto the arm of the couch, watching them all move around me — still joking, still filling the room with noise and presence and ease.

Same guys I'd known since college.

Same laugh.

Same stories.

But I wasn't in the center anymore.

Didn't need to be.

That used to be my spot — the one who held the energy, cracked the line that made everyone fold.

Now?

I was good just listening.

Good just being here, still in it, but not leaning on it to remind me who I was.

Ty eventually flopped beside me, drink in hand, shirt still halfway open.

He nudged me. "You ain't say much."

"I'm saying enough."

"Jo not here?"

"She's in town. Linking with her cousins."

Ty nodded slow. "She real chill."

"She is."

He sipped. Thought about something.

Then looked at me.

"You feel different," he said. "Not weird. Just... like you got space now."

"I do."

"You solid?"

I nodded once. "Yeah. Solid."

He tapped my glass with his. "Good. I like this version of you."

Before I could answer, Shawn shouted, "Yo! Where's my cufflinks?!"

Dev tossed them across the room without looking. "Same place you left your attitude."

The whole room cracked up.

Ty stood, stretching. "Aight, I gotta get dressed before they call my name and I'm still in socks."

Shawn checked his reflection again. "Yo, group photo at 3:45. No excuses. I want it clean."

"Damn, now he a director too," Dev muttered.

But we moved.

Ties were knotted.

Shoes polished.

Cufflinks clicked in place.

Music switched to a classic — something old, soulful, with drums that made you stand up straighter.

We stood in the mirror. All of us.

Black suits. Straight shoulders. Clean lines.

Not boys anymore.

Not really.

I looked at myself last.

Didn't feel proud.

Didn't feel fake.

Just... still.

And for the first time in years, that was enough.

* * *

The suite door clicked shut behind us, and for the first time all day, the air felt still. The kind of quiet that doesn't ask anything of you. That just lets you exist.

We stepped out in loose formation, a slow-moving group of Black suits and polished shoes easing toward ceremony. Ty and Dev led the pack, Ty with his sunglasses still on even though the sun was starting to drop, Dev pretending he wasn't three shots in already. Shawn's cousin walked next to me. Said something about the view. I nodded but didn't really hear it.

I was watching the light.

That late afternoon glow had settled across everything. Soft gold pouring through palm trees. Long shadows cutting across the stone path in sharp lines. Even the breeze felt warmer. Not strong — just enough to lift the linen at the edge of someone's jacket and move it like the scene had a pulse.

The path was white stone.

Fresh. Clean. Like it had been rinsed just before we came out.

Flowers lined both sides — hibiscus and marigolds, red and orange and almost too bright to be real. Someone had spread petals along the edge like punctuation marks.

To the left, the ocean sat open — flat blue stretching out toward the sky. No boats. No noise. Just shimmer.

It didn't crash or wave.

It just… breathed.

To the right, the clearing.

The ceremony space.

Dozens of white chairs had been laid out in perfect arcs facing the altar. Each chair wrapped in sheer fabric, tied with a bow. Soft ivory linen, fluttering like they wanted to be wind.

The altar itself was simple: two posts draped in gauze, with shells strung across the top.

Nothing flashy.

Just enough.

A woman in a navy dress adjusted the placement of one of the chairs, then stepped back and squinted — like it mattered whether it was straight when hearts were about to break anyway.

I slowed down.

Let the others keep walking.

Let them carry the jokes and shoulder bumps forward.

I needed to feel this.

The air was thicker here.

Not heavy — just full.

Like it knew what was coming.

My feet sank a little in the grass as I stepped off the stone. Shoes too clean for dirt, but I didn't care.

The music started — faint at first.

Steelpan and strings.

Something island and soft and laced with sentiment.

Not loud enough to distract. Just enough to open your chest.

Then I saw her.

Tiff.

Near the second row, half-turned toward the altar, half in her own world.

Gold dress.

Deep neckline. Open back.

Shoulders bare, glowing like she'd been kissed by the last ten minutes of sunlight.

The fabric hugged her like it knew her body better than anyone else in the room ever had.

Like it had secrets to keep and wasn't planning to share.

Her hair was swept to one side — soft curls pulled back just enough to show her neck, but loose enough to say this wasn't for you.

She wasn't looking around.

She wasn't posing.

But I saw her.

And she saw me.

Her eyes met mine like she'd been waiting to time it right.

No smile.

No wave.

Just a look.

Long enough to make something in my stomach tighten.

Short enough to make me wonder if I imagined the weight of it.

Then she turned.

Back to whoever was talking.

Back to the front.

Back to pretending she hadn't just knocked the air out of me without moving.

I inhaled slow.

Let the breath fill every corner of my chest.

Held it.

Released it through my nose.

I wasn't nervous.

Not like I used to be.

I just knew now — what you feel, you feel.

Whether you act on it or not is another thing.

I kept walking.

Shawn was already up front, posted next to the officiant — crisp black tux, white rose on his lapel, looking like someone who practiced this moment in the mirror too many times but still couldn't believe it was real.

The rest of the crew fell into place, groomsmen lining up to the left. Shawn's cousin joined them.

I stood off to the side, watching.

Rows filling up.

Sundresses. Linen suits. A baby fussing. Aunties fanning themselves with printed programs that said *Forever Starts Today*.

I looked down at my shoes.

Remembered the last time I wore a suit for a wedding.

Mine.

Indoor venue.

Cold light.

Too much pressure on the playlist.

Everything rehearsed.

Everything half-felt.

Even my smile.

I was there. But not in it.

Standing at the altar with hands sweating and a voice that sounded like someone else's.

Telling myself this was love.

Telling myself just make it to the reception and smile through the rest.

That wasn't this.

This had breath.

This had color.

This had wind.

And it had nothing to do with me.

I let my shoulders drop.

Felt the warmth on my neck.

The weight of the suit across my chest.

The echo of Jo's kiss still soft on the side of my mouth.

And I just stood there.

Still.

Steady.

Watching the day unfold — not like it was mine to control, but like it was finally safe to witness something without needing to name it.

* * *

Everyone stood. The music shifted — something warm and stringed, the kind of melody that moved slow enough to feel sacred but wasn't trying too hard to be holy. A live guitarist somewhere off to the side plucked the chords gently, just behind the rhythm, like he knew the moment needed space more than volume.

Then she appeared.

Nia.

At the top of the aisle, arm linked with her father's. Her dress wasn't extravagant. No sequins. No heavy train. Just simple, elegant white, fitted at the waist, with soft fabric trailing behind her like a breath being pulled forward. The veil sat low across her face, but you could still see her smile — small and real and trembling at the edges.

Phones came up. Guests angled in their chairs for better views. An auntie whispered too loudly about how good the dress fit her hips.

But my eyes went to Shawn.

He looked like someone had unplugged him. Mouth parted, not smiling, not breathing — just frozen. His hands were at his sides. Palms open. Not twitching. Not wringing.

Just… waiting.

I'd never seen him still before. Not in college, not in meetings, not on the strip. But right then — he didn't move.

Nia stepped slow. Not gliding. Not floating. Just walking like she'd earned every step. The wind pulled the veil back slightly, revealing more of her face. Shawn inhaled when it happened — deep, like his lungs had forgotten how until that second.

The music slowed. The guitarist dropped to just a hum of chords.

And she reached him.

The officiant nodded for everyone to sit. Chairs scraped gently against the ground. Cousins settled. Toddlers hushed. A hush rolled in like a curtain.

And then they were there.

Side by side.

Facing the altar.

Facing us.

Facing themselves.

I felt the sun shift across my back, heat wrapping around my neck and collar like a slow hand. I watched the way Shawn glanced at Nia out the corner of his eye, like he was afraid looking directly at her might knock him down again.

I remembered that feeling.

But not like this.

Mine had felt like stage fright.

Like reciting lines I'd memorized but never rehearsed in my heart.

This?

This was different.

Their hands found each other.

And the officiant began.

"Friends, family, loved ones near and far…"

I barely heard the words. My eyes scanned the rows in front of me, across to the left, and that's when I saw her.

Tiff.

She hadn't moved much since the ceremony started. Sat up straight. Hands folded in her lap. Ankles crossed at the knee. Her dress still shimmered faintly, catching whatever light filtered through the trees. Hair still tucked just right. Face calm, unreadable.

But her eyes?

They found me.

For just a second.

While the vows were being spoken.

While Shawn promised forever.

She looked at me.

Not soft.

Not cold.

Just aware.

And I knew — in that glance — we were both doing math.

Running the same emotional tab we hadn't spoken about since landing on this island.

What are we?

What haven't we said?

What does it mean that we haven't said it?

Then she turned away.

And I looked back at the altar.

Shawn was reading his vows from a folded paper. His voice cracked once. Nia squeezed his hand. He recovered. People smiled. Someone near the front wiped a tear.

The officiant asked for the rings. Dev stepped up, hand in pocket, passed them over with a wink and a bow. Laughter rippled through the guests. The tension broke.

Shawn slid the ring on her finger with slow hands. She did the same. Their fingers lingered, pressed palm to palm like a private pact.

The officiant raised his arms.

"And now, by the power vested in me..."

I tuned out.

Not because I didn't care.

Because I was full.

Full of memory.

Of air.

Of space I'd finally made room for.

They kissed. The crowd stood. Applause. Music rose again — louder this time. Joy spilling in all directions.

Shawn and Nia walked down the aisle hand in hand, both grinning now, both trying not to trip over the moment. Ty threw a fist in the air. Dev clapped so loud his ring hit his palm.

I stayed seated for a beat longer.

Breathing slow.

Letting the weight settle before I stood and followed the joy.

* * *

The reception glowed. Not bright. Not loud. Just glowed — warm and honey-colored under the hanging lights strung across palm trees. The courtyard had been transformed. Tables wrapped in white linens. Candles flickering in clear glass. Platters of seafood and callaloo and fruit arranged like someone actually gave a damn about presentation.

People moved easy now.

Jackets were off. Shoes unbuckled. Laughter loosened.

The kind of joy that didn't need permission. The kind that hums under your ribs and makes you lean into the person beside you just to say *yo, this feel good, right?*

I was posted near the back corner of the courtyard, drink in hand.

Rum punch, top-heavy with Wray & Nephew.

Sliced orange floating on the top like garnish. Glass sweating down my palm.

I wasn't hiding.

Just standing still.

Observing.

Dev had already lost his tie and was telling a story that required full arm movements and two fake Jamaican accents. Ty was deep in conversation with a bridesmaid who kept laughing a little too loud. Shawn and Nia were doing the rounds — arm in arm, still glowing, smiling like they couldn't hear anything but each other.

And for once, it didn't feel like a show.

The DJ dropped "Poison" and the courtyard erupted before the beat even landed. Voices went up. Hands flew to the air. Chairs scraped as people jumped to their feet, instinct moving faster than thought.

Then came the line.

Alphas first — three deep, black suits loosened, gold watches flashing as their shoulders bounced in unison. Their hop was clean. Tight. Like they'd rehearsed in silence and could do it blind.

"AY-YO!" one of them called, voice sharp, chest out.

The crowd echoed back — deep, guttural, already moving.

Phones came out. The path cleared.

The Deltas answered next, coming from the far side of the courtyard, already locked in formation. Red dresses hit just above the knee. Sneakers laced.

They didn't dance in — they declared themselves.

Hands slicing air. Elbows wide. Heads high.

"Ooo-OOP!" cracked through the beat, and the energy spiked again.

AKAs followed like a breeze behind a blaze. Pink and green. Step soft, line tight.

They didn't need to stomp. They strolled.

Glided past the crowd like they'd been crowned and were just circling the court.

It wasn't competition.

It was communion.

The DJ blended seamlessly into "Knuck If You Buck" and the whole courtyard shouted like someone dropped the floor. Uncles started filming. Aunties started testifying. People on the outskirts jumped in, then jumped out just as quick.

You could feel it in your knees. In your chest.

History wasn't just being remembered — it was being performed.

Not for show.

For them.

That's when I heard her.

"Yuh always look like yuh studyin' people."

I turned.

Jo was beside me — not out of place, not announced. Just there.

Hair loose now, soft curls brushing her shoulders. Red lipstick. White fitted dress that clung at the waist but fell soft at the hips.

She wasn't dressed for attention.

She just wore herself well.

She sipped from a plastic cup and raised her eyebrow when I didn't answer.

"I am," I finally said. "It's how I stay present."

She smirked. "Mi swear you write dat down in yuh Notes app."

I laughed. Couldn't help it.

She looked out across the courtyard, watching a couple sway by the speakers.

"Mi just stop by fi show face," she said. "Mi bredrin dem a keep a house party up in Ironshore. Mi might roll through for a likkle."

I nodded. "You driving?"

"Nah. Dez know somebody already out that side. Him link mi up wid a ride."

There was nothing guarded in her tone.

No distance.

Just rhythm.

She took another sip. "Mi figure yuh good now. Yuh got yuh people."

"I'm good," I said.

She didn't move right away.

Just stood there with me.

Let the quiet settle between our feet.

Then she leaned in and kissed me on the cheek.

Firm. Soft. Lasting just long enough to say *you still mine, but I'm not staying*.

"Mi find yuh tomorrow," she said.

"Cool," I said, voice lower than I meant it.

She turned.

Slipped through the crowd.

Didn't stop to say goodbye to anyone.

Didn't wave.

Didn't look back.

* * *

But someone was watching.

Across the courtyard.

Left side. Near the end of a table half-shadowed by a swaying palm.

Tiff.

Sitting like a still frame.

Wine glass in hand.

Leg crossed at the knee.

Face unreadable.

But her eyes were locked on me.

She hadn't looked at Jo.

Hadn't reacted when she walked up.

Or when she left.

She'd been watching me.

And she didn't look away when I noticed.

Didn't smile.

Didn't blink.

Just held the stare.

Like it wasn't even about Jo.

Like it was about me finally running out of excuses.

I tipped the glass back.

Finished my punch.

Felt the weight of it slide down warm.

The DJ transitioned to something harder now — riddim lifting, hips moving, heels sliding off under tables.

But I didn't move with it.

I turned and slipped away from the noise, off to the edge of the courtyard.

Toward the trees. The breeze.

Somewhere I could think.

I stood still, hands on the railing, looking out at the dark shapes of the resort disappearing into night.

And then — footsteps.

Soft.

Slow.

Intentional.

I didn't turn around.

I already knew.

She didn't say anything at first. She just stepped up beside me at the edge of the courtyard, slowly. The only thing louder than her heels was the air between us.

I could smell the wine on her breath. Faint citrus. Something floral. A note of tension she hadn't spoken yet.

She stood there a second.

Not touching me.

Not facing me.

Just… standing.

We looked out together.

Palm trees swaying against the dark.

The glitter of the resort lights dancing on the edge of the pool in the distance.

The music behind us kept pulsing — muffled now, but steady.

Laughter. A broken cheer. The scrape of chairs and the stomp of a new line hop starting up again.

I didn't move.

Neither did she.

Then finally—

"You got a second?"

Her voice didn't break.

Didn't rise.

Didn't try to dress itself in anything polite.

Just real.

I didn't answer.

Just nodded.

Subtle. Tight.

She started walking first.

Heels clicking against the stone path.

Measured. Controlled.

That same poise she always had when she was trying to walk off emotion she wasn't ready to unpack.

I followed.

We slipped past the edge of the reception — away from the lanterns and the half-finished plates.

Past the bar.

Down a narrow walkway lined with trimmed bushes and low lights sunk into the stone.

Neither of us said a word.

The further we moved from the music, the more I could feel it creeping in — the weight, the silence, the everything we hadn't dealt with.

Tiff didn't look back.

But she slowed up enough that I could catch up beside her.

Not behind. Not in front.

Beside.

The walkway opened into a small garden alcove — string lights woven through tree branches, an empty bench against the wall, the hush of the sea somewhere just beyond the hedge.

She stopped walking.

Turned slightly toward me.

One arm folded under the other, wine glass still in hand, her thumb running slow circles along the rim.

I looked at her.

Really looked.

Dress still flawless.

Makeup barely moved.

But her eyes—

Tired.

Not from the night.

From the space between us.

She didn't speak.

Didn't have to.

I took one breath.

Stepped forward.

And sat on the bench.

She stayed standing.

Looking down at me.

And I knew—

This conversation's not about what happened tonight.

It's about everything we let slide before this moment.

23

Excavation

I wasn't planning on going out that night. The plan was me, a half-finished bottle of Appleton, and takeout from LanZhou's. Stir-fried intestines, heavy on the garlic. House special stir-fry with hand-pulled noodles. Still warm in the bag, grease soaking faintly through the bottom like a promise. A couple Red Stripes tucked behind leftover pasta and a jar of pickles I should've thrown out weeks ago.

It was a Thursday. Or a Tuesday. Didn't matter.

I was deep in the kind of stretch where time didn't move unless you made it.

The TV was talking to itself in the corner—volume low, screen soft with that golden filter USA Network loved to use. Monk was pacing in a beige-walled living room, hands twitching at the edges of a coffee table no one else had noticed was off-center.

He kept muttering: "It's not the blood. It's the shoes."

And sure enough, thirty seconds later, he was on the floor examining a scuffed pair of wingtips like the answer had always been there, just waiting for him to stop pretending it wasn't.

I'd seen the episode before. Still watched it again.

Felt like watching myself—some guy everybody thought was doing too much, when really he was just trying not to let the world crush him in silence.

That's when Shawn texted.

Yo. Prom over. We celebrating. Teachers wildin'. Come through.

Ain't like you doing shit.

He wasn't wrong.

I set the phone down face-up on the counter. Took one last bite of the noodles—chewy, perfectly oily, just the way I liked 'em. Then rinsed out my glass, slow. Didn't even need to—but the sound of water hitting the sink made the room feel less empty for a second.

I stood there with the cabinet open, hand hovering over the Appleton like it might answer something. Then I closed it. Walked to the living room. Turned the TV off mid-episode. Monk was still muttering something about symmetry when the screen went black.

I looked around.

The silence came back fast.

Not heavy.

Just... familiar.

That's what did it, really.

Not the invite.

Not the drinks.

Not even curiosity.

Just the fact that nothing in that room needed me.

And I needed to feel needed.

Even for a night.

* * *

Downtown Atlanta was still sweating from the day. That sticky kind of heat that clung to your collar and made even the night air feel personal. Traffic had thinned, but the city still moved—Uber horns, sneaker soles on concrete, heels wobbling on cracked sidewalks. A girl in box braids fixed her lip gloss in a side mirror. Somewhere across the street, a man laughed too loud and called someone "ma" like he meant it.

Embr Lounge was already humming when I walked up. Low-end bass leaked through the doors like it was trying to escape. Security scanned IDs like they were reading backstories. The bouncer gave me that quick up-and-down—then the nod.

Inside was all red light and black velvet. Matte walls. Gold trim. Perfume hanging in the air like intention. Hookah smoke curled into chandeliers overhead while bottle girls danced past with sparklers like they were carrying secrets.

Shawn's section was near the DJ booth. He spotted me, stood, dapped me with that half-grin he always wore when the night was already doing what he needed it to. Didn't say much. He just handed me a drink.

I leaned back, let the liquor sit on my tongue before swallowing. The bass rattled through the leather. Laughter spilled in from the next section over. I wasn't really listening. I just let the noise wash over me.

Trying to remember why I came.

And then I saw her.

She was sitting on the back edge of the booth. One leg crossed. Fingers wrapped around a glass like she had all night to finish it. Didn't look rushed. Didn't look pressed. She wasn't trying to be seen. But she wasn't missing anything either. Eyes moving slow around the room like she was waiting for the part of the night worth remembering.

And when her gaze landed on me—

It was like she'd been expecting it.

No smile.

No flinch.

Just... recognition.

"You Bruce, right?" she said.

I hadn't even answered yet, and she was already leaning slightly forward—like the space between us was negotiable. Like the music, the bottles, the people—none of it mattered now.

"You Bruce, right?" she repeated.

A little louder this time, but still with that softness, like she didn't need confirmation to know she was right.

I nodded. "Yeah."

Took a sip of the drink Shawn handed me.

She watched me like she was judging how I drank it.

She cocked her head, amused. "Figured. I've seen you before—in some old pictures with Shawn. Think we were at the same spot last year for his birthday too. That lounge on Edgewood."

I tried to remember. I really did.

But all I could come up with was a dim room, too much laughter, and wings I barely touched.

"I remember the wings," I said. "Spicy as hell."

She smirked. "Figures. All that personality and you remember the chicken."

I shrugged. "I'm a simple man."

"You don't seem simple."

"And you don't seem like a teacher."

That got a laugh out of her—not loud, but real. She leaned in a little more.

"Special ed," she said. "Middle school. Keeps me humble."

I looked at her. Really looked this time.

Not just at her legs crossed and her necklace resting right in the dip of her collarbone, but her eyes.

Clear. Curious. No performance.

"You like it?" I asked.

She paused. "Some days."

I nodded.

"What about you?" she asked. "What do you do when you're not chasing wings and forgetting parties?"

"Consultant," I said. "Used to work in corporate supply chain. Left it alone a while back."

She raised an eyebrow. "That sounds vague and suspicious."

"It is."

We both laughed. She tilted her head slightly and said, "So what now? You just exist?"

I met her eyes. Held them a second longer than casual allowed.

"Trying to," I said. "Trying to figure out who I was before I became everything I was supposed to be."

That stopped her.

Just for a moment. Like something in her shifted.

Then she raised her glass and tapped it lightly against mine.

"To remembering who we were," she said.

I clinked it back.

"To forgetting who we weren't."

* * *

We kept talking. About history—Black revolutions, diaspora fractures, the lies they printed in textbooks.

"Did you know the first successful slave rebellion that formed a state was in Bahia?" she asked.

I leaned in. "Haiti. 1804."

She smiled. "No. I'm talking before that. Brazil. The Palmares."

I blinked.

Okay.

She sipped slow, her lip gloss smudging slightly at the rim. "See, most people don't know 'cause they don't care to. We live in a country that sells amnesia."

"And we spend our lives buying pieces of ourselves back," I said.

Her eyes lingered on me a little longer after that.

"You always talk like this?" she asked eventually.

"Like what?"

"Like you're already in the middle of a documentary."

I laughed. "I get that a lot."

She grinned, then leaned in even closer, lips barely a breath from my ear.

"Well... I like documentaries."

And just like that, the temperature changed.

The lounge had faded. Not literally—it was still loud, still full, still thick with perfume and sweat and static. But for me, none of it mattered anymore.

It was just her.

The shape of her questions. The rhythm of her logic.

The way she didn't flinch from ideas, only pressed into them harder.

We were two drinks in by now. Maybe three.

Her leg had uncrossed and re-crossed again, closer this time. Her eyes hadn't left mine in ten minutes.

She swirled the ice in her glass and asked, "What's your favorite era?"

The question came out casual—but I knew it wasn't.

It was a door.

One you only opened when you wanted to see what someone worshipped when no one was looking.

I didn't answer right away. I just smiled.

"Prohibition," I said finally.

She raised a brow. "Really? Liquor and lawlessness?"

"Not just that," I leaned forward, elbows on knees. "It was chaos... but intentional. A whole country trying to pretend it had morals while drinking in basements and fucking in jazz clubs. Black folks building empires on bootleg, running nightclubs under segregation, feeding culture from the margins while America acted holy."

I paused. "It was Black brilliance with no blueprint. Illegally excellent."

Her lips parted slightly. She didn't speak right away. She just nodded like the taste of what I said lingered on her tongue.

"That's sexy," she said.

I raised an eyebrow. "The era or my description?"

She smiled, slow. "Both."

Then she set her drink down, leaned in closer, and said,

"Mesopotamia."

"Come again?"

"My favorite era," she said. "Mesopotamia. Sumer, Akkad. Fertile Crescent. Cradle of civilization."

I blinked. "Did not have that on my club bingo card."

She laughed. "That's 'cause most people hear Mesopotamia and think of some brown land with bricks. But it was more than that. It was the first time humans tried to organize chaos. They made laws. Cities. Agriculture. Trade. Written language."

She held up a finger. "Cuneiform. The first receipts."

I laughed. "You deadass just turned me on with the word 'receipts.'"

She winked. "That's 'cause you're a sapiosexual."

I didn't deny it.

She went on, voice lower now.

"But it wasn't just the systems. It was the attempt. These people were fresh out of the wild, still half-savage, but trying to build order. That tension? Between instinct and structure? That's where all the sex is."

My mouth was dry and it wasn't from the liquor.

"Okay," I said, adjusting slightly in my seat. "You might be dangerous."

She leaned in even closer, her voice a whisper now.

"Maybe. Or maybe I'm just what you've been waiting for."

We sat there, the air between us humming.

This wasn't casual anymore.

We were peeling each other open, one era at a time.

No touch yet. No kiss.

But my heart was pounding like she already had her hand on it.

She took another sip, set her glass down, and let her fingers trace slow circles on the rim.

"I ever tell you," she said, eyes still on mine, "I used to want to be an archaeologist?"

I smiled. "That tracks. You're literally trying to excavate me right now."

She laughed. "Exactly. I like ruins. I like things people gave up on too early."

"Why?"

She looked down for the first time all night. Not long. Just enough.

"Because I feel like one sometimes."

The joke didn't come. I waited for the smile, the punchline.

But it never landed.

She shut up for a second. Not the awkward kind. The heavy kind.

"People see me," she said, finally. "They think confident. Loud. The girl who doesn't need anything from anybody."

She met my eyes again.

"But that's curated. That's the armor. I'm a soft bitch, Bruce. I just hide it well."

I didn't know what to say right away.

Didn't need to.

She kept going.

"You ever build your whole personality around not needing to be disappointed?"

I nodded.

Too fast.

She clocked it.

Gave me a soft smirk, but her eyes stayed serious.

"Yeah. Thought so."

Something shifted in my chest then.

Desire didn't leave—but it got quieter.

Made space.

Because I didn't just want her.

I wanted to know her.

To pull the rest of that truth out of her mouth, gently.

To earn it.

"You're not a ruin," I said finally.

She tilted her head.

"You're a blueprint."

She stood.

Didn't ask. Didn't wait.

She just gave me that look—chin tilted, mouth curled at the corner like she knew something was about to break.

The DJ faded the current track out mid-beat.

A second of silence.

Then—

"Ayo, ladies…"

The crowd stirred.

"Y'all know what the fuck time it is."

Bass clicked once. Lights dipped redder.

"Fellas, get the fuck out the way—this one ain't about y'all."

And then—

Dun...

Dun...

That violin hit like a siren.

Sharp. Lean. Ancient.

Like a church bell that only bodies could answer.

The second dun dropped and the club exploded.

"CASH MONEY RECORDS TAKIN' OVER FOR THE '99 AND THE 2000!"

Tiff turned to me, eyes glinting.

"You better come on," she said.

No question in her tone. Just certainty.

She was already halfway to the dancefloor before I could answer.

The crowd roared, but it all went underwater for me.

Because Tiff was already halfway to the floor—hips already loaded, hands already lifting her hair off her neck like she needed space to breathe.

I followed, slow.

Didn't rush.

Didn't speak.

She didn't wait.

Didn't look for approval.

Didn't check to see if I was behind her.

She just danced.

Dropped low like gravity owed her.

Rolled her hips like she could crack the floor open beneath her.

Arms loose, lips parted, ass moving in hypnotic sync with every bass hit.

And for the first full verse—she didn't touch me.

It was just her.

Her body. Her beat. Her rules.

And it was the sexiest fucking thing I'd ever seen.

I stood still—heat rising in my chest, dick pressing hard against denim, trying not to adjust mid-room.

And then—mid-swing, mid-verse—she looked over her shoulder.

Locked eyes with me like she'd known I was melting and decided to finish the job.

Took one slow step back.

And backed.

That.

Ass.

Up.

Right into me.

* * *

The contact wasn't aggressive—it was confident. Measured. Intentional. Her ass met me like it had been waiting for me all night. The curve fit just right against the throb I couldn't control anymore.

I moved with her. Hands steady on her hips. Breath caught in my throat. She rocked slow at first, like teasing. Then harder. Then right. Back and forth. Up and down. One hand slid behind her to hold my neck. She looked forward again like she hadn't just changed the temperature of the room.

And I?

I wasn't thinking anymore.

Wasn't narrating.

Wasn't calculating.

I was feeling.

And fuck, I was losing.

The lights dimmed one shade lower, and the bass kicked deeper. Tiff didn't just keep dancing—she slowed down. Pressed her full body into mine like she was trying to leave an imprint. She didn't rush the rhythm. She owned it. Ass heavy against me. Back arched into my chest. Arms looped around my neck like a leash I didn't mind wearing.

Miguel crooned soft through the smoke:

"All of my bitches got friends..."

Her hips rolled with the words—slow, sensual figure eights that made my thighs tighten. She wasn't just dancing on me. She was dancing with my restraint. Testing it. Breaking it. The scent of her sweat mixed with something sweet—mango or honey, I couldn't tell. Didn't matter. I was high off it.

"And they bad, they bad..."

She leaned forward, grinding deeper. My dick pressed hard into the crease of her ass, and this time she stayed there. Settled. Shifted. Then moved. Again. And again. I gripped her hips—thumbs grazing skin under the hem of her dress. She guided my hands lower without words. Fingers brushed the top of her thighs—bare, soft, warm. She kept swaying, breathing deep and steady like this was normal. Like we weren't seconds away from crossing the line.

Her mouth was close to my ear now.

Didn't say anything.

Just breathed.

And I swear—that breath alone had me throbbing so hard I almost lost my footing.

"So we good..."

She turned slowly, one leg slipping between mine, her thigh tight against my length. She stared at me—eyes glossy, mouth slightly open, lips glossed and parted like a question.

I wanted to kiss her.

Right there.

Right in the middle of the floor.

But I didn't.

Because this dance?

This was the kiss.

"It's enough for the clique..."

The beat pulsed again and she grabbed the back of my neck. Pulled me down just enough to whisper against my mouth, not into it.

"You good?"

I swallowed.

"Not even a little."

"Whole squad gettin' rich..."

She smiled.

Real slow.

And rolled her hips once more—long, deep, locked.

I almost moaned.

* * *

The song was still playing, but the world had gone numb. We weren't dancing anymore. Just breathing, together. Our bodies still touching in places that told the truth, even if our mouths hadn't. Her eyes met mine— calm, unreadable, but deep. Like she'd already made a choice and was just waiting to see if I could keep up.

She looked around, slow. One glance to the bar, then the booth where Shawn and the rest were half-laughing, half-lost. Then back to me. And with that same even voice, barely above a whisper—

"You tryna get outta here?"

It came soft. Bare. No wink. No smirk. Just air and intention. But the way she said it? Like she already knew the answer. Like she'd been giving me the chance to catch up all night. Like this was the moment the night became real.

I looked at her. Really looked. Sweat glinted at her collarbone. Her lip gloss was mostly gone. Her breath was still shallow from the wine she'd just laid in my lap. She wasn't performing anymore. She didn't need to. And fuck, I loved that.

I didn't answer right away. Didn't want to break it with a dumb joke or some line I couldn't live up to. I just let my eyes move over her—slow, grateful.

Then I stepped closer. Our foreheads touched, light. Like a secret. I leaned in—not kissing. Just speaking low, right at her lips.

"Yeah," I said. "Let's go."

She nodded once. No smile. She just turned, still holding my hand, and started walking toward the door.

And me?

I followed. Not like a man chasing a woman. Like a man walking into a decision he'd already made the moment she first said his name.

* * *

(Bruce's mind drifts, a quick, almost disorienting jump back to the present, before snapping back to the past's unfolding urgency.)

I blinked. The bass from the club still pulsed in my chest, but for a split second, I was back in the garden, the cool air on my face, the weight of a different kind of truth pressing down. Then, the memory snapped back into focus: the urgency in her grip, the heat of the club, the unspoken promise of a night that refused to be contained. We were moving. Fast. Out of the noise, into the quiet, a taxi ride that blurred into the closing of a hotel room door. There was no hesitation. No second thoughts. Only the sudden, overwhelming need to shed everything that wasn't real.

"Fuuuck, Bruce—"

Her voice cracked, high and broken, knuckles white on the sheets. Legs wide, shaking, toes curled hard into the mattress as I beat the pussy like it owed me back rent. I was deep. Too deep. That thick, slippery kind of grip where the walls sucked me in and tried to keep me.

"Goddamn, this pussy is—" I hissed through clenched teeth, slamming in harder.

She cut me off with a laugh. A fucking laugh. Wet, cocky, breathless.

"That's all you got?" she panted, glancing back over her shoulder with sweat stuck to her cheek. "You fuckin' or playin', Bruce?"

Oh.

Bet.

I gripped her hips harder. Adjusted my stance. Thrusted in slow once—long, deep, until she whimpered—and then let that shit go.

Clapping.

Smacking.

Sloshing.

I was hitting it like I hated it. Like her talking back was a challenge and the only answer was more dick.

*"Oooh shit—shit—*fuck you," she gasped, burying her face in the pillows as her thighs buckled again.

And then it hit—

A sudden squirt.

Then another.

Then it just poured.

Splashing down my shaft, down her thighs, drenching the bed like a busted pipe. She moaned so loud it was almost a scream, one hand scrabbling for the headboard, the other caught in her hair.

I pulled out fast—dripping, soaked to the base—and flipped her over in one motion.

She was still panting, tits rising, nipples hard and glistening with sweat.

"Clean that shit up," I said, nodding down to my dick—still glistening, coated in her slick.

She smirked.

Didn't even blink.

Sat up on her elbows, grabbed the base with both hands, and devoured it.

No teasing.

No warm-up.

She licked her own cum off me like it was dessert.

Slow swirls.

Heavy eye contact.

Then she spit on it, let it drip down her tongue, and took it deeper.

"Shiiit," I groaned, eyes rolling back.

She pulled off with a pop.

"You gon' nut already?" she taunted, smirking while she jerked me in one hand. "You lookin' like you ready to fold."

I grabbed her by the throat.

"Turn the fuck around."

She grinned.

Didn't move fast enough.

So I spun her, bent her over the edge of the bed, and drove back in—one stroke, no mercy.

She yelped, but it turned to a moan fast. A hungry, soaked, choking moan as I pounded her from behind. The cheeks clapped loud enough to echo. Pussy still squirting—short bursts now, rhythm with every thrust.

I leaned down, mouth to her ear.

"Talk that shit now," I growled, hand wrapped in her hair.

She tried.

But I was too deep.

Too thick.

Too locked in.

All she could do was take it.

She was still dripping when I pulled out—pussy fluttering like it missed me already. Her body trembling against the bed, one leg dangling off the side, breath coming in ragged waves. I stepped back to catch mine.

She didn't move at first. She just stayed there—ass still arched, thighs glossy, hair stuck to her spine. Then she turned her head, looked at me with eyes that had no shame left in them.

"Let me taste it again."

Her voice was raspy. Destroyed. But hungry.

I walked over slow, dick still glistening, still hard, still slick with all the mess we'd made. She sat up on her knees, wiped her mouth, and opened it. Wide.

I slid in slow, let her tongue cradle the head, then pushed deeper. She moaned. I groaned. Then she grabbed my ass with both hands—and pulled me in. Balls to lips. No warning. I jerked forward, thighs flexing.

"Shit—Tiff—"

She gagged once, then again, spit bubbling at the corners of her mouth. But she didn't back off. She stayed there. Throat wide. Nose buried. Her hands digging into my skin like she needed something to hold while she drowned in dick.

I started to move. Small strokes first. Testing her. Then faster. Harder. Until the sound was just wet and ruinous—gag, suck, slap, drip. I looked down and saw tears sliding from her lashes. Eyes still open. She took it all. Then I pulled out with a wet gasp and a thick strand of spit connecting us.

She coughed.

Smiled.

And said, "Now open up my ass."

Fuck.

I grabbed the lube off the nightstand—hadn't used it in a while, but I kept it. Something about her made me want to be ready for everything.

She flipped over, arched again. This time wider. Pussy still swollen, glistening. But her other hole? Tight. Waiting. Perfect.

I got on my knees. Rubbed the lube slow, let her feel every part of me between her cheeks before pressing in.

"Breathe," I said.

She nodded, face in the pillow.

I pushed.

She gasped. Not a scream this time. Just a low, guttural moan that made my whole body shake. The tip slid in. Then a little more. Then a little more. She reached back and spread herself wider.

"Give me that shit."

I gritted my teeth, grabbed her waist, and sank in—inch by inch until I was seated deep in her ass. And she was moaning like it was heaven.

Her ass clenched tight around me, trying to fight it, trying to hold me out. But I pushed deeper. And deeper. And deeper—until my balls pressed against her soaked pussy and I was buried to the base.

"Shiiit," I hissed, head tilted back, chest rising hard.

"You feel that?"

She didn't answer with words. Just backed into me—slow grind, small circles—like she wanted more. Like she wanted all of it.

"Dick not even that big," she mumbled into the pillow, voice smug and half-broken. "Could've taken this shit in the club."

Oh.

I snapped.

Grabbed her hips, pulled her back, and started fucking her. No rhythm. Just pounding. Her ass bounced wild under me, cheeks clapping, spit flying from her mouth with every thrust.

"Say that shit again," I growled, slamming harder.

"Talk now, bitch."

She screamed, one hand gripping the sheets, the other fisting her own hair.

"Is that all you got?" she choked out, voice high and shaking.

"Fuck me like you mean it, Bruce. Stretch this little asshole out—make me shut the fuck up."

So I did. I buried one hand in her throat, the other wrapped under her body to rub her clit as I fucked her harder than I ever had anything in my life.

Raw.

Heavy.

Messy.

Every time I pulled out, I watched her hole cling, trying to hold me in. Every time I sank back in, she moaned louder. Sweat dripped from my chin to her back. Our skin stuck together, slippery and wet.

"Take this fuckin' dick," I growled into her ear.

"Open that nasty ass up, bitch."

"I am," she panted.

"Shit—don't stop—**cum in my fuckin' ass, Bruce—don't be a lil bitch now—**fill me up."

My stroke stuttered.

I was close.

"Yessss," she moaned, reaching back to grab my wrist.

"Nut in this ass. You know you want to. I can feel that dick twitchin'. Go ahead—make this fuckin' mess."

I lost it.

Thrusted once.

Twice.

Buried deep.

And exploded.

Groaned loud as I filled her—pulse after pulse of thick, hot cum spilling into her. She squeezed around me like her body wanted to drink it all.

Then she pulled off—slow—and dropped to her knees behind me.

"Still drippin', huh?" she smirked, grabbing my spent dick, sticky and leaking. She wrapped her lips around the head and sucked—slow, greedy, moaning like the taste of her own ass and my nut was everything she wanted.

Licked the shaft.

Swallowed the tip.

Sucked till she got the last drops.

I nearly collapsed.

We dropped back onto the bed, soaked and destroyed. Breathless. Silent. Soaked in sweat, spit, squirt, and cum. The sheets were ruined. The room smelled like everything we'd just done. And I couldn't feel my legs.

I looked over at her. Eyes closed. Lips swollen. Ass still twitching. Fucked. Raw. Real. Mine.

* * *

I blinked. Back in the garden. She was still standing. Same posture. Same poise. The night hadn't shifted at all—only I had. Still tasting her. Still hearing her. Still feeling her shake around me.

She didn't move. She just stared down at me, thumb still circling the rim of her glass.

312

Then—finally—she spoke.

"How you been?"

No smile.

No shade.

Just... the question.

I looked up at her. And for a second, I didn't know how to answer.

24

When Did We Stop Telling the Truth

"How you been?"

She said it like it was casual. Like we were old coworkers running into each other at a gas station, not two people who once fucked like we couldn't breathe and then stopped speaking like it never happened.

I didn't answer right away.

I just let the question float. Let the night keep pulsing behind us—music, laughter, footsteps on tile.

She stayed standing.

I could feel her eyes on me, but I didn't look up yet.

Finally, I said, "Been alright."

Simple. Measured. Not too open. Not too closed.

She didn't nod. Didn't respond.

She just let it sit.

Then she sat beside me. Slow. Careful. Like she didn't want to shift the air too fast.

We both stared ahead now. At the hedges. The lights. The sky.

She sipped her wine.

"You brought her here?"

There it was.

Not heat. Not judgment. Just the question.

"I didn't bring anybody," I said. I kept my voice even.

"I just didn't send her home."

Tiff didn't blink. Didn't say anything for a long second.

Then finally, "Fair."

And that was it.

Another pause.

I glanced at her, just long enough to study the outline of her jaw, the soft press of her lips against the glass, the way her heels were planted flat on the stones like she was trying to stay grounded.

"You still smoke?" I asked.

She smiled, barely.

"You still lie?"

I almost laughed.

But I didn't.

Because she wasn't joking.

I leaned forward. Elbows on knees.

"When did we stop telling the truth?"

The words came out quiet. Not bitter. Not even sad. Just... tired.

That was the moment. The air shifted. Like we both felt something unlatch.

And that's when the memory came back.

Not the loud ones. Not the wild ones.

Just that night. That one dinner. When we still thought we could handle it.

"When did we stop telling the truth?"

I didn't mean it like an attack. Didn't even mean it like a question, really. Just... one of those things you say out loud because it's been echoing in your chest for weeks.

She didn't answer. She just let the silence sit. Let it breathe. Like we both knew the truth but neither of us wanted to name it aloud.

I stared at the way her thumb moved around the rim of her wine glass. Soft. Thoughtless. Familiar.

* * *

315

And I remembered—

One night. One dinner. Warm light. Small table. Her lips slick from red wine and pepper soup.

The last time we thought we were still being honest.

The lighting was dim but golden, the kind that made dark skin glow and every silence feel intentional. Candle flickering between us. Steam rising from the egusi. She was sipping red wine like it wasn't already the second glass, and I was working slow through my jollof.

We hadn't said much in the last few minutes. But it wasn't uncomfortable. Just... settled.

Tiff was looking past me, at the art on the wall—vibrant brushstrokes of kings and ancestors in burnt orange and oxblood. Her gold hoops caught the light every time she tilted her head.

"Can I ask you something?" she said finally, still not looking at me.

I wiped my mouth with a napkin. Nodded.

She leaned back in her chair, still scanning the paintings like she was talking to one of them.

"You really good with this being open?"

Her voice was soft, like it didn't want to disrupt the air too much. Like it wasn't loaded.

I set my fork down slow. Swallowed. Thought. Not because I didn't know, but because I did—and it still felt like saying it made it real.

"I am," I said.

She looked back at me. One eyebrow raised.

"You sure?"

"I don't need to own you."

That made her smirk. Like she'd heard that before—just never from someone who might mean it.

"But?" she asked, tilting her head, voice teasing.

I sipped my beer. Shrugged.

"But I need honesty. Real shit. Not performative transparency—just... don't let me find out through a comment section."

She laughed into her glass. "Noted."

I looked at her for a beat. Let my eyes hold.

"You?"

"Me what?"

"You good with it being open?"

She didn't answer right away. She just shifted a little in her seat. Bit the inside of her cheek. Looked down at her lap, then back at me.

"Yeah," she said eventually. "But open can get… blurry."

"How so?"

"'Cause people say it like it's just sex. But it's not. Not always."

She traced her finger around the rim of her glass.

"Sometimes it's the way somebody makes you laugh. Or how they listen. Or remember your food orders without you telling them. That's the shit that fucks with me."

I nodded. Because I knew. That was the part I protected, too.

"Yeah," I said. "That's where the real danger is."

* * *

She looked at me, then looked away again.

"You ever caught feelings while being open?"

The question felt like it was made of something more delicate than words. Like it had history behind it.

"Yeah," I said.

"Did you tell her?"

"Nope."

She smiled like she understood that.

"I didn't want to hurt her," I added.

Tiff sipped again. "Sometimes not saying it is worse."

"Sometimes," I said. "But not when the rules were soft from the start."

That made her hum. Not quite agreement. Not quite disagreement either.

She reached over and stole a piece of fried plantain from my plate.

"You want to know everything?" she asked. Still chewing. Still cool.

"Not everything," I said. "But the real stuff. The shit that could shift us—I want to hear that from you. Not the internet. Not some passive post. You."

She tapped her fingernail on the edge of the plate.

"I post to provoke," she said. "Sometimes I like seeing who reacts."

I leaned back, looked at her. "And what reaction are you hoping for?"

She looked right at me this time.

"Yours."

That hit something in me I didn't want to show. So I smiled, but didn't say anything.

She reached for her wine again. Sipped like it wasn't a confession.

"You got a good heart, Bruce."

I shook my head.

"Nah. I just listen close. And I don't pretend not to care."

She stared at me a little longer than expected. Then looked down at her glass again.

"Dangerous combo."

"Why?"

"'Cause you'll love somebody before they've even decided who they want to be."

We sat in that for a second. Longer than a second. Neither of us moved.

And then she said, quieter this time—

"But I'm glad you're here."

And I was. Even if I couldn't say it out loud.

We were trying that night. Both of us. Saying the right things. Believing we could handle the weight.

But somewhere between that table and this moment... something changed.

It wasn't one night. Not really.

It was a string of them. Late calls. Slurred "you up?" texts. Panic attacks in parking decks. Muffled sobs on voice notes. And me—always me—being the one who picked up.

Even when I was tired. Even when she didn't ask how I was holding all her weight.

I never said no.

* * *

I think the beginning of the end came on a Thursday. I was on the couch, plate of cold noodles in my lap, Monk playing on low in the background. Some scene where he couldn't walk into a room without turning every lamp the same angle. It made me laugh—until it didn't.

I opened Instagram. Just scrolling.

And there she was.

Tiff. Slicked up in the backseat of someone's car. Hair damp, lips glossy, camera tilted low like it slipped on purpose. She was giving head. Sloppy. Loud. Sucking the soul out of somebody that wasn't me. Hooked to the beat of a song I didn't know she was pushing. For her OnlyFans. For her bag.

No warning. No check-in. No, "Hey, just so you know…"

We were open. But I wasn't invisible.

I didn't bring it up. Didn't text. Didn't ask her if it was recent, if it meant anything, if she meant for me to see it.

I just watched it twice.

Once to understand.

Once to see how it felt to be a stranger.

She used to talk about land. About buying property in Jamaica, maybe Ghana. About taking her mama to Accra for the Year of Return. She used to read Baldwin out loud. Debate capitalism over brunch. She had a plan. A fire. Something still tethered to purpose.

Now it was OnlyFans links. Viral mess. Cheap liquor. And this need to be seen that only made her more hollow every time she hit "post."

And me?

I was still there. Still showing up. Still pretending it didn't gut me to watch her become unrecognizable.

She came over the next night.

Didn't mention the Story. Didn't ask if I saw it. She just dropped her bag, took off her shoes, asked what was for dinner.

I said nothing.

Warmed up leftovers. Poured her a drink. Rubbed her feet while she vented about a homegirl who bailed, a man who ghosted, a venue that underpaid her again.

And I just… listened.

But I wasn't in the room anymore.

* * *

Next morning, she shuffled into the kitchen in one of my hoodies. No pants. Bare legs. Told me I was good to her.

Kissed my cheek like always. Drank the tea I made. Sat in my kitchen like none of it was different.

And I smiled.

Because I always did.

But inside?

I almost said, "I miss you." But I didn't even know who I was talking to anymore.

That was the morning I let go.

Not loud. Not bitter. Just….

I stopped trying to hold the shape of something she kept shifting.

I stopped trying to save someone who didn't want to be seen.

* * *

I blinked.

Back in the garden.

Same bench. Same dress. Same thumb circling the rim of her wine glass like the motion kept her anchored.

She hadn't moved. Neither had I. But something in the air had shifted.

She looked out at the hedge, the lights tucked into the stone path, the shadows that stretched just past the edge of everything.

Then, without turning her head, she asked—

"You still want to go to Kingston?"

Simple.

Like we were talking about a restaurant. Like the trip hadn't been planned in a version of us that no longer existed.

I didn't answer right away.

I just stared out at the sea. Still couldn't see it—just heard it beyond the trees. But I swear the tide was louder now.

Finally, I said, "Yeah. We said we would."

* * *

She nodded once. Didn't smile. Didn't press.

She just let the night take it.

And for the first time since she walked up... we both sat still.

Not as lovers. Not as friends.

Just two people who once meant something. And still had the map, even if the destination didn't make sense anymore.

25

No Escape

The quiet didn't last long. Tiff shifted beside me. Picked up her wine glass, but didn't sip it. She just turned it in her hand like she was trying to hold onto something.

"You really had her out here like that?"

I didn't move.

"Like she belonged next to you. Like you couldn't even pretend I ever meant anything to you."

I exhaled slow.

"Tiff—"

"Nah," she cut in. "Don't 'Tiff' me. You had her holding your hand like she owned a piece of you. Like I ain't never been nothing but a fuckin layover."

Now I looked at her.

"You wanna do this here? Right now?"

She laughed, bitter. "I didn't choose the setting. You the one brought your little tropical rebound to a wedding full of people who know what the fuck we used to be."

My jaw tensed.

"I didn't bring anybody. She was already here. I didn't ask her to show up. I didn't plan shit. But she treated me like I mattered—which is more than I can say about you the last few months."

"Oh fuck off, Bruce."

She stood now, heels scraping stone. Didn't care if it made noise. Didn't care if anyone heard.

"You didn't bring her? That's your defense? You let her pull you around like you hers. You let her kiss up on you like you ain't never had nobody before. You think that shit don't sting?"

* * *

I stood too.

"She ain't the one who posted a video sucking dick on social media for the whole fucking timeline to see!"

Boom.

Her eyes flared.

"And there it is."

"Yeah. There it is. You wanna talk about embarrassment? Let's talk. You posted your throat working overtime like it was a fuckin trailer drop. No heads up. No check-in. Just dropped it like new music."

"Because it was promo, Bruce! For my work. That pays my bills. Which, last time I checked, you don't contribute to."

"That's what we calling it now? Work?"

She stepped in close.

"What do you care anyway? Thought we were open. Thought you didn't need to own me. Ain't that your little line?"

"We were open, not stupid. That was violating."

"I told you I was on OnlyFans!"

"You didn't tell me I'd be finding out through Instagram like everybody else. You didn't tell me I'd be watching a woman I loved choke on somebody else while trying to remember what your laugh used to sound like."

She blinked. That one hit.

But I was already in it.

"I used to replay your voice notes when I couldn't sleep. I used to light incense you left at my place and pretend the scent was your fuckin presence. And while I was doing all that, you were out here spitting on dicks for

323

retweets."

"Fuck you, Bruce."

"Oh, we cussing now? Good. Let's get it all out. Let's stop pretending we civilized."

"Fuck you," she said again, louder. "For making me think I was safe with you. For pretending you gave a fuck, then moving on with some barefoot island bitch who don't even know your middle name."

My hands balled into fists.

"You think Jo's the problem? You think this is about her?"

Tiff stepped back and waved a hand.

"You know what? Fuck this."

And she turned to walk away.

"You always do that!" I shouted. "Every time it's too real, you run! You throw fire, then vanish in the smoke and act like the ashes ain't yours!"

She froze.

Turned back. Slow. Walked up till we were damn near nose to nose.

"You think you know everything. But you don't know SHIT."

By now, someone had turned their head. A couple by the garden steps paused. A DJ switch dropped too loud—then dipped again.

But we didn't care.

We were breathing hard.

Chest to chest.

Neither of us blinking.

And for a second—just one second—

I swear I saw it.

The crack.

The sorrow.

The truth trying to claw its way out.

But it wasn't ready yet.

So we stood there.

Burning.

* * *

She was still in my face. Breathing like she'd just run ten miles through rage. I was breathing the same. Not out of anger anymore. Just... spent.

I looked down first. Not because I was backing down. Because I was tired of holding my chest out like I was still trying to win something.

She stepped back. Not far. Just enough to break the gravity between us.

Then, softer—almost like it surprised her—

"I didn't wanna be this."

Her voice cracked on the word "this." She blinked hard. Once. Then again. Like she was trying to clear it before it fell.

"You think I wanted to become this version of me?"

She shook her head.

"I was never like this. Not when we met. Not when I used to come to your place after work and fall asleep before my shoes were off. I was still me then."

I stayed silent.

Didn't rush it.

Let her keep going.

She looked past me. Out into the dark where the garden met the trees.

"My sister's getting beat. Every other week, she calls me whispering from the bathroom. Scared. But won't leave. I been sending her money I barely got just so she can say she has options—just so I don't feel useless."

Her voice didn't rise. Didn't wobble.

It just... sagged.

"My mom ain't got heat. The landlord's trying to push her out. I paid her gas bill with promo money from that video you hate so much."

She finally looked at me.

"I didn't post that shit 'cause I'm proud of it. I posted it 'cause I'm drowning. And if I can't scream, I can monetize the silence. That's the world we live in now, right?"

I didn't have words yet.

Couldn't find the shape of a response that didn't feel like apology or shame or pity.

So I just let her talk.

"My uncle died. The one who used to pick me up from dance class. I couldn't even go to the funeral 'cause I had a fucking hosting gig that paid my rent. So yeah—I been spiraling. And maybe I didn't wanna tell you. Because you were the one place I didn't have to be the strong one. And I knew if I opened up, I'd fall apart."

I stepped toward her.

Slow. One foot at a time.

Like I was approaching a cliff.

When I was close enough, I said,

"You could've told me."

"I couldn't," she said. "I didn't want you to see me like that."

I looked her in the eyes.

"I been seen you like that. I just didn't know why."

She blinked.

"I thought you stopped caring."

"I never stopped caring," I said.

"I stopped knowing how."

Another silence.

But this one didn't burn.

It... breathed.

Then she whispered, "You really loved me?"

I nodded. No pause.

"Still do."

That cracked her open.

"You loved me and still agreed to be open?"

"I only agreed because I thought I couldn't have all of you. I thought you didn't want that."

Her eyes welled.

"I didn't want open either," she said.

"I just didn't think you'd choose me if I asked for more."

And there it was.

The marrow.

The thing we never said out loud because saying it meant risking the whole damn thing.

* * *

I looked at her.

"You were my soft place, Tiff. My anchor. When the divorce fucked me up—when my life collapsed, when I didn't know who the fuck I was anymore… you were the one person who made me feel like I could survive it."

She pressed a hand to her chest. Like it physically hurt to hear.

"I didn't know that," she said.

I nodded.

"I know. And I ain't say it either. Because I didn't wanna lose you."

She looked at me like she forgot why she ever pulled away in the first place.

Then she stepped in.

Not bold.

Not certain.

Just close.

Close enough for her hand to find my wrist.

Close enough for me to feel the breath slip out of her mouth and land on mine.

And when we kissed—

It wasn't slow.

Like something giving out.

Her lips moved like she was trying to remember the shape of me.

Like she didn't trust it, but couldn't stop.

My hand found her waist.

Not to pull her in—

just to feel if she'd let me.

She did.

And when her fingers curled in my shirt—tight, desperate, like she was drowning again.

327

I knew this wasn't about closure.
It was about everything we never said.
And maybe we weren't gonna stop.
Not tonight.

26

Where I Been Needing It

Her fingers were still in my shirt. Breath tangled. Mouths still parted like we hadn't decided to stop—just paused to remember where we were.

She looked at me.

Like she saw every version of me—the man who held her down, the man who let her go, and the one standing here now, still holding on.

Then she pulled back. Not far. Just enough to breathe. Her hand slipped down my chest, slow.

And then she said it—low. Plain. Like a dare dressed as a choice.

"We could stay out here and kiss each other 'til our lips go numb…"

She let it hang.

Then stepped in closer, leaned into my ear—voice dropping half an octave:

"Or you could follow me inside… and put that big dick where I been needing it."

She pulled back, eyes locked on mine.

Didn't smirk.

Didn't blink.

Then she turned.

Walked down the stone path like she knew the night belonged to her now.

Didn't check to see if I was behind her. She didn't have to.

* * *

I followed.

Didn't rush.

Didn't speak.

Just let the air thicken around us—the party still echoing somewhere behind the trees, the moon sliding behind clouds like it didn't want to watch.

We took a side path I hadn't noticed before. Her room was tucked behind a bend in the garden—hidden, light spilling soft beneath a row of palms.

She didn't pause when we reached it. She just opened the door like she'd done it a hundred times before.

Walked in.

Barefoot now.

I followed.

Closed the door behind us.

Inside, the air was warm. Still.

And her—

standing in the middle of the room, back to me, hands on her hips like she was deciding what to do with all this energy.

* * *

She turned around.

Didn't say a word.

Just walked up.

Slow.

Her fingers reached for my shirt again.

Not to grip this time.

To undo.

One button.

Then another.

Eyes never leaving mine.

She didn't ask if I wanted this.

And I didn't need to tell her I did.

I kissed her again before she could turn around—hands on her jaw, mouth open, breath shared like oxygen didn't exist outside of us. She moaned into it, soft at first, then deeper, throatier, like her body remembered this better than her mind did.

She tried to reach for my pants but I caught her wrists.

Held them still.

Pressed her back against the wall.

"Nah," I said against her mouth. "I'm going first."

She smirked like she knew what that meant.

But her eyes widened when I dropped to my knees and yanked her dress up all at once—no finesse, no teasing.

"Bruce—fuck—"

Already breathy.

I pulled her panties aside and went straight in—no warmup, no warning.

Tongue deep. Broad. Firm.

Flattened and dragged across her clit like I was writing a memory in cursive.

She buckled.

Thighs clenched my head on instinct.

And I didn't move.

Just held her there.

Let her ride my mouth like it was hers to lose herself on.

The bass from the room's Bluetooth speaker hit right then—

"Clouded" by Brent Faiyaz.

I been thinkin' maybe...

I been goin' crazy...

Yeah. That part.

I was already too far gone.

I spread her wider, pulled her leg over my shoulder.

Started sucking—messy, wet, shameless.

"Shit—fuck, Bruce—oh my—"

She jerked once, hard, grabbing my hair with both hands like she needed to hold on to something real.

Then she squirted.

Violent.

Airborne.

That first jet slapped my cheek, then sprayed down my neck and chest—hot, sweet, wild.

"Goddamn," I muttered, wiping my mouth with the back of my hand and grinning up at her.

"You a fuckin' geyser now?"

She couldn't speak. Just gasped and half-laughed, gripping the wall like it was holding her up.

I didn't wait.

Pushed her leg higher.

Buried my face again.

Licked up everything she gave me—let it drip into my beard, onto my collarbone. Didn't care.

She squirmed, tried to close her legs again.

"Move, Tiff."

"Can't—sensitive—"

"Don't care."

I growled it against her clit and kept going.

Flicked my tongue faster.

Then slower.

Then sucked it into my mouth like I was tasting her soul.

She came again.

Didn't scream—just shook.

Her whole body stuttering.

Then I moved lower.

Slid my tongue down, deeper between her cheeks—

licked that tight little ring like I'd done it a hundred times before.

She froze.

"Bruce—Bruce—"

"You know I been missed this ass," I muttered, voice rough in her crack.

Then I spit on it.

Spread her wider.

And went back in.

Slow, circular, deliberate.

Her hips started grinding.

She was moaning now—low, dark, broken.

"Eat that shit, baby. Fuck—fuck yes…"

I looked up at her while I did it—her eyes rolled, her lips parted, hair sticking to her face.

Then her voice dropped.

"You wanna come up here and get your dick sucked now, or you wanna keep making puddles on my floor?"

* * *

I stood.

Didn't speak.

Pulled my pants down just enough and she dropped to her knees before I could blink.

No warm-up.

No tease.

She opened her mouth and took me deep—spit and heat and tongue everywhere.

"Shit—"

She grinned with her lips wrapped around me, then pulled back with a pop.

"You quiet now?" she said, licking her lips.

Then she went lower.

Licked my balls, sucked them one at a time—wet and slow—then slid her tongue further.

Teased me.

Got under me.

Hit that spot.

I shivered. Couldn't even fake it.

"Damn, girl…"

She came back up, eyes gleaming.

"You shaking already?" she said, wiping her chin. "I ain't even started yet."

I pulled her up from her knees like I was lifting something sacred. But I wasn't gentle. Turned her around. Bent her over the bed. Pushed her face into the sheets. Not rough—just enough to remind her what I'd been holding back.

"Keep that ass up."

She arched without hesitation. That ass… I gripped it in both hands and spread her wide. Still wet. Still glistening. Her whole body gleamed under the low lamp like honeyed sweat and sin.

I slid back inside—slow, deep, steady. She moaned low, then gasped as I bottomed out.

"Fuuuck—you ain't even warn me."

"Wasn't no warning last time either."

I leaned over her back, lips against her ear.

"You gave me that pussy like you were trying to make me forget who I was."

She looked over her shoulder, face half-pressed to the pillow.

"And did it work?"

I slammed into her harder—once, deep. She choked on a breath.

"Yeah," I growled. "You ruined me."

Then I started moving.

Heavy strokes.

Her body met every thrust like it remembered the rhythm better than we did.

I grabbed her hair, pulled her up slightly.

"Say you missed this dick."

"Fuck yes, I missed this dick. Missed you stretchin' me like this—missed

334

how full you make me feel—"

She started to come mid-sentence. Her legs gave. She fell forward and I caught her hips, held her in place, kept fucking. Her thighs were soaked. The sheets—drenched.

I slid out. Flipped her over.

"Open them legs," I said.

She obeyed.

Head back.

Hair stuck to her cheeks.

I lifted one leg over my shoulder and slid back in—slow, cruel, full.

She screamed.

No words. Just sound.

I moved deeper.

Deeper still.

"Stretchin' this pretty pussy out," I muttered, watching her fall apart.

She started squirting again.

Not soft—forceful.

Spraying the sheets, the floor, my chest.

"Goddamn, baby—"

She slapped my chest.

"I—I can't—Bruce, I can't stop—"

"Then don't."

I grabbed both legs, held them together, and fucked through it—through the mess, through her shakes, through the puddle forming beneath us.

The sheet couldn't take it.

It was drenched.

Unusable.

I pulled out.

She lay there—panting, drenched, twitching.

Then she laughed, breathless.

"You...you broke the bed, Bruce."

I looked down at the soaked mattress.

"You did that."

She grinned.

Eyes wild.

"Then let's go drown Lora's bed too."

* * *

We stumbled into the second bed—Tiff leading the way, still half-naked, dripping down her thighs. I laid her on her stomach, pulled her hips up.

"Don't move."

She looked back, biting her bottom lip.

Then I slid in again—this time deeper.

Wetter.

Wilder.

Flat strokes while she lay with her cheek pressed to the sheets—fingers gripping the headboard. She kept coming. Over and over. Body convulsing. One hand between her thighs, rubbing herself as I hit it from behind.

"Bruce, I'm gonna—fuck, I'm gonna—"

She screamed into the mattress.

Soaked the second bed too.

And I didn't stop.

Didn't let her catch breath.

Not yet.

She collapsed on her side—wet, shaking, breath stuck in her throat like she couldn't find the next one. I slid in behind her. Wrapped one arm under her chest, pulled her close, pressed my dick between her thighs and dragged it through the slick heat until she whimpered.

"You done?" I whispered against her neck.

She laughed.

Low. Ragged.

"Hell no."

Then she rolled over. Climbed on top. Straddled me like it was hers again. She reached between us, slid me back inside.

And rode.

No warm-up this time.

Just bounce. Grip. Wet.

Pussy still pulsing around me like it couldn't get enough.

My hands found her ass.

I guided her up and down—let her fuck me at her rhythm.

She gripped my chest for balance, but her hips never slowed.

"Fuck—fuck, Bruce—feels too good—"

She came again.

Hard.

Left a flood on my stomach.

Slid back, collapsed over my thighs.

Then she licked her lips.

And went down.

Took me in like she was mad at it.

Gagging.

Spit trailing down my shaft.

Balls slick from her tongue.

She sucked hard, then pulled off and looked up at me.

"You want it all?" she asked.

Voice gone. Face glowing.

I nodded.

She went back in.

Faster.

Sloppier.

Hand twisting at the base, lips working overtime, spit everywhere.

Then she slipped lower.

Sucked my balls again, then lower—tongue teasing my ass, wet and slow.

I twitched.

"Goddamn, girl—"

She came back up smiling.

"Thought you ain't like surprises."

"You tryna kill me."

"Not yet."

She climbed back on, planted her feet, and rode me deep.

Flesh clapping.

Juice running.

Her eyes locked on mine like she wanted me to see every drop that left her.

"Don't look away," she said.

"I want you to see what you did to me."

She came again.

Again.

And again.

Each time left a new trail across my thighs, my chest, the sheets.

Then I sat up, grabbed her hips, flipped her to all fours.

"I want it now," she said.

Voice gone.

I grabbed the vibrator from the nightstand—Lora's, probably. Didn't matter.

Pressed it to her clit.

And slid in her ass.

"Shiiiit—Bruce—fuck—"

I gripped her waist and went deep.

Long strokes.

She screamed into the pillow, clit pressed hard to the buzz, ass clenching around me.

"Keep that toy there," I growled. "Don't move it."

She obeyed.

Trembled.

Body went rigid.

Then she came one last time—

back arched, scream caught in her throat, the kind of orgasm that short-circuits the whole body.

And I lost it.

Pulled out fast.

Stroked once—twice—then exploded.

Thick.

Hot.

Ropes of cum shot across her back—her ass, her spine, her shoulder blades.

More than I even thought I had in me.

We didn't speak right away. She lay there on her stomach, breathing deep— body twitching every few seconds like the orgasm hadn't fully left her system. Her back was streaked with cum. Her thighs glistened. The sheets were soaked straight through.

I sat on the edge of the bed, still catching my breath, still half-hard.

Then I stood.

Didn't say anything.

Just walked to the bathroom and turned on the shower—hot.

The water hit my skin like a confession.

I stood under it for a while.

Let it run down my face, my chest, my hands still shaking from how tight she'd held me.

Her moans were still in my ears.

Her voice, her spit, her scent.

All of it.

I wasn't trying to rinse her off.

Just... calm the electricity in my body.

When I stepped out, she was still there.

Eyes closed. One leg bent. Fingers trailing lazy lines across her hip like she was tracing a memory she wasn't ready to let go of.

I walked over.

Bent down.

Pressed a kiss to her shoulder.

She turned her head, met my eyes.

Then lifted up—barely—and kissed me on the mouth.

Not hard.

Not hungry.

Just… honest.

We held it for a second.

Then she exhaled.

"I need a shower too," she said.

I stood. Nodded.

She didn't rush. She just slid out of the bed slow, body glistening under the soft light.

I watched her walk to the bathroom.

Didn't say another word.

Just got dressed—slow, careful—and let the door close behind me.

27

No One Knows, But Everyone Knows

The bass hit first. Even before we opened the door. Low and thick—it sounded like it had been waiting on us.

Inside, the reception was full-on glowing now. String lights everywhere. Couples grinding slow near the DJ booth. Uncles leaned back in chairs with shirt buttons popped open. Laughter cutting through the music like it had its own beat. The whole room smelled like cake and sweat and rum punch.

Me and Tiff slipped back in without saying a word. No handholding. No extra smiles. But the heat was still on us. I could feel it in my chest. And in the way her dress stuck to the small of her back now.

* * *

We moved casual—like we ain't just flip a bed and flood the sheets in Lora's room.

Dev spotted me quick. Already grinning. Already halfway through his cup.

"Aye—look who finally came up for air," he called out, waving me over.

I shook my head, dapped him up.

"I was literally gone for a drink."

He looked at me. Sipped slow. Grinned again.

"That's wild. 'Cause the bar's right there and you came back smelling like secrets."

I laughed, tried to brush it off. But he wasn't done.

"Yo," he leaned in, voice low, "you movin' like your knees still recovering. You good?"

"I'm straight."

"You sure?" He pointed at my shirt.

"You missed a button, my boy."

I looked down. Fixed it.

"Mind your business."

Dev just laughed and turned back to his drink.

Didn't say nothing else.

Didn't need to.

That afterglow wasn't easy to fake.

And honestly? I wasn't even trying to.

* * *

Tiff had already peeled off toward the bar. Didn't look back. Didn't have to. We were still moving like we shared a frequency no one else could hear.

I posted up by the edge of the dance floor, drink in hand, watching the energy swell around me. People were loose now—heels off, shirts damp, arms in the air. The DJ transitioned smooth into "Essence," and the whole floor moved like honey—slow, waist-led, sticky with heat.

Tiff reappeared a few songs later.

She wasn't dancing.

Not yet.

Just standing by Lora and a few bridesmaids, swaying slow with her cup to her lips.

Her eyes caught mine for half a second.

Not a full glance.

Not a stare.

Just a check-in.

Like: *You good?*

And I was.

Still floating.

Still tracing the shape of her moans in the back of my mind.

Dev nudged me again, this time with a toast.

"To redemption sex," he said.

I laughed, clinked glasses.

Didn't deny a damn thing.

* * *

The music dipped under just enough to hear a voice come through the mic—smooth, confident, practiced.

DJ:

"Aight, aight—before we get too lit, we got some words comin' from the fam. Y'all show some love real quick for the groom's big brother—G!"

Applause broke out. A couple frat calls echoed in the back.

Then G stepped forward—clean white linen, gold chain low on his chest, that calm-but-playful energy only an older brother can carry. He took the mic, grinned, waited for the noise to settle.

"Now I ain't tryna hold y'all from the dancefloor… but I do got a mic, so…"No warning

(laughter)

"First off, I just wanna say—Shawn, you did it, bruh. You found somebody who ain't just beautiful, but patient enough to deal with your dramatic ass."

(more laughter, a few loud 'facts!' from the groomsmen)

He glanced at Nicole, then back at Shawn.

"For real though—watchin' y'all come together these past few years been a blessing. Y'all been through long distance, job switches, lost people. But you kept showin' up. You didn't just fall in love. You chose it. Over and over."

"So here's what I got for you—and y'all can hold me to it: You gon' argue. You gon' get tired. You gon' wonder why the hell you even got married in

343

the first place. But if you remember this—you not doin' it alone—you'll be alright."

He raised his glass.

"To Shawn and Nicole. May this be the easiest part of y'all forever."

The room erupted—cheers, clinks, somebody screaming "toast toast toast!"

Then the DJ brought the music back up, rolling smooth into "Get You" by Daniel Caesar.

* * *

The music dropped with no warning—just horns and heat. That Lil Jon energy. Raw. Aggressive. Announcing itself before the beat even landed.

"WHO YOU WIT?!"

Somebody from the back yelled out:

"AYO SIX!"

Then came the claps.

Then the stomp.

Then the chant.

The Alphas mobbed up fast—black and gold everywhere, already bouncing like the floor belonged to them. Shawn was at the front. Tie gone, shirt unbuttoned halfway down, mouth wide open as he shouted:

"ICE COLD!"

He wasn't drunk. He was charged. Lit from the inside. His line brothers fell in behind him—tight formation, locked arms, bounce timed to the bass. They hit the floor like they never left undergrad. Chest out. Shoulders rockin'. Eyes locked in like this wasn't a reception—it was a probate.

The crowd lost it.

Phones up. Aunties screaming. Bridesmaids ducking for safety and grabbing their heels.

Bruce stepped back, posted up near the edge. He wasn't Greek. But he knew power when he saw it.

"That shit look like tradition and testosterone had a baby."

The whole dancefloor pulsed as the line stomped through it—turns tight, steps sharp, synchronized with the kind of pride that didn't need explaining. Shawn hit a move, dropped to one knee, threw up the sign, then popped up smooth and called out:

"Nicole—get your ass over here!"

Laughter. Cheers. The DJ hyped it from the booth.

Nicole shook her head at first, but she couldn't resist. She stepped in. Got low. Matched him step for step like she'd been rehearsing in secret.

That's when the floor erupted.

People ran in to surround them. It turned into a full-blown Greek celebration.

"This what it look like when legacy marries love," Bruce thought, sipping slow.

He scanned the room.

Saw joy.

Saw heat.

Saw Tiff standing off to the side again, arms folded, watching with a half-smile.

She looked centered. Still.

Like all of this was hers too.

Then his eyes drifted—just a little.

And there she was.

Jo.

Across the room.

Watching him.

Black dress.

No makeup.

Hair pulled back like she came for peace, not attention.

She wasn't dancing.

Wasn't talking.

Just watching.

Me.

Her face didn't say much.

No smile.

No judgment.

Just... still.

I froze.

For maybe a second.

But long enough.

She nodded once. Small. Like a punctuation mark on something we never finished.

And that's when I felt it.

Tiff.

Watching me.

From across the floor.

She didn't say anything.

Didn't make a scene.

Didn't even move.

But something in her eyes shifted.

Like the light dimmed just a bit behind them.

She turned back toward the bridesmaid, laughed at something that wasn't funny, and started dancing harder—arms up, head thrown back like she was trying to drown whatever just hit her.

And me?

I couldn't move.

Couldn't even lift my cup.

Because Jo was still looking.

And now, she wasn't alone.

The room kept moving. DJ was deep in a soca set now—flags waving, drinks spilling, heels long forgotten.

Tiff was still dancing.

But something was different.

Before, she'd been in sync with the night.

Now? She was trying to outdance it.

Arms looser. Laugh louder.

NO ONE KNOWS, BUT EVERYONE KNOWS

Almost like she was proving something to the air.

I slid closer.

Not right behind her. Just enough to say something low—something only she'd hear.

"You good?"

She didn't turn.

She just kept moving, eyes locked on the bridesmaid in front of her.

"Why wouldn't I be?" she said, barely glancing over her shoulder.

I stepped back.

Watched her for a beat.

The curve of her mouth was still soft, but her eyes weren't checking for mine anymore.

Not the way they were earlier.

She tossed her braids off her shoulder and kept dancing.

Like I wasn't standing there.

Like my hand hadn't just been wrapped in her hair a half hour ago.

Dev eased up beside me, cup in hand, breath short from laughing.

"Yo, you good?" he asked.

I nodded. Didn't answer.

Because I knew what this was.

I'd felt it before.

That moment when somebody takes their heart off the table—but acts like they never put it down.

And Tiff?

She was still in the room.

Still in the rhythm.

But not with me anymore.

* * *

The music was still going. Bodies still grinding. Cups still clinking.

But something in me had already stepped out of it.

I needed air.

347

Told Dev I'd be right back, but we both knew I wasn't coming back in.

I slipped out through the side terrace.

Walked past the hedges into a little stretch of quiet—just me and the garden lights buzzing against the dark.

Sat on a bench.

Rolled my shoulders.

Let the sweat on my back start to cool.

The night felt thick with everything I wasn't saying.

Tiff's voice.

Jo's eyes.

The way the music kept trying to keep me in a moment I'd already drifted from.

I stared out at nothing for a while.

Listened to the tide in the distance.

Tried to breathe.

The walk back to my room felt longer than it should've.

Not because the hallways stretched—but because I didn't want to reach the door.

Tiff's text still sat open on my phone.

Hope you have a great night.

That fake-soft tone.

Polished like closure.

Heavy like a goodbye that didn't want to beg.

I didn't respond.

Just tucked the phone in my pocket and let my footsteps echo.

Past other rooms. Past laughter. Past music still thumping through walls.

I slid the key into the lock.

Turned it.

And froze.

Lights low.

Not off.

Just dim enough to cast a golden hue over the room.

There was music playing. Something slow. No words—just keys and bass that knew how to wait for a body to move.

And her scent.

Not the one I remembered from the club.

Something softer now. Like coconut and skin after rain.

Then I saw her.

Jo.

* * *

Already inside.

Leg crossed over the other, heel dangling loose off one foot.

She was sitting on the edge of the bed like it belonged to her.

Black lace.

Not trashy. Not dainty.

Structured. Bold. Cut high on the thigh, hugged low at the waist.

Straps framed her chest like she knew exactly how much to offer without handing over everything.

And heels—

Black, glossy, nothing simple.

Like she came dressed to say I knew you'd be here.

Her hair was swept to one side, loose curls falling over one shoulder.

Lips full. No gloss. Just soft.

Eyes locked on mine like she'd been waiting for this exact second to arrive.

She didn't smile.

Didn't blink.

Just tilted her head slightly and said:

"Mi nah come fi compete, yuh hear?"

I didn't move.

She stood.

Slow. Deliberate.

Walked toward me like the floor agreed with her.

"Mi nah here fi be louder dan she... or softer. Mi nah try be some version yuh can manage easier."

She stopped a few inches from me.

Close enough for the heat to rise off her skin.

"Mi come 'cause di way yuh look at mi—like mi still inside yuh chest.

An mi feel it.

Even across di room.

Even after all dis time."

I swallowed.

Couldn't speak yet.

She reached up.

Ran one finger down the side of my neck.

Not teasing—just claiming.

"Mi nuh know wah dis is, Bruce.

But mi nah leaving 'til mi find out.

Not again."

She leaned in—

Pressed her lips just under my jaw.

Not a kiss.

Not a pull.

Just a mark.

A decision.

28

Mi Still Deh Yah

I didn't expect the lights to be low. Didn't expect the room to smell faintly like coconut and citrus—like skin that had already showered, lotioned, settled. Didn't expect the music either. Something soft, slow, barely audible.

But I knew she was there before I saw her.

Jo.

Standing by the edge of the bed. Heels still on. Long legs smooth beneath black lace that caught the light every time she shifted her weight.

Not performing. Not posing.

Just… present.

Her eyes found mine. No smile. No drama.

"Mi still deh yah."

* * *

Like it was a fact.

Like she didn't need to ask permission.

Like she wasn't afraid of whatever I was carrying when I walked through the door.

I shut the door behind me. Dropped the key on the table. Didn't move at first. I studied her in the soft amber wash of the lamp near the bed. How the shadows hugged her hips. How her arms stayed loose at her sides. How her lips didn't part—not yet. How one heel dipped slightly inward when she shifted—like she was grounding herself before saying too much.

"You didn't have to wait," I said.

She tilted her head—not sass, just softness.

"Mi wasn't waiting. Mi came."

She took a step toward me.

Barely.

"If yuh done wid me... just seh dat. But mi know seh no woman can tek mi place. Only borrow space."

Her voice didn't flinch.

Neither did she.

I didn't know what this meant. Didn't know if reaching for her would feel like betrayal or redemption.

But my body moved anyway.

We stood like that—close enough to feel each other's breath.

But neither moved.

Not yet.

"Yuh look tired," she said.

Not pity. Not softness. Just observation.

I nodded.

Then walked forward, slow.

Closed the space between us.

Let my fingers graze her wrist.

"I never said I was done."

They didn't touch right away. Not fully. I let my hand slide from her wrist to her fingers. Held them. Jo didn't squeeze. Didn't pull away. She just let our hands rest there—joined, unmoving.

* * *

I led her to the bed. Not to lie down. Just to sit. Side by side, our backs against the headboard, our legs stretched forward, ankles brushing.

The music was still playing—Lila Iké's "Second Chance", slow and heavy like wet silk. That aching sway, her voice curling around the bassline like a whisper you weren't supposed to hear.

I didn't know the name at first.

But I knew the feeling.

That ache. That almost. That if only.

Like the track itself had seen two people come close and drift—then choose to stay for just one more night.

For a long stretch, neither of us said anything. Jo tilted her head back, eyes closed, her breath slow and steady like ocean rhythm. Her leg was warm against mine, bare at the thigh, still and steady—like she'd always belonged in that silence beside me.

I stared ahead—at the TV turned off, the shadows on the wall, the light catching the curve of her collarbone.

It wasn't awkward.

It just... was.

Eventually, Jo spoke. Her voice was low, almost playful.

"You remember that night at the party?"

I turned toward her, eyes soft.

"I remember the way you looked at me before you even said a word."

Jo smiled, eyes still closed.

"Mi saw yuh watching me. Yuh didn't blink."

I chuckled. That crooked kind of laugh that carried more weight than humor.

"I thought you were gonna disappear after that. Like you weren't real."

"Mi nah ghost," she said. "Mi spirit."

That hit something in my chest.

Because she was right.

Jo didn't haunt—she hovered. She held. She witnessed.

Still looking at the ceiling, she added, quieter this time:

"From the first night... mi know yuh was searching fi something yuh couldn't name. An' mi never try fi be yuh answer. Just... company pon di walk."

I didn't respond right away.

I just let that settle.

Then:

"You were more than company."

I paused.

"I ain't felt like myself in a long time. But with you? I stopped pretending. I almost…"

I stopped.

Jo didn't push.

She turned her head slowly. Looked at me. Really looked.

I met her gaze.

The space between us folded.

And finally, she said—

"Good."

A beat passed. Then another.

"Yuh heart is yuh own," she added. "Mi never wanted fi hold it—just touch it and leave it warmer than mi found it."

I didn't answer.

* * *

I just reached over and kissed the inside of her wrist.

Soft. Steady.

The song faded, but Jo's breath moved in rhythm with the echo—slow and syncopated, like she wasn't listening with her ears, but with memory.

The silence that followed wasn't heavy anymore.

It just felt like truth.

My lips lingered at her wrist. A breath. A pause. And then her fingers curled under my chin, lifting my face to hers.

"Mi see yuh," Jo said. Not like a confession. Like a ceremony.

I leaned in. Not fast. Not hungry. Just full. Our mouths met with no need to rush. No fight for control. No hands grabbing or breath catching. Just lips parting, tongues brushing—like we'd been waiting to remember how.

She tasted like red wine and warm breath. Her skin smelled like mango oil and fresh cotton. Warm. Clean. Like she'd been waiting without waiting.

* * *

Jo reached for my shirt. Pulled it up slow. Not because she was teasing. Because she wanted to feel every inch of me again, deliberate. Like reading braille.

I helped her, letting the fabric fall behind me. Her eyes moved down my chest. She didn't smile. Didn't comment. She just looked.

I watched her too. Her hips still in lace. Her heels still on. Her breathing steady. But her eyes—those eyes—looked like they were memorizing me.

I slid my hands around her waist. Ran my fingers up the lace, over her ribs, behind her back. Found the clasp. She didn't flinch. She just exhaled. The strap loosened. She rolled her shoulders free.

Then climbed into my lap. Not straddling. Not grinding. Just settling. Her thighs bracketed mine, soft but sure. Her warmth pressed against me—no friction yet, just fire waiting.

Her forehead rested against mine. I closed my eyes. Held her. Let my palms slide down her back. Let the moment hold its shape.

It didn't feel like claiming. Didn't feel like guilt either. Just presence. Just grace. Just...Jo.

When our lips met again, it was wetter. Warmer. I kissed her like the silence was breaking open and everything I couldn't say was sitting behind my teeth.

She pulled back slightly, her voice low.

"No pressure, right?"

I nodded.

"No lies either."

"Mi not here fi lies."

Her nails dragged gently along the back of my neck.

"Then touch mi like yuh mean it."

355

29

Just This. Just Us. Just Now.

She said, "Then touch mi like yuh mean it."

And didn't say another word.

Didn't move.

Didn't undress.

Didn't perform.

She just waited.

Not for permission.

For presence.

I stepped toward her like my body already knew what my mouth hadn't dared to admit—that this was it. Not an ending. Not a beginning. Just this—whatever this night could hold, however long it would last.

I brought my hands to her waist, hovering first.

Then settling.

My palms met the smooth warmth of her sides, just above the lace.

She was firm there. Tense.

But not from fear.

From intention.

I let my thumbs slide gently along her hips, then up the delicate ribs I'd studied with my eyes but never touched.

Jo stood still beneath me.

Not frozen.

Just open.

Her breath shallow but steady, chest rising slow.

She smelled like citrus and something floral underneath—mango oil maybe, mixed with the soft scent of sweat from hours of dancing.

Real. Alive.

When I leaned in, I didn't go for her mouth.

I brought my lips to her collarbone first.

Pressed a kiss there, slow and closed.

Then another.

Then lower, just above her breast.

Her skin tasted like lotion, wine, and salt.

Jo let her hands fall to my chest—flat, not pulling—just feeling me.

Her fingers drifted down my sternum, over the fine trail of hair beneath my bellybutton, stopping at my waistband.

But she didn't tug.

Didn't ask.

She just looked at me.

I met her eyes and held them.

"I'm not gonna rush this," I said, voice low.

"Mi not going nowhere," she whispered back.

I reached behind her, brushing the backs of my fingers across the clasp of her lingerie.

Waited.

She nodded, once.

I unhooked her.

The lace gave way without protest, straps slipping down her arms like secrets she no longer needed to keep.

She let it fall to the floor but didn't look down.

Didn't cover herself.

Didn't explain her body.

She just stood there, naked in her heels, waiting to be seen.

My gaze moved slow.

The curve of her breasts.

The softness of her stomach.

The faint stretch marks on her thighs that caught the light and made them shimmer like river lines on a map.

Her skin was a deep bronze, kissed darker from the sun over the last few days.

I knew it'd fade.

But not tonight.

I stepped closer.

Closed the space.

Let my bare chest meet hers, warm skin to warm skin.

My breath synced—then staggered—then synced again.

"I don't want to forget this," I murmured.

Jo brought her mouth to my ear.

Her voice was a hush.

"Then don't."

I kissed her.

And this time, it was full.

Not a peck.

Not a test.

But a mouth pressed to mouth, open, patient, tasting each other like prayer.

My lips moved slow.

Tongues met without fighting.

We kissed until the kiss no longer felt like a thing—we were just... breathing through each other.

Her hands slid around my back.

My arms wrapped around her waist.

We held.

And held.

She was the first to break the kiss.

Only to whisper, "Touch mi."

And I did.

* * *

I dropped to my knees. Not like a man begging. Like a man finally ready to listen. Jo didn't move. Didn't shift or pose. She just stood there, watching me with a stillness that wasn't nervous—it was knowing. Like she already trusted what came next.

I ran my palms along her calves. Her skin was soft, warm, slightly dewy from the heat of the room. I felt the give in her muscle. The faint tremor in her thighs. Kissed the inside of her knee like it meant something. Like it always would.

I moved slow. Not because I was unsure. But because I didn't want to miss a single inch of her. My hands followed the length of her legs, up her hips, over the thin lace that barely covered her.

I looked up at her.

And she nodded.

That was all.

I hooked my thumbs into the sides of her underwear and dragged them down slow—so slow they barely made a sound as they passed over her skin. She stepped out of them and didn't look down. She just let me look.

There was a tiny scar below her navel. Faint, curved. I wanted to ask about it—but didn't. Just filed it away with all the other truths about her.

She smelled like mango oil and something deeper—earthy, floral, lived-in. The kind of scent that made you lean in twice without meaning to.

I kissed her again.

Higher now.

Then finally, lower.

I brought my mouth to her—slow and deliberate. Tongue flat. Pressure steady. She inhaled—sharp and shallow. One hand braced on my shoulder, the other gripping the edge of the dresser behind her.

I found my rhythm—not a pattern, but a presence. I let my tongue work in circles, then long, slow strokes. Let my hands press into the backs of her thighs, feeling the heat rising off her.

She moaned—but low.

Not for drama.

Just because it moved through her.

Her breath shifted.

Her hips started to roll.

I didn't chase the moment.

Just stayed with her.

Fully.

There was a point—I didn't know how long in—when her fingers tightened. Her thigh trembled. And her voice broke—not loud, just raw. That's when she folded forward, forehead resting on the back of my head, breath hot against my scalp.

No words.

No gasps.

Just stillness.

And the slow melting of someone letting go.

I stayed with her until her grip softened. Until her breath slowed again. Until she lifted her head and looked down at me with eyes that weren't just open—they were present.

I rose.

She brought her hands to my face and kissed me.

Long.

Deep.

No urgency.

Just the flavor of what we'd made together still warm on my lips.

Her fingers went to my waistband.

Undid the button.

Zipper next.

I stepped out of my pants.

Stood there.

Fully exposed.

Not tense.

Not hiding.

She didn't ogle.

Didn't bite her lip or make a sound.

She just looked.

Like she was taking inventory of a man who'd finally stopped running.

She took my hand.

Walked us to the bed.

Not sexy.

Not slow-motion.

Just certain.

Jo climbed in first.

Laid back.

Her body open but not sprawled.

Her knees slightly bent.

Her curls spilling over the pillow like vines in moonlight.

She looked up at me—half-lidded, flushed, and so real I had to close my eyes for a second just to take it in.

"Mi glad it's yuh," she said softly.

That was it.

She opened her arms.

"Come lie wid mi," she whispered.

And I moved toward her—slow, steady, like I'd been waiting my whole life to arrive here.

* * *

I crawled into the bed like it might disappear under me. Not timid—just careful. Every movement a decision. Jo lay back against the pillows, one arm still open, the other resting at her stomach. Her legs parted just slightly. Not invitation. Just ease. Her breath was steady now, like waves just after high tide.

I moved between her, chest to chest, our skin touching with that first soft shock of heat. She wrapped both arms around my back, pulling me in—not with force, but with finality. Like she wasn't trying to hold me forever. Just long enough.

361

We kissed again.

Long.

Slow.

Open.

It felt like all the nights we could've had, folded into one. All the almosts. All the times I thought about reaching out and didn't.

I kissed her like I knew that part of myself was ending tonight.

Her thighs framed my hips. I moved carefully, my hands sliding beneath her to lift her, align her, feel her. I didn't rush entry. Just stayed there, forehead pressed to hers, my length resting at her opening.

Felt her warmth.

Felt her waiting.

Jo whispered, "Tek yuh time."

I did.

I slid in slowly—inch by inch, breath catching with every heartbeat. Jo exhaled like she'd been holding that breath for days. Her legs curled around me. One hand traced the back of my head.

We didn't move. Not at first. Just stayed like that. Joined. Still. Like we were remembering the shape of each other from lifetimes ago.

When we started moving, it was slow. Measured. I pushed into her with the kind of rhythm that felt like conversation. No thrusts. No pounding. Just a soft, repeated *I'm here*.

Her body met mine without resistance. She rocked with me. Held eye contact. Let me see everything.

I buried my face into the curve of her neck. Whispered things I didn't know I'd been carrying.

You feel like home.

I forgot what this could be.

Thank you.

She didn't respond with words. Just her body. A breath. A moan. A pull.

We moved through it together—waves and stillness. Hands clutching. Fingers threading. Mouths open, not for words, just for breath.

I slowed the rhythm. Buried deeper. Held her gaze. Jo was close—I could feel it. Her body trembling in my hands. Breath stuttering. Eyes wide, lips parted, like her soul was pushing to the surface.

Still, she didn't let go.

She was holding it.

Waiting.

"Yuh close?" I whispered, voice hoarse.

Jo nodded, breath shaky.

"But mi nah come 'til you come too."

That hit my chest harder than anything had in years.

I pressed my forehead to hers.

"Look at me."

She did.

Eyes locked.

No fear.

No flinch.

Just fire and trust.

"Stay wid me," she whispered.

"I'm right here."

The rhythm picked up—still slow, but deeper now. Their hips moving in perfect, unspoken agreement. Kisses breaking and returning between moans. My hands sliding beneath her, pulling her closer like I needed her soul against my skin.

Jo's breath hitched. Her mouth opened—but no sound came, just air and ache.

And I let go with her.

Held on with her.

Let it rise in me and crash between them—together.

We came as one.

Not like an explosion.

Like returning home.

I trembled against her. Held in her. Felt every pulse of her around me, like she was memorizing me from the inside out.

Jo pressed her palm flat against my chest. Right over my heart. Fingers splayed, warm and steady. Like she was grounding herself in it. Or maybe saying goodbye without words.

I'd never felt more present in my body. Never felt so known without having to explain a thing.

She kissed the center of my forehead.

"Mi glad it's yuh," she said, soft.

I couldn't speak.

I just wrapped my arms around her and held on.

We didn't say anything else.

We just lay there.

Skin to skin.

Eyes barely open.

Hearts still full.

We stayed like that—my weight on her, her hands on me—for longer than made sense. Until our breathing matched again. Until the sweat cooled. Until there was nothing left to say that hadn't already been felt.

And when we finally slept, it wasn't in fear of losing anything.

It was just sleep.

The kind you only earn after telling the truth.

We stayed wrapped in that truth until sleep took both of them without asking permission.

* * *

When I opened my eyes again, the light had changed. Not bright. Just soft—filtered through curtains pulled halfway closed. It was morning, but the kind that didn't demand anything yet.

I woke slowly. Body sore in the best way. Chest warm. The smell of her still on my skin.

Jo was curled beside me, one arm draped over her stomach, one knee bent slightly outward. Her lips parted in sleep. Her breath steady.

I stayed like that for a moment. Just watching her. Like I could memorize her body language and carry it home with me.

Then the buzz started.

Phone.

Under the pillow near my feet.

I reached for it quietly, careful not to shift the bed.

Tiff.

Three missed calls.

Four texts.

Another missed call.

I didn't open them.

Didn't need to.

The preview said enough.

Where are you

Seriously Bruce?

You just gon disappear?

I turned the phone over, face down. Held it there in my palm. Felt the weight of it grow heavier even though it was still.

When I looked back toward Jo, her eyes were already open.

She hadn't moved.

Wasn't frowning.

Just... watching me.

She didn't ask anything.

Didn't flinch.

Just said, voice calm:

"Mi going fi bathe."

I nodded.

Didn't stop her.

Didn't reach for her.

Jo slid from the bed, bare feet soft against the floor. Gathered her robe from the back of the chair. Tied it slow. Then disappeared into the bathroom without looking back.

The door closes.

Not slammed.

Not soft either.

I lay there, phone still in hand, screen dark now, heart flickering.
Not regret.
Just the grief of a moment that can't stay untouched.

30

One Name, Two Silences

The light in the room was warm now. Not hazy like dawn, not sharp like noon. Just golden. Steady.

I sat on the edge of the bed, slipping on my shorts, while Jo stood by the mirror adjusting the loose knot on one of my button-ups—blue, half-wrinkled, still carrying my cologne from the night before. She wore it like it was hers.

No words had passed yet.

But nothing felt unsaid.

Jo tied the shirt once more at her waist, then turned and tilted her head.

"How mi look?"

I smiled.

"Tastefully stolen."

She rolled her eyes and walked past me, brushing her shoulder against mine as she moved toward her sandals.

As we passed the bathroom, Jo reached up and fixed the loose collar on my shirt without a word. Just two fingers, a slight tuck. Like she'd done it a hundred times before.

We stepped out together.

The walk to the restaurant was quiet, but not stiff. The kind of silence that holds hands with memory.

The resort was already alive—plates clinking, children running, music floating light from the speakers overhead. Tourists in straw hats. Locals in uniforms. The sea in the distance, low and eternal.

We found a table near the edge of the patio. Jo sat cross-legged, barefoot in the chair, her sunglasses tucked into her hair. I grabbed two plates from the buffet and brought them back full—fruit, ackee, dumplings, eggs, too much meat.

Jo smirked.

"Yuh always pile up like yuh nuh know food free."

"I like options," I said, biting into a piece of melon. "And I got company."

She picked a slice of mango off my plate without asking and popped it in her mouth.

We ate in rhythm.

Slow.

Savoring.

At one point, Jo laughed mid-bite at something I said about the tourists doing the Electric Slide too early in the day.

"Mi cyan tek unuh," she said, shaking her head.

I just smiled.

Watched her mouth curve.

Watched the sunlight dance on her skin.

Then my phone buzzed.

I didn't check it right away.

Second buzz.

Then a third.

Jo glanced down at the table.

I flipped the phone over, screen down.

Went back to eating.

I didn't check it.

But I knew who it was.

Jo didn't comment.

Didn't shift her energy.

But something in her quiet said enough.

She leaned back in her chair.

Looked out toward the ocean.

Let the sun touch her face.

The moment held.

For a second, I thought we'd made it through the morning untouched.

Then—

The sunlight shifted—just a little.

I squinted toward the edge of the patio.

A figure moved toward them.

Steady.

Familiar.

* * *

And then Jo looked up too.

Tiff stormed across the patio like the concrete owed her something. Not rushing—but every step had violence in it. Slides slapping. Fists clenched. No pause. No blink. No greeting.

I looked up and saw her too late.

Jo followed my eyes. Then looked back at her mango.

Tiff didn't wait. She stepped right up to the table like she'd been holding this fire all damn morning.

"Oh, so you just out here eatin' breakfast? Smilin'? Chill as fuck like you ain't got six fuckin' messages from me? You deadass, Bruce?"

My fork was still halfway to my mouth.

"Tiff—"

"Nah. Nah, don't Tiff me now. Answer the fuckin' phone, Bruce! That's all I wanted! A text. A fuckin' 'hey I'm alive.' But you ghostin' me like I'm some random bitch?"

Jo wiped her fingers slowly with a napkin.

Didn't flinch.

Tiff turned on her.

"This the reason you couldn't fuckin' respond?"

I stood halfway.

Voice low.

"Tiff, you really wanna do this?"

She laughed—sharp and empty.

"You know what? Nah. Lemme guess. Y'all been chillin'. Fuckin'. Vibin'. Playin' house with this bitch like the rest of us just supposed to disappear."

I stepped around the table.

"Tiff—stop—"

"Nah, fuck that. You think this shit cute? Think I wanna be out here lookin' dumb? You got me fucked up."

Jo sat up straighter now. Still calm.

Still watching.

"Mi nah disrespect yuh," she said. "But mi not di reason him cyan talk."

Tiff's eyes cut.

"Girl, shut the fuck up. You don't know shit about what the fuck is going on."

Jo tilted her head.

"Clearly neither do yuh."

I tried to say something again. Too late.

Tiff pointed straight at me.

"You just disappeared like that night ain't mean shit? Like we ain't just fuck like we still fuckin' matter? Like bein' here together don't change the fuckin' rules?"

Jo stood up.

"You lucky a jus words mi deal wit," she said, voice low, accent thick. "Mi should bruk mi foot off inna yuh bloodclaat mouth."

My body went stiff.

"Tiff—Jo—please."

But Jo wasn't done.

"Mi tek care of yuh man? Yuh man? Mi nuh own him. Mi nuh want him bad enough fi argue wit a woman who cyan even keep him honest."

Tiff scoffed.

"You don't know what the fuck we been through."

"And mi nuh want to. But yuh nuh go disrespect me cause yuh cyan control yuh emotions."

Tiff clenched her jaw.

Chest rising.

Jo stepped back, then looked to me.

"Mi done. Handle dat."

She walked off—no tears.

No drama.

Just fire in her stride.

Tiff stared at me.

Eyes wet.

Hands clenched.

Breath caught.

"I would've given you everything," she muttered. "You just had to fuckin' ask."

Then she turned.

Gone.

I stood between two plates.

My stomach tight.

My mouth dry.

The patio dead silent.

Even the birds had stopped singing.

* * *

Jo was already walking fast down the path when I caught up behind her.

"Jo," I called out.

She didn't stop.

"Jo—wait."

She slowed—barely.

I came up beside her, still breathless, heart pounding with things I hadn't planned to explain.

Jo kept her eyes ahead.

Jaw set.

Her silence loud.

"Just give me a minute," I said. "Please."

Now she stopped.

Turned.

Her face wasn't angry.

It was done.

"Mi nuh like mixup," she said flat. "An mi nuh fight over man."

"I know. You shouldn't have had to be in that."

Jo crossed her arms.

"Then why mi did end up in it?"

I sighed.

"I didn't expect it to go like that. I should've handled it better. That's on me."

She scoffed softly.

Not bitter—just tired.

"You know mi hate drama," she said. "So mi really try hold it down. But she come loud, inna mi face, and you? Just standin' there like mi invisible."

I shook my head.

"You weren't invisible."

"Could've fooled mi."

She turned, took a step like she was ready to leave it all behind.

Then paused.

"You leaving tomorrow, right?"

I nodded slowly.

Jo didn't look at me.

"So spend the day wid whoever yuh need to. Mi just cyaan do embarrassment and vibes inna the same space."

I stepped closer.

"I'm not letting it end like that between us."

Jo gave a short, humorless laugh.

"It not up to yuh anymore, is it?"

She looked at me again.

Something flickered. Not softness—recognition.

"Go fix what yuh need to fix," she said. "If you want come find mi later, mi nah run."

Then she walked off.

No performance.

No drama.

Just real.

I watched her go.

Then turned toward the railing—toward Tiff—toward whatever fire still needed my name on it.

* * *

Tiff hadn't gone far. I found her near the boardwalk railing, staring out at the waves like she was daring them to crash harder. Her arms were tight across her chest. Eyes locked on the horizon. Sunglasses gone.

"Tiff," I called.

She didn't turn.

"Tiff," softer this time.

She spun around.

"Don't."

I stopped.

"Don't walk up here like that shit back there ain't just fuckin' happen. Like I'm crazy for reacting."

"I'm not."

"'Cause I will go the fuck off again, Bruce. Don't play with me."

"I'm not. I just—"

"Don't say you sorry."

I exhaled.

Waited.

She turned back toward the water.

"I ain't mad you fuckin' somebody else," she said. "That's not even it."

I stayed quiet.

"I'm mad you didn't fuckin' tell me. I'm mad I had to find out with an audience. That I'm out here callin' you, worried something happened—only to see you chillin', laid up, actin' like none of this shit meant anything."

"I didn't mean to—"

"No. You didn't want to deal. That's what the fuck it was. You wanted the peace without the cost. The comfort without the consequence."

She turned now.

"You had me out here lookin' like some needy ass bitch, Bruce. After everything we been through. After everything I held you through."

I stepped forward.

"You're right."

Tiff blinked.

"I fucked up," I said. "You needed clarity and I gave you silence. You deserved a heads-up, and I let you walk into that shit blind."

She didn't interrupt.

"But I wasn't tryin' to hurt you. I was tryin' to survive myself."

Tiff's face shifted slightly—confusion, then something like grief.

My voice dropped.

"I've been breaking, Tiff. Quietly. For a long time. And you were always the one holdin' me up. Even when you were barely standin' your damn self."

She looked away.

"I didn't know how to say I needed to stand alone. That I couldn't keep leaning on you to make me whole."

She wiped at her cheek fast.

"And Jo," I said, "she ain't saved me. But she let me fall apart without tryin' to fix it. She didn't ask me to be strong. She just saw me. And for the first time... I let myself see me too."

Tiff stared at the sand.

"I didn't ghost you to hurt you," I continued. "I ghosted you 'cause I didn't know how to be with you without performing. Without trying to be the man you deserved when I was still tryin' to figure out if I even deserved to be here."

"You coulda just said that," she whispered.

"I was scared."

We stood there.

The sea loud behind them now.

Like it knew what silence had cost.

I looked at her.

"I love you. Still. I just didn't know how to hold that and not drown under it."

Tiff met my eyes.

And for the first time, the anger fell away.

"I just needed to matter, Bruce."

"You do."

She looked down.

Then back up.

"Maybe I wanted you to lean on me," she said, "'cause I didn't know how to stand up alone either."

She looked out at the water, jaw tight.

"You ever wonder why we keep doing this? Same dance, same burn."

She didn't look at me.

"Some of us run. Some of us just stand still pretending we ain't stuck."

She said it soft — like it was a secret she didn't want back.

I didn't respond.

I just stepped forward and let my wrist brush hers—light, intentional.

She didn't pull away.

I didn't respond.

I just stepped forward and let my wrist brush hers—light, intentional.

She didn't pull away.

We stood like that a moment longer.

Then Tiff asked, "So what now?"

I exhaled.

"Jo got weed. We gon' drink. And enjoy this beautiful ass scenery while we still got it."

That got the faintest smirk from her.

Then a head shake.

"This shit gon' be awkward as hell."

"Yeah," I said. "But maybe peace is supposed to be."

* * *

Jo was exactly where I left her. Sitting on the low stone planter near the bend in the path, one leg tucked under the other, face tilted toward the ocean breeze like she hadn't moved, like she wasn't waiting—but still noticed when I returned.

I walked up slow.

No swagger. No mask.

Just me.

Jo didn't speak.

I sat beside her, not too close.

Hands on my knees.

Shoulders still heavy.

We sat like that for a moment.

No music.

Just wind.

And the sound of joy happening somewhere else.

"I went after her," I said.

Jo nodded once.

"She good now?" she asked.

"I think we both said what we needed to."

She didn't look over.

"I didn't ask you to wait," I added. "But thank you for waiting anyway."

Jo exhaled.

"Mi did need fi cool off. Mi cyaan deal wid mixup."

I nodded.

"I wouldn't have blamed you if you left."

"But mi did want fi see if yuh would come back."

I looked at her.

"I'm here."

"Mi see dat."

We sat in it.

I glanced past the path for a second.

Behind them, maybe thirty feet back, Tiff stood in the shade, not approaching.

Just watching.

Waiting.

"She's over there," I said quietly. "Didn't want to assume anything. I told her if you were open, we could just… have a day. Peaceful. Chill. You, me, her. Nothing forced."

Jo didn't turn to look.

She just stayed facing forward.

"Tiff good?" she asked.

"As good as she can be. She listened. I listened. That's a start."

Jo nodded slowly.

Then:

"Mi nuh inna mixup. But mi nuh fraid of it either."

She turned her head just slightly—enough to meet my eyes.

"If it get weird, mi gone. But if everybody can act like dem have sense…"

She shrugged.

"We can see."

I smirked.

Small. Honest.

I stood, turned slightly, and gave Tiff a small nod.

A gesture.

Not permission—just presence.

Jo pulled out her pouch and passed it to me.

"Start di day proper."

We sat in silence while I broke it down.

The breeze still coming soft.

Tiff approached slowly now.

Cautious, but not hiding.

She stopped a few steps away, arms crossed but face calm.

I looked up from the grinder.

Stood.

"Jovel," I said, voice low but clear. "This is Tiffany."

I turned slightly.

"Tiff—this is Jovel."

Both women nodded.

Nothing warm.

Nothing fake.

But a name is a bridge.

And sometimes, that's enough to start with.

I sat back down.

Finished rolling.

Jo handed me a lighter.

Tiff took the bottle.

And the chapter closed not with peace—

But with a blunt, a name, and a breath held between three hearts still learning how to be seen.

31

The Kanye Shrug

The sun was already warming the edge of the pool when I lit the blunt. I didn't say much. Didn't need to. Just passed it to Jo, who sat beside me in a lounge chair wearing oversized shades and that same knot-tied button-up from the day before. Tiff was stretched on a towel to my left, legs crossed at the ankle, scrolling with one hand and sipping juice with the other.

They hadn't planned to be out here like this.

But somehow, it made sense.

Quiet.

Warm.

Everyone still here.

The blunt came back around. I took another pull, exhaled slow, and leaned my head back. The sky was too blue. My mind too still.

Then I heard it—footsteps and a voice I knew too well.

"Bruuuuce! Aye—yo!"

Dev.

I cracked a smile before I even looked. Dev was walking past with two of the other guys, all in swim trunks and half-sleep.

Dev clocked the setup instantly—Jo, Tiff, blunt in hand—and damn near tripped over his own feet.

"Bruh… what the fuck?"

I just grinned.

379

Shrugged.

The Kanye shrug.

Jo smirked behind her shades. Tiff didn't look up, but she exhaled through her nose like she was trying not to laugh.

Dev pointed.

"I ain't even gonna ask," he said. "You… you a wild boy."

"Mind your business," I said, grinning.

The other guys just kept walking, shaking their heads.

"Y'all need prayer," one muttered.

Jo leaned in, whispered with a slight grin, "Dat one talk like him never do worse."

I chuckled and passed her the blunt.

Tiff finally spoke without looking up.

"You know they gon' be talking."

I exhaled.

"Let 'em."

At one point, Jo passed the blunt to Tiff without looking. Tiff took it, held it a second too long — then passed it back without a word.

But this time, when she spoke, she didn't look at me. Just straight ahead.

"They gon' talk — but they don't know half the story, do they?"

She tilted her head just enough to meet Jovel's eyes behind the shades. A flicker of a grin — quick, gone, but real.

Old shit. New shit. Both of them choosing not to drag it out here.

Jovel matched it. No words. Just that quiet acknowledgment that maybe, for now, this mess was theirs alone to hold.

I noticed. But didn't say shit.

Some bridges didn't burn. They just smoldered.

I noticed.

But didn't say shit.

Some bridges didn't burn. They just smoldered.

I looked at them both—Tiff sunbathing, Jo now sitting up, legs swinging slowly off the side of her chair.

And I just… took it in.

The women.

The weed.

The sky.

The fact that they were still here—not healed, not fixed, but not running either.

What a fuckin' week, I thought.

* * *

I didn't say anything when I left. I just stood up from the pool chair, slipped on my sandals, and walked. The weight didn't hit me until I reached the edge of the beach—that stretch where the tile ends and the sand starts to forget how to hold your steps.

I stood there a second, toes curled just inside the dry grain.

Then kept walking.

No towel. No phone.

Just me.

The breeze was soft today. Like it knew the fire had finally cooled.

I walked until the noise behind me faded. Until it was just waves and birds and that soft sound of the sea tapping the shore like it didn't mean anything.

But it did.

Everything did.

I stood at the edge of the tide, staring out at the horizon that looked exactly the same as it did the day I landed.

And yet—

I didn't.

A mosquito landed on my forearm, bit me before I could slap it away. I watched the tiny welt rise. Maybe I needed that — something small, real, reminding me this skin was still mine.

I closed my eyes for a moment. Let the sun warm my eyelids. Tried to remember who the fuck I was when I got here.

I thought of that first morning.

381

Alone.

Confused.

Still smelling like Delta's recycled air.

Still holding everything I didn't know how to name.

I remembered standing in the kitchen one night in Atlanta. Lights off. Just me and the hum of the fridge. Wondering if my kids still talked about me when I wasn't there.

That memory hit harder than expected.

My jaw locked without me noticing. Shoulders tense. Like even now, part of me was still bracing for impact.

I came here burnt out.

Not just tired.

Burnt the fuck out.

Trying to outrun the version of myself who only knew how to be useful.

The provider.

The protector.

The man who always held it together—even when it was bleeding through his goddamn shirt.

I'd called it strength.

But it was survival.

The tide didn't care. Maybe that's freedom.

Jo saw it before I did.

Saw the cracks in my armor and didn't try to patch them.

She just sat in the silence.

Let me melt.

Let me fucking breathe.

Tiff... she carried me too long.

And I—I let her.

Because it felt good to have someone who never asked for the truth if the lie came wrapped in consistency.

But now?

Now I was standing barefoot in another country with two women who should've both left me by now.

Still showing up.

Still offering peace, even if it tasted awkward in their mouths.

I wasn't afraid of burning anymore.

I was afraid of what came after—

When the fire was gone, and there was no one left to blame.

The ocean kept moving. Didn't care what I'd done. Didn't care what I was becoming. It just came and went. Soft. Steady.

And maybe that was the point. Not putting the fire out — just not running from the burn.

I dug my heels into the wet sand. Felt it swallow my feet, cool and rough and real. No more pretending I could stand on water.

I didn't pray. Didn't speak.

I just let the waves break over my ankles. Salt on my skin. Wind in my teeth.

For the first time in years, I wasn't pretending at all.

I was here.

Finally real.

Finally mine.

* * *

The room was quiet when I walked in. Windows open, breeze lifting the curtains just enough to make them dance. It smelled like rosemary, sweat, and incense.

Jo was sitting on the edge of the bed, folding my shirts into neat, square stacks. Barefoot. Hair pulled back with a scarf. Still in one of my tees, no bra.

She didn't look up when I stepped in.

She just kept folding.

"You pack quiet," I said.

She smiled faintly.

"Mi used to pack fi mi modda dem. Yuh learn how fi be gentle wid tings yuh cyaan replace."

I sat on the other bed.

The overhead fan ticked and groaned, pushing stale incense smoke across the room. The smell clung to my shirt, even clean.

Watched her.

Didn't speak.

The silence wasn't heavy.

But it wasn't light either.

After a moment, she looked at me.

"Mi cyaan lie… mi wasn't ready fi yuh leave."

I didn't move.

She folded another shirt. Slower this time.

"Mi nuh expect none of this," she said. "Mi see yuh di first night and mi think, 'He look like him running from fire.' But mi neva know yuh would walk straight into mine."

I swallowed.

"You were the fire," I said.

She looked at me then.

Eyes full now. Not tears yet. But close.

"Mi try play it cool. Play it easy. Tell miself it was vibes… but den mi start feel things. Start wait fi yuh come in di room. Start care when yuh didn't speak."

Her voice cracked slightly.

"Now yuh leaving… and mi cyaan unsee yuh."

I stood. Walked over.

Sat next to her.

I reached for her hand—gentle.

She didn't pull away.

"You didn't just give me space," I said.

"You gave me permission to be silent. And broken.

And that silence didn't scare you."

I looked at her.

"You ever wonder why I never asked you for anything?"

She nodded slowly.

"Because I felt like I already owed you for what you didn't ask of me."

I exhaled — that bitter laugh again, gone as quick as it came.

"I'm trying, Jo. Trying to be better. But God knows I'm scared I'll run again."

She didn't flinch. Just brushed my thumb with hers, eyes soft but sure.

"Mi know," she said. "Dat's why mi nuh hold yuh. Just remind yuh."

Jo's eyes finally broke.

Just one tear, then another.

She wiped them away fast, but didn't hide.

"Mi nuh cry fi most man," she whispered.

I leaned in, forehead against hers.

We sat there—eyes closed, breath shared.

She reached into her bag.

Pulled out a single item: a torn matchbook from the first club they met. Written on the inside, in her handwriting:

"When fire meet fire, it nuh always burn—sometimes it free."

She closed it in my palm.

"No souvenirs," she said. "Just reminders."

We stood.

She pulled me in again.

Held me tighter.

Longer.

This time she kissed my neck, then my jaw, then finally my mouth.

Slow.

Full.

But final.

No tongues.

No second round.

Just presence.

We walked down together.

Tiff was already downstairs, by the front desk, hugging Lora tight. She glanced up as they entered.

Saw Jo.

Saw me.

Said nothing.

Jo said nothing either.

At the counter, the woman behind the desk looked up and asked with a soft smile,

"Yuh enjoy yuh stay?"

I looked back.

At Jo.

At Tiff.

At the ocean through the lobby doors.

"Yeah," I said. "I needed it."

* * *

Dez was waiting outside, leaning against the car with his arms crossed and sunglasses on. Tiff climbed in without a word.

He studied me for a second, thumbed the ash off his cigarette.

"Mi son called last week. Mi ain't pick up."

A shrug, half-smirk. "Some roots too deep fi pull, eeh?"

He didn't wait for an answer. Just nodded toward the car. "Ready?"

The stone driveway was still warm under my sandals. Heat climbing up through my feet like it didn't want me to forget where I'd been.

I turned to Jo.

We didn't hug again.

Just stood there.

Looking.

Jo reached out and fixed the collar of my shirt—one last time.

Just like the first morning.

Then she said—

"Yuh still carry fire. Just… remember which parts fi let burn."

I nodded.

"Yuh gon' be good," she added. "Mi know it."

I kissed her cheek.

Held her wrist for a second longer than necessary.
Then stepped back.
Climbed in.
Closed the door.
As Dez pulled off, Jo stayed there.
Didn't wave.
Didn't smile.
Just stood with arms folded, face calm but unreadable.
And I?
I looked back.
Watched her until the driveway curved.
She didn't wave. I didn't either.

32

The Drive to Kingston

The road rolled out in front of me like it had stories to tell and no rush getting to the ending.

I sat behind Dez, window cracked, elbow resting on the ledge. I wasn't thinking. Not yet. Just watching the trees lean with the breeze, like even they knew this stretch of land was different. More jagged. More alive.

Tiff was beside me. Face turned toward the window, sunglasses on. Not distant. Just… still.

The hum of tires on pavement, wind dragging itself in through the crack, and somewhere in the background, Peter Tosh singing "Coming in Hot" low from Dez's Bluetooth speaker.

Nobody said shit for a long time. And that was okay.

Then Dez spoke.

"So," he said, like we'd been mid-conversation, "did yuh listen?"

I looked over. Dez kept his eyes on the road, but the smirk was there.

"To the island," Dez added.

I didn't answer right away. The wind carried the silence for me.

"I did," I said finally. "Had to get quiet first."

Dez nodded. "Yeah, man. Jamaica nuh shout. She whisper. And if yuh too loud, yuh miss di whole fuckin' sermon."

I cracked a smile. Let the sun catch my face.

Dez shifted in his seat, one arm hanging out the window as we passed a battered green sign: Bog Walk – 5KM.

"Yuh feel different," Dez said. "Yuh step lighter. Yuh face… it settle."

I didn't respond. Didn't need to.

Dez kept going.

"Mobay test yuh. It pretty on di outside, but it rough underfoot. Whole heap of distraction. Energy wild, tourist loud, locals louder."

He glanced at me through the rearview.

"Kingston nuh care 'bout your feelings. She give yuh di raw, no chaser. History in di walls. Politics in the potholes. If yuh soft, Kingston spit yuh out."

Tiff chuckled low. "Sounds warm and welcoming."

Dez grinned. "Nah, man. Kingston real. Yuh feel her bones. It di place weh Bob Marley get shot and still go play di show next night."

I blinked. "What?"

Dez nodded. "Yuh never hear dat? 1976. Smile Jamaica concert. Gunman come to him yard, buss shot. Man get grazed, still go perform next day. Say he do it 'cause people who try hurt di world nah tek no day off."

Tiff pulled her shades down slightly. "Damn."

"Yuh see mi?" Dez said. "Kingston built fi warriors. Artists. People wid fire. If yuh reach Kingston and leave unchanged, is 'cause yuh neva show up proper."

I leaned into the doorframe a little more. Let Dez's words stretch.

We passed a cliff now—sea way off in the distance, flashing between trees like memory. Fishermen posted up on rocks like gods with coolers.

Tiff finally spoke again. "So what should we do when we get there?"

Dez tapped the wheel like a drum. "Go Devon House. Eat di ice cream. Vanilla wid rum cake if yuh smart. Go sit pon di wall at the harbor and watch sun set low."

He turned slightly, just enough to catch my eyes again.

"And if yuh brave… go Trench Town. Feel di roots. Where music born and revolution walk still."

He paused. "But only if yuh really want to hear yuhself."

* * *

Nobody said anything after that. Just breeze. And birds somewhere off deep in the canopy.

I didn't feel restless anymore.

Didn't feel like I was losing something or about to fuck it up.

Just felt still. Not because everything was fixed.

Because I'd stopped trying to fix it.

Tiff adjusted in her seat and pulled out her phone, but didn't open it. Just held it in her hand.

The road curved again—soft and winding. Bush thick on both sides now. No more sea in sight.

Dez turned the music down to a whisper.

Then, almost to himself, he said—

"Every man come to Jamaica to run from somet'ing. But if yuh stay long enough, yuh realize… yuh neva was running. Yuh just tired of pretending."

I didn't move. Didn't speak.

Then Dez added—soft, but sure:

"Yuh different now," he said. "Mi see it. Just don't forget who yuh had to burn fi get here."

I looked out the window. Sea gone now. Just bush, and dust, and curves that knew how to hold silence.

I didn't know who I was gonna be when we got there. But for the first time in years, I wasn't scared to find out.

The road curved again. Sharp this time. And just beyond it—Kingston waited.

A new fire. A new chance to face it.

Dedication

For my father, Bruce *'Buckeye'* McMullen Sr. —
I didn't get to know you long enough, but I've felt you all my life. When I was lost, stuck, hurting — I called for you, and you showed up in ways only I could feel. You never really left me. You kept me steady when I didn't think I'd stand again.

For my stepfather, Robert *'Puppie'* Evans III —
You didn't have to step in, but you did. You didn't have to love me like your own, but you did. You gave me a man's shoulders to lean on and taught me how to carry my own weight when the time came to stand alone.

I hope you both can see me now — standing here, doing my best to be the man you'd both be proud to claim. I hope I've made you proud. I hope you know I never stopped trying.

And to **every man** who ever stepped in — friends, family, coaches, teachers, mentors — who stood beside me and poured their strength, their lessons, and their belief into the boy I was and the man I've become — thank you for shaping the man I am today!

About the Author

Bruce C Bee is a storyteller from Richmond, Virginia, now based in Atlanta. After walking away from corporate America, he traded the cubicle for backstreets, new cities, and lessons found in places most people overlook.

His writing is raw, unfiltered, and rooted in the truth that stories don't need polish to leave a mark. *Burn Me Whole* is his debut novel.

You can connect with me on:

🌐 https://www.brucecbee.com